Praise for *Demons Prefer Blondes*:

D1538250

DEMONS
like it Hot

SIDNEY AYERS

sourcebooks
casablanca

For my grandmother.
You were always there
to help me recognize my dreams
and always made me smile
with your own fascinating stories.
I know you're smiling from above.
Love you always!

Prologue

"SO YOU'VE FINALLY DECIDED TO JOIN US?"

The loud voice boomed in Matthias Ambrose's ears. He shoved his hands into the pockets of his camouflage cargoes and paced along the dais. The council, consisting of the Paladin's oldest and fiercest demon warriors and delegates, looked down their noses at him.

He felt inferior, weak, and little. A common occurrence as of late... ever since his last job. A job he wished he never took. He deserved whatever hellish mission the Fore-Demons had in store for him.

"I have." In the seven hundred and fifty plus years since he'd been demonized, he'd learned one thing. The less he talked, the better. Short and simple. End of story. The less he opened up, the less he'd show his weakness. And that was the last thing he wanted at this moment.

"Very well, Ambrose. Step forward." The high-demon stood and clapped his hands. "I need to summon your handler."

Matthias rolled his eyes. Of course the Fore-Demons controlled their assets just like the CIA did. "Summon away, my lord."

"Do I sense some sarcasm in your tone, Ambrose?" The demon clucked his tongue. "I can always reassign you to another mission. How does Siberia sound?"

Knowing the Fore-Demons and their nonexistent

sense of humor, he wasn't kidding. Might as well play along. "Cold."

"Ahh, still as witty as ever." The elder demon scraped a withered hand through his white beard. "Unfortunately, now is not the time for jokes. We have serious problems on Earth and we need all the help we can get—including yours." There was no mistaking the contempt in his voice.

He controlled the snort that threatened. As if he was the truly evil one. If they only knew the truth. Maybe then the almighty Fore-Demons Council and their ever-so-virtuous Paladin wouldn't be so quick to make assumptions.

What in Hades had he gotten himself into? He had never needed to prove his worth to anyone before. Now it was the only thing that drove him. He wanted to belong. He wanted to help. It unnerved him.

And it was all *her* fault. How could one simple job cause him to doubt his own existence?

He was a paid mercenary. He'd never chosen a side. Now he was ready to jump on the Paladin bandwagon. Why now?

The answer was simple. *Serah SanGermano*.

The moment his eyes had met hers, his world had spun out of control. And when he saw the mark on her hand, he knew exactly why the Infernati wanted Serah SanGermano. The two dots separated by a long slash showed him all he needed to know. She was a Pure-Blood. Despite his fear at the discovery, other emotions roared inside him. The scar only accentuated her beauty. Because of her, he'd almost failed his last mission. The only comfort was that when it was all done and over,

Miss SanGermano wouldn't remember a thing. He'd made certain of it.

The curse of his demonic existence—the ability to remove all memories and thoughts. He could swoop in, do his business, and no one, not even one of those blasted slayers, would remember a thing. Part of his heart constricted at the thought. Why would he want her to remember him? He'd nearly sent her to her death.

From the fight she and her chimp of an imp put him through, he was lucky to make it out alive. She was a spitfire for sure. That sort of fight would only get her in trouble—especially in the Infernati's clutches.

Infernati. He hated them more than ever. They were evil. They had taken advantage of him. They had found a weakness.

Never again. He'd not let his guard down. But then there was Serah. Her curly brown hair that framed her face. Bright eyes that sparkled like the most vibrant sapphires left him entranced. Steamy sexuality rolled from her every move, yet still an aura of purity surrounded her. Confusing and intoxicating. *Dangerous*.

He had to stay away from her, yet she needed protection. An imp, no matter how feisty he was, would not do. Not with the battle he could feel brewing. Then again, with Rafael Deleon and the bevy of demons in Connolly Park, Serah would be well protected.

Why couldn't he stop thinking about her? He hadn't thought about a woman in that way since that fateful day over eight hundred years ago. He drew his lips tight. Now was definitely not the time to draw up the past. He wanted to concentrate on his future. A future where he could fight evil… preferably on his own. Alone.

"Are you done brooding, Ambrose?" The dark, rich tone prickled in his ears.

Matthias's head snapped up. He ground his teeth and clenched his fists tighter. If he was here it could mean only one thing. "What the hell are you doing here?"

"Ambrose, you will respect your fellow Paladins if you wish to join us," the only female of the Fore-Demon council admonished. To iterate her point, she threw back her arm and launched a warning fireball whizzing just past his shoulder.

Rafael Deleon shrugged and leaned against the marble dais. "No worries, Councilwoman Astra. He has his reasons, I'm sure." He turned back to Matthias. "As for your question, Ambrose, I could ask you the same thing."

Taking in Rafael's countenance, Matthias blinked. Was this the same man? Where he had once been brutally formal and uptight, his aura now remained peaceful and serene. He could try to mask it behind all his pomp and arrogance, but Matthias knew better. The rumors were true. He'd fallen in love with the half succubus he'd been sent to protect. Blasted odd; he'd always thought love a weakness in demons. Yet here stood Rafael Deleon, as proud and strong as ever.

Matthias raised his chin. "I don't need to answer to you, Deleon."

Rafael snorted. "I beg to differ."

"Are you a member of the Fore-Demon Council now?"

"No."

"I only answer to them or who they choose for my handler."

Raking a hand through dark hair, Rafael turned to the council. "So you haven't told him yet?"

"We were just about to, Deleon," Astra said with a flick of her barbed wings. "He seemed too deep in thought."

Rafael nodded. "I might as well do the honors." With a devilish smirk he turned to Matthias. "Ambrose, you will answer to me because I—much to my chagrin, I assure you—am your handler."

Handler? Deleon? Why? This couldn't be. He needed a mission somewhere far away from Connolly Park and Serah SanGermano. With her best friend's demon lover as his handler, all his hopes slipped away. "I cannot agree to this."

"Why ever not?" asked the elder demon. "Deleon is a one of the finest Paladins and he needs your help."

"My reasons have nothing to do with Deleon and are personal in nature."

"If you let your personal grievances sway your decisions, then you will never succeed as a Paladin. If you want to prove yourself to the cause, you will accept Deleon as your handler."

Exactly what mission was he signing up for? What was so urgent that the great Paladin Rafael Deleon needed his help? After all, wasn't he the one that was prophesied? "Fine. I accept Rafael Deleon as my handler." As soon as he muttered the words, he was certain he'd regret it.

As if reading his mind—which he was certain they were—the Paladin council stood and nodded to him.

An indiscernible smile crept across Astra's lips. "Very wise decision, Ambrose. Now it is time to hear your mission. Deleon, do the honors."

Rafael nodded in return. "Thank you, my lieges." With stony silver eyes he glared at Matthias. "Your mission is this: You will guard my fiancée's best friend: Serah SanGermano."

The frozen tundra of Siberia sounded better after all.

Chapter 1

"*MON DIEU!* THE FONDUE!"

"What?" Serah SanGermano clutched her grand-mother's watch, its warmth flooding her body, and spun around. Flames shot out from the burners, flickering and taunting. Heat continued to flood her every pore. Her cheeks, fingers, and toes tingled. Every receptor fired in her body. She sucked in a breath. Would it ever stop?

"The stove broke!" Edie, her sous-chef shouted, her French accent thickening. She fumbled with the knobs, twisting and turning each direction. "*Merde...*" she mumbled beneath her breath.

Flames licked, flicked and taunted. More pans bub-bled, threatening to spew their contents.

Oh God, not the vichyssoise too!

Serah shook her head to clear her jumbled thoughts. What in the hell was going on?—and she did mean hell. She had her reasons. But there was something different about this. Something unnatural, yet no evil lingered. She had a nose for it—literally.

She'd always believed in the netherworld and the occult. She never knew just how close it was—until now. Now those demons wouldn't leave her alone. An imp here, a ghoul there. Nothing terribly harmful. They mostly just liked to stir up trouble. More or less just a nuisance in her busy life. Thankfully, she had Lucy, her half-succubus friend, and Lucy's demon fiancé, Rafe, to help her. Who would have guessed that not all demons are bad?

More energy pounded its way through her body, filling her with intense heat—a heat she didn't need or want. She shook her wrist, the silver band with its tiny diamonds sparkling and flashing.

Stupid watch. Nonni told her to wear it at all times, that she'd be there to help Serah claim her destiny. Well, where was Nonni now? Gone, and it was all her fault. Serah shuddered as she stifled a sigh. She'd always love her grandmother, but she couldn't bear it anymore.

"You do something, Ms. SanGermano!" Edie flailed her arms back and forth, words so colorful they could only mean something she shouldn't dare repeat spewing from her mouth.

More heat shot into Serah's wrist and her head buzzed. Something wasn't right, but she had a business to run. People were counting on her. She had customers to take care of. She couldn't let them down.

A giant bubble of chocolate popped in the air, coating Edie and her purple, custom-made chef's jacket in gooey chocolate. With that, another gush of chocolate erupted. Chocolate sprayed in every direction, all over the floors, the walls and ceiling... everywhere. Serah reached for a towel and lunged for the fondue pot, her Jimmy Choos slipping across the slimy chocolate coating the floor. Bad choice in shoes, she knew, but she had a client to meet with.

"Aiee!" Serah shouted as her legs slipped beneath her. Pitching forward, she threw her arms out in a futile attempt to catch herself. She only slipped more. With an unceremonious plop, Serah landed face first in the ocean of chocolate. Who knew one pot could hold so much chocolate? She loved the decadent treat, but this much and she'd end up in a diabetic coma.

"Damn it," she muttered beneath her breath. What the hell was going on? Swiping the sticky sweet liquid from her face, she crawled toward the counter. She gripped the edge and pulled herself up. Without thinking, Serah swiped chocolate-coated fingers through her curls. *Ugh!* The rich sweet scent of cocoa clung to the air. She rubbed her nose, her fingers smushing into more sticky warmth. It certainly gave new meaning to *brownnosing*.

Chocolate continued to gush in the air like Old Faithful. More pots rumbled and shook, threatening to spill their contents. Serah sniffed the air, hoping to catch a whiff of evil demon. Not a rotten egg in the vicinity. Just great. She didn't need this. Not now. Not ever.

Serah glanced down at the watch, the diamonds sparkling—taunting her, its unmerciful warmth spreading everywhere, down to the tips of her toes.

Sorry, Nonni, but I just can't wear it anymore.

With that, Serah ripped off the watch and shoved it into the pocket of her jacket, where it would be safe— for now. After all, it was her grandmother's watch. She had wanted her to have it. Serah couldn't disrespect her memory. Not after everything she'd given up for her.

Edie shook her head, chocolate drops flinging from her chef's hat and normally red hair. "I no sign on for zis, but I see you need help." She stomped toward the utility closet and threw open the door. "Ve must clean now. Before Health Department cloze uz down." With a smile, she wheeled out the bucket and mop. "I did not think people used zeez s'ings no more."

"Mop's always been good to me. I just can't part with him."

"After this mess, he might be the one who parts company." The thick voice wafted through the air, along with the faint hint of lemon. Kalli Corapolous sauntered in, her tall, buckle-down boots squishing in the chocolaty layer coating the floor. Flinging a purple dreadlock to the side, she scanned the kitchen. What in the hell was she doing here?

"I've come to clean," she said on a whispered breath. "I noticed a spike in otherworldly powers and came as soon as I could."

"Do you mind?" Serah asked, her voice taking on a tinge of irritation. Her best friend, Lucy, told her all about Kalli's demonic gifts.

"Mind what? The look on your face said it all. No mind reading necessary." Kalli smiled, a warm smile despite the Goth getup she chose to wear. "Lucy's on her way too."

Great. Just what she needed. Everyone meddling in her life. She didn't need help. Nothing was wrong. So she had a few unfortunate mishaps with a few minor imps and wraiths. Big deal. They'd seen worse.

"Just a little mishap with the fondue pot." Serah smiled, twisting a finger in a chocolaty curl. "I was experimenting. I read somewhere that chocolate and its antioxidants were good for your face and hair."

Serah popped a fingertip in her mouth and smacked her lips. The rich chocolate exploded on her tongue. Damn, Edie made a killer fondue. Too bad it was now sprayed across the kitchen. What a waste of fine chocolate.

Kalli's gaze narrowed and she pursed her lips, the

silver loop in her lower lip jutting out. "I'll have to ask Lucy about that. I'm still getting refreshed with my hair-styling skills."

Well this was an excellent way to change the subject.

"So has Lucy actually let you style hair yet?" Serah leaned against the counter, her arm landing in yet another puddle of chocolate. "Ick."

Her question apparently fell on deaf ears. With a wary eye, Kalli continued to scan the shop. "Where's Edie?"

"In the back room filling a bucket. Something tells me we may need more than a mop though?" Serah forced a chuckle.

Kalli nodded, her expression stern and stony. "What happened, Serah? And tell me the truth. I can smell bullshit a mile away."

"Nothing happened. The fondue got a little too hot and boiled over. No imps, demons, or wraiths around."

"There might not be demons, but something strange is going on." Kalli turned to her, her amethyst eyes sparking. She grabbed her by the shoulders. "You and I both know this isn't normal. You need help."

A huff escaped Serah's lips and she placed her hands on her hips. "The only thing I have going on is a rehearsal dinner and if I don't get everything done, then my business is shot."

She spun away from the counter and plodded to the sink. A quick turn from Serah, and the faucets roared to life. Squirting some soap into her hand, Serah lathered up. With a splash of water to her face, she scrubbed away the chocolate. She'd probably have blackheads for months now. She scrubbed her face harder.

"If you scrub any harder, your skin will fall off." Her

best friend's normally smooth and silky voice grated in her eardrums. Now that Kalli had her reinforcements, she was due for an earful.

With a sharp twist, Serah turned off the water. Steeling herself against the admonishments of one and a half demons, she gripped the edge of the sink. Then again, the human half of Lucia Anne Gregory was just as formidable as the succubus half—if not more.

She turned to her friend and mustered the most confident and collected tone she could. "Lucy, everything's fine. As I was telling Kalli, it was just an accident."

"Pbbbt... A big accident." Edie pushed her way into the kitchen, the yellow mop bucket sloshing in front of her. Pulling the lever, she released the wringer and yanked out the mop. Like a French ninja, she swung the mop from one hand to the other. Drops of water flung from the yarns, ricocheting against the wall. Passing her hand across her face, she brushed off some of the drops.

"I've got some *industrial* cleaners, Edie. I'm sure Serah won't mind you taking off early." A sly smile spread across Kalli's lips. She turned to Serah and narrowed her gaze. "Right, Serah?"

"Uh, yeah." Serah balled her hands into tight fists. "You can take the rest of the day off, Edie."

Edie arched an auburn brow, her lips pressed firmly together. "Everyzing iz okay? You sure?"

"Yes."

She nodded. "Okay. Don't forget to feed *le chat*."

Serah smirked. *Le chat* was quite able to feed himself. The cat, who had adopted her as his own, was way too intelligent for his own good. Why did all the strange beasts wind up on her doorstep?

"This is getting old really fast," Lucy ground out as soon as the door clicked shut. Raking a hand through her always perfectly styled hair (one of the few benefits of being part sex demon), she rolled her tongue between her teeth. Her hazel eyes sparked as she shot Serah a penetrating glare.

Serah threw her hands up in frustration. "What now? How many times do I have to say it was an accident?"

"Rafe says you're hiding something."

"So can he read minds now?"

"Not funny."

"So speaking of your other half, where is he?"

"He's meeting with the Fore-Demons to discuss our impending nuptials and... other matters."

"Don't tell me you need their permission to marry."

With a roll of her eyes, Lucy grabbed the only stool not coated with chocolate and took a seat. "Like I'd listen to them anyway."

"You are the Sex Princess, after all."

Being the daughter of the Sexubi King definitely had its advantages. Then again, it had its disadvantages too. Serah saw what could happen if Lucy's powers were unleashed. Pheromones from hell. Thank goodness she'd learned to control those powers, or she'd never be able to go out in public. Then again, she and Rafe did enjoy their *privacy*.

"It's *Sexubi* Princess. Big difference." Her gaze softened. "Seriously, hon. We're worried about you."

Were they suggesting she have herself committed? Then again, some days that's what she thought she should do. The odors that barraged her night and day. The imps who liked to play. Luckily, with the protection charms they insisted she use, she was safe. Then again how good was a protection charm when it couldn't protect her from herself?

Chapter 2

THE PRINCESS GOT HER WAY.

Then again, even if she wasn't royalty, Lucy would still get her way. One of the reasons Serah loved her so much. She never gave up.

"We're going to talk about this privately." Lucy dragged her toward the door leading to her office.

"I work better alone, anyway," Kalli said, flinging the fondue pot into the sink.

"Don't you remember anything from that day?" Lucy asked as she kicked the door shut. She flopped into the leather, high-back chair and steepled her fingers. As if on cue, she tapped her foot. Impatience certainly wasn't a virtue. Then again, she was part sex demon. She probably didn't need to worry about virtues.

"What day?" Serah asked nonchalantly. She slung herself into her chair and kicked her feet up on her desk. Swiveling the chair from side to side, she flashed her friend a sweet smile. Of course she knew what day. They'd been through this before.

"I told you I don't remember. One moment I'm on the phone with you, the next I'm being yanked by my coat by a man who's too blond for his own good." If it wasn't for the cinnamon and sewer smell that lingered in the air, she might have been attracted.

"We don't have time for this, Serah." The greenish-amber glow of Lucy's gaze sliced into her. "This is the third time this month Kalli and I have come to your rescue."

"Maybe I irritated some demon king," Serah said. "It's nothing, really. I have Mr. Whiskers to protect me now anyway."

Lucy rolled her eyes, something she was way too good at. "The hell it isn't." Lucy wrinkled her nose. "Mr. Whiskers? What kind of name is that?"

"Whoever had him before cut his whiskers." She balled her fists. Who in their right mind did that to a cat? "It seemed appropriate."

"Poor guy. Speaking of the little ball of fur, how's he handling his new home?"

"Too well. He's already out chasing the Persian tail next door."

"Sounds like a cat." Lucy scraped fingers through her mussed hair. "I thought he was neutered."

"I have no idea. Nothing surprises me anymore." She blew out a breath. "So what other matters is Rafe discussing with the all-knowing Fore-Demons?"

Lucy looked down to the floor and let her gaze roam to the wall. She punctuated her review with a small sigh. Serah knew that expression well. She was hiding something.

"Another mission, huh?"

Lucy shrugged. "I guess."

"Is there another demon outbreak?"

Lucy scooted the chair closer and leaned over the desk. "I don't know. Is there?"

Serah contained her gulp. Did she know? God she hoped not. She wanted a normal life, away from imps, ghouls, and demons—present company excluded. "How would I know?"

"Serah, you know how much I hate beating around the bush." Her friend's hazel eyes sparked and swirled. Her fingers gripped the side of the desk as her knuckles whitened. Even before unlocking her succubus nature, Lucy was a force to be reckoned with. But now, the potent energy rolled from her every pore. Frightening, yet amazing just the same. "So spill it."

Why did Lucy have to be so damn astute? Then again they were best friends. They'd known each other for over twenty years, so reading each other had become second nature.

So did bullshitting. And Serah could BS with the best of them. Taking a deep breath of air, she leaned in to challenge Lucy's stern glare. "I have nothing to spill."

"Except a pot full of chocolate," she muttered. "Oh wait, that was more than a spill." Resting back in the chair, Lucy heaved a sigh. "This is serious, girl. I'm worried about you. Something's going on. I know it. And I know deep down inside you know it too. What about the Bernstein's Bar Mitzvah? Pork Rolls? Even I'm not that stupid."

Oh no. Not the Bernstein's. Leave it to Lucy to bring up her most infamous culinary catastrophe, and Serah's first run-in with malevolent minions of hell. Apparently some of these demons didn't like her much. Why else would they have replaced her chicken kabobs with pork instead? Thank goodness she tested all the food before she served it, and thank the gods for Kalli and her magical "cleanup" abilities. Crisis averted.

"For crissakes, Lucy. Did you smell demons when you came in? If there was a demon in my kitchen, they would've left a bigger mess than an exploding pot of chocolate, don't you think?"

"Fine. I'll wait until Rafe gets here. Maybe he can get the information out of you."

Serah shrugged. "I'll tell him the same thing. I don't know what's going on." Not a complete lie. She knew an occasional demon or imp enjoyed giving her a hard time, but this wasn't a demon. This was all Serah. Something inside her made the pot erupt like Mount Vesuvius. White-hot energy streaked through her, radiating to everything around her. Uncontrollable. Scary, yet exhilarating—And she didn't like it one bit.

Matthias sheathed his sword. This had to be some cruel joke at his expense. The Fore-Demons knew his secret. They were deliberately toying with him. He'd rather be a mercenary for an eternity than weakened by her hooded sapphire gaze. Never mind that gaze was framed by a sinfully sweet oval face. Shifting to ease the discomfort his tight blue jeans suddenly caused, he stifled a growl. Not in front of Deleon. He was the last person who needed to know what was going on.

The door to his personal chambers flew open, a cold burst of air spiraling around him. Rafael Deleon strode into the room, slamming the oak door behind him. With a steely gaze, he scanned the room. "Are you ready yet, Ambrose? We haven't got all day." Rafael swiped a strand of dark hair from his face. With a snort, he glanced down at the gold watch on his wrist.

Odd. He remembered the old pocket watch the brute had always taken such good care of. Perhaps

Rafael Deleon was succumbing to modern inventions after all.

"Where's your pocket watch, Deleon?"

He shrugged. "I wanted something newer, and it was a gift from Lucy... my fiancée."

And succumbing to human emotions as well. To each their own. If it was what Deleon wanted for himself, then so be it. Matthias, on the other hand—he'd given up his humanity a long time ago. There was no way he'd ever get it back. Which was fine by him. He wouldn't know what to do with it anyway.

"How touching." Matthias said with a chuckle. "Who knew that the ever-so-staunch and severe Rafael Deleon would fall in love."

"I wouldn't say staunch, Ambrose."

"Oh what would you call it then?"

"I had a stick up my ass."

And he'd grown a sense of humor too. Well, good for him. "Sometimes a stick serves a purpose."

"A purpose maybe, but uncomfortable still the same." Rafael's gaze grew serious. "If you truly want to be a Paladin, the stick serves a better purpose elsewhere."

"We'll see about that."

Rafael crossed his arms and leaned against the alabaster wall. "I'm sure the idea of protecting a human leaves little to be desired, but Serah SanGermano isn't just any human. There's something special about her. Plus, we need your help locating the assassin who was hired to kidnap her."

Matthias's blood, had he been truly alive, would've run cold. He struggled to rein in every bit of calmness within his body. This would not go well. His first mission as a Paladin trainee would end in failure. Perhaps this was what the Fore-Demons had planned.

Deleon was right about one thing. Serah was not just any woman. She had power. That much he could tell. He was lucky he was able to wipe her memories. If only he could wipe his own. If only he'd never taken the mission in the first place. The Infernati, however, drove a hard bargain.

If Deleon knew the truth, he'd be beyond pissed. He'd probably send Matthias back to limbo for an eternity. The mad side of him sank. The sane part of him cheered. Limbo was a better fate than guarding Serah SanGermano. Matthias stifled the chuckle that threatened. The only thing Serah truly needed protection from was him.

He balled his hands into tight fists. He wouldn't let Deleon see him in such a weakened state. That was the Paladin way, as he remembered. Never succumb to your emotions. Then why in the hell was Deleon still a Paladin. He'd succumbed to the most infamous emotion of all.

Love. He'd loved once before. He'd be twice damned if he'd do it again. The only thing love brought him was an eternity of anguish and guilt. And the hold Serah SanGermano had on him wasn't good. He'd felt that way once before. Nearly eight hundred years ago.

He finally found his voice. "Mercenaries don't generally move in the same social circles. What makes you think I can find this one?"

"I'm sure you have connections, Ambrose. Business and networking contacts?"

"When you've done this as long as I have, it's no

longer a business... it's my life." *Time to lighten the mood*. Or at least try to. "And I turned in my DAMN card centuries ago."

Rafael arched a brow. "DAMN?"

"Demon Assassin and Mercenary Network."

"Ridiculous."

"Tell me about it, considering there is a big difference between the two. By the way, I'm a mercenary, not an assassin."

"Is there really a difference? You're both paid to kill people."

Leave it to Deleon to bring him down a few notches. "I'm a hired soldier, not a hired killer." *But not far from it*.

"Fair enough. Thank you for the distinction."

Apparently Deleon wasn't thrilled about this mission either. Matthias would give him kudos for that. He was pretty damned astute. Two reluctant heroes? This would be interesting, if not suicidal.

"I didn't sign up to baby-sit a mortal. I've over a half century of demonic combat skills. I could be better use elsewhere."

"I'm not disagreeing, Ambrose." Rafael flexed as he crossed his arms. "But the Fore-Demons chose this mission for you." Much to Deleon's disappointment, it seemed.

"They've made mistakes before."

Rafael shrugged. "True, but the mistakes always managed to work themselves out." His expression grew stern. "I'd rather have someone else protecting Serah, but the Fore-Demons chose you, so I am bound to honor their decision."

"So dedicated to the cause."

"To a fault. Truth is, I don't trust you. You haven't chosen a side in over seven hundred years. You're a mercenary. The only things guiding your decisions have been wealth and self-preservation. Why all of the sudden now?"

"I have my reasons."

"Are they honorable or just self-serving?"

Matthias returned his answer with stark silence, his jaw ticking with aggravation. The less Rafael knew the better. He drew his lips straight.

"Until you can answer that question, I'll have my doubts. Make no mistake, I will be watching you... like a hawk."

"I appreciate that, Deleon. It shows your dedication. Don't worry. My decisions, although personal, are honorable."

"Very well. I'll still be watching you."

"As my handler, I wouldn't expect anything less."

Deleon took a controlled gulp of air. "Good. We'd better get going. The sooner we get you into your duty, the better." His face turned to stone.

Matthias stifled a groan. Not only did Rafael Deleon not trust him, he didn't even trust himself. This would prove a tough mission, indeed.

Chapter 3

"YOU MAKE A GOOD FONDUE." KALLI STRODE INTO THE room, broom in one hand, chocolate-covered strawberry in the other. With a quick lick of her lips, she plopped the remaining strawberry into her mouth. "I wonder if this is what heaven tastes like."

"Heaven could be closer than you think. With your miraculous cleaning abilities, that has to count for something." Serah flashed a confident smile. "And I'll pass your compliments to Edie. It's her recipe."

"No wonder she was flipping out," Kalli replied. "No worries. Your chocolate pot and its heavenly contents are intact. The kitchen is clean." She turned to Lucy. "Is everything under control?"

"For now."

"Good." Kalli turned to glance at the clock. "I have a haircut in an hour. So if everything's fine?"

"Rafe is due back anytime. We'll be fine."

Kalli nodded. "I've got a few minor things in the kitchen to take care of and I'll be on my way." She spun on the heels of her clunky boots and sauntered out of the room.

Lucy stretched out her legs. "Seriously, though. This is getting tiring. You're hiding something and I don't like it."

"I told you I don't remember anything. Have I hidden anything before?"

Lucy coughed. "Do you want my honest answer?"

They'd known each other for over twenty years, ever since Nonni and she had moved from Chicago. There wasn't much they could keep hidden from each other, no matter how hard either of them tried—which was why this was so difficult.

The more Lucy pried, the more she chipped away at the truth. And truth could be scarier than fiction. What if one of the demons Lucy and she had loosed managed to possess her? Maybe that's how she was able to smell demons. She just hoped she didn't go Linda Blair on everyone. That stuff only happened in the movies, right?

Then again, so much crazy shit had happened that night, anything was possible. Nonni always warned her that demons existed. Serah always thought she was just babbling a bunch of nonsense. But after that night, she realized how true it was.

But what if it was something else? What if she was a demon too? Then again, from the conversations she'd heard between Rafe and Lucy, only those demons who'd been blessed could sense that hideous odor. Did that mean she was blessed? Was she a Paladin and didn't know it or was she just a freak of nature? The way her life seemed to be going, it was safe to believe the latter.

"Earth to Serah." Lucy pushed her lips together and slammed her hands to her waist. "So have you had any new revelations?"

Revelations? Ha. From the looks of it, that's where they were heading. Hurricanes, earthquakes, volcanoes. Oh my, was this the end? She hoped not. She had a helluva lot of stuff on her bucket list. Saving the world from herself was not on that list.

"Nothing new, unfortunately. Like I said a million times, you'll be the first to know when I do."

"If Kalli doesn't pick it up on her radar first."

Kalli and her radar. Oh, Serah knew it wasn't a real radar, but it still impressed her just the same. Anywhere in Connolly Park there was some sort of demonic activity, Kalli was there to either kick ass or clean up. Quite impressive.

"Trust me. Kalli's radar won't see any unauthorized demons here."

"And I never expected demons to destroy my salon, either."

"But—"

A blast of cold air slammed into Serah, swirling and churning as ice crystals danced in the air. Fog rolled up and filled the office. Goose bumps bubbled up, making the hairs at the back of her neck stand at attention. If she didn't know better, she'd think the AC was on the fritz. But she knew that the churning ice and fog meant something else—Rafe was on his way. And from the size of the ice storm brewing in her office, he wasn't alone.

"Get out of the way, Serah. You're standing in Rafe's poof space."

Poofing was what Lucy called *Peragrans*. Apparently it was Latin for traveling. Now Latin, a language Serah thought was dead, reared its ugly head. She never was any good at it in Catholic school. Lucy, on the other hand, could speak and read it better than those holier than thou nuns. And she didn't even need to study.

"Is it always like this?" Serah asked, frost rolling from her mouth. Ice sliced through the air. Winds gusted and spun around them. She caught her breath and pushed her way to the corner of the room. She'd never seen a *Peragrans* before, only heard Lucy's stories. Lucy only traveled once and said that was enough for her. Being only half-demon, it really sucked all the energy from her. For Rafe, and many full-blood demons, though, it barely affected them.

"Not usually. I've never seen a double poof before." Lucy yanked at the pink sweater clinging to her curvy form. Dark blonde hair whipping in the wind, she steadied herself. Well at least Serah wasn't the only one affected by the winter storm brewing in her office.

"I know it's almost December, but isn't this a little strange?"

Lucy managed a chuckle, despite the ice pelting her face. "Sorry, but that word is no longer in my vocabulary, along with weird, fucked up, and a few others."

"Point made," Serah gasped out.

Ice and snow still spun as two bulky figures formed in front of her eyes. Winds whipped and wound around, and the frost bit at her skin. She pulled her arms closer in an attempt to keep warm, but the cold remained relentless, surrounding her, slicing into her chef's jacket.

The winds died down. Ice and snow drifted and melted away. The bitter cold evaporated into the mists. All that remained were two ice-covered hunks. All the descriptions Lucy had given her in the past few months did not compare to the volatile beauty she saw. Sure it may have been cold enough to freeze off an extremity or two, but fascinating just the same.

With a flick of his head, Rafe flung ice and frost from his hair. Dusting off the leather jacket that clung to his every muscle, he let his silver eyes gaze around the room. Spotting Lucy, a wide smile arched his lips. Even though he tried to hide it with all his pomp and pride, he was a man in love. And there wasn't anyone but Lucy worthy of that love.

Just like that, Serah's dreams of a spinster sisterhood went up in smoke.

Then it happened. The other hulk shook the ice from his thick, massive body. Any words she wanted to speak died on her lips. Her breath caught. Her heart thumped. She could only stare. Then his gaze met hers. Eyes the color of the darkest onyx burned into her, sending shivers racing from her head down to her toes. Not because it was cold, but something else. Something dangerous.

Biceps flexing, he flung the remaining chunks of ice from his short, light brown hair. A well-chiseled chin under a pair of strong, yet unsmiling, lips. Wonderful. Another demon with an attitude. But there was something about this demon that unnerved her. No hint of Infernati scent lingered in the air, yet her senses were on full alarm.

"Where are we?" His voice, deep and baritone, hit her like a brick. Her breath caught again. Her legs turned to mush. What the heck was happening? What was the deal with this Adonis standing in the middle of her office?

"Serah's office, it appears." Rubbing fingers against the stubble on his chin, Rafe scanned the room. "Don't tell me there was another *incident*."

Arching an eyebrow, Lucy flashed a wary glance at Serah. "No imps or demons involved this time, fortunately. I wish I knew what was going on." She glanced at the man and back to Rafe. "So everything's been arranged?"

For some reason Serah didn't like the sound of that. She squirmed in her pumps and rubbed the tips of her fingers together. What exactly had they arranged?

"Yes, sweetie." With a quick peck to her cheek, Rafe took Lucy in his arms and crushed her to him. "I missed you."

Lucy ran her fingers through Rafe's hair. "I missed you too, Rafie-Poo."

The mystery man cringed. Well, they had one thing in common. The intense aversion to public displays of affection and silly nicknames.

Serah snuck another glance at him. Hot damn. He could give Rafe a run for his money in a Mr. Universe competition. Here she thought Rafe was sculpted. This guy, though… holy shit! An army green T-shirt strained against well-defined pecs. The faint outline of his abs traced down to the waist of his olive green khakis. A pair of black lace-up combat boots completed his outfit. G.I. Demon reporting for duty. Go figure, even demons had Rambo tendencies.

She thought they all wore leather. Rafe always did. The image of this man in black leather flashed in her mind. Her mouth watered. God, she hoped mind reading wasn't this guy's demonic talent. Can you say awkward?

Jaw rigid, he crossed his arms. Stoic and silent, he turned and strode toward the window overlooking the not-so-rapid River Rapid. Muscles rippled with each move he made. This afforded her another view of his *ass*ets—just as well formed as the front. He grabbed the windowsill and exhaled—the first sound she heard him utter since the three words he spoke earlier.

A mixture of emotions collided inside. Part of her

melted at the sight of this rock-hard specimen of a man. The other part, the more sensible part, wanted to run away in fright. Today, however, sensibility would win. She would make sure of it.

Serah finally managed to speak. "So who's your friend?"

Rafe scraped a chunk of hair from his brow. "Not a friend—a colleague." He turned to the other man and crossed his arms. "I suppose introductions are in order."

The guy growled—a common sound where demons are concerned—and, keeping his well-endowed backside to her, pulled away from the window. Whoever he was, he sure didn't want to be here. But if what she heard about the Fore-Demons was true, most Paladins never ended up where they wanted. Karma, she guessed.

"Ambrose, enough brooding already. Join us now."

Ambrose? A name to go with the face. A name to go with the attitude too, apparently. Stuffy and arrogant—a common affliction among demons. Brooding was the understatement of the century. This guy was as unyielding as a concrete wall. Not a real good conversationalist either. She snuck another glance. He jerked his head, as if the very sight of her would turn him to stone. Little did he know, he didn't need her help with that. He did it well enough on his own.

The usual lack of interest from men didn't normally affect Serah, but for some reason this man's blatant unconcern left her frustrated, angry, and even a little disappointed.

Two could play this game. His pride seeped into her. With a haughty lift of her chin, she crossed her arms. Lips pursed, she angled an attempt at a nonchalant glance. In a not-so-Oscar-worthy performance, she drew out a long annoyed huff and spun away from him. Melodrama was another of her fortes.

Lucy arched her brow and snuck her a surreptitious glare. "Wow, is it just me or did it get even more icy in here?" She turned her glance back to egomaniacal asshat. "Definitely a cold front for sure."

Rafe strode to the guy and gave him a healthy tug of the shoulder. "You'll have to forgive him. This is a new type of mission for him."

"Welcome to Earth," Lucy said, extending her arm. "I'm Lucia Gregory. You can call me Lucy."

He nodded and took Lucy's proffered hand. "A pleasure to meet you, Lucia."

Ouch. What a way to break out the formalities. Too bad he didn't know how much Lucy hated being called by her given name. Wars had been started over less trivial things.

Serah decided to break the ice—almost literally. "Lucy. Only her mother and her cronies can get away with calling her Lucia." She stuck out her arm and offered him her hand. "And I'm Serah SanGermano, Lucy's friend."

The man's onyx eyes met hers again. This time they lingered. Even within their abysmal darkness, a heat burned. Despite the fire burning in his eyes, shivers and chills crept along her skin. He hesitated, then allowed his fingers to brush along hers. A shock of electricity replaced the chills. She should've pulled her hand back, but she couldn't. His fingers encircled her hand and his grip grew firm.

Heat rocketed through her. She stifled the gasp that

was near bursting from her lips. Her head spun. All this from a touch? What the heck was going on?

He hesitated again then shook. "Seraphina."

Serah contained the cringe that threatened to release. And here Lucy thought her given name was horrendous. Hers took the cake. What were her parents smoking when they named her? Something that made them fly, apparently. Little did they know, she was no angel. There was only room for one of those in this town. Then again, knowing Connolly Park and all its weirdness, there were probably more.

Lucy snickered. "Seraphina? You gotta be joking."

"Shut up," she muttered. With a yank, she pulled her hand from Ambrose's grip. Quite a feat too. "If I hear you mutter anything more about how much you hate your name, I'll knock you upside the head."

"I didn't know it was secret. My apologies."

More importantly, how did *he* know her real name? Maybe it was his demonic talent common one at that. At least two demons she knew had the ability to read minds. One of which was in the kitchen working her *magic*.

"Guess it isn't anymore." *Poor Nonni.* She always told Serah to keep her name a secret. Heck, she was all for that. She hated that name. It made her feel like one of those chubby-cheeked little angels. Who would've known her secret would be let out of the bag by a six-foot-four wall of pure male muscle with dark, black, swimming eyes.

Damn it! This was nuttier than she originally thought.

"You know so much about me, yet I know so little about you."

"I am Matthias Ambrose. I'm here on a mission."

More missions? What now? She angled a teasing glance at Lucy. "Don't tell me you opened another box of demons."

Lucy snorted. "Nope. I added not opening up creepy chests on my list of New Year's resolutions. Remember?"

"Oh yeah." How could she forget those crazy resolutions? Serah's was to avoid buying anything creepy. So far, so good. It was almost December and she'd managed to avoid A-Line Road Antiques, the New Age shop, and the local mission store. Wherever creepy things abounded, she tried her hardest to stay away. She even found a way to block Amazon and eBay on all her computers at home and at work. Who needed fire walls and Internet security, when you had Demonware 2.0?

"Well, I have a kitchen to run, I'll let you all go off to wherever demons go to discuss their missions."

"We're discussing the mission here," Rafe said, his gaze stern and steely. "With you."

"But I'm not a Paladin. Heck, I'm not even a demon."

Matthias's eyes sparked, albeit only briefly. "But you are something."

"Of course, I'm something. I'm one kick-ass caterer." No way in heck would she be anything else. She saw what Lucy went through. Even though everything worked out in the end, she didn't wish the same for herself. Lucy was smart, if not a little lucky. Serah, on the other hand? She wasn't so fortunate. She struggled all throughout grade school and high school and the closest she'd ever come to Lucky were designer jeans. And after looking at that $100 price tag, she didn't feel quite that lucky at all.

Matthias drew his lips straight, his dark, abysmal gaze penetrating. "I didn't come here to play games, Ms. SanGermano."

Despite the anger and frustration welling inside, Serah returned her own penetrating gaze. "Well, that makes two of us, Mr. Ambrose." She turned her gaze to Lucy and Rafe. "What the hell is going on?"

"Since you won't tell us, and we can see you are in obvious danger, the Fore-Demon Council, Lucy and I have decided you need protection."

"From a few imps? Come on. I'm fine. Really. Look. Kalli got it all cleaned up already."

"No, Serah. There are forces out there worse than imps and goblins. Neither of us were harmed when my shop exploded like Old Faithful on steroids. Not a scratch on any of our heads when glass went flying. Tell me that's natural?"

"I'm lucky?"

"More than lucky," Rafe inserted. "You can speak with imps. I've seen how you act when a demon is near. You hesitate. Your eyes widen. You become more alert than any other human I know. You are Pure, and Matthias is here to protect you."

"Pure?" It might have been a while since... well. But she certainly wasn't pure. "You *definitely* got the wrong girl."

"Your blood is pure." Matthias's onyx eyes continued to swim, hinting at her other not so pure portions. Her body shook and shivered, goose bumps popping from her skin.

She struggled to tamp down the sudden rush of adrenaline. Something about this guy sent her body into overdrive. Her heart thumped, sending more waves of electricity. She sucked in a deep breath. "Now I know you all are out of your gourds." She forced a chuckle. "I'm on the River City Blood Bank's 'Do Not Drain' list. Apparently not pure enough for them."

"Or too pure," Matthias muttered. He raked a hand through his shorn dark blond hair. Despite the militaristic facade, something in his face sparked. He angled a glance at her and just as quickly jerked his head away.

"If I'm so pure, why do you keep looking at me like I'm a zombie ready to eat your brains?"

His face filled with alarm. "You've seen a zombie?"

"Dude, this is the twenty-first century. Ever heard of a thing called a movie?"

"Zombies are no laughing matter, Serah. They are mindless humans controlled by demons."

She should have known. It seemed every monster or supernatural being was actually a demon or some sort of minion. Sirens, faeries, and vampires—to name a few more. "I didn't know." Although she probably should have. "Are there any monsters that aren't demons?"

"Look at the world," Rafe added. "Every culture, every continent, every religion has a belief in demons. It isn't a coincidence."

She wouldn't argue there. "Coincidence is something I've learned doesn't really exist." She crossed her arms. "However you all are overreacting. Seriously."

Taking a deep breath, Lucy shook her head. "You want serious? I'll give you serious. Serious is having your salon explode. Serious is finding out your father is still alive and is the King of Sex Demons. Serious is almost getting married to some stinky, egomaniacal demon. I'm quite aware what serious is. This—whether you choose to admit it or not—is very serious."

Matthias's eyes widened, apparently shocked by Lucy's rant. With a slow, meticulous nod, he moved in closer. "I would listen to your friend, Ms. SanGermano."

Lucy raised her chin and crossed her arms. Letting out a long huff of air, she leaned against the high-back chair. "Just humor us here. Even if what you say is true, a little extra protection never hurt anyone." With a waggle of her brow and a lopsided grin, she threw a sidelong glance toward Matthias.

Rafe grumbled and nudged Lucy on the shoulder. "Lucy, please." He angled lower and whispered something in her ear.

With a nonchalant shrug, she whispered back. Tossing Matthias another scrutinizing glare, she scrubbed her fingers through her chunked hair. "Take care of her, Matthias, or I'll kill you."

"I will," Matthias replied, his voice stony.

His onyx glare continued to slice into her. Her stomach was tied in knots and her breath caught. He might not smell of Infernati, but he was still dangerous. He unnerved her. His entire presence seeped into her, drowning her. Part of her wanted to run away in terror. The other part screamed for something else—something she hadn't had in a while.

A little extra protection might not hurt—*my ass*.

Chapter 4

"SO NOW THAT WE'VE GOT EVERYTHING SETTLED, WE should head back to the shop. Kalli deserves a break." Lucia laced her arm in Rafael's and pulled close to him. It amazed Matthias how much trust and love the two had for each other.

"Should we leave him alone with her? They just met."

"They have to be alone eventually. So why not now?"

Rafael's silver eyes sparked as he angled a glance at Serah.

"Why don't all three of you vamoose? I already have protection."

"Your chimp of an imp isn't going to protect you from the evil coming this way." Matthias crossed his arms and turned a stern glare at her. "The Paladins need you safe. They need your help to fight the Infernati."

Serah shrugged, then raised her chin. "Squeaky's moved on to bigger pastures. And I'm a lover, not a fighter."

"Oh. What form is of protection do you have now?"

"I have Mr. Whiskers," she spat out.

"Mr. Whiskers? What kind of name is that?"

"He's a cat."

"You call that protection?"

"He is a certified attack cat. He's good with his claws."

"A cat is no match for an Infernati assassin."

"He has claws. Twenty of them, to be exact. And they're razor-sharp too."

"Twenty?" Matthias asked.

"Polydactyl, or so I've been told."

Matthias grumbled. She definitely needed more protection. "Where is Mr. Whiskers now if he is such a good protector?"

"He's at my house."

Matthias's jaw tensed. Either she was clueless or just plain reckless. Either way, she needed someone to defend her. "And that's why I'm here." He leaned in, his jaw set and his nostrils flaring. Perhaps he could scare her into submission. He might not have wanted this mission to start, but now he knew its severity. He'd read the reports Deleon had given him. She was more stubborn than he thought. She was smarter than she gave herself credit for too. He sensed the energy surrounding her. He saw it in the spark in her eyes. It radiated from her every pore, hot and heavy, and seeped into his being. That sort of power needed to be controlled. She needed more than a bodyguard. "Your life depends on it."

"Oh, well." Her gaze glowed like two molten sapphires. His heart, despite the control he tried to muster, thumped in his chest, sending all the blood rushing to his groin, where an altogether different organ throbbed. Bloody hell.

She could very well be her own worst enemy—and his complete and utter downfall. One thing was obvious. The Fore-Demons wanted him to fail. And, with his previous history, it didn't surprise him one bit. He'd heard stories about the Fore-Demons and their cryptic ways. Perhaps they knew more than they let on. Mayhap they believed he was doomed long before he even joined the ranks. He had news for the Fore-Demon Council. He would not back down. If he was meant to fail, he wouldn't go down without a fight. Serah's protection depended on it.

"Oh well?" he ground out, grabbing her by the shoulders. Heat pounded its way from the tips of his fingers and slammed him in the head. His whole body reeled with energy. Calming the rush of energy and emotions rushing through him, he sucked in a breath. "Your friend saved your life, did she not?"

Serah's gaze widened. Her body trembled against him. He loosened his grip on her shoulders, reluctant to let go completely.

"Yes," she whispered. She lowered her gaze to the gray, carpeted floor. Even though it had only been gone for a mere second, Matthias already missed that sapphire gleam. Maybe she was finally coming to her senses, because God knew he was surely losing his.

"Damn, Ambrose. We wanted you to protect her, not have her cowering in fear." Lucia shook her head. "What the hell?"

"She needs to accept what she is. Acting stubborn and ignoring the truth isn't the way." He glanced around the room, seeing Lucia's and Rafe's piercing gazes. Uttering a low growl, Matthias scrubbed his chin. "This isn't the sort of mission I'm used to."

Serah's head snapped up, affording him another glance at the jewels he desperately tried to avoid. "What sort of mission are you used to, Ambrose?"

Matthias's heart quickened. Good God! Did she remember? She might have been strong, but his powers were strong enough to make even a demon forget, which was why his services were always in high demand. He always wondered why the gift of erasing his victims' memories was important. After all, they usually ended up dead or banished to the deepest dregs of hell. There, memories were often fleeting.

But not everyone's memories were so fragile. Those with stronger powers often remembered, and Serah was powerful. He needed to tread carefully. He couldn't have her remember. Not just the kidnapping, but something else. Something he should have never done, something he swore he'd never do in over seven hundred and fifty years as a demon. He had let his emotions get in the way. He had fallen victim to her charm. He needed to keep his distance—a virtually impossible task.

But he had no choice. This mission was no longer about him finding his place. It was about keeping Serah safe. He could not fail. He owed her that much, after all the horror he'd allowed to befall her earlier.

"Well?" Her sweet, sultry voice broke his thoughts.

"I'm a tactical expert."

Her gaze roved up and down his body, sending more heat spiraling through his veins. He strained to swallow the lump forming in his throat. "I should have guessed. Military fatigues and all."

"He didn't have time to change," Rafe said, his voice annoyed. "We'll have to go shopping later."

Matthias cringed. Some things still hadn't changed over the years. Shopping was one of them. Merchants might have improved their wares over the centuries, but the outcome was still the same—overpriced rubbish.

"I hate shopping," Lucia grumbled. "I'd rather have a root canal… with no anesthesia."

Serah chuckled. "You're just jealous of my mad shopping skills." It amazed him how, despite the tension of the situation, everyone remained chipper. He should've been unnerved, but the laughter seeped into his system. His jaw twitched as he struggled to control the smile brimming on his lips. He couldn't show weakness.

Serah scrunched her brow, her gaze quizzical. "The constipated look doesn't become you at all."

"I don't see the humor in this," he said, forcing a gruff tone. The fact was, the humor was infectious, like a disease that crept in when you least expect it. He was practical. He was tactical. He didn't have time for laughter. It left you open. It left you vulnerable. He needed to be alert if he wanted to keep her alive.

"Laughter is the best medicine, you know." Serah let out a long sigh. "Seriously, Lucy. This guy's stick is wedged so far up even a proctologist can't help him."

Everyone broke out into laughter. Everyone except him.

Matthias wasn't that familiar with mortal medicine, but he was familiar with ancient languages, so he had a good idea what a proctologist was. And hopefully he wouldn't be meeting one any time soon—stick up his ass or not.

"I'm so glad I dropped out of med school," Lucia drawled.

"Whatever. You would have kicked ass as a surgeon, but the women of Connolly Park thank you for your sacrifice." The sarcasm rolled from Serah's mouth and permeated his senses. What was it about that subtle wit that drove him mad?

Lucia chuckled. "The only thing I sacrificed was my insanity. You know how much blood scares me."

With that, an irritatingly high-pitched falsetto rent

the air. Lucia dug in her pocket for the source of the annoying tune.

"Justin Bieber? For real?" Serah covered her ears, grimacing in mock horror.

Lucia fumbled with the gadget. "It was the only thing I could find annoying enough to force me to answer the phone."

She pressed a button. "What's up?"

Matthias contained his groan. God, how he hated those silly electrical contraptions that modern mortals allowed their lives to revolve around. He wished things were as simple as they were eons ago. But times change, people changed, and so did their technologies. In this day and age, technology was a necessary evil.

"Oh, really?" Lucia blew out a deep breath. "Wow. Just wow." Gripping her phone tight, she paced the office. "All right. We're almost done here anyway."

Rafael's eyes glinted. "What's going on?"

Lucia covered the phone. "Hairstyling emergency. Frankie accidentally dyed someone's hair blue." She blew out a loud breath of air. "Where's Kalli?" She paused briefly. "Oh, okay." She shook her head. "Gerardo, you know that's not safe. Even angels have their limitations. Rafe and I are just about done. Everything's settled. We'll be right there."

"What now?" Rafael asked with a groan.

"Kalli sure picks the best time to stock up on supplies," said Lucia.

"What about Gerardo? Can't he do anything?"

"You know as well as I do that angels aren't supposed to use their powers on humans. Looks like we're the next line of defense."

"Bloody hell." Rafael turned to lock gazes with Lucia. "I really don't like leaving him alone with her so soon. But I've seen some of your irate customers."

Lucia stuffed the phone back in her pocket. She turned to her friend, sternness etched across her face. "We're not finished talking."

"I figured as much," said Serah, as she steepled her fingers, hunched her shoulders, and allowed soft sigh to escape.

Matthias's mind reeled. Angels? Here in Connolly Park as well? Angels and demons, congregating in one area? This did not bode well. Something big was brewing. Something he didn't want Serah to be a part of. He wanted her safe, protected. He would not fail her.

It was his fault she was in this mess. Had he not delivered her into the Infernati's clutches, they would have never found out about her powers. He'd signed her death warrant. He wished he'd signed his own instead.

"Gerardo's only a guardian angel. No worries, buddy."

"How—"

"The tension in your jaw. The narrowing of your gaze," Serah said with a shrug. "It's pretty much written all over your face."

Then again, she was a Pure-Blood. From what he'd heard, they were excellent at reading expressions, even those of people they barely knew. Matthias struggled to rein in the churning emotions boiling to the surface, realizing again that they weren't complete strangers.

Serah crossed her arms, her gaze adamant. "He's harmless."

Not good enough of an answer in his book. "Angels,

even those of the guardian variety, don't usually social-
ize with demons."

"She needed guidance. He saw no one guiding her,
so he stepped in."

"How nice of him."

In his previous dealings with angels, he'd learned to
avoid them at all costs. But now, since he was training
to be a Paladin, that would have to change. After all,
he'd need an angel's blessing. Was it worth it? He snuck
another glance at Serah. She twirled a corkscrew curl
around a pink-tipped fingernail. Hell yes, it was. And
when he was done, he'd erase himself from her memory
again. Too bad he couldn't erase her from his.

"Gerardo was a blessing." Lucia raised her chin.
"And one damn good stylist. Angels aren't that much
different than Paladins." She flashed Matthias a smile.
"Relax. Today's his last day. He's being reassigned."

"That's mildly comforting," Matthias muttered.

Lucia shrugged. "We both want to keep the
Infernati from taking over." With that she looped her
arm in Rafael's. "We'll have to continue this conversation later."

"If you need anything, you know how to reach us."
Rafael flashed a surreptitious glare. "Take care of
her, Ambrose."

"I will."

"Good." He led Lucia to the door. "I could always
travel there, you know."

"Yeah, that's a great idea," Lucia muttered.

"Good point. That swirling ice storm could scare the
bejeezus out of your clients."

"No kidding," Lucia said with a smirk.

"Call me if you need anything." Lucia allowed Rafael to escort her out the door. The door slammed behind them with an ominous thud.

"Guess I'm stuck with you."

Matthias's heart clenched. He ground his teeth. He should be relieved that she wanted nothing to do with him, yet it only filled him with regret. "I cannot let you out of my sight."

"I hope you don't plan on joining me in the shower. That would be awkward."

Matthias struggled to control the beating of his heart. Just the thought of water rushing through her dark cascade of curls and down her lush, naked body sent more desire ripping through him. He needed to get her out of his system. Fast, before he exploded. No, he didn't plan on joining her in the shower. That would be too dangerous.

"There's no need to worry, Matt. It's okay to call you Matt, right?" There was no mistaking the challenge in her glare. Bloody hell and Hades.

"Pardon?"

"Gerardo. Like Lucy said, he's being reassigned." A forced smile spread across Serah's lips. "I'm planning his going-away party. I really can't have any unwelcome interruptions."

"I didn't ask for this either, Ms. SanGermano. I have better things I could be doing with my time." Like trying to forget he'd almost delivered her to her death.

He wished he had the ability to turn back time. He'd do things differently. Too bad time travel wasn't one of his demonic talents. He'd gladly go back in time and tell them no—even if it meant losing one of his own.

Chapter 5

WOW. SHE THOUGHT THOSE WORDS WOULD HAVE brought relief, but they had the opposite effect. All she was to him was an inconvenience. Then again, she, herself, had just said the same thing about him. What was it about this guy that sent her sensors into hyperdrive? Regardless of the aura of danger that surrounded his not-so-frequent moves, another, more-mysterious aura shimmered deeper in him, leaving her utterly intrigued.

And she didn't like it at all.

"When will your inadequate idea of protection be returning?"

"Mr. Whiskers may be small, but I wouldn't call him inadequate."

"A cat can't follow you everywhere—like a true bodyguard can."

"I was fine on my own. I'm sorry my friends dragged you into this mess. They tend to overreact anytime anything weird happens to me."

God love 'em. Not that she didn't appreciate a little friendly intervention now and again, but it was starting to seriously dampen her cooking mojo. If she wanted to succeed, she needed her mojo intact, and having a six-foot-four, rock-hard giant lounging around wouldn't help things either. Even if he was a giant jackass, he was still a distraction.

Matthias scraped a hand through his light brown

hair, his onyx gaze narrowing. "Your friends care about you." He opened his mouth to say more, but instantly shut it. He took cautious steps toward her, his eyes smoldering.

Her breath caught. A huge lump formed in her throat. Sweat beaded on her palms. Her heart thumped a wild beat. Images flashed in her mind. Matthias's gaze was burning into her, closer and closer. His strong arms wrapped around her. The ridges of his glistening pectorals pressed into her. His fingers wove through her curls, pulling her closer to him. His strong lips brushed against hers. Her mind swam. Dear Lord.

"What the hell are you doing?" she demanded.

"Nothing."

Sure it was nothing—to him, maybe. She should have known the power of suggestion was his demonic trait. "Yeah, right. If you do that again, I'm going to imagine my knee in your nuts. Got it?"

"What happened?"

"Like you said—it was nothing."

Matthias's onyx gaze grew solemn. His face was as immobile as granite. He grabbed her by the shoulders and glared. "What happened?"

Like she was going to tell this man her mind was fantasizing about him—even if he did suggest it. She wouldn't let him know he got to her. "I'm sure you know. Don't you demons know everything that goes on in a human's head?"

"I don't read minds, Serah."

"Sucks to be you, then." As his grip relaxed, she pulled herself free and spun away. "Whatever you're doing, I'd appreciate you doing it to someone else."

"I'm not doing anything! I swear…"

A sarcastic chuckle burst from her lips. "Swear to God?"

"You know as well as I do that a demon cannot swear to God."

"But you're a Paladin, right?"

Matthias lowered his gaze to the carpet below. "Not yet."

"Wow. The Fore-Demons sent me a Paladin-in-Training. Priceless."

Matthias cracked his knuckles. "I have centuries of combat and tactical experience. I once was an armed guard for Napoleon Bonaparte."

"Oh, and look where he ended up."

"He deserved it." His gaze hooded. "Besides, I protected him earlier in his reign."

"And that makes it all right?"

Matthias shrugged. "I've lived a long time. Even demons do things they aren't proud of. I wouldn't expect you to understand."

Oh, she understood, all right. More than she wanted him to know. Regret—well, it could be her middle name. Her heart clenched. She sucked in a breath. She needed to be strong—for Nonni. She reached into her pocket and clasped her hand around the watch she had so callously discarded earlier. The diamonds warmed against her skin, and peacefulness seeped into her pores. Yet she wasn't at peace. She would never be.

"Yeah. You're right. Being a human and all," she fibbed. Quickly caressing her grandmother's watch, she pulled her hand from her pocket.

"I have some questions about what happened this afternoon. I need details so I can gauge the situation." Narrowing his gaze, he motioned her to sit. "Please."

The last word strained his lips. She stifled a chuckle. He apparently hadn't muttered the *P*-word all that often. Then again, a man of his size and strength probably didn't have to beg for much.

"Since you asked so nicely." She swayed toward the desk that took up most of the corner and sat down. Following her lead, he took the seat across from her. With a soft click, she shut the laptop and leaned in. "Interrogate away. From the looks of your getup, I'm sure you're good at it. Or is truth serum your demonic talent?"

Matthias snorted. "I see you are a witty woman, Ms. SanGermano. I appreciate that, but this is serious, whether you choose to believe it or not."

"Fine. Sorry. I'll cooperate." She shifted in her chair. If he glared any harder, she'd catch on fire.

"Good." Sitting in the office chair he dwarfed, he stretched his legs. Even in that brief, uncomfortable shift, she caught a glimpse of the pure muscled strength that rippled through his entire body.

And here she thought *the questions* would make her uncomfortable. She gulped down a breath of air. Get it done already, so she could get this guy out of her sight—and away from her overactive hormones.

"Did you see anything when the explosion occurred?"

"Nothing out of the ordinary. Just the flames burst a little."

"Hear anything?"

"No. Just Edie, my sous-chef, screaming."

He scratched his chin. "Smell anything?"

"No. Just the smell of horribly expensive chocolate erupting."

"Taste anything?"

"No. But the chocolate would have tasted good, had it not exploded."

"Feel anything?"

Had he seen her hand in her pocket? Did he know? The way the word rolled off his lips left her uneasy. "Well, Mr. Ambrose, I felt a lot. You would too if you watched ten-dollar-a-pound chocolate erupt before your eyes." She held back her sigh of relief. She couldn't show him any hesitation.

"Really?"

"It all happened so fast. I really didn't pay any attention. My main concern was Edie. If that stuff had ended up on her, she'd have been in the hospital with third-degree burns."

"Fair enough." His thoughtful expression lingered. "What about these other incidents?"

"A tiny little imp changing chicken into pork?"

"What about this ghoul and this goblin that Rafael reported?"

Damn it. He wouldn't let up. Then again, that was probably part of his tactical experience. "What's next, waterboarding?"

"I do not condone the use of torture." A flash sparked in his eyes. "I have more productive ways of obtaining the truth."

She bet he did. The temperature in the office rose another fifty degrees—at least that's what it felt like. She didn't like the way he made her feel. She sucked in a gulp of air. Who was she kidding? The naughty part of her loved it. *Down, naughty girl. Not now!*

She snapped back to reality. "Doesn't surprise me."

"How so?"

"You're not a small guy, for one. And that glare could melt an iceberg. And the stern expression—well it's stronger than the ones my grandmother showed me when I misbehaved."

"Niceties do not get you far in my position." He reached down to grab a huge duffle bag and stood. With an unceremonious thud, he dropped the bag on the desk. With a quick yank of the zipper, he spread the bag open. Grabbing a Glock, he slid in a magazine and stuffed it in the holster on his hip. Snapping the holster in place, he grabbed another magazine and shoved it into a pouch on his waist. Another snap, another weapon—this time a dagger. Unsheathing it from the ruby-and-sapphire-bedecked scabbard, he twisted the weapon in his grip, and the silver-etched blade flashed. She'd never seen anything so beautiful in her life. Vines were carved from hilt to tip and rosebuds had been etched into the shiny silver. Rubies and sapphires spiraled around the hilt.

Not an ordinary weapon for a mercenary. Then again he wasn't any mercenary. He was a demon. And he wasn't any ordinary demon. He was a built like a brick shithouse—luckily he didn't smell like one. And, heavens, his face was strong and angled. Not unattractive—if you were into the Delta Force type. Or was that Demon Force. And from the way her hormones flared, she was becoming that type. Not good. Hormones and hollandaise did not mix—at all.

"Admiring the blade, are you?"

Among other things. It was safe to assume he couldn't read thoughts—thank goodness—because her thoughts would make even a eunuch blush.

"It's not the type of weapon I'd expect from someone in camouflage."

"It was given to me by my mentor." His dark eyes glinted, and something similar to remorse passed over his face. He strapped the scabbard to his belt and slammed the dagger in. Without another word, he hoisted the duffle over his shoulder. "A few centuries back."

Well, if that wasn't a conversation stopper, she didn't know what was. And he obviously wanted to keep his distance, which was—much to her recently active hormones' chagrin—fine by her.

"All right, already. I know you're old, dude. No need to keep beating that in."

"I was not."

"So you say." She tucked a stray curl behind her ear. "But if you plan on wearing those weapons into the mall, security will be on you like white on rice."

"Normal humans shouldn't be able to see my weapons."

"What's that supposed to mean?"

"It means you need to realize—no matter how hard you try to hide it—you are not normal."

"I've got news for you. No one is normal. Everyone is unique in their own special way. Even century-old demons."

"Centuries."

"You know what I mean." Curiosity bit her in the butt. "How old are you exactly?"

"I was born in 1194."

Whoa! He was a lot older than Rafe... by at least

three centuries. "When did you die?" He couldn't have been that much over thirty.

He opened his mouth to answer, then shut it, a deep scowl etched on his face. "I prefer to keep my previous life private, Ms. SanGermano. No offense."

Irritating, yet that aura of mystery nagged at her. Why in the hell was she so interested in him? "Fine, but the mall closes soon, and you definitely need some less conspicuous clothes. I didn't tell Lucy, but I'm trying out for *American Chef*."

"What?"

"I'm trying out for *American Chef*."

"I forbid it."

"Well, you know, you're not my dad, and last I checked I was twenty-nine years old. I'm old enough to make my own decisions."

Not one of her most brilliant and well-thought-out ideas, but she needed the publicity. And, unfortunately, there was a kill clause in the contract. She couldn't back out now.

"I sort of signed a contract. The host of the show is meeting me tomorrow."

"This isn't safe."

"But now I have a big bad bodyguard to protect me, so what's the big deal?"

"I'll need to discuss this with Rafael. This complicates matters."

"It's *American Chef*, not *Hell's Kitchen*." And thank goodness for that. If there was one chef that could be a demon, Gordon Ramsay was it.

Matthias stood to his full six-foot-four height, his eyes smoldering. "I don't care if it's the bloody *700*

Club, inviting the public means inviting trouble. You don't need any more trouble."

No, what she didn't need was a huge hulk of a man—*scratch that*—demon, controlling her every move. Being a bodyguard and protecting her was one thing. Ordering her around like a child was another. She wasn't a teenager. She was an adult.

"I need publicity. I've had a dry spell. This TV gig will bring in more business." She stood to her full five-foot-six stature in a pathetic attempt to meet his glare. "As for *The 700 Club*, Pat Robertson will be the last person on my invite list." She brushed a finger along her cheek. "How do you know about television? I figured you'd been too busy dealing with your demonic military company."

"Just because I'm a demon doesn't mean I don't keep track of modern religion and political beliefs. I need to stay on top of trends if I'm supposed to blend in."

She let the sarcasm roll off her tongue. "Well, you're doing a smashing job so far. Because everyone in America feels the need to dress up like an extra from *Apocalypse Now*. No pun intended."

"I didn't have time to get civilian clothes."

"I'm sure Rafe would lend you some of his clothes but something tells me leather really isn't your thing." And she doubted he'd fit Rafe's pants anyway. Her heart thudded again. Her breath caught. Muscles bunched and rippled with his every move. She trained her gaze lower—to his hands. They were big, yet elegant—well, as elegant as a military man's hands could get.

Hands like that could grip parts of her body tight. What? Where did that come from?

He gripped the side of the desk. Any tighter and the dark mahogany would splinter. Hands like that could kill.

Serah gulped. She needed to keep her distance from him. He was a demon—and a rather large, dangerous one at that. And the aura of mystery that surrounded him didn't help matters much either. The way he avoided her questions meant one thing. He was hiding something. Then again, he was a mercenary. Not the most honorable job in the world—or the netherworld.

But, first, she needed to get him in new clothes. "The mall is going to close soon, unless you'd rather shop at the Super M-Mart. They're open twenty-four hours a day. Not as expensive, but cheaper quality."

"Money is no issue."

She snorted. "I figured as much. Green's Corner it is. There's a designer big and tall shop in the shopping center. I've obviously never shopped there." But the live models in the window always got her attention— you'd have to be dead not to notice them. Then again, none of those men had anything on Matthias. Centuries of battle experience—human and demonic—would do that to a man.

"Is this necessary? I happen to like my clothes."

"I just think it would look awkward to have you dressed like Rambo. My customers might not like it." Not to mention the T-shirt he wore strained too tight against the ridges of his muscles. She needed to concentrate. Him standing there in military gear twenty-four-seven wouldn't help matters at all.

"Fair enough." He crossed his arms in front of his chest. His words came out strained. "I am at your mercy." His gaze seared and his jaw remained firm. Hard. No softness anywhere.

Her heart continued to thump. She swallowed the lump that kept forming in her throat. No, he'd never be at her complete mercy. Men—demons—like him never were. And for some reason that naughty corner of her didn't mind that one bit. The sooner she got this man into some normal clothes, the better—for the sake of her practical side.

Chapter 6

"Watch out!"

The command echoed in her eardrums. She slammed on the brake, sending her new GMC Terrain screeching. She wasn't known for having the best driving skills, but having such a bulking presence with her sent her mind reeling and her car swerving. *Focus, girl. Don't let him get to you.*

Too late. He already had—in more ways than one.

"Sorry." She adjusted her sunglasses and pulled down the mirror. "Sun was in my eyes." No need telling him the truth. He'd make up his own assumptions anyway.

Shrugging, he pulled out his own sunglasses. The *Top Gun*-style aviator glasses nearly completed his military guise. Just add a wide-brimmed hat and he'd make a perfect gunnery sergeant. "Just be careful. I can't have you getting hurt on my first day on the job."

His brusque tone sent shivers through her body. Her lower lip trembled. As if she really cared that all he was concerned about was his damn mission. He had made it clear that he didn't want to be here, any more than she wanted his protection. Why did that thought rip at her insides?

"That wouldn't be good at all, would it?" she asked, her tone biting. With a little more force than needed, she turned left onto A-Line Road. The SUV's tires screamed in reply. Good Terrain. Just the response she wanted.

Matthias gritted his teeth and clung to the handle. What was with these demons and their aversion to driving? Even Rafe had a similar reaction to Lucy's driving, and she wasn't nearly as bad behind the wheel. Who was she kidding? She was tons better than Serah.

"Damn it, woman," he said through clenched teeth. "Deleon didn't mention you needed protection behind the wheel too."

"Must have slipped his mind." Just like it slipped his mind to tell her they were hiring a bodyguard—a bodyguard she didn't need. She yanked on the steering wheel, sending him crashing against the passenger side window. With a grunt, he shook his head.

"Unholy Hades. Who did you bribe to get your license?"

She slid into the right lane. "I got it out of a Cracker Jack box. I wouldn't talk. You probably learned to drive on a chariot."

"I'm not that old."

"Could have fooled me. You sure act like it." With another hard right, she turned into Green's Corner. As she drove by the abundance of shops that lined the shopping center, she glanced over at Luscious Locks, Lucy's salon.

"Is that where you and Lucia unleashed Belial's minions?"

If that wasn't a barb, she didn't know what was. "Yes, that's where Lucy opened the chest. And for the record, I tried to stop her."

"I apologize." He turned to face her, his gaze penetrating into her pores. "I know it wasn't you who opened the *Arca Inferorum*. You're too pure."

"I'm not a virgin." Oh, dear. Did she just say that out loud? Like he wanted to know about her sex life, or lack of it for that matter. It was a pretty boring story at that.

Matthias blew out a deep breath, his brow creasing with frustration. "Your soul is pure. Even certain intimacies do not diminish that."

How about sex with a demon? Not that she would have a chance to find out. He was too uptight and militaristic. Not her type at all. Yep, that was her story and she was sticking to it.

"Fine, whatever you say." With that, she turned into the nearest parking spot and slammed on the brakes. Matthias pitched forward, then back, and the seat groaned. With a small smile curving her lips, Serah shifted into park and turned the key. "We're here."

He shifted in the seat and unhooked his seat belt. "I don't know what I need to protect you from more—the Infernati or your driving."

Oh, he had a sense of humor. "Neither," she said, pulling the keys out of the ignition. "That was for show. I'm not nearly that bad." *But not by that much.*

"I'll do the driving from now on." With calculated precision, he swung the door open. "The sooner we get this done, the better."

If he planned on acting this stiff through the entire ordeal, she couldn't have agreed more.

"My sentiments exactly." Flinging her seat belt off, she ripped open the door. Shopping with Lucy had always been a chore. This would prove to be pure torture.

A loud hiss rent the air followed by a high-pitched shriek. *For God's sake. Not now!* Matthias sprung from car and clutched the dagger strapped to his belt. "Serah! Stay in the car."

Two balls of fur flew in the air and attached themselves to his T-shirt. Claws flying, they swept at his arms and face. Matthias swung out his arm, sending a black-and-white ball of fur flying.

"Reooooooooooooooow!" came a screech.

The fluffy white Persian lifted her paw, long sharp claws, ready to slice.

Serah flew from the car and pounded her fist on the hood. "Inanna! No!"

Inanna's long fluffy tail slashed back and forth and her bright green eyes flared. She gave a low menacing hiss.

You are in danger. I sense a darkness about him. Inanna's Middle Eastern accent sang in her mind.

"It's okay, Inny. Go home," Serah said, as she stood tall, hands on her waist.

Mr. Whiskers moaned as he rolled on the ground, dust and dirt coating his black-and-white fur.

"Meowwwwwww," he groaned out.

Ah thooght Ah was yer new bodyguard! Mr. Whiskers sprang to his paws and shook dirt from his head. "Grrrrrrrrrrrrrrrrrrrowl." He angled his head and licked his hind leg. With a reluctant shrug, he sidled next to his Persian kittyfriend and winked.

Matthias swept a piece of shredded fabric from his arm. "Mr. Whiskers, I presume?"

Mr. Whiskers sat on its hind legs and extended a paw. With the swiftness even a normal cat shouldn't possess, he extended each claw.

"Don't let the size fool you. Mr. Whiskers is one badass cat."

With wary steps, Mr. Whiskers slunk toward Matthias. With a predatory gleam flashing in his green eyes, he continued to circle.

"Mr. Whiskers, cut it out. For real, he's with me."

Inanna growled low, sliding down Matthias's chest. Her claws slit the rest of his T-shirt into shreds.

With a soft snort, Mr. Whiskers turned to Serah and puffed out his chest. His green eyes flashed with question. *Why him?*

She shrugged. She seriously didn't know. He didn't want to be there. She didn't really want him there. Then again, that was usually the Council's MO. "I honestly don't know."

"You can talk to them, can't you?"

Great. Another of her secrets was out. "Just call me the Animal Whisperer." She smirked. "And before you say anything, plenty of *normal* people can talk to animals."

Matthias nodded. "You're right."

"He's harmless. He's here to protect me."

Mr. Whiskers scratched his kitty whiskers and narrowed his eyes into a thoughtful glare. *Ah dorn't buy it.*

"I will keep Serah safe."

Mr. Whiskers nuzzled protectively against Serah, a look of concern spread across his kitty face. *Ah don't trust him. How dae ye ken he's tellin' the truth?*

"He's a friend of Rafe and Lucy."

Wha'ever. Ah still don't trust him.

At least she wasn't the only one. But she had other reasons for not trusting him—personal reasons. Everything about him raised her adrenaline level. His voice, his gaze... his body. His scent. It was hard to describe. Woodsy notes with a ginger undertone. If only she could bottle some of that and sell it. Totally intoxicating. Now she needed protection for sure, from her overactive libido.

Then again, maybe Matthias was the one who would need protection from her naughty thoughts. Never mind. There wasn't anything that could loosen his stiff ass up. If there was, well, pigs would be sighted flying over a glacier in hell.

She would have said when hell freezes over, but she knew better. "Well, whether you trust him or not doesn't matter. He's here and obviously is in need of new clothes." Thanks to Mr. Whiskers's and Inanna's claws of fury.

"I am here and can hear perfectly, you know."

As he raked a hand through his shorn hair, one of the tears in his T-shirt ripped further, affording her a quick glance of the outline of one massive pectoral. Like a Greek god. Hell, his body would put Adonis to shame.

Fine. See ye later. With the flick of his long black tail, Mr. Whiskers sidled next to Inanna and slunk along her fur-puffed body.

Serah cringed. PDAs were bad. PDAs involving cats was on a whole other level of wrong. "Enough, Whiskers."

Wha'ever, he meowed over his shoulder. *Yer're just jealous*. Slinking further down the sidewalk, the two cats twisted their tails together.

Yuck.

"Hardly," Serah muttered. "Jealous? Of a cat? Yeah, right!"

But she still loved the little guy regardless.

"How about this?" Serah held up a crinkled black shirt and tossed it onto the pile of clothes stacked in Matthias's arms. He rubbed the crisp fabric in his fingers, smoothing it out. "It's wrinkled."

"It's linen. It's supposed to be that way."

Not the linen he remembered. He leaned in toward her. "So you're telling me humans enjoy looking sloppy and unkempt?"

"It's casual." She grabbed the price tag and shook it in front of his face. "And expensive, so I'd be quiet if I were you."

"Whatever," he grumbled beneath his breath.

She moved to a pair of jeans. "How about these?"

"Too constrictive."

One of Serah's eyebrows swept up. "Really?"

"I need room... for my weapons."

"Oh yeah, I forgot how big your weapons are."

Was that an innuendo? He couldn't tell. Her expression remained noncommittal. He contemplated asking her. But if it wasn't, then she'd think him depraved—more than he already was.

She put the pair of tight jeans back and pulled out a pair of cargo-cut jeans. They looked worn, but loose, and they had plenty of pockets. Perfect for combat. "How about these instead?"

"They look a little frayed in places, but the pockets come in handy."

"That's how people wear their clothes now."

Yes, it was confirmed. Humans had become unkempt. But if he wanted to fit in, that's what he would wear. "They will work just fine, then."

Good. She grabbed up a few more in different colors

and tossed them onto the mound of clothes. If the piles in his arms grew any taller, he'd start leaning like the Tower of Pisa.

"I suppose you'd like some in khaki too?"

"As I said earlier, I am at your mercy, Serah." Truth was he really was. He was completely out of his element in this shop. Give him a military surplus store, on the other hand, and he could be busy for hours—especially the military surplus stores he shopped at. Try buying silver-tipped throwing stars at the local store.

"Okay. Khaki, olive green, and tan it is." She grabbed them and stuffed them in her own pile. She then snuck a pair in black.

How long did she expect him to be here? "Isn't this a little excessive?"

"Better to have options. We aren't buying everything. You still need to try them on." She passed by a display of folded T-shirts. Picking one of every color, she shrugged. "Didn't they tell you about my shopping problem?"

"Shopping problem."

"I like to shop."

"A lot of women enjoy shopping. I think the term is *shopaholic*."

Serah snorted out a chuckle. "That's putting it mildly. But you just put a recovering shopaholic in undiscovered territory."

He'd been warned about her uncanny hobby of buying anything under the sun. He just never thought it would include men's clothing. "But these clothes aren't for you. You can't possibly get enjoyment from that."

"Trust me. I can." She plopped another shirt on her

mound of clothes. "I'm just amazed they have clothes big enough to fit you."

"I don't know whether to take that as an insult or a compliment."

Her sapphire gaze sparkled. "Take it however you want." With that she turned and flagged down the salesman. "We need a changing room. I hope there isn't a limit." She turned to Matthias and leaned in. "If there is, you can use that enrapture thing on him."

Matthias reeled. Back in the day he'd have had no qualms about using the demonic skill that allowed him to get humans to bend to his will. But now he was a Paladin. Skills such as temptation and enrapturement could only be used when times were dire. Trying on clothes did not constitute a dire need to alter the human psyche.

"Paladins only use their demonic talents in an emergency." He hefted the pile up. "Buying a wardrobe, although necessary, isn't urgent."

The salesman nodded and ambled toward them, swinging his key chain. "We normally have a limit." He examined Matthias from head to foot. "I can make an exception for a fellow serviceman. I used to be a Marine." He stood tall and saluted. "Semper Fi. Hooah!"

"Thank you," he mumbled.

"You'll have to forgive him. He's been in the field too long. Right, Matt?"

"Something like that."

"So what division are you?"

He did not come to this store to share war stories. And he sure as hell had stories that would curl the man's teeth as it were. The less these humans knew, the better.

"Special Forces," he said, his voice firm. "I can't talk about it."

The clerk nodded, a secretive spark in his eyes. "Oh! Off the grid. Fair enough."

Matthias offered a stoic nod and crossed his arms. No words were necessary.

The salesman pointed toward the back of the store. "This way, please."

"Jeez. Can you be any ruder?" Serah asked under her breath. She brushed past him, leaving the heady scent of orchids mingling with spice behind her, invading his space. That damn fragrance. It was too intoxicating. His body reacted accordingly. Muscles tensed, blood flowed. Things became hard. Too damn hard.

Serah stopped at a rack and thumbed through the garments. "Hmm." With a curious gaze, she snatched up a pair of red-and-black polka-dot silk boxers.

Matthias blinked. *Hell and damnation, no*. Just the thought of her running her fingers through something worn so close to his intimate parts sent jolts of excitement pounding through his body. And he'd never worn such exquisite fabric ever. Even when he was human. He was born a commoner, after all—not a prince.

He yanked the garment from her hands and shoved it back on the rack. "I'll choose my own undergarments, thank you."

Rolling her eyes, she turned away and reached for something on another display table. "Fine. I should have known you'd be a tighty-whities kind of guy." With that, she threw a plastic package of men's briefs on top of his already overabundant stack of clothes.

Bloody hell. He couldn't even pick out his own underwear? Then again, he didn't know what the hell he was doing. "Those seem, umm… confining."

"Oh, so you take this commando role seriously huh?" Serah twirled a curl around her finger. "Doesn't surprise me one bit."

"You aren't surprised often, as you're so apt to point out." Curiosity got the best of him, and he promptly inserted foot. "Why doesn't it surprise you?"

"Rafe's a commando guy too. Must be a demon thing."

Had she been intimate with Deleon? The man was attractive enough. He gritted his teeth. Fire burned inside. Not a fire of desire, but something more animalistic. Jealousy? What the hell was coming over him?

"You've seen Deleon naked?"

Serah's eyes widened and her mouth gaped open, then she threw her head back in roars of laughter. "Heck no. Lucy would have my hide. We're best friends. We do talk. Don't you have any friends?"

"No."

"That sucks."

"I lived a solitary life. It's the mercenary way. Fewer people to trust."

Not that he hadn't had acquaintances over the centuries, but people—including demons—changed over the years. It was better to keep his distance.

"I'm sure that isn't the Paladin way. You're not a mercenary anymore."

"Part of me will always be a mercenary." With that, he brushed past Serah—not before sneaking a pair of those silk boxers into his pile.

Tighty-whities? Not all the time.

Chapter 7

HE STORMED INTO THE TINY COMPARTMENT THE salesman held open for him. The flimsy door crashed behind him. A grunt of frustration reverberated against the walls as hangers clanked against each other. And Serah thought Lucy was a grumpy shopper. Matthias was ten times worse—if not more.

"Sorry. He hasn't gone shopping in a while." Serah contained her chuckle. "Well, that is if you don't count the surplus store."

"Certainly looks like he's in good hands." The clerk peered down to where Matthias's combat boots peeked from underneath the door. With a grunt, Matthias kicked the back wall.

"Might I interest you in some shoes while you wait?"

"Sounds great. Something nice enough to wear with slacks, but still masculine enough to kick ass."

The clerk's eyes lit up. "I know just the pair. Be right back." With that, he jogged off toward the shoe section.

"Damn it!" Matthias grumbled and grunted. Kicking his camouflage fatigues around his ankles, he cursed some more. He mumbled something in Latin. The way it spit from his mouth, she probably didn't want to know what it meant.

"Everything okay?" she asked in a singsong voice. She ambled toward the stall and leaned against the door.

"I hate shopping."

"I figured as much."

"Take off your boots. It'll be easier."

"And if there is an *issue*?"

"I saw you ward the shop." He seriously needed to lighten up. He was ten times worse than Rafe when he had first landed on Earth. And Rafe—he was pretty bad himself. "I think I'm safe, Matty-boy."

He snorted in displeasure. "I feel naked without my boots."

"A few minutes of *nakedness* won't hurt." Her body shivered just thinking about it. What the hell? She never thought the body-builder physique attractive... until Matthias Ambrose poofed into her office.

Now her hormones were roaring. There was no way she could concentrate on anything with him lingering about. Even with his Neanderthal ways, he seeped into her. *Damn it*. What was she going to do?

With a loud exhale, he dropped his clunky combat boots to the floor. Then down went his camouflage cargoes. Her breath caught. He was getting undressed, and only a thin layer of wood separated them.

She caught a glimpse of his feet as he roamed around the tiny compartment. Large feet. She gulped, remembering what she heard about men with large feet. Not that she should care about that particular myth.

But her mind wandered anyway, wandered up his hard, toned calves, to the rocks of his thighs. Her imagination was out of control. She could feel her hands roving over each cord and tendon, feeling his muscles flex beneath her touch. It was as if she'd touched him before. Like she knew exactly which curve and plane to brush her fingertips across. Every receptor in her body flared.

Her heart thumped in her chest. Waves of hot energy washed over her, like she'd just been thrown in the oven. If she didn't stop this, she'd surely burn to a crisp.

Her fantasy view traveled upward, to the tighty-whities that did little to conceal the bulges. Especially that particular bulge. Curse her imagination. It couldn't even imagine him naked.

Man he was good, and a tease to boot. "I know you're doing it again."

"Doing what?" he asked, his silky smooth voice melting her to mush. He pushed open the door and stepped out. Even the loose khaki cargoes couldn't hide the rippled muscles that bunched and flexed beneath. He smoothed his hands over black linen, in a futile attempt to straighten the crinkled fabric. Curls of dark brown hair peeked from the open collar, also affording her another glance of the contours of his pecs. Serah swallowed the lump in her throat.

"Not to your liking?" he asked, scrubbing his hands across the stubble on his chin. He turned around to glance in the full-length mirror and raked his fingers through his trimmed hair. Oh God. Not that view. The khaki accentuated the hard planes of his buttocks. Her mind would be off on its wild tangent if he didn't get out of her sight.

"It looks good," she finally managed. More than good, but she couldn't tell him that. She collected her thoughts. "Why not try on a few more so you can choose what you want?"

"I'm not that good with fashion, Serah. I'll need some help."

Trust me, you don't need any help. He could wear

a burlap sack and it would look good on him. She was a caterer, not a fashion consultant. Was it her fault her tastes normally ran on the designer side? Not to mention bizarre at times. "Seriously, fashion is overrated. Just wear what makes you feel comfortable."

"I know what makes me feel comfortable, and according to you, that's not an option."

"Touché." Serah flipped her curls back and raised her chin.

"Miss?" The clerk's friendly voice broke her thoughts. "How about these?" Several shoe boxes were stacked in his arms, and he held out a pair of Doc Martens. "I've got a few different styles to choose from."

"So what do you think, Matt? Comfortable enough for you?"

"I suppose I can try them on." He marched toward the clerk and took them from him. With that, he stomped back into the changing room and slammed the flimsy door behind him.

"I hope none of your customers are as brusque as him."

The man shrugged. "I've seen worse, actually."

"Yikes." Serah took a couple of the boxes from the guy and sat them on the love seat. "Thanks for your help. We should be all set."

"No problem. Let me know if you need anything." The guy strolled off toward the cash register.

With a small sigh, she plopped down into the softness of the cushiony love seat. She closed her eyes and leaned her head back. A short nap wouldn't hurt. She'd had an exhausting day. He'd warded the shop anyway. She was safe.

But she wasn't safe from her overactive imagination.

He was shirtless again. His hard body pressed against her, her fingers gripped tightly around his arms, his biceps rippling against her fingertips. His mouth, gentle yet demanding, sucked, nibbled, and nipped at her neck. She wrapped her arms around his neck, pulling him closer. His tongue swirled along her earlobe. Of course he would know her secret spot, she'd pulled him there. His hands, large and calloused, roamed over the swell of her breasts, and down to her thighs, ready to begin their journey back upward.

Her breath caught and her pulse skyrocketed. A soft murmur escaped her lips. Part of her wanted to expand on this fantasy; the other, more practical side struggled to tamp down her libido. She couldn't afford the embarrassment of orgasming in public.

Forcing her eyes open, she jumped up from the couch. "Stop it!"

Throwing open the door, Matthias growled. His shirt was unbuttoned, and it fell off his shoulders, exposing the breadth of his chest. She bit her lip. "For the tenth time, I'm not doing anything." His look of frustration molded into one of concern. Onyx eyes searching, he gripped her shoulders. With an odd gentleness, he raised her chin to look up at him.

"What happened, Serah?"

"Nothing. Just a dream."

"What did you see?"

She gnawed her lower lip. She couldn't tell him the truth that he was making her hormones go bonkers. He was probably an incubus or something. Then again, as territorial as her kind was, Lucy could easily detect another Sexubi. Serah still laughed at the name. Had he been a Sexubi, the introductions would not have been so pleasant.

"I... I forgot."

Matthias jaw ticked. "I know you don't trust me, but I am here to protect you. At least trust that."

Serah crossed her arms. So he thought she didn't trust him. Well, it wasn't a complete lie. More like she couldn't trust herself. He was like her own demon-sized helping of molten lava cake. That sort of deliciousness always ended up in disaster.

"I know you mean well. I just think your being here is unnecessary."

"Necessary enough that the Fore-Demons sent me. That should be proof enough."

"I've heard how these Fore-Demons operate." Serah yanked her head away. She couldn't let herself fall into the pool of that intense gaze again.

"I'm new to taking orders from the Council, but I do know they have their reasons. You are special. You need protection."

"Seriously, this is getting old." Serah reached down to pick up one of the shoe boxes, but stopped in her tracks.

The faint hint of sewer and cloves wafted to her nose. *Not now. Not in front of him.*

Her stomach roiled as the odor grew stronger. Her nose twitched. Shivers of revulsion crawled across her skin. She couldn't let him see her like this. Otherwise her cover would be blown more than it already was.

Hard muscled arms wrapped around her, pulling her against Matthias's rigid chest. Her breath caught, as the heat radiated between their bodies. Her body, against her own better judgment, molded against his. *God, all that hard muscle*. It felt too good. "What the hell?"

"Shh," he whispered, his breath teasing along her earlobe. With stealthy—too stealthy by Serah's standards—footsteps, he backed into the changing room and slammed the door shut with his foot.

"Do you sense it?"

Serah forced a mask of bemusement. "Sense what?" she managed.

"Don't play ignorant with me, Serah. I saw your reaction."

These demons were too smart for their own good. She clenched her fists. This one especially. How was it that he could read her so well?

"You grabbed me so tight, what other reaction did you expect?"

"Stop it, Serah. I saw you tense before I grabbed you."

"You read into things too much. And you barely know me."

"Centuries as a demon have taught me how to gauge people's reactions. You smell the demon, same as I."

Serah narrowed her gaze. If he wasn't a full Paladin, how could he sense the Infernati?

"I thought you weren't officially blessed as a Paladin yet. How can you smell demons?"

Matthias crossed his arms and leaned in, his onyx gaze burning. "I'm a trained mercenary. That's all you need to know." He turned away and swept up the clothes in his arms.

"Wow. You expect me to trust you to protect me, and you can't even answer a simple question?"

"It *isn't* simple."

The odor of sewer and thick spice grew stronger. Serah's stomach continued to roil. Whoever this demon was, he was powerful. They always left the strongest scent. Imps and wraiths, on the other hand, she could tolerate. Now she was on the verge of losing her lunch.

"Whatever. We need to get going." She looked down at her grandmother's watch—a quarter to eight. "The store closes in fifteen minutes."

"There is a demon out there. A powerful one."

"That's not fair to Charlie out there. I'm sure he has things to do."

"It isn't safe. For you, and especially him."

"This is nuts. You are all overreacting." With that, she reached for the door handle and tugged. It wouldn't budge.

"What the fuck?" She yanked and pulled some more.

"I'm sorry, Serah, but I need to protect you." And, just that quickly, an icy swirl of wind, snow, and ice misted around him. And—*poof*—he was gone.

Chapter 8

MATTHIAS SWIPED FROST, SNOW, AND ICE FROM HIS shoulders and head. Backing against the cold concrete of the building, he made his way toward the darkened alley. He knew Serah would be irritated but it was the only way he could keep her protected while Balthazar lingered.

Balthazar. He recognized that reek anywhere. Once Belial's right hand man, he hardly ever traveled from the *comforts* of hell. He preferred to work from the pits. This confirmed Matthias's suspicions—Serah was in bigger trouble than he thought.

But Balthazar hadn't always been Belial's lapdog. He was once a friend—

A mentor. Matthias gritted his teeth. *His* mentor. He'd taught Matthias everything he knew about being a mercenary. But even mercenaries were vulnerable.

He'd never thought his friend would fade into the darkness of the Infernati. How wrong he was.

He inched along the side of the building, creeping slowly down the alley. Hand firmly gripping his dagger, he continued his stealthy movement.

"I taught you those moves, you know." The familiar baritone voice he used to revere as a friend's now pounded in his ear. His friend was gone. Then again, he already knew—ever since they had last met in Belial's chambers in hell.

Balthazar sniffed the air, sucking in a deep breath.

With a devilish wink, he licked his lips. "Mmm. The Pure-Blood is nearby. So you've come to finish your mission, I hope?"

"What's it to you?"

"You have too much at stake to act so bloody glib."

"As far as I'm concerned, I upheld my part of the bargain. I delivered the package as requested. Belial broke his end of the deal when he locked me up."

Balthazar snorted, the sound reverberating against the concrete surrounding them. "And what part of the bargain said you could try to break Serah SanGermano free?"

"When a customer doesn't pay, I take my services back." Not a complete lie. But deep inside, he knew it was more. There was something about that woman that stirred him in ways he never knew. It went against everything he'd learned over the years. Every emotion he tried to keep contained fired where Serah was concerned. Lust, anger, frustration, and other strange feelings he hadn't felt before. It unnerved him.

"Don't tell me you've fallen for her." Balthazar clucked his tongue and waggled his finger. Light blond hair whipped in the air as he shook his head. "You've lost your touch."

Matthias was done playing Balthazar's games. "What brings you to Earth?"

"There's a nasty rumor circulating around hell that you've joined the Paladins. I've come to dispel said rumor."

"And if I have?"

"Then I have no choice but follow through with our demands."

Matthias gritted his teeth and clenched his fists.

Belial, even from the pits of departed demons, managed to be the bane of his existence. He'd always hoped whatever hold Belial had on his friend would dissipate when he was vanquished. Another thing he'd miscalculated.

"Belial is dead. You don't serve him anymore."

"I serve someone else now."

"I remember a time when you wouldn't serve anyone. I am truly disappointed."

Balthazar shrugged, his now-red, beady eyes sparking in the dim moonlight. "Oh well, my friend. Have it your way."

"You are not my friend. My friend is long gone."

"So be it, Ambrose. But heed my words. Your mission still stands. Bring me Serah SanGermano or your last remaining descendant will die in three days."

"How do I know you're telling me the truth?"

"Your wife… she was with child when you left for the Crusades."

Matthias drew his jaw straight. He hated talking about his demonic turning. How he took a Saracen blade in his chest. How he crumbled to the ground, his blood pooling. Just when he closed his eyes, she appeared. *An angel*, he'd thought. Little did he know, she was far from being an angel.

"I want proof."

"Have I lied to you before?"

"I trusted the man who mentored me, not the monster standing here now."

"Have you joined them or not?"

"Why does it matter?"

"It matters because your descendant will die."

Matthias's heart sank. The world's existence

depended on the last Pure-Blood's safety. He needed to protect Serah no matter the cost. Without her, the world was doomed.

He hated what he was about to say, but Serah needed protection. "If I have to sacrifice one descendant for the entire world, then so be it."

"You *have* joined them!" Balthazar chuckled, deep and sardonic. "You fool. You are setting yourself up to fail. That's what those self-righteous Fore-Demons want."

"Do you really think I care what the Fore-Demons want?"

"You should, Ambrose, because it isn't pretty. Especially for you." Balthazar arched an eyebrow and traced a long finger down the thin patch of hair on his chin.

"The cryptic bullshit doesn't suit you, Bal."

"Balthazar. Bal is dead. Thank the Dark Master."

Even the strongest of those not aligned would eventually turn. Their minds warped, they would fall into the dark abyss that was hell. It was only a matter of time. He'd make his decision before his thoughts were tainted.

"No, thank you."

"Would you rather thank God?"

Matthias yanked his dagger from its sheath.

"I'd rather thank myself." With that, he prepared to slice—old mentor or not.

Chapter 9

HE HAD HIS NERVE! SHE PUSHED AND PULLED THE flimsy door. She pounded and kicked, imagining it was Matthias instead. The wood would not budge. Then again, as solid as Matthias was, he probably wouldn't either.

"Get me out of here!"

Jangling the keys, the salesman wiggled the handle. "I'm trying, miss. The lock is stuck."

No friggin' shit. "Try harder," she said through gritted teeth, pounding her fist on the door.

Sweat dampened her forehead and her breath caught. Her heart thumped in her chest. Her head was swimming as she brushed the beads of sweat from her brow. She sucked in another ragged breath.

The heat built up and the walls closed in, suffocating her. She *had* to get out of there. Gasping for air, she shook and rattled the door. Teeth clenched, she slammed her fists into the flimsy wood.

Bastard.

Anger boiled deep inside, warring with the fear. Not a good mix at all. She clenched her fists and closed her eyes. If only her grandmother were here. She'd know what to do. She always did. But Nonni was gone. She swallowed the lump. It was her fault.

Nonni, I need you.

She closed her eyes again and threw her head back, flinging and flailing her wrists.

She peeled an eye open and snuck a gaze at the sparkly band. Gritting her teeth, she grumbled beneath her breath. Why wouldn't it work? Then again, it seemed to have a mind of its own. It only worked when it wanted—such was her life, a never-ending case of Murphy's Law.

Please, Nonni.

As if it were an echo from her past, her Nonni's voice called to her from the faint recesses of her mind.

Breathe in and out from one to five. With each count let the peace envelop you.

One. She sucked in, allowing warmth to creep into her pores.

Two. She imagined herself floating in the air.

Three. She floated higher, the air around her getting clearer.

Four. More energy surrounded her, seeping in.

Five. She fell backwards, into her own personal cloud of softness. *Completely relaxed.*

Warm energy zinged into her wrist. She opened her eyes. The watch glowed warm and energizing, not hot and overbearing as before.

You can do anything you put your mind to. Her grandmother's voice faded with the breeze. With a reluctant smile, she rubbed the watch. The diamonds glistened, no longer taunting sparks, but welcome reminders of her grandmother. Nonni might not have been there in body, but her spirit was plentiful. Nonni would get her out.

She reached out and grabbed the handle of the door and yanked. With a reluctant groan, the door creaked open.

The clerk breathed a sigh of relief. "Thank goodness. I thought I'd have to call a locksmith for a minute. Never seen that happen before."

"Neither have I." She'd seen weirder. But for the clerk's—and her already dwindling—sanity, she kept that to herself.

Thanks Nonni. A mental breakdown averted—her own.

She grabbed the mountain of clothes and toddled toward the other items piled high on the floor. Fumbling with the other stack, she tripped over a shoe box and staggered forward.

"He is so dead."

"He had to secure the perimeter," the salesman said with a chuckle. Too bad he didn't know he wasn't far off from the truth. "Let me help you." He scooped up the other pile and jogged to the register.

Grumbling beneath her breath, Serah trudged to the register. With an unceremonious grunt, she heaved the clothes onto the counter. The scent—scratch that—odor continued to linger in the air. Whatever or whoever this demon was, he was strong… and nearby. Screw Matthias and his one-man army. She was through playing the damsel who wasn't quite in distress.

"An emergency came up. Do you do deliveries?"

The salesman shook his head. "Not usually."

Flashing a smile, she reached inside her purse. She flicked open her gold lamé wallet and drew out her credit card and a crisp fifty-dollar bill. "What if good ole Ulysses helps you?"

"I'm supposed to take my girlfriend out for dinner."

She dug around her wallet again and slid another bill across the counter. "And if Andy joins in?"

The salesman's eyes lit up. "My girlfriend will understand."

"You're a lifesaver." She pulled out a business card and scrawled her address on the back. Who needed enrapturement when dead presidents worked just as well? "I need them delivered to 1564 Creekside Drive." She then drew him a map on the back of the business card. "Someone will be there to pick up the delivery."

"Sounds good. Pleasure doing business."

Serah nodded, grabbed her cell phone, and mashed the familiar numbers.

"Hello?" Kalli's voice boomed.

"Kalli. I need someone to pick up a delivery from the clothing store. Can you do it?"

"What's up?"

"Something came up and this store is about to close."

"Fine."

"Thanks! I owe you."

"Lucy told me about all your IOUs."

"Whatever, bye." She clicked the phone shut and shoved it in her purse. She knew she'd been a little short with Kalli. She'd make it up to her later. With that, she opened the door and rushed outside.

The odor clung to the air, burning her nostrils. Her stomach lurched. Like the reek of a giant sack of broccoli and cauliflower gone bad, it would not dissipate. A rotten egg or stink bomb here and there, that she could handle. This scent, however, made the River City sewer system smell like roses. She scooted against the cold concrete wall, her steps stealthy.

Armed with an unexpected burst of confidence, she

crept toward the alley, the odor acting like a beacon, drawing her closer.

On quiet tiptoes, she rounded the corner. Ready and alert, she scanned the dark alleyway. Shadowy figures paced back and forth, sizing each other up.

A creepy chuckle chilled her to the core. Evil. Her heart pounded in her chest. Shivers of energy crackled through her. She stood alert… ready. What the hell was going on?

"Would you rather thank God?" The voice, low and sinister, sent her hair prickling on end.

The sound of metal scraping against metal echoed through the alley. A hint of silver flickered in the moonlight. Matthias's voice boomed. "I'd rather thank myself."

What the heck? Thank himself? Why exactly was he here? Serah clenched her fists. She should have known. It was only about his own advancement. At least Rafe had a reason when he came here.

"You could always thank me, you know. I'm the one who made you a cold-blooded killer."

"I've never killed anyone in cold blood. Everyone I've fought or killed deserved their fate."

"So much for that. You've gone soft."

"No, I've grown smart."

"Hardly."

She scooted along the wall, edging closer. Maybe Nonni's watch still had some juice left in it. Please?

Scrape! The sound of her heels grinding against pebbles screeched in her ears. *Oh, hell no.* She scurried backwards. Away from the two demons.

A heavily muscled arm encircled her, pulling her

against a brick wall—at least that's what it felt like. Stony and cold. "Look what we have here." The voice, deep and sardonic, sent her blood curdling and her stomach heaving. Maybe it was his cologne—or lack of it. "You have upheld your end of the bargain."

"What bargain?" Serah breathed out.

"You'll have to ask Matthias," he whispered, his fetid breath inching along her ear. "Pretty little thing." He took a strand of hair and curled it around a talon. Sniffing along her neck, he licked his chops. "Good enough to eat."

The only thing this monster would be eating was a knuckle sandwich. Preferably one served up by her.

She angled a glance toward Matthias. Lips firm and straight, his facade remained stony and indifferent. His dagger was poised, and his intense glare never wavered. What the hell was he doing? Was this all a sick twisted plan? And she'd walked right into their trap. She should've known he was too good to be true.

"Are you just going to stand there? You're a bodyguard. Do something."

His lips curved slightly into a frown. "I can't."

"What the hell?"

The demon's grip grew tighter. "He really can't." He yanked her head to face him. Lips spread wide into a sardonic smile, and his green cat-eyes glinted. "He never finished his last mission."

She had to do something. Matthias, standing there like a giant pile of granite, wasn't helping. He obviously had his own agenda. Whatever it was, at this particular point she didn't care.

"The package was delivered. Let her go."

"Not to my boss's specifications."

She closed her eyes and concentrated on the watch. Perhaps Nonni could guide her and help her out of this mess. After all, she'd helped her out of the dressing room.

And into this walking septic tank's arms. Then again, she'd done that all by herself. Luckily for her, his scent wasn't nearly as bad as the last Infernati prick who manhandled her—but not by much. Then again, the more evil you were, the bigger the stink. Made perfect sense.

Serah closed her eyes. Maybe she could channel Nonni again. She had to get out of here. *Please, Nonni?*

Accept your destiny. Her grandmother's soothing voice echoed in the breeze. Not this destiny shit again. Even in death, her Nonni's words always remained cryptic.

Don't deny yourself like I did. Swear to me.

So she had. Anything to ease her grandmother's suffering.

But since then, her grandmother's words haunted her. Almost as if she were there in her mind, spurring her on. Catering was her destiny, though. She had loved cooking, ever since she was a child. Cooking was in her blood—not all this purity stuff. What a crock.

Pure-Blood? Yeah, right. Maybe her grandmother, but not her. She wasn't good enough to fill her grandmother's shoes. She couldn't even speak her grandmother's native language. How dumb was that?

Her ever-present inner self reared its annoying head. *But what about the door? How did you do that?*

It was a fluke. That's all. She might have believed in all that supernatural stuff, but that didn't mean she wanted to be a part of it. Look at Lucy. If it wasn't for Rafe, she'd probably be a raging nymphomaniac, sexing the life out of innocent men. But, knowing her friend, she'd probably aim for the not-so-innocent.

"Cat got your tongue?" The evil demon whispered in her ear, his cold stony fingers tracing along her lips. Screw the watch. She had the perfect opportunity to get out of this mess on her own. A little bit of trickery went a long way.

She drew out her tongue and traced his fingertip, the contact sending shivers of revulsion coursing through her. She murmured and pressed closer to him.

Matthias drew a deep breath. "What are you doing to her, Bal?"

"It's all her. She wants me. How does that make you feel?"

"I feel nothing."

Serah's heart fell at those words. What the hell?

"I know you too well, Ambrose. I remember that look well. Try all you want to hide it."

"This woman means nothing to me."

"Really now. I beg to differ. I should have known you'd fall for the Pure-Blood charms. You were always too noble."

Fall for her charms? What the hell was this guy spewing? Unknown frustrations rammed their way through her body. Whatever trick this guy was playing was working.

Bal, or whatever his name was, swirled his rank tongue along hers. Sour milk and spice rolled across her tongue. She bit back the urge to retch—quite a feat.

It amazed her how she managed to control her disgust and anger. She angled a gaze toward Matthias. His gaze burned and lips curled into a snarl. He raised his arm, silver glinting. He wasn't doing nearly as well. So much for Mr. Cool-and-collected. What was up with that?

Bal pushed his tongue inside her mouth. She now had her chance. With as much strength as she could, she bit down hard. Slamming her stiletto heel down hard into his foot, she wrenched herself free from his grasp.

"Bloody bitch!" He lunged forward.

Swiping the metallic tang of his saliva from her chin, she gasped. The blood stung her mouth. She coughed and sputtered, her mind reeling.

"Serah, move!" Matthias's shout echoed through the alley.

Heart pounding against her rib cage, she sidestepped Balthazar. Rummaging through her purse, she dug around for anything she could use as weapon. Palming the silver letter opener Lucy had insisted she carry, she slammed it into Balthazar's shoulder.

A loud, agonizing roar ripped from his mouth. Thick, dark blood pooled from the wound. He snorted in anger, his snarl morphing into something dark and hideous. Fangs glinted in the moonlight as he hissed viciously. The sound grated in her ear.

A hand, strong and demanding, crushed around her shoulder. Sizzles of electricity raced through her. Matthias yanked her out of Balthazar's way. Eyes blazing, his jaw ticked.

"I said move."

With that he hauled her down the darkened alley.

Turning the corner, Serah looked over her shoulder. With an eerie chuckle, Balthazar swirled away in a mist of ice and snow.

Another cold blast slammed into her chest.

"Matthias, do you forget who I am?" Balthazar smirked, brushing off the shards of ice from his tailored jacket. "We can do this all night."

Matthias pulled her away and bolted toward the parking lot. Balthazar just laughed some more, poofing away again. Absolutely ridiculous.

"Over here!" a strong feminine voice called. Serah angled a glance. The door stood wide and inviting, a hand beckoning them toward. Serah peered up at the signage and cringed.

Wisdom of the Goddess. What? That store had been closed for almost a year. When did it reopen?

Matthias snaked an arm around her waist and hauled her toward the open door.

Then again, resolutions were meant to be broken, right?

Chapter 10

THIS WASN'T GOING TO BE EASY. ANY TIME SHE WALKED into this shop some weird piece of jewelry, a statue, or some other strange item always called to her. She didn't like breaking resolutions, even if they were silly. She pushed and pulled against his hard, unyielding body.

"I can't go in there!"

Matthias turned her to face him, his onyx eyes smoking. "We have no choice."

She gulped. "What about one of the other stores? There's a bakery three doors down. I know the owner."

Matthias shook his head and pulled her across the street. "Balthazar will get us before we make it." He scanned the perimeter. "And the shop is heavily warded. It's the safest place."

"But—"

"No buts. You are safer in the spiritual shop."

Props to Matthias for calling it what it really was. New Age? Unless you consider the time before Christ new. But from everything she'd learned about demons and angels in the past year or so, she knew that all religions had a common bond. *Funny, that.*

"I can't go into a shop like that without buying something."

"So?"

"It's like an addiction. All these strange magical items. Worse than clothes shopping."

"Pardon?"

"How do you think I came across a damned chest? It just landed in my lap?"

"Deleon told me the story." With that, he hauled her across the walkway, toward the shop.

Of course Rafe would fill him in on all the sordid details. "Do you think anyone in their normal mind would buy something as creepy as that?"

"In my centuries as a demon, nothing surprises me."

"I'm afraid I might accidentally buy the Necronomicon next."

"It's time to face your inner—uhh—demons." He left no chance of refusal and shoved her inside the shop. "And, FYI—the Necronomicon isn't real."

"But other books are bad, if not worse. Right?"

"Bloody hell." He scooped her up and threw her over his shoulder. "It's just a store, damn it."

Serah pummeled his back and shoulders, watching the ground fly by. "You are the most infuriating and demanding ass I have had the misfortune of meeting." Matthias's body tensed, and he exhaled deeply. The buildings continued to rattle around them. "Save for him."

"Well, I'm glad I'm not the worst," he said, slamming the door shut with his foot. He helped her to her feet and backed away.

The aromas of sandalwood and patchouli wafted through the air, erasing any remaining trace of demon body odor. It soothed and calmed her fraying nerves. Slumping against the door, she sighed.

It always amazed her how the simplest of scents could calm her, even in the most stressful situations. She angled a glance out the window.

Balthazar paced back and forth outside, pounding the windows and growling. His face contorted in a primal scowl. This was definitely one of those stressful times.

"Whew. That was a close call." The rich, thick, feminine voice echoed through the shop. Firm, yet ethereal. Definitely not a demon, but was she human?

The zing of metal scraping metal echoed through the room. Matthias's gaze remained alert as he readied his dagger. "What the hell are you?"

"Not a demon, so put that silly dagger away."

Matthias kept his dagger poised. He stood stony and alert. "Show yourself first."

"Very well." With a snap of her fingers, the shop filled with light. She leaned against one of the counters, spinning one of the jewelry displays. Despite the aura of secrecy that radiated from her, her smile remained friendly. Peace and tranquility wafted toward them with her every move. Her dark hair was wound in a severe bun, and she pushed a pair of reading glasses back up the bridge of her nose—not what one would expect of the proprietress of a pagan store.

She smoothed the wrinkles of her knee-length, gray pinstripe skirt. "Are you both done gawking?"

Matthias's gaze narrowed, yet he sheathed the dagger. To Serah's utter disappointment, he wrapped his arm around her and drew her closer. He took this protection thing way too seriously.

Then there was that naughty side, the side that enjoyed his corded muscles rippling against her body. And it seemed that part of her began calling the shots. How could she concentrate?

"Well, what are you then?" Serah managed in a short breath.

"Demons aren't the only things with powers that rove the world, you know." She threw Matthias a knowing glance and snickered. "Seriously, you're going to suffocate her, Matthias. Believe what you want, but I am here to help."

Matthias grumbled and loosened his protective hold. Serah's naughty side pouted. Her sensible side blew out a huge gust of relief. "What are you?"

Serah glanced around the shop. She sighed in contentment. The store had everything of the unusual variety. Incense sticks, cones, and scented oils. Potions and spell books and grimoires filled its spacious walls and shelves. Statues, medallions, and stones of every kind were intricately placed on several tables. She ran her fingers across a bowl of rose quartz, peace surrounding her.

"When'd you reopen? I thought this store was closed for good."

"The man that ran the store before wasn't selling authentic merchandise." The woman clucked her tongue. "I hate when people try to capitalize on religion."

She motioned them toward a seating area in the back. "Now, only those who are at peace with their spiritual side are allowed in. You're getting there, slowly but surely."

"So that's why Balthazar couldn't enter?"

"Exactly."

Matthias shrugged. "How did I get in?"

"You're the Pure-Blood's protector."

"And what exactly are you?"

"Someone who wants to help. Does it matter?"

"In my line of work, I've learned to trust very few people."

"And that will be your downfall."

"So I guess you are some sort of sorceress?" Serah turned to Matthias. "Do they exist?"

"Only in fairy tales and fantasy."

"For deities sake, Matthias. I thought you would recognize me."

With that she spun around, her pinstripe skirt and cardigan sweater swirling into a long, flowing, gauzy fabric, her dark brown bun loosening and cascading down her back in rivulets of blonde. A gold circlet was wrapped around her head, and beautiful beads and pearls framed her face. Eyes, the most vibrant shade of green, sparkled mischievously. This woman, whatever she was, was hotter than hell, yet no steamy sensuality radiated from her.

Serah narrowed her gaze. She could only wish to look so beautiful. "Yet you say you aren't a sorceress. You really had me fooled there—for a second."

Matthias's jaw ticked. "She's no sorceress."

"Yeah, right."

"She's a goddess."

Then again, she should have figured.

"Goddess?" Serah arched a brow. *What the hell else was this town hiding? The Ark of the Covenant?* Then again, with her experience in antique chests, that wouldn't be a big surprise.

Matthias clenched his fists and his jaw ticked—judging by the scathing gaze he aimed at the goddess, he knew her well.

"But I thought they all were converted to demonism."

Matthias groaned. "Not all."

"If all of us were converted, there wouldn't be anyone to pray to." She chuckled. "Aren't you going to introduce us?"

Matthias scrubbed his fingers across his chin and paced in front of the expansive sofa. "Serah SanGermano, meet Minerva. The—"

"Wisdom?"

"Well, you know who I am, so that's a start." She smiled and removed the winged headdress, setting it on the gold-trimmed end table. "And wisdom is subjective."

"I don't always feel so wise all the time. Is there a crime in that?"

"Wise people learn from their mistakes. Have you?"

"I've learned to not spend time in metaphysical, antique, and secondhand shops." She got up from the seat.

Matthias grabbed her wrist, the contact sending electrical impulses shooting through her body. "Minerva never shows herself unless there's a reason." He turned to face Minerva, his voice stony. "What exactly are your reasons?"

"Your debt has long been paid, Matthias." She traced a finger down his cheek.

Serah's nostrils flared. She bit her lip and clenched her fists. "What sort of debt?"

Minerva's eyes widened, and a singsong chuckle burst from her mouth. "Oh! I had something he wanted, and he had something I wanted. It was a fair trade."

What exactly did he want? What else was this demon hiding? She didn't like it one bit. Minerva sat there behind her nondescript facade. She liked this supposed goddess less every moment. The sooner she could get back home, the better. Matter of fact, the sooner she could get the hell away from malodorous demons and mysterious goddesses, the better too.

"It's really not my place to discuss," Minerva said with a flip of her golden hair. "You're here because I have my own debts to pay."

Matthias lunged forward and yanked Minerva to face him. "I won't let you take her."

Serah blinked. Was she really in that much demand? Then again, Balthazar seemed to want her. She just assumed it was him trying to get under Matthias's skin, but something else flashed in the walking cesspool's eyes that scared her to death.

She stifled the chuckle. Had he actually suggested Matthias was attracted to her? Yeah right! As if some muscle-bound giant was interested in her. Heck, someone that built didn't dare eat the stuff she was fond of cooking. She was Italian, after all. *Can you say carbohydrate central?*

Minerva hissed and with a light push sent Matthias flying back against the back of the sofa, the impact sending them both reeling.

Holy shit! What did they want from her? A catered three-course meal with devil's food cake for dessert? That was all she was probably good for.

"I owe one of my dearest friends. I promised her I would deliver something."

"Don't let us stop you." Matthias crossed his arms and leaned into the sofa.

"Good, now that we have that all out of the way." Minerva steepled her fingers and rose from the chair. She snapped her fingers and a golden tray with three glasses of red wine appeared on the table. She plucked two of the glasses and handed them to Serah and Matthias, the red liquid sloshing. "Wine?"

Serah hesitated. She glanced toward Matthias, who was equally hesitant.

Minerva's lips spread into a wide smile. "Lambrusco. A little birdie told me it was your favorite." She thrust the glass out to Serah, giving her no chance to refuse. "Of the Dolce variety too."

Serah took the fine crystal glass into her hand, allowing her fingertips to trace along the etchings. How did this woman know sweet Lambrusco was her favorite? Maybe she really was Minerva. "Thank you."

Minerva nodded. "You're welcome."

Bringing the crystal up to her nose, Serah inhaled the deep, heady scent. Whatever vintage it was, it was exquisite. She took a sip. Despite the slight dryness, the delicate fizz burst along her tongue and the delicious notes of berries swirled in her mouth. It was amazing.

The goddess turned to Matthias and shoved the glass in his hand. "I don't care if it isn't your favorite. You demons need to broaden your tastes."

Matthias grumbled. His eyes shooting daggers, he took a healthy sip of wine, gulping visibly as he swallowed. "Happy now?"

"Very." Minerva swished toward the back hallway. "Now if you will follow me?"

Matthias rose from the sofa and placed his hands on his waist. He dwarfed the goddess by a good six inches. Either he was brave or just incredibly stupid. If this woman was truly a goddess, no one in his right mind would dare challenge her. Gods had smote people for less. "What sort of debt, Minerva? And don't dance around the subject."

Minerva only chuckled and patted Matthias on the shoulder. "If you were anyone else, I'd kill you. But I promised someone I'd keep you safe."

"Me?"

"Well, you are her protector after all."

Serah groaned. Were people this wise always so mysterious? Then again, she always knew Nonni had been wise beyond her years, and she was as mysterious as they came. "So what do I have to do with your promise? I'm just a caterer, born and bred in the Midwest."

Minerva shook her head. "You are so much more, Serah SanGermano. Come." She held out her hand. "I'll show you."

A spark of truth flashed in her green eyes. Serah nodded and took her hand. With no more effort than lifting a paper off a desk, Minerva pulled her to her feet. "This way," she said, extending her hand toward the darkened hallway.

Matthias grabbed Serah's elbow, the instant jolts of energy not so foreign anymore. "I don't trust her. She's been known to be very manipulative. I won't have you hurt her on my—"

"First day on the job," Serah said with a roll of her eyes. "You said that already. Besides, I think if she planned on hurting me she would have done it already."

"Precisely!" Minerva interrupted. "You are much more valuable alive," she added with a wink.

"Valuable to whom?" asked Matthias.

"To you, I imagine," Minerva snickered.

Matthias glared.

Serah simply scratched her head with bemused wonder. "Are you working for the Infernati or Paladins?"

Minerva shrugged. "I work for myself and the occasional human or demon"—she punched Matthias's shoulder—"who can pay me a price."

"How do I know you aren't being paid by Infernati right now?"

"Matthias can answer that."

Matthias balled his hands into tight fists, as a flash of remorse altered his gaze. Serah wanted to comfort him. She'd never seen any man with that sort of pain in his eyes. It tore her up inside. *What the heck?* "The Infernati keep you prisoner until the debt is paid."

"And this obviously isn't a prison." Minerva crossed her arms and lounged against one of her ornate tables. "Will you follow me now? We haven't got all night."

"I haven't got anything better to do," Serah said, angling a glance toward the front of the shop. "Balthazar has us pretty much blocked in for now."

Minerva shook her head. "You have so much to learn. You won't need to use the door to exit the shop."

Serah sighed. Leave it to a goddess to show Serah her shortcomings in the IQ department. "No need to rub it in, oh wise goddess. I already know I'm not the smartest person in the world."

"There is a difference between being smart and being wise. Smarts are learned, but wisdom you are born with. However you chose to use that wisdom... well, that's up to you."

Serah clasped her hands in front of her. "One of my teachers said my prospects weren't that great."

Minerva huffed. "Thereby proving that not all

teachers know what they are talking about. You're an awesome caterer, right?"

"I don't like to brag."

A mysterious smile spread across Minerva's face. "See? You are wise!" She turned to Matthias. "This is for Serah's eyes only."

Matthias moved forward and grabbed Serah's arm. Jaw rigid, he shook his head. "You might not be Infernati, but I still don't trust you."

"I swear on all that is wise, I don't plan to harm her."

Matthias crossed his arms, keeping that same stony look.

Minerva threw her hands up and blew out an exasperated breath. "Fine. You can stand guard outside the door. That's the best I can do."

Matthias offered a slow, reluctant nod. "But I warn you, if I sense the tiniest bit of harm, I'll take you down."

"I wouldn't expect anything less out of you, Matthias. How's that favor working out, by the way?" She smiled and placed her hand on his shoulder. The touch sent an instant flame of anger inside Serah—she didn't like it.

Matthias jerked away. Serah's inner jealous bitch went back to her little corner. Jealous? What the heck for? He wasn't her type. "It works well, thank you."

"Good. I'm glad we could work together." She flashed a knowing smile.

What exactly did she do for him? Jealous bitch stirred from the recesses. "What if I don't trust you?"

"What would your dear Nonni say about that?"

"Nonni?" What did her grandmother have to do with this? "She died almost two years ago."

With a frown, Minerva's gaze traveled to the floor.

Not something Serah would expect from a woman full of wisdom. "A terrible loss."

"You knew Nonni?"

A wan smile formed her lips. "Quite well. She was one of my best customers. A true friend."

Serah's eyes widened. She always knew Nonni was spiritual. But Nonni was, like most people in their quaint town, a devout Catholic. A New Age shop was the last place the fine parishioners of St. Vincent's Catholic Church would step into. Even from beyond the grave, Nonni surprised her.

"Don't look so surprised dear. Your grandmother was a great woman who understood the spiritual balance of the world. One of the wisest too."

Serah wasn't buying all this wisdom baloney. *Me?* One of the all-wise and knowing Pure Persons Network? Yeah, right! "And then there's lil ol' me."

"Stop, Serah," Matthias ground out. "There is nothing little about you."

"As to ol'—the only thing old about you is your soul," said Minerva.

"Great, my soul is a Geritol-popping, walker-pushing dinosaur. I'm surprised it's able to keep up with my body."

Minerva groaned. "Don't play dumb, Serah. You know what I meant."

Matthias rolled his eyes, albeit only a little. "Now is not the time to be cracking jokes."

Serah held back the snort that threatened. "Is there ever a time for jokes with you?"

"When you are safe from the Infernati that will never rest until you are killed."

"It'll be a while, I guess."

"Just get this over so you can return to the safety of your home."

"Sir! Yes, Sir!" Serah said, flashing her favorite salute, the one-fingered kind. With that, she padded behind Minerva toward the back room.

"So is this where you go to do all your secret goddess stuff?"

"Very funny." Minerva twisted the knob and opened the door. "Unfortunately, it's just a sitting room used for private readings."

"Tarot readings?"

"Among others." Stepping into the room, she flipped the switch. Bright fluorescent lights illuminated the room. Rows of books lined the back wall. Old grimoires as well new ones were stacked from floor to ceiling.

In the center of the room sat a simple circular table covered with a plain white tablecloth. Serah scrunched a brow. For a room used to predict the future, it looked *ordinary*.

"Something wrong?"

"It just wasn't what I was expecting."

"We don't need all those fancy embellishments. Our readers' and psychics' work speaks for itself."

"Fair enough." Serah turned to see Matthias standing in the doorway. Hands on his hips, he stood tall and proud. It was a wonder he even fit through. She turned back to Minerva. "So are you going to give me a tarot reading?"

With a dramatic flourish, she plopped into one of the seats. She reached across to grab the tarot deck.

Minerva's hand stopped hers. "Not tonight." She

grabbed the tarot deck, shuffled the cards and placed them on the stand behind her. "What I have is much better than a tarot or rune stone reading." Twirling a golden lock of hair around her finger, she flounced to an old, worn-out armoire. Paint chips peeling off of it and the door creaked as Minerva pulled it open. She mumbled to herself as she sorted through dozens of boxes in myriad sizes and shapes.

"I know it's here somewhere. She asked me to keep it hidden." She pulled out a false bottom and continued her search.

"Who?"

She pulled out an antique box and brushed off a layer of dust. Carved vines were etched across the sides of the tiny box. Serah stepped back and drew her lips straight. *Hell, no*. She'd had enough of creepy boxes and chests to last a lifetime. "Sorry. I don't want it."

"Good, because I wasn't giving the box to you."

Matthias, sensing Serah's unease, stepped forward, hand clasped on his dagger. Did he ever let go of that thing? "Is everything okay?"

"Everything is fine, Matthias. Save the dagger for someone who deserves it." Minerva drew her fingertips across the latch and lifted it, the old metal creaking in protest. "I'm giving you what's inside. The chest stays with me."

"Maybe I don't want what's inside either."

Minerva simply shook her head. "Oh, you'll want this. Close your eyes and open your hand, Serah."

"Is it necessary for her to close her eyes?" Matthias stalked into the room and grabbed Serah's arm. He turned her to face him, concern flashing in his dark gaze.

"You don't need to do this. Minerva sometimes uses her wisdom to trick the unsuspecting."

"I can hear you perfectly, Matthias." There was no mistaking the annoyance rolling from the goddess's tongue. She shook her head. "Men!"

She turned back to Serah. "I knew Angelica SanGermano. We were good friends." She took a seat and set the box on the table.

"How come I never heard about you?"

"You weren't ready. You needed time."

"Time for what?"

"To accept your destiny." She pushed a folded piece of paper across the table. "This will explain things better."

Chapter 11

WITH CAUTIOUS FINGERS, SERAH TOOK THE NOTE AND unfolded it. Her grandmother's familiar handwriting scrawled across the page. Serah's fingers trembled. The note was dated two days before she passed away.

> *My dearest Seraphina,*
> *I hope this note finds you in good health. I know you have many questions. I wish I had been there to better explain things to you. I did what I thought was best to keep you protected from harm. Now I am not so certain I made the best decision. As I watched you grow into the beautiful young woman you are, I knew you had the gift. It was terribly selfish of me to keep you sheltered from the life you deserve. You're a great cook, don't get me wrong. But you are destined for greater things. It's not too late. Embrace that destiny. Make it yours. Make your Nonni proud.*
> *Love,*
> *Nonni*

Serah could only stare at the letter. She would have tried to say it was a fake, but the handwriting said it all. She'd know Nonni's signature anywhere. The way she swirled the *n*'s and dotted the *i*'s. There was no way to forge it.

Then again, Minerva was a goddess, and goddesses had powers—strong powers from what she could see. "How do I know you're not playing me?"

Minerva chuckled. "You'd already be dead. Now open the box already."

Matthias unsheathed his dagger, the scraping sound echoing in her ears. "If anything happens to her, I'll send you to—what did the Romans call it? Tartarus."

"I'm hardly a sinner, but you have my word, Matthias, she will be safe." She sauntered toward him and snatched the dagger from his hand. "I am getting sick of this thing. Have some manners, Ambrose." She tossed the dagger to the corner of the room.

Matthias grunted but backed away. "I'll still be watching you, Minerva."

"I wouldn't expect any less from the Pure-Blood's protector." She swirled in her skirts and came back to the table where Serah sat. "And if I meant you any danger, Matthias would have already run me through. Right, Matthias?"

"She can be trusted—for a while."

"Thank you, I think." Minerva took Serah's hand in hers, the warm peaceful energy soothing her fingertips. "See? I mean no harm. Now, Serah, please close your eyes."

Sera nodded. Maybe she planned to do a séance. She had so much she needed to tell her grandmother. But most of all, she wanted forgiveness. Slowly, she drew her lids closed and held her hands still for Minerva. "I'm ready."

"Wonderful." The sound of the latch popping up echoed in her ears. She resisted the urge to peel one of her eyes open and sneak a peek. Remembering the last time someone opened a chest, it was best to follow the goddess's direction.

The lid clicked shut. Minerva took her hand again, still as soothing as before. Matthias, surprisingly, remained dead silent. Maybe she gave him a magical muzzle.

"Do you truthfully accept your destiny and whatever comes with it?"

"Yeah, sure."

"You don't sound too confident, Serah. I am being serious."

"If it brings me closer to Nonni, I accept."

Minerva clucked her tongue. "Fine, but remember what I'm about to give you will work only if you fully accept what you are."

Serah nodded. "I will."

Minerva opened Serah's palm and placed a pendant and chain in her hand. The metal was warm, not cold—silver. She could feel the encrusted stones tracing paths across her skin. Warm energy flowed through her body, similar to what she felt when she held her Nonni's watch.

"Can you feel it?"

"It feels like a necklace."

"Is that it?"

"Yes. Can I open my eyes now?"

Minerva blew out a breath. "Angelica told me you'd be stubborn. Yes, you can open your eyes."

Serah looked down at the necklace she held. Not a pendant, as she originally thought, but a locket. A circle of chipped diamonds surrounded the shiny silver surface. Dangling from a plain silver chain, it sparkled and shined, despite the stones' poor cuts. She looked down at her watch—the similarity in the arrangement of the stones almost knocked her senseless.

She finally exhaled. "This belonged to Nonni, didn't it?"

"It did. Now it belongs to you."

"It's just a necklace. Why couldn't I have it sooner?"

"You aren't fooling anyone, Serah. You know why. And if you don't accept your destiny, the Earth is doomed."

Chapter 12

MINERVA COULDN'T HAVE SAID IT ANY MORE succinctly. Maybe all Serah needed was a kick in the ass from a goddess. He fought the smile that threatened to curve his lips. No way would he show emotion. Emotions were a weakness, often taken advantage of.

Matthias would not let Minerva have the upper hand. Too much was at stake.

Unfortunately, Serah shrugged. A deep roar of laughter burst from her lips. "I find it hard to believe that a simple caterer is destined to save the world."

God's teeth. He knew she'd be stubborn, but this was worse than he thought. He clenched his teeth, and his words came out strained. "You are far from simple."

He reached for her, his hand brushing hers. Jolts of electricity flowed between them. A soft gasp escaped her lips and her lids fluttered across her eyes, which were clouding over. He'd seen that look before. Desire. His loins tightened, pressing uncomfortably against the briefs he had tried on earlier. They were called tighty-whities for a reason. He struggled to control his gulp.

A brief hint of recognition flashed in her gaze. As if a lightning bolt had zinged through her, she gasped. Yanking her hand from his, her sapphire gaze grew stormy and her lip trembled. "I don't know what you're doing, but stop it already."

Matthias's blood grew colder than it already was. He had not done anything, save for touch her. He tamped down the paranoia creeping through his body. Did she remember? He hoped not. None of his victims, demon or human, had ever remembered. His unfortunate skill made certain of that. If she remembered, it meant one of two things. Either he was losing his powers, or she was stronger than the Fore-Demons realized.

He didn't know which was worse.

"I only touched you, Serah."

Her gaze burned a hole in his already blackened heart. "Then don't touch me again."

"I can't guarantee that, and you know it. It's my duty as your bodyguard to protect you—and if it requires *touching*"—he paused and narrowed his gaze—"then so be it."

She turned and stormed away from him, hand still firmly clasping the locket. "Well, pray you don't have to," she said with an exasperated breath and a dramatic flip of her hair.

Matthias turned to Minerva. Not only was the goddess wise, she was known for her candor. He would get to the bottom of this one way or the other.

"So why is this necklace so important, other than belonging to her grandmother?"

This evening, however, candor was fleeting. Minerva shrugged and twirled a golden lock around her manicured finger. "That is for Serah to find out. When she accepts her destiny, all will be revealed."

"Destinies are overrated." Serah grumbled, frustrated by the clasp she was fumbling with.

"A little help?" she asked in a huff.

Minerva shook her head. "Once the locket is in your hands, I cannot touch it. Bad things will happen."

Serah arched a brow. "What sort of things?"

"Let's just say a disaster of biblical proportions." Minerva plopped down into her chair and propped her elbows on the table. "Only the pure and those who have been blessed can touch it now." Minerva flashed a cryptic smile. "Matthias will have to do the honors."

Just one touch could be his downfall. Minerva was too wise for her own good. He crossed his arms. "She doesn't want me to touch her." And to be honest, he didn't need the drama that would come from that touch, nor the excitement. But that animal deep inside him wanted it. Badly.

She was a Pure-Blood, and he was a demon. It was a union destined for disaster. He might not have been Infernati, but he wasn't all that good either. As a mercenary, he straddled the line of good and evil. One wrong move, and he could have chosen the path of his mentor. He restrained his cringe. He would not join Bal—in this life or the next. Even the farce of a blessing he received from a not-so-innocent angel straddled the line of good and evil.

"Damn it!" Serah's grumble pulled him from his thoughts. Arms twisting behind her neck like a contortionist, she struggled with the necklace. "Fine—please help?" Her reluctant request matched the unease swirling in her gaze. Then again, could he really blame her?

With slow, meticulous steps he came to stand behind her. Far enough away to prevent any discomfort. He flashed a surreptitious glance downwards. Well, discomfort for her, at least.

She turned to meet his gaze and thrust the necklace at

him. With just as quick a spin, she turned back around and gathered her mass of curls in her hands, baring that beautiful, porcelain neck. *Ahh, hell. This was not going to be easy.*

He inched closer. Who knew assisting a woman with a simple bauble could be so difficult? Then again, this bauble was anything but. And this woman—well she wasn't simple either. Difficult, stubborn, and too sexy for her own damn good.

"I'll keep the touching minimal," he whispered in her ear as he quickly swept a stray hair away from her neck.

She stiffened, a tiny gasp escaping her lips. "Just hurry," she said with a ragged breath. *Oh hell.* His blood was ready to boil.

"Awkward," Minerva said, obviously amused at the reaction. Chin perched on her godly hands, she flashed an all-too-knowing smile. Were they pawns in a bizarre game of amusement? Then again, she was a goddess. Humans and demons alike had always been a source of amusement for the gods. They certainly enjoyed their *sport.* He imagined it would be the same now, even with their fleeting numbers.

"I fail to see the enjoyment in watching such a mundane task as clasping a necklace."

Minerva shrugged. "You would, Matthias." She lowered her hands to the table and stretched back in her chair. "We gods could find amusement in watching paint dry if we wanted."

"That doesn't surprise me at all." He turned back to Serah's neck, the pulse at the base of her throat tempting him to lower his head and trace the contours with his tongue. Like he had several months ago.

Who knew someone so pure could tempt even a demon?

This was becoming an obsession. Even when she wasn't near, she always managed to seep into his dreams and drive him mad with desire. And in those dreams, he was less than gentlemanly. A Pure-Blood was innocent and deserved better.

And dreams like that were better not to come true.

With an abrupt grunt, he placed the necklace around her neck, and clasped it shut. And just as abruptly he let the chain fall against her neck. "There." He turned to glance at the clock on the far wall. Nearly ten at night.

The stench of Balthazar still clung to the air. Leave it to Balthazar to still linger. Balthazar was never one to give up when he wanted something. Persistence—one of his better traits. At least that part of him had stayed intact. "Got anything that can get us to Serah's without running into Balthazar's wretched claws?"

"I have many tricks up my sleeves." Minerva fluttered her gauze-draped sleeves and arose. With a smirk, she winked at Serah. "Then again, so do you. Claim your destiny."

Serah shrugged. "I have a destiny. To run the most successful catering company in the River City metropolitan area." Her sapphire eyes narrowed. "Not sniff out stinky demons like some stupid bloodhound."

"Is that all you think you're good for?" Matthias could give a damn about his promise not to touch her. She needed some sense knocked into her. He reached out and grabbed her by the shoulders. The fire leapt across his skin as jolts of electricity ripped through his body and right to his cock. But he needed to say it, and this was the only way to break through. He could forego a little comfort for now. He lowered his intense gaze to hers. Defiance, not usually a trait Matthias found pleasant, swirled in the blue depths of her eyes, but with Serah it was more than pleasant. It was goddamn hot.

He managed to find his voice. "Trust me, there's more to it than that."

Serah yanked herself from his grasp. "There always is." She leaned against the doorjamb. "Let's just go home. I'm tired and I have a big day tomorrow."

She still plans to try out for that silly show even after their run in with Balthazar? Is she nuts? "You are not auditioning."

"I signed a contract. I have to. I doubt I'll get the show anyway. I'm just a caterer from a small Midwest town. They probably want someone more elegant."

She was elegant enough. She could get the job on looks alone. Did the woman not know how beautiful she was? Unfortunately for Matthias, that only added to her innocent charm.

"Would you like me to audition?" Minerva smiled. "Then again, I never was any good in the kitchen. That was more Edesia's specialty."

"As much as I would love a goddess in the kitchen, I think I can handle it. I've got demon-boy here to protect me if anything goes wrong."

"What did your friend say about this?"

"Lucy? She doesn't know."

He didn't like it one bit. "Why haven't you told her? Don't friends share important news like this?"

Serah twirled a curl around her finger. "The rules of

the contest were very specific. I signed a confidentiality agreement. I'm only telling you because, well, you're my employee."

"Fine. But as soon as anything otherworldly happens, I'm pulling the plug."

"Fine. As for demons, the shop is warded. And they can't come in if they aren't invited. Trust me—I won't be inviting them in."

"Glad you both got that settled. Now, you haven't got all night," Minerva said. She held a blue stone, with laces of gray flowing across its surface, in her hand. "Take this stone. It will help you travel."

He'd never seen such a beautiful stone. "I'm unfamiliar with this stone."

"It's a fairly new discovery—to humans at least. It's called angelite."

Matthias stifled the cough deep in his throat. He glanced at Serah. She simply rolled her eyes.

"I should have figured," Serah said. With a reluctant sigh, she took the stone, allowing Minerva to close her fingers around it.

Minerva took three slow steps backward and clasped her hands together. "To activate the stone, close your eyes. Take five deep breaths to clear your mind. Then simply visualize yourself where you most want to be."

"Nothing is that easy." Serah let out a hearty chuckle.

Minerva shrugged. "With that sort of attitude, you're right."

If only Serah would acknowledge just how important she was. How powerful she could be if she just believed in herself. Matthias tamped down the desire to throttle her then and there. He wasn't angry. He was frustrated.

He balled his fists and clenched his teeth. His words, meant to be firm, came out as an angry growl. "Stop trying to fight it, damn it."

"Fine!" Anger swirled in her eyes. "But seriously, I might be able to smell demons, but this whole Pure-Blood shit... it's a bunch of... well, *shit*."

"Try me," Minerva said with finality.

Chapter 13

THE WORDS CAME OUT LIKE A CHALLENGE. ANYTHING to prove this goddess wrong. Then again, her being the goddess of wisdom would only add to the challenge. The anger simmered away, as determination took over. She clenched the stone tight in her hand and slammed her lids shut.

So she could go anywhere she wanted, eh? She'd always dreamed of lounging on a Tahitian beach sipping mai tais. "I know exactly where I want to be."

"Is it just like normal *Peragrans*?" Matthias asked, as if in tune with her devious thoughts. Then again, the way he invaded her fantasies, he probably was.

Minerva nodded. "Yes, minus the Ice Capades routine."

Oh well. Didn't hurt to try. The rules of *Peragrans* were pretty straightforward. You could only teleport to a place or person that you were familiar with. At least she wouldn't freeze her ass off. "So that means my back-up trip to Matthew McConaughey's place isn't going to happen either, huh?"

Matthias blew out a breath of air. "Correct." Ice laced his voice.

"Bummer."

She inched an eyelid open and snuck a covert glance at Matthias. Still wearing the wrinkled linen shirt and loose cargoes, he stood tall and proud; his lips remained straight and severe. Biceps bulging, he crossed his arms as he leaned against one of Minerva's oak bookcases. Her breath caught. Even the loose linen shirt couldn't hide the pure strength that rippled through his body.

Who needs Matthew McConaughey?

What the hell was wrong with her? He was an insufferable asshat. He looked at her like she was his last meal and a leper at the same time. It agitated her beyond words.

But every time he touched her, it was like molten lava flowing through each and every vein. She should've been afraid but instead she was intrigued. Too damn intrigued, and she didn't like it.

And from what she could see, he didn't either.

Which further fueled her ire.

"I have a thing for Matthew McConaughey, if you haven't guessed."

"Matthew McConaughey?" Minerva said with a snort. "Actors are so overrated."

"Let's get this over with," Matthias barked. "I didn't come here to discuss actors."

Wow. The way he barked, you'd almost think he was jealous. Yeah right! "Heck, I didn't want to come here at all."

"Can't we all just get along?" Minerva grabbed Serah by her sweater sleeve and pulled her to stand next to Matthias. "Time for a group hug."

She might have been wise, but Minerva was weird as hell. Bemusement filled Serah's face and Matthias's brow scrunched. An awkward minute of silence followed.

"Too much?" Minerva grinned.

Matthias offered a slow nod.

"Oh, well. Maybe next time?"

"Uhh... sure," said Serah, stone still secure in her hand, as she patted Minerva's back. "Next time."

"I sense some sarcasm." Minerva's lips curved downward into a mock frown.

"They don't call you the goddess of wisdom for nothing."

"More sarcasm!" Minerva beamed. "A trait often attempted, but only mastered by the truly witty."

"Wit and wisdom go hand in hand, huh?"

"Of course."

"Sarcasm and wit serve a purpose, but don't you have a stone to use?"

Party-pooping, another one of Matthias's demonic talents. Despite Minerva's odd tendencies, Serah liked the goddess. Matthias, on the other hand—it didn't take a mind reader to see the aura of distrust that swirled around him.

Then again, he didn't seem to trust many people. Probably an occupational hazard. Serah blew out a breath of air. Did he trust her? Probably not, or he wouldn't be hovering over her every move.

Like she should care.

"Okay, here goes nothing." And she meant that in the literal sense. Like a stone could just zap her here and there. Maybe if she was Lucy or Kalli. Not this pure demon detector that they thought she was. But might as well give the demon and goddess a show.

She closed her eyes again and took in the first breath of air. Nothing funny yet. She exhaled and took two more breaths. Still nothing. Three down, two to go. She took breath four and still felt as normal as she had before she held the stone. No biting cold swirls nipping at her

nose. She sucked in as much air as her lungs could hold
and blew it out in a slow breath out her nose.

"There's no place like home." All that was missing
were the ruby slippers.

Still nothing. If she had transported herself clear
across town, she would have felt something. A pinch?
Wind through her hair? A TSA agent giving her a much-
too-thorough pat down?

Slowly and deliberately, she opened her eyes—and
wished she kept them closed.

"Wha' the hell?" the high-pitched screech pierced her
eardrums. "Where did ye come frae?"

There sat Mr. Whiskers on her black Italian leather
sofa with a tub of popcorn between his cute kitty
legs. One paw held a cigar, smoke wafting from it,
and the other held a lowball glass of scotch. Serah
just shook her head. She should have known the cat
wasn't normal.

Interesting mix, though.

Even more interesting location.

"No smoking in my house!" She grabbed at the cigar
in Mr. Whiskers's paw. "Cuban cigars? How the hell
did you get these? They're illegal." She put her hands
on her hips. "You can talk? What in the hell are you?
The Cheshire Cat?"

"Guess the moggie is oot o' the bag. Ah was sent tae
tak' over the chimp's job." Mr. Whiskers pinched his
cigar out. "Ah'm sorry. Ah thought ye'd be gone fer a
while. The packages hae been delivered. Kalli just left."
He shooed his paw at her. "Now move. Yer blockin'
ma view. Mel Gibson is gettin' ready tae moon the
Sassenach dogs."

A cat with attitude. Who would've known. Then again, he was Scottish.

"Aren't you a little shocked that I am standing here?"

Mr. Whiskers arched a whiskered brow. "Only fer a second. Ah kent ye had it in ye. Ah'm jist a wee pisht ye did it in front o' the tellie." He pushed a button on the remote that sat next to him and paused the movie. With a high-pitched sigh, he flicked his now-unlit cigar.

"At least you have better tastes in movies than my last imp, even if they're a tad historically inaccurate."

"At least they got most o' the accents right." He swirled his scotch and took a sip. "Ah love guid Scottish whisky. It's the water o' life, ye ken?"

"I'm more of a Cabernet kind of girl."

"Wine is weak."

"Whatever, Whiskers." She plopped into the sofa next to the demon cat and grabbed a handful of popcorn. "What's your real name?"

"Farquhar MacTavish, at yer service."

Serah cringed. "I could get arrested for saying that name in public."

"Jist call me Farquie. That's wha' Inanna calls me."

"So where is your hot Persian tail? Is she special too?"

"She is." He sighed. "She has tae spend time wi' her human. Who kent keepin' a secret imp identity could be sae hard? Inanna says she makes her wear silly pirate costumes an' forces her tae sleep wi' her." Farquhar cringed. "Ah tellt her tae start peein' oot of the box. Mebbe she'd send her tae the beastie shelter."

"Ouch. I didn't realize she had it so bad."

Farquhar shrugged. "She'll be fine. So where's th' mercenary turned Paladin?"

"How long does it take to *poof*?" She preferred to use the layman's term. Butchering was an understatement when it came to her speaking Latin.

"Depends on how far awa' he is an' if he's been here a'fore. Travelin' tae an unfamiliar place can tak' a while. Five or ten minutes."

Serah relaxed. "Then I have some freedom. Thank God."

She threw a popcorn kernel up into the air and opened her mouth to catch it. Instead a sharp burst of wind swirled around and sent the popcorn spinning and pinging against the wall. She slammed her mouth shut, shock pounding through her system.

"Damn, Serah. He's guid."

Five to ten minutes, her ass.

And like that, freedom zipped away with each frigid gust.

She didn't know whether to be relieved or pissed. And that's what really pissed her off.

Chapter 14

MATTHIAS BRUSHED OFF CHUNKS OF ICE AND SNOW from his shoulders. He hated the *Peragrans* and the brutally icy portals. One of the small sacrifices for a minute or two of travel. It was certainly better than the alternate... especially when you were in a hurry.

And he'd left her alone too long.

Then again, she wasn't completely alone. Sitting next to her on the sofa was her wannabe protector. And to make matters worse, he was sipping scotch and smoking a cigar. Not a bodyguard, more like a sidekick. A very inept one at that.

"How'd you get here so quick?" Serah asked, pushing a piece of popcorn between her lips.

"Och aye. How did ye?"

"I am a trained warrior with over seven hundred and fifty years of experience."

"Wha'ever," the cat meowed out. He set his cigar on an ashtray sitting next to him on the sofa. Taking one final swig of the amber liquid in his glass, he tossed it back. "Ah spoke tae Rafe. He says ye'r clean. I'm still watchin' ye though."

Matthias gritted his teeth. He should have known it was more than a cat. And a Scottish one, to boot. Things couldn't get any stranger. "Another imp?"

"Och aye. Farquhar MacTavish at yer service."

"This is ridiculous," Matthias grumbled.

"Ah guess he's gettin' the guest room?" Farquhar narrowed his eyes into a penetrating glare. "Wow. Kickin' the kitty tae the curb."

"You have to start acting like a cat, damn it."

"Lickin' ma crease, pissin' in a stinky box, an' chasin' ma feckin' tail?" Farquhar puffed up his fur. "I'd say I'm daein' a damn guid job."

"Since when do cats smoke cigars and drink…" She looked at the label on the bottle on the table. "Glenfiddich? Where'd you find the money for that?"

"Nae jist any Glenfiddich. Forty-year single-malt." He grinned, whiskers turning upwards. "Ah hae ma ways."

This was absolutely ridiculous. How could this pint-sized ball of fur protect her if all he did was sit back with fine scotch and Cuban cigars and watch movies all night. And where was he getting Cuban cigars? Weren't those illegal?

Then again, he'd seen Farquhar and his lady friend give him the slicing of the century earlier. That, oddly, counted for something.

He wouldn't give the imp the benefit of the doubt.

"So you got the all clear?"

"Unfortunately."

"Then you are relieved of your duties. Go, be a cat."

"This is crazy."

So was talking to a cat. "And meow, damn it."

"Meow." Farquhar extended his middle claw. With a not-so-graceful leap, he plopped to the floor. Tail swishing back and forth, he dropped into the pet bed in the corner. "Dinnae get on ma bad side, Ambrose."

"Don't get on mine, and I won't get on yours." He turned back to Serah whose mouth fell open in shock.

"Wow. Impressive."

"Why's that?"

"Mr. Whiskers—Farquhar doesn't listen to many people. Not even Rafe."

"Just like a cat."

Farquhar's head popped up. "Ah can still hear ye."

"Take the guest room. Tonight only."

"Fine." Farquhar moseyed over to the entertainment center, climbed up on his back paws and pressed a button on the DVD player. He pulled the DVD out of the open turntable and spun the disc around a clawed finger. With quick flick, he sent the DVD flipping up in the air and caught the DVD on the tip of his tail. "Gie me ma scotch, buddy."

"I think you've had enough. You're a cat."

"Ah'm an imp. A powerful one. Dinnae make me go medieval on yer crease."

"Here's your scotch, Farquhar. We'll talk more about this later." She laid the bottle in front of him.

"Wha'ever." With that, he batted the bottle down the hallway and toward the second door on the right. "Ah'll still be watching ye." The door slammed shut behind him.

"Blood and damnation. I've never met a pair of more obstinate beings, human and demon combined."

He yearned to sit down next to her and put on a less violent movie. Something more to Serah's liking. To pluck some popcorn from that bucket and feed it to her one kernel at a time. To pull her close to him and—bloody hell. He moved to take the spot vacated by Farquhar earlier.

"Pair? You aren't all that amenable either."

With a disgruntled groan, he opted to take the recliner instead. This wouldn't be easy. "I have reasons. I've lived a long life. I've seen enough death and destruction. I will not sit idly while the world's only possible chance at salvation lounges here and ignores her calling."

"All I know how to do is cook. How do you expect me to save the world from demons? Feed them to death?"

This was getting futile. He couldn't touch her, though. Too many sensations zinged through him. And from the look he glimpsed in her eyes, she felt them too. And then there was the fact that she had *touched* him. And she still lived.

"What happened when you touched me earlier?" he asked. Oh, something had happened, all right. But not the normal thing that happened when a human touched a demon without permission—agonizing pain, and some-times, death.

"I already told you nothing happened."

"Exactly."

Serah sank into the sofa and averted his glance. "Maybe Rafe or Lucy put a protection spell on me."

"Good try, but no. Enrapturement only works on *normal* humans."

"Maybe you're wrong and they did cast a charm on me."

"Rafael and Lucia gave me their word. You are un-enrapturable."

"Maybe I'm not human."

"What makes you say that?"

"Everything started after Lucy opened the chest. Maybe I'm possessed."

"If that were the case, you wouldn't have

demon-sense. Only those who are pure—or blessed— can smell the Infernati odor."

Serah leaned in, question flashing in her gaze. "And if you're not a blessed Paladin yet, how can you?"

Matthias ground his teeth. He wasn't proud of his past. He'd done things that would send any respectable person packing. At the time it seemed right. After all, he needed to survive. "I've worked for some unsavory people."

"You already mentioned it." Serah leaned back into the sofa. "If you want my trust, then you need to be honest with me. I get the feeling you're hiding something."

"My past is not pretty, Seraphina." The moment he spoke her real name, his heart plummeted. A frown creased her lips and she exhaled a deep sigh. "I have killed many, Infernati, Paladin, and humans alike."

"And yet the Fore-Demons allowed you to join?"

"Maybe they want more amusement in their ancient demonic lives."

"Amusement?"

"Maybe they enjoy watching me suffer."

"So protecting me is torture? Is that what you're saying?"

More than she knew. Torture in the most tantalizing ways. God, the things he wanted to do to her. His loins throbbed in response. He turned his head away.

"If you don't care for me, then have them reassign you. I hate being treated like an inconvenience."

The gauntlet had been dropped. He clenched his fists. "The feeling, my dear, is very mutual." Maybe it was time to show her just how inconvenient she was.

He hauled himself to his feet and snaked his arm around her curvy waist. Pulling her against him, he angled her head to meet his gaze. Her sapphire pupils sparked in challenge, a challenge the certifiable part of him had no qualms about accepting. Grasping the curls at her neck, he continued to take in her beauty. What harm could one searing kiss do?

Just one kiss. To put her in her place.

Hah! He wanted to put her in to many places—mainly his bed.

Her heart thumped against his. A soft gasp broke the silence. She pushed a hand against his chest. It was as if he were struck by lightning. Energy zinged through his body through every receptor. Then again, lightning probably didn't feel this damned good.

"What—"

He didn't give her a chance to finish her sentence. With a quick sweep, he brought her lips to his. Sizzling energy exploded between their skin. Much to his delight, she did not pull away. She inched her arms around his shoulders, friction sparking between their bodies. Fingers laced in the hair at the nape of his neck, she pressed closer as her lips parted. Acquiescence never tasted so good. Like fresh plums and—warm buttered popcorn.

His tongue sensed her acceptance. As if on its own, it swept along her lips and pressed into her warm, inviting mouth. Who knew fruit and popcorn could taste so good. His greedy tongue danced along her equally eager tongue, sending all his blood rushing to his groin. He throbbed against the heat that pressed so intimately against him.

He didn't want to stop.

He moved his mouth lower, nibbling on her lip. Tongue-laving against the rosy softness of her skin turned to nipping. He moved his mouth lower, to her chin. The pulse at her neck thumped. He was doomed. He didn't care.

Without further thought, he traced his tongue along her neck. Flicking and flitting, he swept his tongue along the pulsing vein. Right to the tip of her earlobe. His hands worked up and down her body, tracing the curves of her full breasts.

Another tiny moan reverberated against his lips. Her hands moved to the collar of his linen shirt and to the first button. With eager ministrations, she plucked it open. Tracing fingertips through his exposed chest hair, she moved to the second button and inched open the wrinkled shirt. Roving hands over his pectorals, her fingers brushed against his scar. The one scar that had brought him into the life as a soulless demon. His body jerked in response. He couldn't let her touch him there. The one part of his body that could corrupt her own.

This isn't right.

With an abrupt pause, he pulled away. He would not risk her innocence. And from the way her hands moved against his skin, that was where they were heading.

He steeled himself for the slap that was soon to follow.

It never did. Serah backed away, speechless. Curls cascading around her face, she brought her fingertips to her swollen lips. She flexed and unflexed her fingers. Her body trembled.

"I'm sorry, Serah."

"What just happened?" she whispered.

"I kissed you."

She narrowed her blue eyes into a penetrating glare. "Don't fucking do that again."

You better believe it. That was one thing he'd never let happen again, no matter how much he wanted it. It was too dangerous. Even if they had a past. To be good at your job, you needed to keep your emotions in check. He couldn't let her get under his skin.

She blew out a long sigh and brushed a stray curl from her cheek.

Then again, perhaps she was already there… eating away at his heart.

Her body continued to shiver. She wrapped her arms around her body. *God, this was too much*.

"Did I hurt you?"

"No."

He needed to wipe her memory again. But with both the necklace and watch, how easy would it be? Even with the watch, it seemed his charm was fading. She was getting stronger. It was only a matter of time before she remembered everything.

"Did something happen?"

"Yeah, something happened." With that, she spun around and stormed down the hallway and slammed a door behind her.

It was too late. She already remembered. His mission was doomed.

Chapter 15

Something happened, all right. She liked it too much.

Scraping a hand through her hair, she leaned against the door. She could still feel his lips, hot and hard, on hers. His tongue fencing with hers. His body, all corded and sinewy, pressing against her. His scent. How could she have missed that exotic smell before. Like citrus, ginger, and other exotic spices. It was sensual, it was delicious. It was—familiar?

She would have never forgotten such a scent. It was a strong scent, but not overpowering, like some of those colognes men doused themselves with. Not cloying at all. It drove her crazy. She wanted more.

She'd smelled it before.

"Damn it! I'm going crazy." She'd never seen him before today. But that scent…

Heck, she'd had a long day. She needed sleep. She needed to get his intense dark gaze, his chiseled abs and pecs, and those huge hands out of her thoughts.

Her naughty side licked her lips. Impossible!

She stalked over to her dresser and yanked open her drawer. She pulled out her favorite silk cami and traced her fingertip along the delicate creamy lace scalloping. Would Matthias like it?

Arrgh! She thrust the offending fabric back into her drawer and grabbed a pair of black cotton shorts and a

T-shirt instead. She yanked off her sweater and jeans and quickly changed.

Looking down at the light blue T-shirt, she grimaced. "What's cookin' hot stuff?" was scrawled across her breasts in big, bold, hot-pink sweeps.

She silently cursed Lucy for buying it for her.

Oh well, no one except her could see the silly shirt. She'd make sure of it. She sprinted back to the door and pushed in the button, locking the room against unexpected visitors—especially those of the male variety.

Then again, Matthias could just poof his way in. *Oh hell, it was useless.*

Then again, she had her grandmother's necklace and watch now. Maybe they could help keep that putrid demon at bay.

Seriously, you're going to keep this Fitness *magazine cover model from coming in? Where's your sense of adventure?*

"It died nearly a year ago."

Great. She was talking to herself again. How would she survive the meeting with Daniel Blackburn tomorrow with him lingering around. She wouldn't be able to concentrate. She'd end up making a fool of herself. Her chance at exposure was doomed. And the producer hadn't even stepped into her kitchen yet.

"What the heck am I going to do?" she whispered.

He might have had a job to perform, but she did too. She couldn't afford to fail, not when the thing she loved most was at stake.

She loved to cook. She'd be damned if she'd let some walking hunk of a demon tell her she was meant for something else.

Wow. Was this what Lucy went through when she found out she was half-succubus? But that's where she and Lucy were different. Lucy really *was* part sex-demon. Serah was just Serah. Not a demon, not a Puritan or the like. She was just a caterer. End of story.

"There's only one thing I can do."

It was simple. Keep him out of the kitchen and away from her senses. It was the only logical solution. *If he didn't like it, boo-frickin' hoo*.

And she knew he wouldn't like it one bit.

Hot, moist kisses traveled down her neck to the throbbing base of her throat. A tiny mewl pressed through her lips. Hard strong hands roved up and down her body. Mewls turned to moans as she grabbed the hair at Matthias's nape and pulled him closer.

Matthias?

God Almighty. He had found a way in. And he was torturing her again with that mouth of his.

Oh shut up. You know you like it.

Too much. His fingers lingered along the hem of her flimsy shirt.

"We shouldn't do this," he whispered in her ear, his tongue making a long sweep along her lobe.

As if making up her own script, she inched the shirt up. "I need your help." Lips curved upwards, she pulled the shirt up over her head and threw it against the stone wall. "Please?"

"Seraphina," he whispered. He swept his arms around her waist and dragged her against his hard, very naked chest. "No one that pure can be this tempting."

"Kiss me," she insisted. "Now."

Wow, where had that come from? She traced her fingertips through the curly hair on his chest and moved lower to circle a nipple. Lower still.

He grabbed her hands and pulled them away. "Not like this."

Man, if only he'd let her touch his chest. Not a touchy-feely sort of man, unless he was the one doing the touching and feeling. What was his deal?

Friction zinged in the air. One spark and she'd go up in flames. She angled her gaze upwards, pleading. She had to feel those lips.

Talk about some dream.

And, crazy as it was, she didn't want it to end.

Curse him for invading her mind. Then again, she couldn't complain one bit.

"Like this?" she asked. She moved closer, lip to lip, and traced her tongue along the crease of his lips.

"Bloody hell," he growled. With that, he pushed her against hard concrete, fumbling with her bra straps. He yanked them down over her shoulders. Lips hard and unyielding, he pressed his tongue inside her mouth.

God, she was so hot.

Clenching her fists in a futile attempt to keep her hands off his magnificent body, she gasped against his lips.

His hands moved up and down her body, lingering around her breasts. Like it was his favorite part of her disproportionate body. She wasn't known for her feminine endowments and she curved in all the wrong places, but he didn't seem to care. And that only made her hotter.

"Oh God, Matthias," she moaned, louder than she ever moaned before. Thank goodness she lived alone, or she would've woken the entire house.

The loud pounding pulled her from her salacious dream. Her eyes snapped open. *Oh shit!*

"Serah!" Matthias's voice boomed. "Are you okay?"

She flung off her sheet and jumped from her bed. Stumbling across the room, she grabbed her discarded shirt off the floor.

"I… ahh… well." She silently cursed herself and her stupid hormones. "I'm—"

Matthias crashed through the door, his gaze dark and intense and lips taut.

"Fine," she breathed out, gripping the shirt tightly in front of her. Her scantily clad body was the last thing she wanted Matthias seeing at this point. "A little privacy?"

His gaze moved lower, his eyes sparking. He sucked in a breath. "I heard you call out for me. I thought you were in trouble."

Oh, she was in trouble. And it wasn't the Infernati this time. It was her own undersexed body's fault.

"Jeez! You're hearing things." She fumbled with the shirt that barely covered her naked breasts. "Do you mind? I'm trying to get dressed."

She trained her gaze to the door that dangled from its hinges. "You better have that fixed by tomorrow."

He slowly backed away. "I heard what I heard, Serah, but I can tell when I am not wanted. And the door will get fixed. Believe it or not, I was a carpenter before I was a mercenary."

"Jesus Christ was your idol, I bet."

"No one can live up to him, and anyone who thinks they

can is sorely mistaken." He spun around and slammed the door behind him. It squeaked on its broken hinges.

Serah could only gape in silence. He wasn't as arrogant as she thought.

But he was wrong about something. Very wrong. Contrary to her practical impulses, she wanted him— more than any other man, even Matthew McConaughey.

Chapter 16

HE HEARD HER SHOUT HIS NAME. THERE WAS NO mistaking that. From the urgency in her voice, she was in distress. He had no choice but to bust through that door. Who knew what he would find.

And, whoa, did he find something. Curls tousled, Serah clutched a tiny shirt to her half-naked body. His blood boiled at the sight. It took everything in his power not to crush her into his arms again.

Like he had almost a year ago. Who knew what would have happened in that cell had the Infernati guards not shown their evil faces and taken her away.

And that was where his mission did a complete one-eighty. Something inside him snapped. He went from mercenary to protector in a nanosecond.

He originally thought it was because Belial reneged on his promise. But something else stirred him into action. Something he couldn't decipher. It was dangerous and unnerving, yet caused his body to zing.

Maybe he'd been celibate too damn long.

But it was the only way he could keep focused on his missions. Sex only complicated matters. Even a meaningless tryst could turn a simple assignment into an utter failure. But sex with Serah would be far from meaningless. It would be mind-blowing. And if he wanted this mission to be successful, he needed all his wits about him.

An impossible task. Just looking at her sent his wits flying out the window.

"Curse those bloody Fore-Demons." They knew damn well what they were doing.

A door snicked open. Bloody hell. He didn't want to see her. Not now, not when he still needed to get control of his rampaging body.

"You can go back to bed, Serah."

"Sorry tae disappoint ye." Farquhar whipped his tail against his leg. Daring little imp. "Ah needed tae tak' a wiz. By th' way, wa' was Serah moanin' yer name?"

"It was just a nightmare."

"Seriously?" Farquhar mewed out a laugh. "That was nae nightmare."

"She told me it was nothing."

"Ye expect me tae believe that guff?" Farquhar shook his black-and-white-furred head. "Haven't ye ever... ye ken?"

"Know what?"

Farquhar rolled his round eyes. "Forget it. Ye Paladins need tae get oot more often. By the way, blankets an' spare pillows are in the hall closet. But ye really dinnae need them, dae ye?"

Matthias shrugged. It was uncommon knowledge that demons didn't need sleep to function, but despite the unnatural stamina, handling Serah SanGermano's stubborn streak left him completely drained. He'd never felt so vulnerable in centuries.

"I enjoy a rest every so often."

"Fair enaw." With that, Farquhar sauntered down the hallway and pushed open the bathroom door. "Wha'ever ye want tae believe. 'At wasnae a moan o' distress. If ye try anythin', I'll slice ye frae limb tae limb." He raised his paw and extended his five claws, one by one. "Got it?"

Matthias offered a silent nod.

"Guid." Tail flicking back and forth, Farquhar swished into the bathroom.

"Shit," Matthias muttered beneath his breath. He'd heard her moan like that before. When they were locked up in the Infernati dungeon. There was no doubt now. Her memories were coming back.

She was getting stronger. It was only a matter of time before the truth made itself known. His stomach pitched at the thought. She would hate him.

He couldn't blame her. He deserved it. To be honest, he deserved worse. And when she remembered, the worst was yet to come.

"The Fore-Demons must have lost their minds." If he were one of them, he'd never allow himself to join. If they weren't crazy, then they had a sadistic sense of humor.

Then again, this was the Fore-Demon Council. He'd heard stories about their strange and twisted ways. They obviously knew more than they were letting on.

Damned Fore-Demons! There was no doubt now. They wanted him to suffer. And suffer he would, if it meant protecting Serah.

Nothing in life was simple. And if it was, it was always too good to be true. He paced in front of the couch and scrubbed the stubble growing along his chin.

The blast of wind chimes reverberated against his eardrums.

Reaching into the pocket of his pants, he fumbled

for the mobile phone Deleon insisted he carry. Modern technology was a necessary evil.

He swiped his finger across the green button flashing on the screen.

"Ambrose."

"Is everything in order?" There was no masking the concern in Rafael's voice. "Lucy said she tried calling Serah several times tonight."

"Serah has gone to bed for the evening."

"Already?"

"It's eleven thirty."

Rafael blew out a breath. "She's a night owl. It's early for her. What happened?"

"There was an issue while we were at the store."

"Issue?"

"We were attacked by Balthazar."

Rafael clucked his tongue. "Balthazar? Not good."

"Who's Balthazar?" Matthias heard muffled in the background. Lucia. Thank goodness Serah had such dedicated friends. Who knew where she'd be without Lucia Gregory and Rafael Deleon.

"Hold on a moment, Ambrose." More muffled words ensued. "Let me get more info from Ambrose."

He came back to the receiver. "So what happened, and do not sugarcoat it."

Matthias relayed the entire evening, sans the kiss. If Deleon knew the truth, he'd send him packing back to the Council. He might not have wanted the mission before. Now, on the other hand, he *had* to protect Serah. She needed him. Hell, he owed it to her.

"And what's this about some television show she's signed up for?"

"Television show?"

Of course she didn't tell them. She knew how'd they react.

"*American Chef*?"

"Lucy, do you know anything about *American Chef*?" He heard a faint click. "I've put on the speakerphone."

"Fine," Matthias muttered.

Lucia's voice boomed. "It's a show that travels around America and spotlights different chefs. Serah mentioned signing up for a while ago. Before… you know."

"They're coming here tomorrow for an audition."

"Hell's blood," Rafael growled. "The last thing Serah needs is exposure. Especially if Balthazar is lingering around."

"Who is he?" Lucia demanded.

Rafael sucked in a breath. "Belial's second in command."

"God! Even from the bowels of hell, Belial still manages to be a thorn in our sides."

"He says he serves another."

"Even better." There was no masking the sarcasm in Lucia's voice. "Not only is he vengeful, he works for another Infernati asshole."

"I have everything under control."

"Let's hope you do, Ambrose." The finality in Lucia's voice said it all.

"We will further discuss this tomorrow, Ambrose. Early. Preferably before this TV show comes calling." Rafael left no room for refusal.

"Good. There are other things we should discuss as well."

"Very well." With that the call dropped. Not one for familiarities. Then again, Matthias didn't blame him one bit.

Then again, maybe Deleon knew more than he admitted.

He stalked down the hallway and yanked open the closet door. He grabbed a cotton sheet and flannel blanket and wrenched out a jumbo-sized pillow that was stuffed into the top. He kicked the door shut.

He turned his gaze to Serah's miraculously closed door. "I'm doomed." But just because he might have been doomed, didn't mean the world had to suffer the same fate. He'd see to it. He only hoped Serah could forgive him, because he couldn't forgive himself.

Serah awoke with a start. Warmth tingled its way throughout her entire body. Her toes curled. Whatever Matthias was doing to her needed to stop. No matter how damned good it felt.

She reached over to glance at the clock. Four a.m. She never should've gone to bed so early. She'd never get back to sleep. She glanced at the phone flashing next to her nightstand. Five missed calls. All from Lucy. Even if her friend hardly ever slept, it was still too late to call— Lucy and Rafe were probably *busy*. Lucky little demons.

Then again, they were perfect for each other. Rafe, with his stony reserve and Lucy with her no-nonsense attitude complemented each other perfectly. Truth be told, they were more alike than they realized.

"And they're in love," she whispered. "At least one of us is lucky." Not that she wanted love. She was quite content with her nonexistent love life. Men only complicated matters. And she had a kitchen to run. She didn't need distractions—not now.

Lord knew she already had one huge distraction as it was. Why did he have to be so big and muscular? And why did she have to fantasize about him—camouflage and all?

Her cheeks warmed and her stomach clenched. Moist heat flooded into her loins. No matter how hard she tried, she couldn't stop thinking about that dream. Not the dream—the man.

"He has to go." She'd talk to Rafe in the morning. How hard could it be to find a new bodyguard?

What about Rafe's old partner, Dominic? He was able enough. Then again, he'd been sent back to limbo by the woman he loved. Rafe said he still hadn't fully recovered.

A bodyguard with baggage—the second to last thing she needed right now. Why couldn't demonic protection be easy? Why did her bodyguard have to spawn dangerous fantasies?

Not that fantasies are all that bad.

"Ugh!" She swiped a paperback from her dresser and perused the title. *Private Protection.*

Oh gawd.

She continued her scan of the cover. A bare-chested torso of a man wearing a shoulder holster filled the cover, his gun strategically aimed.

Almost as big as Matthias, but not quite.

"Oh, please," she grumbled, tossing the book to the floor. "I should have bought that Martha Stewart cookbook instead."

Frustration, sparked by desire, ignited like a furnace. She wanted to scream, but that would only fuel her frustrations more. Matthias would burst in like he had earlier. Her poor little door couldn't handle any more abuse for the night. And she couldn't handle any more devious fantasies either.

Why in the hell did he have to kiss her? Ever since then her hormones had gone bonkers. She'd liked the kiss too. That's what really irked her.

With a low groan, Serah flung herself back into bed and bunched her pillows around her head. She couldn't sleep. She'd have that stupid dream again. The sad part of it was it felt so real, as if he really were doing all those naughty things to her. And she loved every minute of it.

Maybe Lucy had given her a dose of succubus after all?

At this rate, her audition would be a disaster.

Then again, that's probably what he wanted. He said it himself. The TV show was a distraction they didn't need right now.

Had she known when she applied that her friend would turn into a sex-demon and she'd end up a whatever it was she was, she would have never signed up.

To be honest, she'd completely forgotten about the show. Then Daniel Blackburn, the host himself, had called. She tried to get out of it, but the stupid contract was ironclad. Like it had been written by the devil himself. No escape clause at all.

Not one of my most brilliantly thought-out plans, that's for sure.

Then again, it wasn't like she'd known that she'd end up a walking demon detector a few months after she sent in the application and contract.

Heck, it was *American Chef*, not *Hell's Kitchen*. Daniel Blackburn seemed harmless enough. And he was kind of attractive in a nerdy sort of way.

Not as attractive as Matthias.

"But he knows how to cook!"

Her naughty self snickered. *So does Matthias—where it matters.*

For goodness sakes! Would this ever stop? Matthias Ambrose was a big, stubborn behemoth who only cared about his mission and becoming a Paladin. He'd made that clear enough—on several occasions.

Even if he kissed her. Heck, he was probably just trying to shut her up. Sadly enough, it worked, in the most delicious of ways.

"Damn it." She fisted the sheets and pulled them up around her head. Squeezing her eyes shut, she tried desperately to put herself to sleep.

Rolling around in her blankets, she pounded the pillows, wrapped her arms around them and pulled one close to her body. Too damned soft.

"Ugh!" she shouted through her pillow.

Not even counting sheep could help her now.

She threw off her sheets and chucked the pillow across the room. Was this the same torture Lucy had to endure? She remembered how much her friend valued her sleep. And now it seemed she was as sleepless as the demons that surrounded her.

"Caterer by day, demon hunter by night." Maybe she was the world's next superhero.

"Spiderman, eat my dust," she mumbled. *Yeah right.*

She looked down at her somewhat flat derriere and wrinkled her nose. Even Spanx couldn't help those pancakes.

She angled a glance to her chest. Those either.

With a shrug, she reached for the remote and turned

on the TV. The image of a man sitting at a Bowflex pulling and tugging at the cables flashed before her eyes. Stupid late night infomercials. Why couldn't it have been the ShamWow Guy and his *incredible* Slap Chop instead?

The bodybuilder continued his demonstration. Lean, corded muscles bunched and flexed with each move. Not a bad body, for sure. But something was missing.

It'll take him a long time to even think about matching Matthias's physique.

Serah threw her arms up in the air and blew out a long sigh of resignation. Even her TV had been infected by him.

Then again, he was the most beautifully sculpted man—and demon—she'd ever laid her eyes on. Too built even for *Men's Health*, yet not too steroid-induced for a bodybuilder magazine. Some of those men—she shuddered at the thought—squeezed and flexed so hard they looked like constipated Incredible Hulk wannabes with no necks, grunts and groans included.

She didn't like them when they smiled. And she certainly wouldn't like them when they were angry.

Speaking of smiles, had Matthias ever smiled a day in his life? It was like his mouth was caught in this permanent glower that not even a plastic surgeon could fix.

For God's sake, stop thinking about him! She slammed her finger down on the channel button. A diet smoothie here, an Ab-Roller there. Late-night television really sucked. Maybe she should just buy the items in hopes that they'd get enough sales and stop advertising.

Yeah, right. They'd probably just come up with some other crazy invention to sell instead.

Then she landed on Duke Nelson's Magic Protein Powder. *For real? And who the hell was Duke Nelson? Like protein powder really gave him that body.* With a low groan, she shook her head.

The announcer continued his overdramatic spiel about the wonders of the Magic Protein Powder. Big, bulging biceps, hot women, a smaller dinghy. "And if you call in the next ten minutes, we'll *double* your order—*absolutely free*!" And then in the next whispered breath, "Just pay separate shipping and processing."

Serah rolled her eyes. She might have bought a lot of things in her life, but very few of them came from infomercials. Then again, she really dug that Combo Cooker XL. Great for those on the go, like herself. If only her clients knew how she cooked at home.

"Have your credit card ready when you call," continued the announcer.

"My credit card is on lockdown. Sorry buddy."

With that, she mashed the power button. The TV faded in response. No way did she need protein powder, even if it was only three low payments of $9.99.

Three too many if you asked her.

Darn, she hated it when she woke up this early. The clock flipped from four to five. "Jeez," she yawned, rubbing her eyes. "Too early to be awake, but too late to fall back asleep." Mornings like this were killer.

With a reluctant groan, she crawled out of the cocoon of her blankets. Quite literally a cocoon, too, the way they curled and twisted around her. But she was no butterfly, that's for sure. Especially not this early in the morning.

But damn, those lips of his moved like butterflies, all

over her body. If it wasn't him enrapturing her, what the hell was in that man's cologne? Something harmful if swallowed, probably.

Maybe a cold shower would help get Mr. Magic Lips out of her mind. And it would wake her up too. Lord knew she'd need all the coffee in the world to make it through the day.

And how was she going to keep him out of the kitchen when Daniel arrived? Lock him out? Not likely, after the show of strength he gave her last night.

She shrugged. She just wouldn't invite him in. *Problem solved.* With a confident smile, she leapt from the bed and pushed open the dangling door.

Today would be a good day after all. She'd make sure of it.

Chapter 17

She held her breath, not quite sure what she would find. Farquhar was still snug in the guest bedroom. The door was still closed. Imps weren't as powerful as demons, and they needed naps every so often. Being a cat didn't help matters much for him either.

Eat, sleep, and poop, she remembered a friend from culinary school say once. *That's all my cat is good for*.

Wait until she met Farquhar. He smoked cigars and swilled down scotch like it was going out of style. The eating—well, boy, could he eat.

"He'd probably eat me out of house and home if he could," she whispered as she tiptoed down the hall.

No way in hell was she going to wake the sleeping beast. Then again, he was a demon. Demons didn't need sleep. Some, like Lucy and Rafe, though, still caught a few Z's every so often. Then again, Lucy was only half demon. Sleep still came naturally for her. Rafe just liked tagging along.

Maybe Matthias was one of those demons who yearned to be human and still partook in human activities. After all, she'd seen him sneak a few pieces of popcorn when he thought she wasn't looking.

Then again, he was a bodyguard. What kind of bodyguard sleeps on the job? Especially one who took the commando role so seriously.

Not many.

Oh well, she had to deal with him anyway. Might as well be now.

She shimmied into the living room and rounded the corner to the dining room. The sooner she got her coffee made, the better.

The sooner she could escape to her shower—alone.

Party pooper.

Yep, that she was.

A low gravelly moan came from the couch.

"Oh no," she mumbled.

Oh yes!

She covered her eyes, but peeked through open fingers.

A hand draped over the couch and the sheet fell down across his chest. Eyes still closed, he swallowed and moistened his lips. He twisted and turned on the couch, the blanket falling away, exposing black silk.

Huh?

Red polka dots.

Her cheeks warmed at the sight. Muscles bunched and bulged against the delicate fabric. Her gaze moved upward. Something else pressed against the fabric, the boxers barely concealing what lay beneath.

Pulling her hands from her eyes, she licked her lips. Her mouth watered and her pulse bobbed. She stood still, transfixed by the view in front of her. She yearned to go over and stroke those magnificent muscles through the silky fabric. Her fingers tingled.

Get control of yourself.

She scanned the room. The clothing they'd bought earlier lay neatly over the easy chair. Shoe boxes and packages stacked in order on the floor. Oh great. A neat-freak. He and Kalli would get along swimmingly.

How'd he sneak those into the clothes when she wasn't looking? Then again, he was a demon. If there was one thing she knew, each demon had one or more tricks up his sleeve. Maybe shoplifting was his. Regardless, she'd make certain he only wore tighty-whities from now on. She shivered, imagining him sprawled across her sofa in nothing but a pair of briefs. Even David Beckham in his skimpy Armanis couldn't compare. Scratch that. He was sleeping fully clothed from now on.

"I'm hopeless," she whispered. Why, oh, why couldn't the Fore-Demons send Kevin Costner instead? Nah, Whitney Houston would get jealous. Then again, Kevin Costner didn't have much of a body. And he was old enough to be her father.

Never mind. He would have worked perfectly. No fantasies to interfere with her sanity.

She padded her way into the dining room and jotted into the kitchen. With a long yawn, she reached up and pulled open the cupboard. She needed something strong if she expected to function the entire day.

Smiling, she grabbed the canister labeled *Extreme Dark Roast*. *Yes, it's that kind of morning.*

She scooped several spoonfuls of coffee beans into the grinder, silently wishing for the miracle to keep Matthias and his scantily clad body from hearing the clamor.

With a quick shrug, she rubbed the locket dangling from her neck. If it worked earlier, maybe it would work again. She closed her eyes.

May the kitchen noises not disturb the demons and imps in this house.

Maybe she should add an *amen* and a *hallelujah* for good measure. The powers that be might like that touch.

She pushed the lid down on the grinder and pressed the button. The grinder roared to life. And no one came to bug her.

"Hallelujah!" she exclaimed with a triumphant fist in the air. She pushed the button again and the grinder came to a halt. She brought her nose to the freshly ground goodness and breathed in.

"Mmm."

She poured water into the coffee maker and flipped the switch. With slow, methodical drops, the coffee-maker bubbled and sizzled to life. Too bad *good coffee* couldn't just come in an instant.

The aroma of warm coffee wafted in the air. She plopped down into the barstool, a soft grin spreading on her lips.

It reminded her of Nonni. Her grandmother had always enjoyed her coffee, especially Italian roast. Serah on the other hand, preferred the darker, more flavorful blends. Usually she'd make an espresso, but she had the sinking suspicion she was brewing for more than one today.

Her stomach roared. Apparently breakfast was in order too. She lugged herself out of the barstool and fired up the stove. If these demons expected something fancy, they were sorely mistaken.

Scrambled eggs and bacon it would be.

She sprayed a healthy coating of olive oil and the pan sizzled in response. There was nothing she enjoyed more than cooking in private.

She whisked her eggs, added some milk and cheddar cheese and tossed the mixture into the pan. Chopped onions and peppers always made a good match as well. A little garlic and pepper and her not so secret ingredient—cottage cheese. Fooled them every time.

The sizzling aromas wafted in the air as she threw some bacon on the griddle. The scents continued to swirl around her. She loved cooking breakfast. She and Nonni had always cooked breakfast together.

"I wonder if demons like toast."

"I'll take rye if you have it."

Pulling her housecoat tight to her body, she spun around. Matthias lounged against the doorjamb, a pair of lounging pants hiding her view from the silk boxers he wore earlier.

Thank heaven for that.

"How'd you get in here?"

Matthias narrowed his gaze. "I walked in."

"I put up a blocking charm. I guess it didn't work."

"Oh."

"See! I told you I'm just your average Midwestern gal."

Matthias scratched his chin. "What did you say in your charm?"

"I prayed that the kitchen noises didn't disturb the demons and imps in this house."

Matthias roared in laughter. It was a nice sound really. He should do it more often. "It was the smell that brought me here, not the noise."

"Oh."

"Smells delicious," he said, stepping further into the room.

"It's just scrambled eggs and bacon. Nothing special."

Matthias gaze sparked. "I've eaten my fair share of bacon and eggs over the years, Serah. None of them smelled this good."

"I'm good at what I do, what can I say?"

"You can be good at other things as well, you know."

"I don't have the time to be your little hero. I have a business to run."

"And your friend Lucia does not?"

"She has Rafe to help her, not to mention Kalli and Frankie."

"What about your sous-chef?"

"Edie? She's good, but there's something off with her."

"I can help." Matthias stood proud. "I have cooked a few meals in my lifetime."

"There's a big difference between cooking for yourself and cooking for one hundred."

"I want to help."

"Okay buddy. Take care of the eggs while I go take a shower. How's that?"

Matthias nodded. "Fine."

"Good."

—m—

Serah, still clinging tightly to her robe, strode out of the room. Matthias breathed a sigh of relief. It was pure torture to not strip that robe away and worship her curves.

He sensed she was self-conscious about her body, and that seemed to only add to her appeal. She was proud, but not too arrogant. It drove him mad with desire.

Why in the hell had he offered to help her? He didn't even know the last thing about cooking. He'd cooked a few meals back in his human days, but as technology improved, cooking methods changed as well.

Eggs frying in a pan, though? That was something he could manage. He reached for the handle and stirred the contents. What were those white chunks floating in the eggs? With a shrug, he set it back down on the burner, a little sloshing outside the pan.

Oil bubbled and sputtered, flames flying out from the burner. In a rush, the flames jumped into the pan.

A shrill beep rent the air, alerting the entire house of his stupidity. Serah would be here any minute.

Matthias shook the pan. Flames only grew hotter and leapt higher. Setting the pan back down, he covered it with the lid. Flames snuck out the sides and as if it were taunting, flicked and flitted. What had he done?

He flew to the sink and cranked the water on full blast. Sprayer poised and ready, like it was his favorite firearm, he pushed in the trigger.

Water streamed and sprayed, sending balls of fire exploding in the air. Matthias burst to attention. Somersaulting over the counter, he grabbed a towel and slapped at the ever-growing flames. Heat and smoke burned in his nostrils, the stench clinging to his nose.

"Bloody hell!" If it weren't for the lack of stench clinging to the air and the protection charm surrounding the house, he'd think it was the Infernati making their presence known. The smoke billowed and the flames leapt and danced from beneath the pan. Why wouldn't it go out?

He flung open closets and cupboards, shuffling and clanging pots and pans. If he knew Serah's eggs would turn into napalm, he would have helped in some other way. Now her kitchen was turning into toast—quite literally.

A flame leapt from the stove and licked his bare bicep.

"Shit!" he grumbled. Even though the scar would soon fade, it still hurt like a bitch. He rubbed his arm and threw down the now-flaming towel. What a disaster. She'd get rid of him for sure.

A spark of determination flashed inside him. He wouldn't let her get rid of him. He'd find a way to make this right. Their breakfast was already ruined. He'd be damned if he let her entire kitchen go next.

"Damn it, where's that fire extinguisher!"

"What the hell is going on?"

Serah burst into the kitchen, a damp towel tightly wrapped around her curvy body. An equally damp towel wrapped around her head, shielding her beautiful curls from his view. Even in a towel, the woman was magnificent. Damn. How could his mind wander to a place like that now? Her eyes, widening in horror, curbed his overactive libido. "Jesus Christ!"

She ripped open a cupboard and yanked out a giant yellow cardboard box with an arm holding a hammer stamped on it. With a forceful shove, she pushed Matthias out of the way. She pulled out the spout and poured its white powdery contents onto the fire, the flames dying and smoke billowing and churning in the air.

"It's a grease fire. Water doesn't work." She sat the box down on the blackened counter and wiped a bead of sweat from her forehead, a charcoal streak forming in its place. "You are not allowed in my kitchen ever again."

"I didn't know," was all he could mutter.

Coughing and sputtering, she swatted at the smoke. "My kitchen is ruined."

Matthias rubbed his chin. *Sorry* wouldn't cut it right now. How was he to know that, over the centuries, cooking would become such a complicated task. Life was supposed to become easier as the world evolved, after all. "I haven't cooked in few centuries. I'm sorry, Serah. I was just trying to help out."

She grabbed the blackened pan from the stove and dropped it into the trash. "Be helpful by fixing the door you destroyed last night. I hope your carpentry skills are better than your cooking." Picking up the crispy towel off the counter, she blew out a deep sigh. "I hope Kalli can clean up this mess."

Kalli Corapolous. He'd heard stories about her and her abilities. Cleaning, mind reading, tracking demons, to name a few. Matter of fact, she'd *almost* tracked him on several occasions. If she was as good as the stories he'd heard, she shouldn't have any problems with a small kitchen.

"Was the mess caused by a demon?"

She shrugged. "I guess so, but she's cleaned up a few of my messes too."

"Because you know of our nature. You were blessed at some time in your life, which makes you even more powerful."

"Fine I'll call her from the shop. I still have to do my hair and makeup. I need to get ready for the audition, and I don't want to be late."

"Makeup?"

"You know, stuff women wear on their faces to make themselves look better?"

Look better? If she looked any better, he would die right then and there. "You don't need makeup."

"Yeah, right, tell that to the rings under my eyes. I only got a couple hours of sleep."

Matthias nodded. So much for a compliment. "What about breakfast?"

"I'll stop by BigBob's on the way to the shop."

"BigBob's?" Matthias shuddered at the name. "Sounds interesting."

"BigBob's coffee is the best. Even better than Starbucks." She scanned the counter, and picked up a half-melted coffee cup, the two *B*'s wilting and melting together. "Looks like I need a new cup anyway." She dropped it into the trash can.

"Fine. What about your furry friend?"

"Farquhar? He can take care of himself."

"Does he always sleep during fires?"

"No, but you were here weren't you?" Serah smirked. "Then again, if you weren't here, my kitchen would be fine."

"Touché."

"Oh, well. Kalli and her magic pail of wonder can fix it, but we are going to have a serious sit-down with Lucy and Rafe, especially if I get the show."

She'd get the show. Despite her stubborn streak, the woman had charm. And, of course, she was beautiful, from those two sparking sapphire eyes to her full pouty lips. And those curves. This Daniel person would have to be blind not to notice.

If only he could be that lucky. "We can discuss this show later. I still don't think it's a good idea."

"I signed an agreement. It's too late."

Matthias crossed his arms. "I can be very persuasive."

"If you enrapture Daniel Blackburn, I'll kick you back to limbo myself. Got it?"

"Fine, but if I smell any brimstone, I can't guarantee I'll be so kind."

She angled her chin high and stood proud—all while wearing that damned towel. He longed to pull

that towel off her too-tempting body and have his way
with her right on the kitchen table. If she continued to
stand there so defiantly, he didn't know how long he
could last. Clenching his teeth, he reined in all his remaining control. She finally spoke. "Fair enough, but
you have nothing to worry about. I doubt the host of a
popular cooking show is a demon. Don't they usually
keep low profiles?"

"Let's hope you're right, Serah." He'd seen some
of those so-called celebrities. If they weren't demons,
then there was no hope for Hollywood. He spun toward the dining area and marched through the doorway. The sooner he got her towel-clad body out of his
sight, the better.

Chapter 18

SHE DIDN'T LIKE THE WAY HE STARED AT HER. LIKE HE was the one she should be running from. Like a tiger ready to pounce on his prey. She scrubbed at her soot-streaked face. Running a brush through her dampened curls, she sighed.

Let's hope you're right? "What a jerk!"

Did he think just because he was big, bad, and muscular he could come in here and control everything? Well, he was wrong. And he almost burnt her house down. He was lucky Kalli was nearby, or she would have skinned him alive—with a silver dagger.

She yanked a comb through a gnarled curl. "Ouch." She flung the comb to the counter and raked fingers through her hair instead.

"I don't need makeup?" What exactly did he mean when he said that? Men, especially those of the demon variety, had no clue. As if all women could look like instant sexpots with a snap of a finger. There was only one woman she knew with that skill, and Lucy was half-succubus anyway, so she didn't really count.

She ripped open her makeup bag and yanked out some concealer and foundation. Truth be told, she didn't really like wearing makeup, especially while standing over hot stoves and ovens all day. By the end of the day, it felt like her face was melting off.

But it was different now. She might be on television.

She didn't want to look like a zombie, especially in HD. Her pores were large enough as it was.

She dabbed a little of the creamy liquid on her hand and patted and massaged it into her skin. A little foundation, eyeliner, and mascara never killed anyone. It wasn't like she was going to the Academy Awards or anything, but she still needed to look somewhat presentable.

"Are you almost done in there?" Matthias bellowed.

"I'm human, not a demon. I can't just *poof* my face together."

"I understand. I just don't want you to be late."

How sweet of him, even when he really didn't want anything to do with the show. "I still need to get dressed. How about just zapping yourself there?"

"What about your employee?"

Damn. In all the excitement, she'd forgotten about Edie. And she still needed to call Kalli as well. She smelled like a barbecue gone horribly wrong and needed some clean-up done on herself too.

"I'll call Edie and tell her to expect you." She snagged the phone from the counter. "I'll tell her you've been hired to oversee security."

"Fine." His loud footfalls echoed down the hall.

She located Edie's number in her contacts and clicked the *send* button.

"'Allo?"

Serah stifled the chuckle. She always enjoyed Edie's strange accent.

"Hi, Edie. It's Serah. I've hired a security company in case I get the show. They're sending someone over." She cringed. She'd never been the best of liars. Maybe it was this purity they seemed to rattle on about.

"Iz everyzing okay? The fondue, no?"

"Everything is fine. The fondue was delicious." Thank goodness it was only a practice run for a wedding next week. "The vichyssoise too. No mess to worry about. The Andersons are going to love it."

"*Très bon*."

Whatever that meant. "The man they are sending... His name is Matthias Ambrose. Rafe recommended him."

"Okeydokey pokey."

Serah arched an eyebrow.

"See you in about a half an hour, okay?"

"Okay. Buh-bye! *À tout à l'heure*."

"Uhh, okay. Bye." She hit the red button to end the call. Serah didn't have the heart to tell her sous-chef of her less-than-apt language skills. She loved listening to Edie speak her native tongue anyhow. She turned to the door. "You can do your traveling now, buddy."

"Fine. What about your friend, Kalli?"

"I'm waiting here for her. I smell horrible and was hoping she could use a fresh can of Demon-B-Gone on me." She brought a corner of the towel to her nose.

Ugh!

She took a quick glance in the mirror. At least she looked decent enough. Scraping fingers through her curls, she shrugged. With a sigh, she turned and snuck through the door adjoining her bedroom.

Ripping open her closet, she tore through her clothes. Nothing seemed right. She pulled out a pair of jeans. Too casual. She grabbed a black lace skirt. Too fancy. She grabbed a fuchsia low-cut halter. Too slutty.

"You should wear this." The spicy scent of ginger

followed his voice. He reached out and plucked a bright blue wrap dress from a hanger. "It... looks professional."

"Umm... thanks." She took the garment from him. She actually bought the dress for the wedding that never happened. The Carlson-Harding fiasco. Thank God, the bride had been sent packing. "Why are you in here?"

Matthias turned toward the door. "I thought I would make myself more useful." He opened and closed the door and it whined in protest. Running his large fingers along the split doorjamb, he shrugged. "It still needs a little more work, but at least it closes."

Serah managed a smile. "Thanks, Matthias." She reached out her hand to his. "I can have Kalli finish up for you. After all, it was demon-induced."

"Oh." There was no mistaking the disappointment in his voice.

"But if you'd really like to practice your *human* skills, that's fine."

"I broke it. There are tools to fix it. I owe you that much."

Serah nodded. "Well, at least you can fix one of your disasters."

"Do you need to keep rubbing it in?"

Serah cringed. "Sorry. I was just trying to be funny. No need to get your boxers in a bunch."

"Boxers?" Matthias shifted in his new clothing, a pair of khaki cargoes and the linen shirt he'd tried on last night. Thankfully, they concealed those sexy silk boxers. What was so embarrassing about silk boxers? A lot of men wore them. Then again he wasn't any ordinary man.

"Underwear."

"I know what boxers are. We saw some at the store last night."

"Fine. You better get poofing… uhh… traveling. Edie's expecting you."

"Are you going to be okay?"

"Yeah. Kalli will have this cleaned up in no time."

"I meant behind the wheel."

Serah grumbled under her breath. Was she really that bad a driver? Did she really need to answer that? With a slight downward curve of her lips, she shrugged. So driving wasn't one of her strong suits. She never really felt that comfortable behind the wheel. But put her behind a stove and she could cook for hours.

"I'm sorry. I was trying to joke too." Matthias reached out to grasp her shoulder. More tingles of electricity zipped through her body, right to her toes.

She jerked from his grasp. What was it about his touch? It was even worse on naked skin. All she wanted to do was drop that towel and let him touch every other part of her body. She bit her lip and tensed all her muscles, wriggling in the confines of the towel. Nothing helped.

She clenched her fists. "I need to get dressed."

Matthias nodded and backed away. "Don't let me keep you. The door is fixed. I'll be on my way."

Without further word, he turned and marched out the door, the hinges still whining in response.

Breathing a sigh of relief, she brought her hand to her still-hot shoulder. She traced her fingertips along the searing flesh. A burn was supposed to hurt, but the heat that radiated from him did anything but. It scared her. It drove her mad. She wanted more.

Exactly what kind of demon was Matthias Ambrose? She would find out—one way or the other.

Chapter 19

IT WAS CONFIRMED. SHE REMEMBERED. WHY ELSE would she react that way to his touch? Like just the soft brush of fingertips would unleash a plague upon her skin. His first mission as a Paladin was destined to failure before it even started.

And that stupid towel. It clung and molded to her body in the most devious of ways. It took every fiber of willpower to keep from pulling that towel from her gorgeous body. Too bad that dress he handed to her would do pretty much the same thing.

Heck, battling his old mentor he could handle. However, throwing Serah SanGermano in the mix only complicated matters. It was quite literally a recipe for disaster.

It was, for lack of better words, a mission impossible.

But this wasn't TV, or the movies for that matter. This was real. Demons truly existed. There were no special effects. Serah could die. She needed his help. He had to protect her.

She needed to accept what she was. Only then would she truly be safe. And he wouldn't give up until then—whatever it took.

"What is it about her?" The moment he first set eyes on her he had to have her—had to possess her. He had to take her in every way humanly—and demonically—possible. Everything about her set his blood boiling.

He hadn't felt like that about any woman before—ever. Even when he was human. He clenched his teeth. *No. I can't go back to those days.* It was too long ago. He wasn't the same man. He was a demon now, had been for almost eight hundred years. Those days were long gone, a faded memory. He needed to forget.

The soft murmur carried from her room. His body tensed and his heart thudded. Lust raged inside him. He gritted his teeth. Curse celibacy.

"I've got to get out of here before I do something I regret."

Tasteful Elegance was as good a name as any for Serah's company. It fit her perfectly. Serah radiated elegance, and he'd tasted enough to know her lips were sweeter than sin.

He'd dawdled too long. He had to go or he'd burst into Serah's room and do something he would regret—again. He closed his eyes and threw his arms up into the air.

"Portals of limbo and hell. Carry me away to the front door of Tasteful Elegance."

With that, the winds whipped around him and sucked him up into the freezing vortex. Ice and snow circled him, carrying him through the tunnel. Ice crystals formed on his lips and eyes. A temporary discomfort—in a minute his feet touched solid earth.

The ice melted from his eyelids, and he slowly opened his eyes. Wiping snow and ice from his head and shoulders, he scanned the area.

"Vhat zee hell?"

A tall redhead, clad in tall black boots and a red sweater dress, with a purple scarf draped over her shoulders, stood not more than three feet from Matthias. Her fingers clenched tight around her keys. Her brown eyes widened with shock, and her mouth gaped open just as wide.

"Edie, I presume?"

"*Sacre bleu!*" With that, the woman crumpled to the ground.

Sacre bleu, indeed.

He didn't think that expression was still used in France. Maybe he was wrong. Putting that thought in the back of his mind, Matthias rushed forward and caught her before her head hit the concrete. He took the keys that Edie still gripped and found one labeled *TE cuisine*.

With the sous-chef in his arms and the key gripped tight, he took determined steps to the door. He twisted the key into the lock and kicked it open.

"Ohhh," Edie murmured as she twisted in his arms.

He needed to act fast.

This was not how he wanted to start his mission. He'd promised Serah no enrapturement, but she'd seen the *Peragrans*—demon travel. Even that little glimpse could be too much. He'd learned a lot in his centuries as a mercenary. The less humans knew, the better.

And what he needed to do wasn't enrapturement. All demons could enrapture. What he could do was something far more powerful, something that had kept him hidden in the shadows for many years. It could be dangerous, but he had no choice, for Edie's sake. If humans knew the truth of what was out there, the consequences were too great. He had to do this. There was no other choice.

Serah would understand—he hoped.

He carried Edie to the side office and placed her on the couch. Smoothing back her hair, he took a deep breath. He made a vow to himself to never use his skill, after what he'd done to Serah. He hated breaking vows, even if it was necessary.

"Humans cannot know about the evil that surrounds them."

He clenched his fists. He hated doing this. He reached out and took hold of Edie's shoulders and closed his eyes. The words rolled from his lips a little too easily for his taste. "You will forget the events that transpired this morning between when you pulled into the parking lot and now. You were up all night working on a recipe and fell asleep."

Edie rubbed her eyes and sighed. "Vhere am I?" she mumbled. Slowly, her lids fluttered open. "Vooo are you?"

"I'm Matthias Ambrose, the security guard."

Edie stretched her arms. "*Mon Dieu!* I came in early and must have fallen asleep. I vas up all night verking on a new recipe for my boss. I am very sorry!"

He still had his touch, unfortunately.

———————

"What the hell happened here?" Kalli swept a purple dreadlock from her face. She sniffed the air. Smoke still rolled from the kitchen door. "This is worse than I thought."

Serah groaned. "Let's just say I learned a lesson."

"Which is?"

"Don't let a demon cook breakfast."

"Some demons are good cooks, you know."

Serah stifled her chuckle. "Let me guess. You were a master chef in one of your previous lives?"

It wouldn't surprise her one bit if she was.

"Hell no. I can't cook a meal to save my life."

"Lucky for you, you're immortal."

"And the fact that I don't need regular food for nourishment."

All demons had to keep up their strength some way or another. Lucy's kind fed on sex. Some needed the sun. Others needed a full moon. She never pressed the subject with Kalli. It wasn't any of her business anyway.

"I still eat occasionally."

"I owe you a meal then. What would you like?"

"Steak tartare."

Serah shuddered at the thought. She'd only made the dish once before in culinary school. Raw meat mixed with raw eggs wasn't her thing. Neither was E. coli. "I should have figured you'd be the carnivorous type."

Serah pulled at the sleeves of the dress that seemed to cling to the wrong curves. Despite the fit, it was a pretty dress. Blues, turquoises, and greens swirled together and blended perfectly. She yanked at the waist, trying desperately to adjust the belt wrapped tight against her body.

"If you keep tugging at that dress, you're going to rip it." Kalli grabbed Serah's hands and pulled them from the fabric. "I'm not a seamstress either, if you get my drift. And you look awesome."

Did she really? Or was Kalli just saying that to stroke her ever fleeting ego? "You sure?"

"Seriously, Serah." Kalli shook her head. "I don't give compliments lightly. Just ask Rafe."

"I'll keep that in mind."

Kalli smiled. "You better." She reached down and picked up a pair of Matthias's cargoes from the chair and unfolded them. "Bigger than I expected." She waggled her brows. What was the deal with her and Lucy? Were they trying to play matchmaker? Well, she wasn't interested. She had news for them. He wasn't either.

"Bigger?"

Kalli plopped into the sofa and kicked up her combat boots. "I was expecting someone a little leaner. He always slipped from my grasp like an eel. I'm surprised someone so bulky could sneak away so well."

"Yeah, he's quite… uhh… massive."

Kalli smirked. "Massive seems to be an understatement. So what's he like?"

"Worse than Rafe, if you can imagine that. If Rafe had a stick up his ass when he first came here, this guy has the entire tree." And that's all she would say. Like Kalli would want to know about her naughty fantasies and the kiss they shared. So his stick wasn't wedged as far up as she let on.

Kalli cringed. "Ouch." Scratching her chin, she leaned against the sofa. "But something tells me there's more."

"You better not be reading my mind."

Kalli shook her head. "Whoever blessed you did a damned good job. I couldn't break through even if I tried."

"So you've tracked Matthias?"

"A few times. He always managed to escape though. The one time I almost had him. My mission was terminated."

"Why?"

"I never asked. Knowing his record, I can only suspect his next job was for one of us."

Serah shivered. Could she really trust him with her life? Someone who quickly changed allegiance at a drop of a hat? "Comforting."

Kalli, sensing her unease, wrapped her arm around her shoulder. "To be honest, I never got an evil reading from him. The Paladins he killed weren't the most righteous of demons."

What did she mean by that? Weren't the Paladins blessed? They were the good guys. They couldn't do wrong, could they? "But I thought they were here to keep earth safe?"

"For the most part. But there are still those who lose sight of the greater good."

"Oh." So much for good and evil. The demons were just as conflicted as humans. Politics remained the same, no matter what realm you were in. Talk about a kick in the pants.

"Does that make sense?"

"Perfect sense, actually. Demons and humans are more alike than we realize."

"I never said we weren't. Which is why I always avoided running for a position on the Fore-Demon Council. Too much backstabbing and too many ulterior vendettas for my tastes. I just don't have the backbone for it."

"Oh puhlease. You have the strongest backbone I've ever seen."

"I don't do well in positions of authority." Kalli smiled. "I'd much rather be in the action than directing it."

She turned to the kitchen. "Let's see the damage."

Serah pushed open the door, and the remaining smoke billowed out. Serah covered her cough and waved the smoke away.

"One demon did all this?" She reached over and grabbed a melted Tupperware bowl from the counter. "Something tells me their warranty doesn't cover this."

"Tell me about it." Serah continued swatting at the hovering smoke.

"Allow me." Kalli opened her mouth and held her arms out. With a giant whoosh, she spun around and the smoke wound its way around her, spiraling into her mouth in a huge vortex.

With a loud gulp, she swallowed. And just like that, all the smoke and stench was gone, including the smell that lingered on her.

"You know, you just made me break my New Year's resolution. I was doing so well too."

"Huh?"

"I gave up smoking."

"Seriously, demons have temptations?"

"Almost as bad as humans, if not worse."

"Sorry, hon. I didn't know he couldn't cook."

Kalli grinned. "You're forgiven. Tasting all that burnt smoke and ash shows me exactly what I'm not missing."

"What's next?"

"I can handle it from here. What I do next will make your head spin—literally."

"Like Linda Blair?"

Kalli smirked. "Worse."

After seeing her self-induced tornado, she didn't doubt it one bit. "All righty then." With that, she pushed the door open with her bum and backed through. "Lock up on your way out."

"You got it." Kalli smiled, shutting the door. A loud clanging of pans and glass rent the air.

I sure hope she knows what she's doing. With that, she grabbed her keys off the coffee table and threw on her coat. *What else could possibly go wrong?*

Chapter 20

SERAH CHECKED THE REARVIEW MIRROR AND PUT the car into reverse. She glanced through the windshield at her grandmother's brick ranch and sucked in a breath.

There was nothing to worry about. The house was safe in Kalli's and Farquhar's hands and paws.

"Everything will be fine."

Serah relaxed in her seat and turned on the radio. Lady Gaga's latest tune rang through the speakers. The bass pounded in her ears. She adjusted the volume.

"Wow. Was the volume up that high last night?"

Matthias's leg probably bumped it. He was kind of cramped in there.

She came to the intersection at A-Line Road, her least favorite corner. Who in their right mind designed the left turns in this silly state? Luckily, it was usually a long light. She had plenty of time to cross so she could use the turnaround. She picked up speed.

She looked down at her dashboard and snapped her head back up.

"What the fuck?"

The light was already yellow. And without any more delay, it turned red. Didn't anyone in this town know how to time the lights?

She slammed on the brakes. Tires squealing in protest, the car shuddered and moaned as the anti-lock brakes engaged. Her car swerved on the dew-dampened road and started spinning. Serah held on to the steering wheel in a desperate attempt to remain in control.

She looked out her side view mirror, her mouth wide open in fear.

"Shit!"

A red minivan came barreling down the road—right at her. Horns rang out. Another round of squeals echoed through the air. The van came to a stop—a mere two inches from her car.

The faint hint of burnt rubber and sulfur lingered in the air. Taking slow, even breaths, she clenched the steering wheel. She should have known demons were involved. Had they always been involved?

"Hey," the woman in the minivan shouted out the window. "Watch where you're going."

"Sorry. The light malfunctioned or something." Malfunctioned, all right. From the undertones of sulfur, she knew exactly what caused the malfunction. Maybe she wasn't near as bad a driver as she suspected.

"No problem. It did seem to change a little quickly. Stupid city lights."

The little boy in the passenger seat wasn't so nice. He stuck out his tongue and flipped Serah off.

Serah rolled her eyes. Kids. Cute when they needed to be, devils when they wanted to be.

"Timmy!" the woman shouted as she rolled her window back up.

Serah put the car in reverse and pulled out of the minivan's way. The minivan pulled forward. Timmy flipped her off again, with both hands this time.

Daring little brat.

Serah smiled and waved sweetly at the little boy. "Wow. Some people's kids," she mumbled to herself.

Oh well. Not everyone is born an angel—or demon for that matter. They probably grew into it. She watched as the van proceeded up the road. Mother wagged her finger at her son. Maybe mom could keep Timmy on the right path—unlike the demon who seemed hell-bent on terrorizing her on a regular basis.

She stuck in the Bluetooth headset into her ear and pressed the button on the side.

"Call shop."

"Calling shop," the automated voice replied in her ear.

"Please enjoy the music as we locate your party."

Serah controlled her laughter. If she was having a party she would sure know where it was. If only she were really going to a party. It would be a heck of a lot easier. Too bad Lucy wasn't here to share in their little inside joke. It was silly, but she really valued their off-the-wall friendship.

Heck, they still used paper-rock-scissors to settle decisions. Then again, the last time they did that was the night she wished she could forget. Lucy, the chest, a legion of demons. She needn't say more.

"If only I'd picked rock instead. This whole thing would've played out so much differently." Lucy's inner succubus might have remained untapped. Serah sighed. Her inner whatever-it-was wouldn't be sending signals to all the demons within a ten-mile radius. They'd be normal—or as normal as they used to be. Then again, would Lucy have Rafe?

At least something good came out of the whole ordeal. Lucy and Rafe had found each other. Seriously, if she could go back in time, she'd tell that man at the secondhand shop what he could do with his weird chest of wonder.

"It's a steal... my ass."

But knowing how meddlesome Lucy and Rafe had become, Serah figured she'd see them soon enough. Heck, they'd probably be there bright and early with the rest of the crew.

The music ringtone continued to play in her ear. What was taking Edie so long? She looked down at the clock. She was usually there at least an hour early.

"Tasteful Elegance. Speak." The deep gravelly voice had the same effect on the phone as it did in person. Her pulse quickened and her breath caught. Damn, even when he was rude, he sent her hormones flying.

She finally found her senses. "Seriously. That's not how a business phone should be answered."

"I saw the number on the display as I answered it."

"It's still rude."

"How can I help you? Is that better?"

"Yes. Much. Where's Edie?"

Matthias sucked in a breath. "There was a situation."

Oh God! They decided to move on to her employee instead? This had gone too far. She took a sharp sweep around the turnabout. Her tires squealed again. She didn't care. The quicker she got to her shop the better.

"What sort of situation? Worse than demons changing traffic lights?"

"What? Are you okay?"

"I'm fine. What's going on?"

"Edie saw my *Peragrans*. I had to run some damage control." He paused. "Your situation sounds more urgent."

"It's handled."

Matthias growled. "I can be there in two seconds if you need me."

She wasn't completely helpless. Did no one trust her? "If you want me to accept this thing you think has been bestowed on me, then you have to let me handle my own situations. All that happened was that I accidentally ran a red light and almost got sideswiped. Almost being the operative word."

"I want you safe, Serah."

Want her safe, or need her safe? She refrained from asking and bit her tongue instead.

She flicked the signal to turn into BigBob's Coffee shop. "I appreciate that. Do you like coffee?" She contained her snort. Did demons drink coffee? Rafe didn't. He said it tasted like burnt sandpaper. She didn't bother asking how he knew what sandpaper tasted like.

"I'll take an extra large Toffee Temptation with a double shot of espresso and energy boost."

Her eyes boggled open. That combination would have a human bouncing off the ceiling and walls. "Seriously?"

"You were right. BigBob's coffee is better than Starbucks."

He never ceased to amaze her. From his massive gladiator physique and strong chiseled face, to his odd tastes in coffee. Did they have coffee shops in limbo? With these demons, nothing surprised her anymore.

"Do you really need an energy boost? I thought you demons didn't need sleep."

"Just get the coffee."

So much for trying to make conversation. "Does Edie want anything?"

"The usual."

"Got it. Be there in ten. Bye." With that, she ended the call. Two people could play this game.

Matthias crossed his arms. He did not like leaving Serah unprotected. Especially after what she just said happened. He clenched his teeth.

"Iz Miz SanGermano on her way?" Edie adjusted the white, muffin-topped hat on her head and flipped her red hair. She had the most intriguing accent he'd ever heard.

"Yes. She is getting coffee. What part of France are you from?"

"Here and zere. Everyvere. Me parents moved a lot. France, Germany, Switzerland, Luxembourg, even Liechtenstein."

"Interesting."

"But France has alvays been my home."

If only he had some sort of truth talent. Something about the redhead seemed off. Her aura, though, was clean. No evil surrounded her. She seemed harmless enough.

"Can you tell me about this *American Chef* show?"

"Very popular. The host!" She fanned her face. "*Très beau. Oh là là!* Daniel Blackburn can *coucher avec moi* any day."

Too much information for his tastes. He needed to research this show more. What better way than a computer? He might have been almost eight hundred years old, but that didn't mean he didn't keep up with the ever-changing technology trends. "Is there a computer I can use?"

"*Oui.*" Edie grinned. "The laptop iz over zere." She

headed to a small desk in the back of the kitchen. She lifted the lid of the laptop and pressed a button.

The laptop hummed to life as the display flashed in front of him. He took a seat and stretched out his legs—as much as he could, sitting at a desk that he dwarfed. The computer chimed and brought up a password entry screen.

"Oh, I forgot ze passvord." She leaned over and typed in a few letters and digits. She clicked the touch pad and stepped back. "Voilà."

Did it really take this long for a computer to load? How many programs did she have running on this machine? "Does this computer always run so slow?"

"Vindows Bista. It needs upgrade, no?"

Edie did not need to say any more. That's what happens when you allowed demons to help program your software. You'd think after the whole millennium ordeal, Bill Gates would have learned. The screen flickered and the desktop appeared. Matthias clicked on the browser icon. After a couple of minutes the web browser loaded.

"Apparently it does."

Edie looked at the clock on the wall. "I need to prep zee kitchen. Can you handle it vrom here?"

Matthias nodded. "I just need to look up info on *American Chef* and this Daniel Blackburn."

"Google has everzing!"

He couldn't argue with her there. "Thank you for the help, Ms. Fontaine."

"*De rien*, Mr. Ambrose. Call me Edie, *s'il vous plaît*?"

"Thank you, Edie."

"Can I call you Matthias?"

He wanted to keep his distance. It was bad enough Serah had already whittled her way into what remained of his soul. He didn't want to make friends. He wanted to complete his mission. Friends and affections only complicated matters. And friends could turn on you. However, civility got you further than gruffness. "If you must."

"I certainly must." A wide smile spread across her ruby red lips.

Matthias nodded. "Then call me Matthias."

"Thank you, Matthias." Edie took his hand in hers and offered a healthy shake. "Oh! Strong grip. You vill make excellent security guard."

He gave a tentative shake and pulled his hand from hers. "You're welcome."

With that, Edie skipped off toward the supply closet, a cheerful hum rolling through the air. She certainly was odd, but that added to her eccentric charm. It was comforting to know that Serah was surrounded by such friendly people—Farquhar included.

He turned back to the computer and typed *American Chef* into the search screen. He clicked the link to the official website. The show seemed innocuous enough. The host simply traveled across America, spotlighting different chefs, restaurants, and caterers throughout the United States. He worked with the show's guests to cook up and serve masterpieces to a rather eager crowd. He clicked a link to a video.

Daniel stood over a metal pan stirring a reddish sauce. The man with him poured in some cherries while Daniel continued to stir.

"You might want to stand back for this, Daniel." The

chef took the handle from him and stirred the mixture on final time.

"Oh, but this is my favorite part," Daniel said with that same pristine smile. He reluctantly handed off the pan to the chef.

"Can't have you burn that handsome face of yours." The chef grinned, giving Daniel a friendly—or maybe a little more than friendly—pat on the back.

Daniel stiffened ever so slightly and chuckled. Not a genuine laugh, but uneasy and awkward.

Matthias arched an eyebrow and pressed his lips together. Daniel wasn't as feminine as he thought. No wonder these women ate this stuff up. No pun intended.

The chef poured some liquid over the top of the cherries and directed Daniel to angle the pan and pour a little over the side.

Matthias cringed. That was a disaster waiting to happen. A disaster he'd witnessed earlier that morning. Clenching his teeth, he held his breath. The pan was going to explode.

The pan lit on fire. Instead of running around the kitchen in a panic, the two men laughed and smiled as the cherry mixture burned in front of their eyes.

Daniel just stirred the mixture and continued the conversation, oblivious to the fact that it was still on fire.

Eventually the fire died out and they pulled two bowls of ice cream out of the freezer. The chef scooped some of the wasted sauce and poured it over the ice cream.

"And that's how you make cherries jubilee." Daniel stuck his spoon into the ice cream and took a bite. "Mmmm. Delicious. Tune in next week when a special guest shows us a new way of making crème brûlée." He flashed that damned smile. "Yes, I love cooking with fire. Until then, live long and cook strong."

Matthias shook his head in disbelief. *People actually watch this rubbish?*

He clicked the link to learn more about the host. A large picture of this Daniel man filled his screen. Long, blond hair was neatly tied at the nape of his neck. He took care of himself. Had a sturdy physique and greenish eyes. His wide, toothy smile seemed genuine enough. There had to be more. He moved the page down to read Daniel's biography.

> *Daniel Blackburn was raised in Chicago's South Side. The oldest of four boys, Daniel struggled through school and work to raise his family and make ends meet.*
>
> *While working as a bouncer at a popular Chicago nightclub, he caught the eye of one of the producers of the reality show,* Princes and Paupers, *where wealthy businessmen trade places with those less fortunate. He was season two's pauper. Daniel became an overnight sensation. It was soon discovered that Daniel had a knack for cooking, stemming from his life being raised by a single mother. He currently hosts the successful cooking show,* American Chef, *and runs a restaurant and winery in a Chicago suburb.*

A true rags-to-riches story. Who couldn't love a guy who bounced back from adversity. No wonder all the women, including Serah, were enamored of him. The man had fan pages galore, according to Matthias's research. He saw the way Serah talked about him, how she smiled when she mentioned his name. There was no masking it.

He snorted. What was so fascinating about a man who enjoyed food? What happened to the days when women swooned over a man with a sword? From the vast array of information Matthias had collected, Daniel was also an avid oenologist, a connoisseur of fine wines who prided himself on his extensive knowledge.

Just like Dionysus. Maybe he had nothing to worry about after all. Hah, him? Worry? Why for?

He skimmed over some other celebrity gossip websites. Nothing about Daniel popped up on the radar. He was a bachelor, had no kids or known lovers—male or female. Not even the popular tabloid magazines or websites had anything on him. But he'd seen how the paparazzi operated these days—that was virtually impossible. They could find something on the holiest of people—including Mother Theresa if they needed to. No one was immune.

This man seemed genuine enough in his picture, but some people could pose and pictures could be altered. He looked through several other photos. Just as genuine as the first. It unnerved him. No one, not even a demon, could be so friendly looking. Something was up.

He'd meet this Daniel Blackburn face to face. Only then would he make his decision. Serah would have to learn how to deal with it. He couldn't have her hurt. Especially if the man with the pristine smile had ulterior motives.

He gritted his teeth. Why the hell did he care so much?

Chapter 21

SERAH BALANCED THE TRAY OF COFFEE ON ONE HAND and scrounged around her purse with the other. She grabbed her keychain and clicked the button on the remote to lock the car.

Besides food, catering had its good points, like the ability to balance any size and shape of tray in one hand. Too bad that wasn't an Olympic sport. She'd *so* get the gold medal if it were. Not that she liked bragging, but she did balance a mean tray now and again.

"Need any help?"

The vaguely familiar voice echoed in her ear. Not an unpleasant voice, but unexpected. She glanced down at her watch. Seven forty-five. Of course he'd be early.

Just her luck. Was Daniel setting her up to get invited in? Matthias would be pissed. Really? Did she really care what Matthias thought? And where was that sulfur smell that always lingered whenever a demon was nearby. If Daniel was a demon, he'd be smelling like a steaming pile of... something.

"I got it. I do it every day." Not a complete lie. Usually she did not have three steaming cups of coffee and a bag of bagels. She balanced the bagels atop the cups and grabbed the doorknob.

"See?"

"Oh, you're talented. At least allow me to hold the door for you."

"You just said I was talented, though."

"True." Without further words, he reached out and plucked the tray and bagels from her hand. "I'm talented too."

"Apparently."

"Serah SanGermano?"

Serah nodded and extended her now-free hand. "Daniel Blackburn? Sorry. I wasn't expecting you until nine thirty."

Daniel took her hand in his. Warm and inviting, not electric and hot like Matthias's. Was that good or bad? She bit her lip.

"Sorry, I was already up and about and I dislike being late."

She finally got her first good look at him. Blond hair hung loosely around a tanned face. He stood about six foot four and the long wool coat he wore did little to hide his wide shoulders. What was the deal with all these tall, muscular guys hopping into town lately? First Rafe, then Matthias, and now Daniel. Luckily, Daniel was of the human variety—from what she could tell.

Serah smiled. "No apology necessary. They always say the early bird gets the worm, right?"

"That's true." Daniel's abnormally crystal blue eyes twinkled. She'd always liked blue eyes, but seeing his up close and personal did nothing for her. Was she secretly turning into a lesbian? Not that there was anything wrong with that, but she'd always had a thing for men. Especially blond-haired, blue-eyed ones who looked like they just stepped off the beach. Something was wrong—very wrong.

"You're much prettier in person."

Even his compliment did little to get her heart thudding the way it thudded when Matthias... *Oh hell no*.

"You're taller than I thought you'd be."

Seriously, that's all she could come up with for a response? Then again, it sure beat *You're not as hot as I thought you'd be*. She needed this television bit. Insulting him would get her nowhere.

Daniel flashed a wide toothy smile. "I get that a lot." He leaned in and brought his face to her ear and whispered, "The secret is the hidden platform the guests stand on."

Again, nothing. It was like her libido had packed up and taken a vacation. Then again, maybe that was just what the doctor ordered. No obnoxious fangirls to make matters complicated or awkward. She'd seen a few of those episodes. The ones where the women—and sometimes men—threw themselves at him—so blatantly obvious and even more annoying. And Daniel handled each with nary a misstep. Who knew, maybe he was gay? "Ahh. Good idea."

Daniel shrugged. "I wish I could take claim for it, but it was all my producer's doing. She's the mastermind behind the show."

"Well, your secret is safe with me." Serah winked. "By the way, the show would tank with anyone else but you."

"Whew. Thank goodness. I value being employed, especially in this economy." He reached to grab the door handle. "And thank you for swelling my already ballooning ego."

The door swung open. Daniel fell forward, catching himself on the ledge. The coffee teetered in his hand. "Whoa!"

Matthias stood in the doorway, arms crossed and gaze narrowed. He lunged forward and grabbed the tray of coffee before it fell to the ground.

Oh shit. This wasn't going to be pretty.

Daniel blew out a huge breath of air. "Wow! Good catch, man."

With a gruff snort, Matthias continued to stand there, blocking the entrance. "We need to talk, Serah." He turned his gaze to Daniel and offered another gruff snort. "What's he doing here already?"

Apparently Matthias had done his research. Sadly for Matthias, that research wouldn't get him very far. She'd already gone down that road herself. Checked out his biography, looked up his picture, scanned the Internet film database to see everything he'd starred in. But no, she wasn't obsessed. She just wanted to have something to discuss with him.

Daniel was the spokesman for boys next door all over the world. He was smart, somewhat funny, and generous to boot. He even sponsored a community center in the neighborhood he grew up in and donated hundreds of thousands of dollars to charities all over the Chicago area. Oddly enough, she wasn't as attracted to him as much as she thought she'd be.

Maybe that gaydar worked after all. And here Lucy had said it was perpetually broken.

"Is it a crime to be early for an appointment?" Serah asked.

Daniel scratched his forehead. "The file said you only had one employee and a cat that thinks he's the boss."

Serah shrugged. "He'... umm... an outside investor."

"Uhh. Okay." Without further invitation, Daniel

stepped into the building. He extended his hand to Matthias. "Daniel Blackburn. Nice to meet you."

Matthias took his hand and crunched his fingers around Daniel's and shook. "Matthias Ambrose."

"That's a powerful grip you've got there, dude." Daniel rubbed his fingers then gave Matthias a friendly pat on the back.

Matthias took a sharp breath. "I work out."

"No supplements at all?"

Serah managed to control the snort that threatened to erupt. Supplements? If Daniel only knew. He'd want nothing to do with those types of supplements.

Matthias simply shook his head and his nostrils flared. "No. I don't need supplements."

Daniel stepped back. "No need to get defensive. But I seriously want that workout, dude. Need to work on my upper body strength." Daniel flexed and grabbed a bicep.

"Looks fine to me," Matthias muttered. "I don't think you could handle my workout, anyway. It has killed bigger men."

Serah thanked the higher power that she was not sipping coffee, because she would have coughed and choked on it. What a way to state the obvious in a totally casual and nonchalant way—*not*.

Daniel raised an eyebrow. "Awkward."

Shrugging, Matthias moved back and allowed Daniel through the hallway. "I value my *investments*. I want to make sure they stay safe and secure."

Was Matthias trying to deliberately sabotage her audition? He did say he would keep her safe by any means possible. Did making her look like a fool in front of a celebrity fall in those realms? Seeing how some of these demons operated, it wouldn't surprise her one bit.

Even Rafe wasn't above a little trickery if it kept Lucy safe. But Rafe had good reason. This man... well, who knew what his reasons were.

"Matthias, why don't you go back to the office and check up on your other investments or look at your stock portfolio or whatever you investors do. I need to show Daniel around the kitchen."

"It's Sunday. The stock market is closed."

Damn, too smart for his own good. She'd never get anything done with him hovering so close. Just having him standing two feet from her sent her senses flying off the radar. She gritted her teeth and sucked in a long breath of air.

"Did I come at a bad time?"

"No!" they both answered in unison.

Bemusement filled the TV star's face. "All righty then." He clasped both hands in front of him and paced back and forth with a nervous gait.

"Matt is a grouch when he doesn't get his coffee," She nudged Matthias in the side. "Right, Matt?" She plucked the humongous-size coffee he had ordered and held it out to him. "Toffee Temptation with an added sugar buzz and subsequent caffeine and energy over-load, right?"

Daniel's eyes widened with excitement. "Wow, just how I like it. Dude, you are the man."

Matthias yanked the coffee from her, a little sloshing out of the lid and down the side.

"Ouch," she yelped, yanking back her hand.

Matthias's expression morphed from frustration to

horror. He reached out and grabbed her hand. "Did I burn you?" There was no masking the concern in his voice. His fingertips roved up and down her palm, sending sparks of electricity through each nerve and fiber in her body. Despite the gentleness, a path of fire followed his fingertips. To say she was hot was a major understatement.

Oh, he burned her all right. Anytime he touched her. A deep, burning inferno that not even a long sip of water could cure. She sucked in a long breath and managed to shake her head no.

"As much milk and whipped cream as the barista added, the contents were not as hot as expected."

But his touch was hotter, probably worse than molten lava bubbling beneath the Earth's surface. Unfortunately, the only relief she could think of was completely out of the question.

Chapter 22

"OUTSIDE INVESTOR, EH?" DANIEL SLUNG HIMSELF into one of chairs surrounding the makeshift dining room. He stretched out his denim-clad legs and slid his hands into his back pockets. "How much of an investment are we talking about?"

Serah drew her lips straight and steepled her fingers. "Enough that he has a say, unfortunately. He wasn't too happy with my decision to apply as a guest."

"Nine out of ten people who've been guests on my show saw a profit increase of around fifty percent." Daniel angled a grin that would make a salesperson jealous. "Your investment just got bigger."

This man was good. Matthias took a sip of his coffee. Was it so wrong to enjoy some of the same things humans did? After all, it allowed him to blend in. The essence of dark espresso, toffee, and cream rolled across his tongue. Sweet, but not as sweet as Serah's lips. Not now! He quickly gathered his thoughts.

"What about the tenth?"

"Can't please them all." Daniel shuddered.

"That bad?"

"Was that the 'Diner Diva' episode?" Serah clenched her teeth and grimaced. "Good God. How did you manage to keep your cool?"

Daniel smirked. "A lot of wine."

"I must have missed that episode." Matthias felt

completely out of place and out of his element. This man could cook flaming bowls of cherries; he, on the other hand, only managed to burn down Serah's kitchen. He and Serah were nothing alike. He glanced at Serah and Daniel, sitting at the table chatting and giggling about different episodes. They, on the other hand, were like two peas in a pod.

"Well, I need to call the producer and check in." Daniel reached over and took Serah's hand in his. "If that's okay with you, Serah."

Daniel called her by her first name already? Matthias gritted his teeth. He should feel happy that Daniel and she were hitting it off so well. Instead, he felt empty and alone. He'd been alone for centuries. Why all of the sudden now?

"Don't let me keep you," she said, a smile brushing across her lips. She let her fingertips linger with Daniel's a little longer than he liked. "I need to speak with Matthias about some issues."

"No problem."

Serah pulled her seat back to stand up.

Quicker than most humans, Daniel burst from his chair and allowed Serah his arm. Great, he could add gentleman to the ever growing list of Daniel's charms.

"Wow! How polite."

"I was taught well, huh?"

Serah blushed. "You sure were."

Matthias clenched his fists. Frustration pounded its way through his body. He wasn't sure what frustrated him most, the fact that Serah filled him with emotions he had no business feeling, or the fact that she and Daniel were hitting it off so well. Too well.

"Will do." Daniel reached into his pocket and pulled out an iPhone. "Can I use your office to make a call?"

"Sure, just through the door there." She pointed to the office in the far corner.

"Be right back." Daniel swiped and pushed some icons on the screen. With that, he strode toward the office.

Matthias grabbed Serah's shoulder and pulled her to the side. "I need to do some recon."

"What?"

"Surveillance."

"You are going to try and listen in on his conversation? Seriously?"

"Seriously. I don't trust him."

"From what I can tell, you don't trust many people."

"A good procedure to follow."

"How can I trust you then?"

Leave it to Serah to emphasize a good point. "Just remember this: I have a duty to the Fore-Demons. I will not fail them."

Serah's lips curved down slightly. "I see."

Matthias bit his tongue. He couldn't get close. No matter how hard it hurt. She was safer with someone else. Someone who had purpose. He was still trying to find his.

"I'm going to see if I can hear anything." He left no room for her to refuse. He marched toward the office and crouched low, pressing his ear against the door.

Just a few words to better understand Daniel's interest in Serah's shop. He pressed closer. He silently thanked whatever deity that decided to bless—or curse—him with extremely acute hearing.

"Hey, Sally." Daniel's voice lacked urgency. Matthias

growled. So far, not so good. He pressed his ear closer to the door.

"I'm here at Tasteful Elegance. Pretty good, so far. Miss SanGermano is pleasant. Her investor—not so much."

"I don't know. Was there anything about him on the application? Well... He doesn't look like the business-man type. Kind of weird but he looks like he'd be more comfortable on *American Gladiators* than a cooking show." There was a brief pause. "His name? Umm... Matt... No... Matthew? Wait... It's Matthias. Yeah, that's it. Matthias Ambrose." He chuckled. "Kind of a stuffy name, if you ask me."

Stuffy? Hah. Humans these days preferred silly names like Taylor, Peyton, and Jordan. They sounded more like surnames, not first names.

Daniel cleared his throat. "I don't think they'll go for that." There was another short pause and he blew out a breath. "I can try. Other than that, everything looks good. I'll call you in a couple hours."

Did that mean Serah got the show? Or was there more going on? Why wasn't the producer here too? Something was off. But he'd seen some of the videos and the website. *American Chef* appeared legit.

The sensual aroma of orchids tingled at his senses. He looked up. Serah stood over him, annoyance cloud-ing her expression. "So you have subsonic hearing too?"

"Something like that."

Serah's breath hitched. "That's nice. Remind me to keep my mouth shut while you're here."

Matthias clenched his fists. "I can't listen in on you, Serah."

"Yeah, right. Tell that to the door you mutilated."

"You yelled my name. That is the only thing I heard. It sounded urgent. I couldn't travel inside, so I used force instead."

Serah shrugged, but something mysterious flashed in her gaze. "Ever heard of knocking?"

"I'm not making excuses, Serah. I sensed danger and I reacted as I was trained."

"Whatever." She leaned over and peeked through the window. She scooted him with her foot. "Better get up. He's making his way to the door."

Matthias lunged up to his feet, grabbed Serah by the waist and took her toward the sink. "How long would he be here for?"

"So you approve?"

Matthias shrugged. "I didn't pick up enough of the conversation to target him a threat. He seems harmless—for now."

"And he didn't smell like Infernati either, right?"

"You already knew that, didn't you?"

Serah slumped against the sink and raked a hand through her curls. Grabbing the side of the counter, she blew out a long breath. "You just don't understand. I just want a normal life—demon-free." She snorted. "Well, free of demons I don't already know, anyway."

He understood more than she realized. He'd felt the same way when he'd lost his life and turned into a monster. He hated himself. He wanted to die. But as years turned into centuries, he'd learned that normalcy was just a fantasy.

Serah lowered her gaze to the black-and-white-checkered floor and shook her head. "I'm sorry. I know you're here for a good reason. I... It's just a lot to deal with all of the sudden."

Matthias knew he shouldn't, but seeing Serah in this state pulled at him. He reached out and brushed a stray curl from her cheek. "I understand. Trust me."

He let his hand linger on her cheek, letting the sizzles spark against their skin. His breath caught. God, her skin was so soft. He traced his thumb across her cheek, brushing away a teardrop.

He looked down at her and gazed into her eyes, bright blue and sparkling. God, she was so beautiful. He wanted so much to kiss her—right then and there.

She reached up, brought her hand to his, and brought his hand closer to her skin. What on earth was she doing? Bloody hell, she was a temptress and didn't even know it. And that made her dangerous.

Then again, he never shied away from danger. Why should he now?

He reached out with his other hand and grabbed Serah's waist, pulling her to him. With gentleness he never knew he possessed, he cradled her head to his chest and laced his fingers through her sable curls.

With slow, tentative strokes, he stroked her hair. He leaned in, his mouth inches from her ear. "I understand... more than you know."

She looked up with those disarming, sapphire eyes and placed her hand on his chest. "So what's your story?"

His breath caught. It amazed him how just a simple touch made his blood boil. If they continued this close of contact, he'd do something he'd regret.

"My story would make your blood curdle, Serah."

With that, he pulled away and stormed toward the door. The brisk winter air would do him some good.

———～～～———

The door slammed shut. Serah blew out a trembling sigh. She shouldn't like the hulking demon, but something drew her to him. She shook her head. She knew he sensed it too. What was his deal? One moment he was tender and in a millionth of a second, he was cold and distant. He was hiding something. As for knowing his past—she wasn't quite sure she wanted to know.

"So he's that kind of investor, huh?"

Serah spun around to see Daniel with his elbow propped on the buffet, a sly smile spread across his lips. "Huh?"

"I saw the way he held you."

Serah gasped and shook her head. "It's not what you think. Seriously. He's too arrogant for me."

Daniel's smirk grew even wider. "Really?"

"Yeah, really."

"Whatever you say. And there's no need to hide anything. I'm doing the show."

"Seriously?"

"As serious as a heart attack. Congrats. I'm just waiting for the producer to call and finalize some things."

Serah nodded. "Don't producers usually come along to these things?"

"Not always. Sally's a little private and prefers to remain in the background. Put her in the spotlight and she'll melt."

"Sounds bad. I can recommend a good psychologist if she needs one."

Daniel grinned. "You don't look like the type that would need a therapist."

Oh, how wrong he was. She managed to keep her snort contained. "Ha ha, very funny. Someone I dated."

"Oh, well Sally's not one to see a shrink, but I can take the name anyway. She's pretty content with her reclusiveness."

"To each her own, I guess. So when do you plan to start shooting?"

"Does tomorrow work?"

"I'll make it work."

"I like your style."

"How long does shooting usually take?"

"Two to three days usually. Unless you're Diner Diva, then we're looking at one week to shoot and three weeks post-production therapy."

"I don't think you need to worry about that."

"Good. And I have to discuss Matthias with you." Daniel blew out a deep sigh. "Sally believes it best if he stays away from the production."

"He's already been banned from the kitchen, so no worries there."

Daniel arched a brow. "Banned?"

"Yes," Serah replied with a nod. "He's a horrible cook."

"Sally doesn't like outside investors. She doesn't want him anywhere near the crew."

Matthias wouldn't like this one bit. She wrung her fingers and bit her lip. "That isn't going to happen." Maybe she should just be as honest as she could with him. She never was much of a liar anyway. "Umm… Matthias isn't really an investor."

Daniel slapped his hands together. "Hah! I knew it. You couldn't hide that electricity between you if you tried."

"Heck no! He's not my boyfriend. We only met yesterday."

"Yesterday? Really?"

Serah nodded. "He works for a private security firm. He's a bodyguard."

"I think you are taking this whole TV show a bit too seriously. Even I don't need a bodyguard."

"Look at yourself. Does it look like you need one?"

Daniel shrugged. "I guess not, but still."

Here comes the hard part. She took in a huge gulp of air and clasped her hands together. "A while ago, in my desperate days, I filled out an online personal ad. One of the guys that responded was a little more into me than I was him." *No one is going to believe this shitty story*. She rambled on. "He sent flowers every day. Then chocolates. Then he would show up at random places. The grocery store, the mall, some of my catered events. I finally put my foot down and told him to leave me alone. One night he broke into my house and drilled a hole in my fishbowl. I woke up the next morning to find my precious Goldie belly-up in an inch of water." She snorted out a fake sob. "It was horrible."

"Oh, my God. That's terrible."

"That day my friend and her fiancé called the security guard company for me. He's here for my protection."

It was either that or tell him the truth, and the truth was too much to believe. She might as well give him a more believable and laughable story. The less people knew about demons, the better.

"Did you file a restraining order?"

Serah nodded. "He waits for the restraining order to expire then starts the madness all over again. It expires tonight."

"And the cops won't do anything?"

"I've tried, but until he acts again, they can't be bothered."

"That doesn't sound right."

"Tell me about it."

Daniel reached out and grabbed her hand. "I'm sure Sally will understand. I'll let her know what the deal is."

"Thanks, Daniel." She leaned over to place a kiss on his cheek. As if she were in a cheesy romantic comedy, Daniel chose that exact moment to move his head. Instead of brushing his cheek, she met his lips instead. And she always rolled her eyes at those parts. That never happened in real life, or so she thought. And then the hero and heroine knew in that precise instant that they loved each other. However, this was anything but romantic. Awkward was an understatement.

Daniel made a sound similar to a dying cow and she squeaked against his just-as-surprised lips. Birds did not sing and there were no butterflies or any romantic ballads. There were no sparks or zaps—absolutely nothing. It was like she was kissing a cousin or brother.

Daniel pulled back and quickly wiped his lips. "Wow. That's a first."

"You've never been kissed on the lips?"

"No. I've never been kissed on the lips by a guest." A nervous chuckle burst from his lips. "Did it do anything for you?"

Serah moved from one leg to the other and twirled a finger around a curl. *Aww heck*. She'd lose the show before they even started shooting. However, honesty was always the best policy. "No, not really."

"Whew, me either." Daniel giggled. "I hate saying this, because you're truly lovely, but it was like I was kissing my mom."

Serah winced. "Good thing your name isn't Oedipus, then."

"You know Oedipus?"

"Yeah, he's a complex character."

Daniel burst out laughing. Finally, someone got her joke. "That's a good one."

"Yeah, what can I say. I try."

"You're smarter than you let on, aren't you?"

Serah shrugged. "I like to read, but all that math and science stuff drives me crazy. Those are more Lucy's expertise."

"Lucy?"

"My best friend. She and her fiancé will be here any minute."

"Oh. We can't have too many people here. You know what they say?" Daniel flashed a soft smile.

"What's that?"

"Too many cooks spoil the broth, you know?"

She never was much for those old proverbs. "Oh, yeah. That." She felt her cheeks warm as a blush took over.

"It makes for a better show when it's a more intimate setting. Plus the kitchen can get kind of crowded, even if it's only two."

"Don't worry about Lucy or Matthias." Serah covered her mouth and giggled. "Lucy can't even boil a pot of water, and Matthias? Let's just say he almost burned down my house. Neither of them will be anywhere near the kitchen, so don't worry about intimacy issues."

A wide smile spread across his lips. "The show is somewhat scripted too. To sort of draw on some of that intimacy. Is that okay with you?"

"Scripted? I didn't know I was signing up for a production of Shakespeare in the Park. Jeez. Now you tell me." She blew out a sarcastic sigh.

"Even reality shows follow some sort of script. Did you know that?"

Serah snorted. It didn't surprise her one bit. "They need to hire better writers, then."

"I won't disagree there. Since I write most of my scripts, I will assume you're not talking about my show?"

"No, I'm talking about any un-real housewife in any big town. Where's the *Real Housewives of the Midwest*?" Serah threw up her fists in frustration. "And don't even get me started on those guidos and guidettes down in New Jersey. Is this where entertainment is taking us? Steroid-popping, orange-skinned idiots?"

Daniel shrugged. "I am one of those stars you know."

Serah's mouth fell open and she gasped. "Oh. But *Princes and Paupers* was a great show. I could see how real you all were. And I can tell the difference between fake bake and a real tan. This stuff now? It's just crap."

"People watch it, though."

"I know. It's just that… I'd rather keep up with a turtle than… well you know."

"It's the days of fifteen minutes of fame, what can I say?"

"To each his own. YouTube doesn't help much either." Fingering the diamond-encrusted locket around her neck, she flashed a smile. He was as friendly off camera as he was on camera.

"Some good musicians have been discovered that way."

Including Justin Bieber, but she kept that to herself. "You have a point. My main issue is with the idiots who make fools of themselves just so their stupid videos go viral."

"We have a lot more in common than just cooking, it seems. I hate that too." Daniel wrapped his arm around her shoulder and gave her back a friendly pat. "Enough chitchat. Let's see this awesome tiramisu I've heard so much about," he whispered in her ear.

No tingles. No shivers. Again, nothing. Her libido was indeed shot.

Chapter 23

MATTHIAS SHOULD HAVE STAYED OUTSIDE. HE SAT AT the desk and mashed keys on the keyboard. He'd seen Serah kiss Daniel. It had been the most clichéd, overly romanticized kiss ever, but he still saw it. He wished he hadn't.

He gritted his teeth. Why in the hell did he feel this way? He was supposed to be strong, to keep his emotions in check. Ever since he laid eyes on Serah, his resolve had gone out the window. He was doomed.

Sera continued to laugh and giggle, pulling out mixing bowls and various utensils. He had no idea what they were or what they were used for, but the way they shined told him one thing. Silver. He relaxed slightly.

Daniel followed her around like a lovesick schoolboy, following Serah's lead. So much for relaxing. All he wanted to do was retch. Unfortunately, as a demon, that was impossible.

Daniel reached up and brushed Serah's shoulder. She smiled at him and tapped him on the back with a wooden spoon.

"Owwie," Daniel yelped in mock pain. He leaned in and whispered something into her ear.

His conscience warred inside. He wanted to tune in and hear Daniel's words, but he wanted to respect Serah's privacy as well. He clenched his fists, his fingernails digging deep into his palms. He didn't care if he bled. It was the only way he could keep himself sane.

"Iz zumzing bozzering you, Mizter Ambroze?" Edie sidled up next to him and took the empty seat next to his. "You seem… vhat iz zee word? Ah… tense."

"I am fine," Matthias ground out. "I'm just checking the perimeter."

Edie nodded. "*Oui.* Security iz hard vork, no?"

Matthias arched a brow. What was with this woman's sudden interest in his job? Serah's employee seemed friendly enough, but he'd learned many things in his centuries of training. Sometimes the friendliest people made the worst enemies. And you didn't know until it was too late. He angled another gaze at Serah and Daniel. They continued to frolic and giggle as she whisked something in the bowl. Daniel placed his hand on her shoulder as she cracked an egg.

And now Edie hovered. It was best to keep his distance. "It's too much hard work for a sous-chef to worry herself with." With that he shut the computer down and closed the lid.

Edie sunk back in her chair and scooted back. "My apologies. I vas just trying to make little talk."

Matthias nodded. "I'm not really that much of a conversationalist."

"Zat's too bad. You look like zomevone who has lots to say." Edie drew her lips straight and steepled her fingers. "Don't vait or it vill be too late."

Great, another cryptic person to complicate matters. There was one thing worse than cryptic goddesses, cryptic humans. This wasn't going to be easy.

"I need to make a phone call." With that, he pushed

the chair back and pulled the phone from his pocket. He mashed his finger into the touch screen and pressed the phone to his ear. He marched to the same office Daniel had occupied earlier and kicked the door shut.

"Rafael Deleon."

"Are you on your way? The TV guy is here." Matthias took a seat at the desk, swiveled and stretched his legs out.

"Lucy's already on her way. I'll poof in back of the store in about five minutes."

Poof? Even Deleon used those silly words to describe the demon travel? Matthias shook his head. Had he not seen how powerful Rafael Deleon had become, he'd say the Paladin was going soft in his life here on Earth with his half-succubus.

"I have questions about Edie."

"The sous-chef?"

"Yes. Can she be trusted?" He leaned around to peer through the blinds. "She hovering. It seems suspicious."

Rafael's deep rumble of laughter echoed in his ear. "Edie is very protective of Serah. Gerardo informs me she's not an angel, so no worries there."

"Noted. I still plan to exercise caution."

"I wouldn't expect anything less, Ambrose. Which is why you were chosen for this mission."

Matthias controlled his sarcastic chuckle. *Among other reasons*, he was sure. The Fore-Demons wanted to make sure they could trust him. What better way than send him back to the woman he had almost helped the Infernati destroy.

Rafael's booming voice broke him from his thoughts. "How about Daniel?"

"He's not an unblessed demon. That's not to say he isn't working with the Infernati."

"He could still be a demon?"

"I'm not ruling it out."

"If he doesn't smell of brimstone, then he's one of us."

Matthias groaned low, hoping Rafael didn't hear. "Not necessarily."

"What sort of angel is just going to bless random demons?"

Matthias adjusted the phone to his ear, his grip tight. One little bit of honesty wouldn't hurt Rafael. "One that is now dead."

And that was all he could say for now.

"You killed that angel, didn't you?"

"No. Be here in five minutes." He pulled the phone from his ear and slammed his thumb on the red dot to end the call.

Between Edie and Daniel, something smelled fishy. And it certainly wasn't salmon. He'd get to the bottom of this. He'd make sure of it.

He slipped the phone into his back pocket and reclined in the chair. Maybe a little meditation would help clear his mind.

The door swung open. His meditation would have to wait.

Serah stood there in the doorway, a pristine white chef's jacket hiding his view of the swirly blue dress he'd suggested she wear earlier. Sadly, it hid her sultry curves as well.

"I didn't interrupt anything, did I?"

"No. I just spoke to Deleon. Lucia and he are on their way."

Serah wrung her hands in front of her. "Yeah... about that..."

Matthias narrowed his gaze. He didn't like the sound of that. "What is it?"

"It's going to get crowded. Daniel and his crew will probably take up most of the kitchen."

Matthias leaned over the desk, and narrowed his gaze. "And?"

Taking cautious steps closer, Serah gulped. "Daniel needs you guys to make yourselves scarce during the recording. They like a more intimate environment."

Intimate? What the hell kind of show were they filming? It was a blasted cooking show, not a romance. His jaw twitched. He gripped the edge of the desk. "That's the most ridiculous thing I've ever heard."

"There needs be some chemistry between the host and guest. Otherwise, it gets boring."

Matthias gritted his teeth. He saw the way Serah and Daniel interacted. Smiles, jokes, laughter. They had enough chemistry already. "You look like you were getting along just fine."

Serah shut the door behind her. "Yeah, he's pretty awesome. And he's clean. I can sense vibes from people and his appears honest and good."

"I'm still not convinced." Sure, Daniel looked like any normal person, but there was just something about him that screamed caution. "Edie as well. How long has she worked here?"

Serah's gaze sparked and her lips drew straight. "Now you have a problem with my employees?" She took a deep breath and paced in front of the desk. "For your information, I hired Edie after my grandmother died. She had very good references."

Matthias bolted from the chair and stormed toward her. She had no idea of the danger she was in. He grabbed her by the shoulders and glared down at her. She glared back, defiantly lifting her chin. His body reacted accordingly. His heart pounded and hot sizzling energy ripped through him. He throbbed against the boxers he still wore. Bloody hell. Who knew defiance could be such a turn-on.

Controlling the emotions colliding inside, he reached and brushed aside one of her curls. "I just want you safe—is that so wrong?"

Serah's gaze softened and lowered to the floor. Hopefully she wouldn't notice the problem that had recently arisen.

"No, you are dedicated to your mission," she said, her voice wavering. "Like all Paladins are."

"Good. So you will tell Daniel I won't let you leave my sight?"

"I'll try, but it's his producer who's calling the shots."

"Is the producer here?"

"No, she's not."

"What she doesn't know won't hurt her."

"I guess," Serah said with a shrug. I'll talk to him."

"That's all I'm asking." He pulled away and turned to look out the window. Trees lined a lazy river. They swayed with the breeze, their leaves of golds, reds, and oranges fluttering in the wind. Breathtaking, but not as breathtaking as Serah. This was getting to be too much. The sooner this mission was complete, the better.

Great. Now she had to worry about Edie too? Who knew what side she was on. Team Daniel or Team Matthias. Wonderful, now she was starting to sound like a vampire- and werewolf-obsessed teenager.

And what was Matthias's deal? In one moment he was tender. The next, he was uptight and distant. If the signals got any more mixed, she'd need a strainer to separate them.

"I'm not done here." She'd get down to the bottom of this somehow. She closed the blinds to the office and turned back around. "What is your deal?"

Matthias scrubbed his hand through his hair and turned one way and the other. Then he looked her in the eyes, his onyx pupils sparking and swirling. "My deal?" he asked, his tone incredulous.

Serah stood her ground. She raised her chin and crossed her arms. "Yes. One moment you are tender and caring." She took a deep breath. "Then next moment you're an uptight ass."

His eyes continued to swim like a dark ocean. His jaw twitched. He clenched and unclenched his fists. "Serah, don't do this now."

"Do what? Have a discussion?" She shook her head. "You are so infuriating. What were the Fore-Demons thinking sending you here?" She took another breath and exhaled deeply. This breathing thing didn't work. She was still stressed as hell.

Matthias stalked toward her, his gaze penetrating. He gripped both of her shoulders, tight but not too tight. "You drive me crazy."

He continued to glare, dark and menacing. At one time a look like that would've sent her running. Now it fueled something else inside her. Something even more dangerous. Maybe she should run after all.

"I—" that was the only word she could get out. Matthias crushed her to his body, his arms wrapping firmly around her back. Her breasts crushed into his rock hard abs, she shivered at the electricity rocketing through her. "What are you doing?" she managed on a gasp.

"This." He slid her up his body, his hands firm but gentle. She closed her eyes, flashes of naked skin on skin filling her thoughts. She reached up and moved to the buttons of the crisp linen shirt. She plucked one, two, then three buttons.

His hands roved up and down her body, finally settling on her ass. How'd his hands get underneath her dress? He lifted her up and set her on the edge of the desk, pushing her back. Papers went flying. She didn't care.

Matthias hovered over her, his dark eyes misting over. With that, he lowered his lips to hers. It was like an explosion went off. A delicious, ecstasy-filled explosion in her mouth. She couldn't help but moan. She returned the kiss with just as much eager excitement. She opened her mouth, allowing him full access. He swept his tongue inside and traced it against hers. Wrapping her arms around his neck, she pulled him closer.

He nibbled sucked and nipped her lip, his hands roaming over her breast to pop one button of her jacket and then the other.

"See how you drive me crazy?" he murmured in her ear with a slow tantalizing lick along her lobe.

If this was crazy, then she was going there right along

with him. She'd never done anything so crazy in her life. God, it felt so good.

Matthias's mouth moved down her neck, licking and nibbling a path down to the base of her throat. Tongue tracing along her bobbing pulse, he inched open her jacket, exposing the dress underneath. He traced a fingertip along an azure swirl.

"You took my advice. Nice."

Serah managed a nod. There was no way she could manage anything else. Her pulse skyrocketed and liquid heat pooled in her loins. If this was what a little bit of kissing and groping did, she didn't know if she could handle anymore. Then again, she did love testing her limits.

She moved her hands along his shirt, over the contours and planes of his chest. Firm muscle grew taut against her touch. Returning to the buttons, she struggled to unhook the remaining ones. She whimpered in frustration.

Too bad she couldn't have been born with fingers of steel like Lucy. She'd seen the amount of clothes those two had demolished together.

"Ahem."

Speak of the devil. Lucy and Rafe stood in the doorway. A wide smirk spread across Lucy's lips. Rafe, on the other hand, scowled, his silver gaze boring into Matthias. He started to lunge forward, but Lucy reached out and grabbed his wrist. She shook her head and Rafael growled, reluctantly stepping back.

"Uhh, it's not what you think," Serah stammered, pulling her chef's jacket closed. Her shaky fingers fumbled with the tiny buttons.

Lucy snorted. "Yeah, it looks like a hell of a lot more."

Matthias buttoned his shirt and stood tall. Scratching the stubble that dotted his cheeks, he blew out a breath. "I'm sorry. It won't happen again."

"It better not," Rafe growled. He turned to Lucy. "Did you encourage this?"

"Heck no. They obviously don't need my help." She shut the door behind her and pushed in the lock. "The next time you two decide to get your freak on, lock the door."

"If he knows what's best for him, there won't be a next time." Rafael crossed his arms and sent Matthias a dagger of a glare. "Duty first, right?"

Finishing the last button of her jacket, Serah snorted. "Just like you put your duty first?"

"This is different."

"How is it different? You came to Earth to protect Lucy." Serah put her hands on her hips and sent Rafe her own slicing glare. "And I know there was a whole lot more than protecting going on between you two."

What the hell? Why was she taking this so personally? She should be thanking Rafe for putting the kibosh on Matthias's and her more-than-intimate kiss. But she only felt one thing... annoyed.

She clenched her fist. She wanted to plant it right between Rafe's glaring eyes. She ground her teeth.

"Serah," Matthias spoke, his tone gentle and reassuring. He took her hand in his, his callused hands softly stroking. "Rafael is right. Intimacies only complicate matters. I apologize for any stress I've caused."

He turned to Rafe. "We've got several matters to discuss and not much time. Let's have a seat."

Rafe offered a brusque nod and allowed Lucy to

choose where she wanted to sit. What a gentleman. At least some demons were. Lucy scooted out one of the guest chairs. Rafe pulled out the other, leaving Serah and Matthias the love seat. How ironic.

"Sorry, I don't particularly care for couches," Lucy said, folding her legs beneath her.

With an arch to her brow, Serah took a seat, scooting as close to the side. "Why do I find that surprising?"

Matthias, thankfully did the same. With a soft grunt, he stretched his legs.

"Enough," Rafe barked. "So what was this incident Matthias told me about earlier?"

"Incident? What incident?" Serah feigned bemusement. From the piercing glares from both Lucy and Rafe, she'd failed miserably. Not surprising at all. "Oh! That incident. It was nothing."

"You were almost killed," Matthias gritted out. "How is that nothing?"

"The woman driving the car was not a demon. Her kid, however…"

"You know how I hate it when you avoid answering our questions, Serah." Lucy leaned in, her greenish-gold eyes flaring.

That look said it all. They were serious. And the only way to get out of this mess was to tell the truth.

"Fine. Somehow an Infernati demon managed to change the timing of the light at the corner of A-Line Road and Lover's Lane. I ran a red light and was almost sideswiped."

"Bloody hell," Rafe growled. "This is worse than we thought."

"How so?"

Matthias blew out a deep breath. "I didn't want to alarm you until we had all the facts."

"What. Is. It?" Serah gritted out.

"Some of the Infernati demons have the ability to manipulate electricity."

Jeez, was there any part of human life not in danger of demons? This grew deeper by the second. "Seriously? What's next? Water Demons?"

"Does this really surprise you? The Infernati will use any means to infiltrate human civilization."

Matthias nodded. "It doesn't help that they have human minions ready to do their bidding."

Rafe sucked in a deep breath. "Any person can be a minion, even someone you've trusted for years."

Matthias moved closer to her and took her hand in his. His grip was strong, protective. "Are you absolutely sure you can trust these people?"

She'd known Edie for almost two years. She was a blessing in disguise. When her Nonni died, Serah didn't know if she could manage the business on her own. She struggled to make ends meet. She was about to sell when Edie literally ended up on her doorstep. With her dazzling red hair and vibrant attire and personality, she was just what Serah needed. How could she not trust her? So her accent was a little off. So what? She was an excellent cook. The fondue was just the icing on the cake where Edie was concerned.

Daniel, on the other hand, was kind and sweet. A perfect gentleman. He seemed honest and sincere. And his aura seemed clean as well. He couldn't be a minion. The Infernati weren't that good. Were they? God, she hated all this conflict.

Serah turned to face Matthias. Even though his eyes were dark, they sparked. Despite her inner, practical self telling her to beware, she felt at ease. Emotions conflicted with each other. Wasn't that what the Infernati were good at? Messing with people's minds?

From all those fantasies he'd been putting in hers, maybe he wasn't as good as he claimed. She yanked her hand from his.

"How do I know I can fully trust you?"

Matthias's face grew stony and his body tensed. His onyx gaze continued to penetrate her mind. Serah shivered. Matthias's facade softened slightly. "I already told you, Serah. If you can't trust me, trust that I will do whatever is necessary to fulfill my mission."

Serah nodded. His response eased her stress—slightly.

Chapter 24

MATTHIAS WISHED HE COULD JUST SINK INTO THE SOFA. He didn't blame her for her lack of trust. It was quite obvious she had a knack for judging people. It was only a matter of time before she would remember everything. If only he could keep his hands off her. Each touch, each kiss brought her closer to the memories. Then again, maybe it was better if she knew.

It would make this mission a hell of a lot easier.

"I think we should try to get more information on Daniel," Rafael said, breaking the awkward silence.

Matthias grumbled. "I've spent the entire morning researching *American Chef* and Daniel Blackburn. Nothing. Not even any parking tickets. No credit report either."

"He is a star, you know," Lucia said with a grin. "Maybe Daniel Blackburn isn't his real name."

"There were no court documents, either, sealed or unsealed." Matthias rested his elbows on his knees and grabbed his temples. God, he hated complications. And celebrities with stage names.

Serah shrugged. "Still doesn't mean he's a demon or working for them. He could just be really private."

Private, his ass. "If he's really private, he sure has a weird way of showing it. And I Googled 'I went to school with Daniel Blackburn' and nothing came up either."

"Huh?" *How the hell did a several-centuries-old demon know the ins and outs of Internet searches?*

"There's always someone who wants recognition, in any crowd."

She couldn't disagree with that. "I was referring to your super-mad computer skills, actually."

"In my previous line of work, computer skills were a necessary evil." Sadly, evil wasn't always a pun either. He'd done some evil things in his life. He didn't deserve someone as pure as Serah.

Rafael cracked his knuckles. "We need to keep a close watch on Daniel. I can set up surveillance. I have some phantoms that owe me a favor or two."

Serah snorted in laughter. Matthias loved her laugh. He'd miss it when his mission was done and she never wanted to see him again. "Phantoms? Seriously? I would have thought ghosts would be demons too."

"Ghosts and phantoms are spirits that never made it to judgment. They need guidance to be led to heaven, hell, or limbo." Matthias turned to Rafael. "How soon can you have them in place?"

"About an hour, two at the most."

"Excellent. I can stay here and monitor things as well." Matthias drew his gaze to Lucia. "What about you? What do you plan to do, Lucia?"

"*Lucy*, damn it. I'm staying here. I don't give a crap what Daniel or his reclusive producer has to say about it."

"Speaking of producers, has anyone researched her?" Rafe pulled out his BlackBerry and punched some buttons.

"Not yet. I only have her name. Sally Lohman." Matthias had been just about to enter her name into the search when Edie invaded his space earlier. "I'll do it once we're done here."

"I'll do it," Lucy chimed in. "You need to focus on Serah."

Matthias stifled his chuckle. If he focused on her any more than he already did, he was done for. "I will stand guard. I, too, do not give a damn what anyone has to say about it."

"I'll be back in two hours," Rafe said. "Hopefully Nigel and Rupert are still at their usual haunt."

Serah rolled her eyes. "Ghosts have weird names."

"They are over two hundred years old."

"Thank God I wasn't born then." She covered her mouth, a wide blush filling her cheeks. "No offense."

She was so adorable when she blushed. So pure. Matthias steeled himself. She was too pure for the likes of him. "None taken."

"None here, either. I'm used to Serah's idiosyncrasies—Ouch! Sorry."

Lucy removed her tennis-shoe clad foot from Rafe's. "Don't even say that hurt."

"You keep getting stronger, and I won't know what to do with you." Rafe swept Lucy into his arms and gave her a searing kiss.

"Oh, I think you know full-well what you'd do." She gave him a playful smack on his arm.

Matthias tried to control his frown. If only he could have such a relationship. So open and free. But he didn't wish his baggage on his worst enemy. He scraped his fingers through his head and angled his gaze to the ceiling.

"Your excessive use of PDA is making Matt here jealous." Serah crossed her legs and gave a sneaky smirk.

"I don't see any portable digital assistants here."

Matthias drew his brows together, consternation filling his face.

Serah blew out a breath and shook her head. "Public displays of affection. Jeez. How can you be so knowledgeable about computers and technology, but not common terms used by humans?"

How could she read him so well? Frustration replaced his consternation. "Talking and sending messages in codes is silly. I prefer to spell out words in their entirety."

"OMG! I N-O!" Lucy said with a wide grin.

Matthias groaned. Serah shook her head in her hands. They had more in common than he thought.

"Well, now that we've cleared the air, I better go hunt down those ghosts." Rafe stood and stretched out his legs. "I think I'll take that sofa next time."

Matthias extended his legs, putting his arms behind his head. Human furniture wasn't made for demons obviously. "Unfortunately, it's no more comfortable here."

Serah crossed her arms, a challenging expression clouding her face. "Are you telling me I should special-order my furniture from now on?"

"Just a friendly suggestion," Rafe said. "But I've really got to go. See you all later."

Serah grabbed her arms and huddled tight. Matthias would have offered her his jacket if he had one. "Something tells me I should have brought my coat. This chef jacket just doesn't cut it when you all decide to use my office as a portal."

"It only lasts a minute or two. Besides, it's Michigan. Aren't you used to the snow by now?"

"Just because I'm used to snow, doesn't mean I have to like it."

"Amen to that," Lucy said with a chuckle.

Rafael nodded. "Good point." He closed his eyes and held his arms up high. "Bundle up. I'm heading out. Time to head on over to Kirby Road."

"Kirby Road?" Lucy shuddered. "Poor ghosts."

"Yeah, you'd think spirits with such dignified names as Rupert and Nigel would choose a more stately area to haunt."

"They hang out at the homeless shelter," Rafe explained. "Even though they're ghosts, they still find ways to volunteer their time."

"Charity is charity, whether someone can see you or not, right?" Serah smiled. "I wonder if they were there when I was serving soup last weekend."

Rafe shrugged. "Maybe they were."

With that, Rafael closed his eyes and raised his arms high. "Portals of limbo and hell. Take me to the corner of Plainview Boulevard and Kirby Road."

With that the winds began to swirl and kick up around them. Icy gusts wailed and whistled as the temperature in the room dropped.

Sleet and snow pummeled Serah's face as the winds churned around them. Her curls whipped and whirled around her face. She shielded her face in a futile attempt to keep away from the snow's violent flurry. If only he could take her in his arms to keep her warm.

Who was to say he shouldn't? After all, it was his mission to protect her. He pushed himself through the ice and snow. He'd keep her warm. She could beat the hell out of him after the frost and ice dissipated.

He reached out and grabbed Serah. Cradling her tight to his body, he crouched over her, his back taking the wind instead of hers. Oddly enough, she didn't resist. She relaxed in his embrace and burrowed closer. It took every fiber of restraint to stop his fingers from tangling his fingers through her sable curls. Damn, how he wanted to.

The winds dissipated. Ice and snow evaporated into a mist around them. Serah sighed softly against his chest, her hands gripping the collar of his shirt. Was she ever going to let go? Hopefully not any time soon.

"So, umm, it's safe now, you know?"

Lucy's words hit him in the face like a bucket full of icy water. Serah jumped back and let go of his shirt. Brushing snow from her hair, she shook her head. "Even a single *Peragrans* is bad. Lucy, you lied. How do you handle all that snow?"

"You get used to it." She tapped her foot on the ground. "Everything evaporates in a matter of minutes."

Matthias reached for Serah's hand. "I'm sorry. You looked cold. I'm here for your protection, including a snowstorm in your office."

"I appreciate it. Really, I do. Thanks, Matthias." Shivering, she brushed a curl from her cheek. "God, that was cold."

"As Lucy said, you'll get used to it."

"God, I hope so. And I pray you don't have to do that very much while you're here."

At least they were making conversation. It was a start. And a nice way to at least try and break the ice again.

"If I need to—as you call it—*poof*. I'll make sure to do it privately."

Lucy smiled. "What a gentleman."

"I do try."

Serah smirked. "You still need a little more work, but I do see promise."

Well, it was something of a compliment. He'd take it. "Thank you, I think."

"You're welcome." Serah leaned against the desk and drummed her fingers on its glossy surface. "So did you want to look up furniture while I finish up the tiramisu with Daniel?"

"I can't protect you from here."

"I know, but I'd prefer to discuss this with Daniel first."

He clenched his jaw. It wasn't safe. She'd be vulnerable. "I need to protect you. What if he tries something?"

"Lucy's here, silly. Trust me, she's good. She's saved my ass several times already."

"How good."

Lucy blew out a mirthful snort. "This good."

With that, she jumped in the air. In a matter of a second, she flipped backward. Balancing on her fingertips, she leapt back up on her feet. To punctuate her threat, she kicked out her leg, her tennis shoe two centimeters from his nose.

Both eyebrows arched up. He'd heard she had excellent martial arts skills. He just didn't know how good. "Amazing."

Serah grinned. "Tell me about it. Lucy could kick Jean-Claude Van Damme's ass."

Lucy shrugged. "I don't like to brag, but it'd be a decent fight."

Modesty was not something he'd expect from a succubus. Then again she was part-human. Her soul was still intact. His, however, was long gone.

Serah's voice broke his thoughts. "Well?"

"Well what?"

"Want to look at furniture for a bit?"

"Why would I want to do that?" Matthias asked.

"Well, if you're going to be here for a while, you should be comfortable, at least." Serah offered him a friendly smile. A genuine smile, not fake. His heart rose. "I was planning on redecorating soon anyway."

"I don't want to inconvenience you."

Serah shook her head. "No inconvenience at all. Look, I know we don't see eye to eye on some things, but I can see you have good intentions, whatever they may be."

"Well. I just…"

"It's no bother, really."

"I mean—ahh…" Matthias froze. What was he doing? He had to remain strong, in control. Bumbling like a buffoon didn't help him any. Did she truly care about his comfort or was she just trying to keep the peace?

Serah crossed her arms, her lips started to curve downward. Oh God, he hated when she frowned.

"Is there any particular style that interests you?"

"Not really." She picked up some magazines from the desk and thumbed through them. "Here are some catalogs I got in the mail. You can try searching online too."

"Sounds good."

"One thing." She waved her finger at him.

"What?"

"Stay away from IKEA."

Lucy and Serah both snickered. "I don't think they're built to handle demons of your size."

"Cheaper isn't necessarily better," Serah added. "But they do make some nice stuff—for normal people."

Matthias nodded. "Ahh. I don't want to break your furniture the moment I sit on it." He set the catalogs down on the table. "You know I could just build you some sturdier furniture."

Why did he just offer her that? He wasn't going to stay here long enough to even attempt such a feat. Although the thought wasn't all together unpleasant.

He didn't plan for the mission to last more than a few days. Until Serah accepted her powers and learned how to use them. He needed an in-and-out mission like he was used to. Get the job done, leave, and never look back. But could he forget? And keeping himself from looking back wouldn't be that easy either.

"That would take too long. Unless your carpentry skills were supersized when you decided to go demon."

Matthias's heart sunk. There was no decision for him. He'd been robbed of his life and his soul. He clenched his fists, fingers digging into the magazines he still held. "Sometimes things get decided for you."

"What's that supposed to mean?"

"Never mind." He turned away to glance out the window. He couldn't let her see his pain. He'd gone so long keeping it hidden. "You and Lucy go. I'll stay here and look at these catalogs." He gripped the windowsill tight. *Please, just go away.* Before he did something he would regret.

"Are you sure? Did I say something to upset you?" He felt her standing behind him. He inhaled sharply. "I'm fine."

She reached out and placed a gentle hand on his shoulder. "I might not know you that well, but I can see something's bothering you. Please?"

He jerked his body straight. "I said I was fine," he barked out.

She yanked her hand away. "Fine. Lucy, let's go."

He kept his back to her. He couldn't turn around. She would hate him. It was better this way.

The sound of footfalls echoed in the room, followed by the slamming of the door. No, he'd never have anything with Serah like the relationship Rafael and Lucy had.

He only had himself to blame.

Chapter 25

"UNBELIEVABLE!" SERAH GRUMBLED. "SEE WHAT I mean? He's got some serious mixed signals brewing in that big head of his." She threw her hands up in the air, her frustration raging inside.

Lucy shrugged. "He seems conflicted, really. To be honest, you should probably keep your distance." Shaking her head, she snickered. "Well, as much as you can, considering the situation."

"I think I'm just going to handle this like business-as-usual, with a few extra spectators."

Lucy grinned, that's the spirit. "Did I smell tiramisu when I came in earlier?"

"Yeah, you did." She adjusted her chef's jacket and headed toward the kitchen. "Daniel wants to do a bit on the origins of tiramisu. He's doing research right now. That should keep him busy for a couple hours."

"What is its origin?"

Serah smirked. "No one really knows for sure. Various experts have different stories. But I know this. It tastes damn good."

"You are bad, you know that?"

"Yep." Serah grinned, giving her friend a friendly punch to the shoulder.

"So who is this lovely lady?" Daniel's smooth voice echoed in her ear.

She spun around. Daniel stood there, a stack of paper

and books in his arms. "Daniel, I wasn't expecting you back so soon. This is my best friend, and reluctant guinea pig, Lucy Gregory."

Daniel nodded. "Nice to meet you, Lucy. I'd shake your hand or hug you, but my hands are little full right now."

Serah's eyes popped. "You've been busy, haven't you?"

"Look at all this information I found! I hope you don't mind that I used so much paper, but I don't have a printer at my hotel."

Serah shook her head. "No problem. I've got plenty of paper to go around." No one person could acquire so much information in a matter of an hour.

"How'd you get all this information so quickly?"

"My assistant emailed me some links. God I love having someone to help me."

"Trust me, I'd never be able to do this job without Edie, so I know what you mean." She glanced at her friend. "Lucy knows too, right?"

"Without my two guys and Kalli, my shop would fall apart." Lucy couldn't help the smirk.

"Literally," Serah added under her breath, audible only to Lucy.

Lucy grumbled and waved her fist in mock frustration.

"I had the mother of all pipe bursts last year. Without them, my shop would have been closed for good."

"Praise be for that, huh?" Daniel shuffled the papers and books in his arms.

"Do you need any help with those?"

Daniel shook his head. "I can manage. I got this far with them. I also took a quick trip to the bookstore, if that's okay."

"That's fine. I had to discuss the arrangements with Matthias, Lucy and Rafe anyway. I'll talk about it with you when your hands aren't so full."

"Cool." He shuffled and stacked the printouts, books and magazines in his arms. "I contemplated writing a book on all this information I found about tiramisu." Daniel sighed. "Alas, someone already beat me to the punch."

He handed Serah one of the books. She looked down at the cover. A plate of fluffy tiramisu sat surrounded by swirls of chocolate sauce. Not to be outdone, a decorative chocolate pansy topped the dessert. To the side, a dollop of cream sat nestled between two plump strawberries. She glanced at the title—*Tiramisu: Lifting up the Mystery, One Bite at a Time*. She should have known there'd be a whole book dedicated to the elusive history of Italy's most delicious dessert.

"Nice presentation, but a little too garish for my tastes." She handed the book back to Daniel. "The only thing I've ever topped my tiramisu with is chocolate-covered espresso beans."

"Dark or milk," Daniel asked.

"Dark."

"Oh God. That sounds so delicious. We have to do it for the show."

"I don't have any on hand right now, unfortunately."

"I passed a candy store on the way to the library. I'm sure they'll have some there."

"The Sweetshop, right?"

Daniel nodded. "Interesting name. Their employees are all of legal working age, right?"

"Yeah, the people in this town have a strange sense of humor."

She pulled the phone from her pocket. "Their candy is to die for. With the exception of the gummies, they make their own candy. I have an open account with the owner. I can have Edie go to pick some up."

At the mention of Edie's name, Daniel's eyes lit up. "Sounds delicious."

The candy or Edie? Maybe she was better off not knowing. She'd keep the conversation focused on the chocolate instead.

"Oh my God! Delicious is an understatement." Serah closed her eyes, imagining the smooth and rich Dutch chocolate truffle she tasted yesterday melting in her mouth. Almost as smooth as Matthias's tongue. *Ugh! Not him again.* Would he ever leave her thoughts?

"That good, huh?"

Serah snapped back to attention. "Yeah, pretty much."

"If their candy is as good as you say, I don't doubt you at all," Daniel said with a grin.

"So you want the chocolate?"

"Of course," Daniel said.

"I'll have Edie get it right away." She prepared to dial Edie's number.

His expression grew serious. "About Edie. Can you give her the day off? It's going to get crowded here with your crew."

"That won't be a problem. She's catering an event for the hotel down the road tomorrow."

Daniel breathed out a sigh of relief. "Cool."

What was that all about? Did Edie make him uncomfortable? She was a bit different, but she was friendly too.

"Do you have a problem with Edie?"

"No," Daniel said with a sheepish grin. "Her accent just creeps me out a little."

"She's lived all over Europe. I guess it's kind of mixed."

Daniel nodded, his expression growing thoughtful. A smile curved his lips. "Fascinating."

Serah grabbed the book on tiramisu and thumbed through the pages. "Guess that book came in handy after all."

Daniel tilted his chin. "They say inspiration is just as important as perspiration."

"How true that is." She headed back into the kitchen and grabbed the stainless steel bowl from the counter. "So are you ready to see my tiramisu in action?"

"Let's do it." Daniel said, waving his spatula in the air.

―⁓―

"So how's the furniture search going?"

Matthias threw the catalog across the desk and snapped his head up. Lucy closed the door behind her and pulled up a seat.

"I could be of better use elsewhere."

Lucy flung herself into the chair. "I'm not disagreeing with you. As you know, we have to take precautions when humans are involved."

Matthias nodded. "I understand. I'm just not used to sitting idly while I could be out protecting her."

"It's just for a while, until we convince Daniel that we need to stay during the production." Lucy smirked. "Trust me, we can be very convincing."

"Are you going to enrapture him?"

Lucy shook her head and sighed. "Unfortunately that is one trait I never got."

"Besides karate, what other skills do you have?"

"I can read and speak Old Latin perfectly. I've been able to since I was a kid."

Wow. What an unusual talent. Then again, with that sort of talent she was indeed valuable. "That's fascinating."

"I used to think it was annoying. Not so much anymore."

"It is a great skill to have." He set his elbows on the desk and stretched. "I assume you had some questions for me?"

"Rafe told me you both were attacked last night?"

Matthias nodded. He knew there wasn't any way to dodge the truth with Lucy Gregory. "Balthazar."

"So you know him?"

"At one time I thought I did."

Lucy arched a brow. "Who is he and what does he want with Serah?"

"He was a mercenary. He was my mentor. He taught me all I know." Matthias pressed his fingers into the table. "There comes a point when even the strongest of the un-sided demons snaps. He and I chose different paths."

Lucy flashed him a warm gaze. "I hope you don't mind me asking all these questions. I just want to know what we're up against. Where did his path lead?"

"He was Belial's second-in-command."

The minute he spoke the name, Lucy's gaze flared. Her face reddened. Her fingers bit into the arms of her chair. "I should have known."

"Balthazar said he now serves another." Matthias steepled his fingers. He could only dance around facts for so long.

"I suppose he didn't do any name-dropping either, did he?"

"If only it were that easy." Matthias ran through last night's events. "We took refuge in the spiritual shop in the shopping center."

"I bet Serah liked that."

"Pardon?"

"She and I made New Year's resolutions. Hers was to avoid compulsive shopping. She banned herself from consignment shops, thrift stores, and the spiritual shop."

"It was the only place open and the only place Balthazar couldn't enter."

"I always used to think Serah was crazy when she talked about that store. Every time I drove by, it was closed. Then I opened the chest."

"The proprietress explained that only those who were in tune with their spiritual side could enter."

"That explains it. I guess my spiritual nature is sex."

"I didn't say that."

Lucy smirked. "I'm joking. But Serah's always been in touch with her spiritual side." Her smirk transformed into a frown. "Then, after she was kidnapped, she told me the store had closed. That's when I first knew something was wrong."

Well, at least that part of his mission was falling into place. She was beginning to accept her true nature. They might have been small steps, but they were steps nonetheless.

"While we were there, the woman gave Serah a necklace. It matches her watch."

"I thought that necklace looked familiar. And that crazy watch. I always knew something was up with it. Did her grandmother leave it for her?"

Matthias nodded, then related the events of that night.

Every detail, from the wine, to the proprietress's true godly nature and her grandmother's letter.

"Minerva, huh? I always knew Nonni had some tricks up her sleeve. She was a good woman and very protective of her granddaughter."

Very protective. So protective she helped hide the mark that proved her Pure-Blood status. Why would she go to all that trouble? Being a Pure-Blood shouldn't be something you kept hidden. The world needed her.

He needed to get to the bottom of this. What better time than now?

"What about Serah's scar. When did you first notice it?"

"Last year, when we… you know."

He'd read Serah's file. She was born in Chicago. The pieces started to fall together in his head. Her grandmother had been protecting her. She kept Serah's mark hidden. She kept her secret. But sometimes secrets needed to be shared.

"This makes sense now. Her grandmother used a cloaking charm to hide her powers. But the great numbers of Infernati in the shop must have activated it."

"What are you saying?"

"The only remaining Pure-Blood was last tracked in Chicago, about twenty-five years ago. The Infernati and their minions burned her to death in her home."

"I remember Rafe mentioning that." Lucy's gaze narrowed. "Where are you going with this?"

"Where was Serah born?"

Recognition filled Lucy's face. "Chicago," she murmured.

"When did she move here?"

Lucy gulped a deep breath. "When she was in pre-school, I think."

"Daniel's from Chicago too."

"Could be a coincidence." Lucy harrumphed. "Yeah, right. So Daniel is our most likely suspect?"

"Exactly."

Lucy smirked. "You know, I'm not really into all this crime drama on television, but that was kind of cool."

"So we are in agreement?"

"The agreement that says you're done looking at furniture?"

"Yes, that one."

"I'd say we are." Lucy rose from her seat and extended her hand. Matthias took her hand and gave a hearty shake.

"I'll call Rafe and tell him to recruit some more phantoms."

"Sounds good. Should I go and get Serah?"

Lucy shook her head. "Let's wait on that. If Daniel is working for the Infernati, we don't want to let on that we know something."

"Good point." As much as he hated the idea of leaving Serah with a potential threat, it was the only thing they could do right now. The less suspicious Daniel was the better. He'd been in situations like this before. He could handle it.

"I can tell you care for her."

Where the hell did that come from? Was it that obvious? Then again, they did walk in at a most awkward moment. He hated complications like this. "What you saw when you and Rafe came in was nothing."

"Tell that to Serah's and your tongues."

"As I said earlier, it will not happen again." Matthias sat tall, his fists balled on the desk. "I thought I heard something. I was trying to protect her. One thing lead to another."

Lucy tilted her head, a lopsided smirk curving her lips. "That's how it always starts."

"A relationship with a human is inappropriate. I don't want to risk the Fore-Demons' displeasure."

Lucy snickered. "You don't want to know what I think of the Fore-Demons. As for Serah, I don't blame you for caring for her. She has this personality that just captures you instantly." She smiled. There was no masking the admiration Lucy had for her friend.

All camaraderie aside, he did have a mission to fulfill. Relationships, physical and emotional, only made matters worse. He couldn't get attached more than he already had. He couldn't have Serah's friend putting these insane thoughts in his head.

He needed to keep his distance. And as a bodyguard that was impossible. And it didn't help matters that Lucy sensed his obsession. Damn succubi. They were too damn smart where lust was concerned.

"The Fore-Demons do what they do for good reason. Don't forget that."

Lucy nodded. "Very true. As for inappropriate relationships, the Fore-Demons had no qualms about Rafe and me."

"Unfortunately, Princess Lucia, you don't count."

She huffed. "Trust me, I'm a princess in name only." She leaned over the desk, her greenish-gold eyes glittering. "And no matter how hard you try to deny it, I know you have more than just a professional interest in my friend." Lucy drew her eyebrows together. "I also can tell you're hiding something. I'm not one for secrets, and neither is Serah."

"Is it a crime that I find her somewhat attractive?" Somewhat? Matthias reigned in the intense desire to snort in laughter. More like "utterly." No... not even utterly. No amount of words could describe how beautiful she was. He drew his mouth straight and returned her glare with another stony one of his own. "And as far as I recall, it also isn't a crime that I keep my private life to myself."

Lucy leaned back and threw her hands up in defeat. "You're right. It isn't." She blew out a long breath. "I just want to make sure my friend is safe."

"You might not trust me, Lucy, but I swear that I will do everything in my power to protect Serah."

"I don't doubt that you have good intentions, Matthias." Lucy steepled her fingers. "But I'm worried that whatever it is you're hiding from will put Serah in danger."

"What I have in my personal life will not affect this mission."

Lucy cracked her knuckles, her glare intensifying. "Let's hope it doesn't."

Lucy's threat, although friendly, was very serious. He was in worse trouble than he thought.

Chapter 26

IF DANIEL WAS AN INFERNATI MINION, HE DID AN excellent job of hiding it. Most of the minions she'd seen and dealt with since her problems started were not the best at hiding their natures. They stuck out like sore thumbs.

Yet, she still remained cautious. Cautiously optimistic, she guessed.

"Hey, where's the alcohol?"

"Didn't you read any of that paperwork you printed?"

A sheepish smile spread across Daniel's lips. "I didn't get a chance to."

"Well, true Italian tiramisu doesn't have any liquor or wine in it."

"What's the fun in that?"

"I was just seeing if you were on your toes. Most the tiramisu recipes I've gleaned during my training either call for Italian brandy or Marsala wine." She traced her fingertip over the glossy surface of the liquor cabinet and opened it. "I prefer to preserve the coffee flavor, so I use this." She reached in and pulled out a bottle of Kahlúa. Tracing her fingertips over the smooth, brown glass, she grinned. "It's not Italian, but it tastes damn good."

"I don't care much for brandy anyway."

"Good." Serah reached for the measuring cup and cracked open the bottle.

She measured the liqueur to the bowl of sugar and espresso and passed Daniel the bowl. "Can you stir?"

"Can I?" Daniel grabbed the wooden spoon from the counter. "I think so."

Smiling he stuck the spoon in the bowl and mixed everything together. "How long do I stir?"

"The sugar needs to dissolve." She headed to the refrigerator and gripped the handle, the stainless steel cool against her skin. "I'll take care of the eggs, okay?"

"Just don't get it on your face." Daniel flashed a toothy grin. "Sorry. Couldn't resist."

She pulled out four eggs and placed them in the Pyrex bowl sitting next to the fridge. Daniel couldn't possibly be bad. Even Infernati and their minions weren't the joking types. But still, she wouldn't let her guard down. Not until Matthias and the others gave her the all-clear.

"Ha ha." She removed the eggs from the bowl and pulled open a drawer. She grabbed an egg separator. She didn't want any accidents.

"Ahh, you're cheating."

"Better safe than sorry. The person who invented the egg separator has my undying gratitude."

"To each her own." Daniel kept busy stirring the liquid mixture, still smiling that wide smile. Maybe he did stand out in a crowd. No one, not even a celebrity smiled that much, even one as attractive as Daniel Blackburn.

Either that, or maybe he was just trying to practice that chemistry he said the show needed. Either way, she had to play along.

She shook the separator and the egg white slipped through the wire rings into the container below. "See how easy that was?" she said, with her own wide cheesy smile.

Daniel chuckled. "So Edie says you used to live in Chicago. Whereabouts?"

He couldn't have broken the ice with a more un-comfortable question. Chicago was so long ago. She didn't remember much as it was. Memories did come in bits and pieces sometimes. Here and there. Wrigley and Soldier fields. Shedd Aquarium. Some images and flashes when she least expected them. Mostly dreams. Sometimes nightmares. She didn't want to talk about it.

"I was four when my grandmother and I moved to Michigan. I don't remember much before that." Frustration fed its way into her system. Her hands shook.

Come on, Serah, he's just making small talk.

Yeah, right.

She cracked the egg on the side of the bowl and flung the egg into the separator. The yolk split in protest, sliding in with the whites. "Damn it."

"Thank goodness we're not taping yet."

Serah flung the slimy egg off her fingers and reached for some paper towels. "Haven't done that in a while. Luckily we're not making meringue." Her nerves more settled, she reached for another egg. Taking extra care, she broke and separated the egg with ease. *Whew*.

"And I thought we'd have a local connection. I'll have to find another thing we have in common."

"Sorry about that. My memories of Chicago… well there aren't many to talk about." She dropped the eggs into Daniel's bowl.

"Oh. Too bad, you would've loved it."

"Chicago's only three hours away. I used to go there all the time during my shopaholic days."

"Shopping isn't all Chicago has to offer."

Could have fooled her. She always felt uncomfortable in that city, despite the killer deals. Something always prickled her skin when she neared the city. Like something lingered there. Something evil. Which was too bad. It truly was a lovely town.

"To be honest, all that traffic freaks me out." No lie there. She could barely manage the roads of River City. Stick her in an even bigger city and she was doomed. She tried it once. Never again. "A couple of years ago, I decided to go to Chicago by myself. I ended up getting in an accident on the Dan Ryan. I won't drive there alone again."

"Not a good time, I bet. Sorry that happened to you." Daniel flashed a reassuring smile. But just how reassuring was it? "I'd be happy to show you around town. You wouldn't have to drive at all."

"That's a nice offer. I'll keep it in mind." She pointed down at the bowl. "These eggs aren't going to whisk themselves." She shoved a whisk into Daniel's hand.

"Oh, man. I'm going to end up with arm strain," Daniel said with a smirk.

"No one ever said cooking was easy." She grinned. "Continue whisking until it's smooth."

"I see how you are, making your guest do all the work."

Serah shrugged. "You're the one who said you never made this before. I was just helping you out."

"Thanks, I guess."

"Seriously, you've been doing this show for how long and you've never made tiramisu?"

Daniel whipped the mixture with expert precision. "I was just waiting for the right moment."

"Guess that time is now."

"I can't wait to see how it turns out."

"You'll have to wait a few hours for the custard to set."

"Well, that sucks."

"I know, right." She looked into the bowl. The frothy mixture formed large, fluffy peaks. "The filling is just about done, so you're almost there."

Daniel tapped the whisk on the side of the bowl, allowing the mixture to plop inside. "What's next?"

"We have to soak the ladyfingers." Serah took a seat at the counter and grabbed the package of ladyfingers. Ripping open the plastic, she sucked in a deep breath. She needed to tell him sooner or later. It might as well be now. "So I talked with Lucy, Rafe, and Matthias."

Daniel set down the whisk and bowl. "And?"

"Lucy and Matthias stay."

"Sally's going to freak," Daniel said with a shake of his head. "But I'll talk to her."

"That's all I'm asking for."

"Okay. Well, let's finish this up. I have a few errands I need to run, so I can use the down time to do that."

"Sounds like a plan." She just hoped Rafe had his phantoms lined up in time.

"I've located Nigel and Rupert." Rafael's voice boomed in the phone. "They said they have about five or six other phantoms that they can send."

Matthias nodded. "Good."

"I know you are not someone who enjoys working in the background, but right now it's for the best."

"I was just going to check on Serah anyway."

"Where's Lucy?"

"She had an important client who came into the shop unexpectedly."

"That's a rather strange coincidence."

"It was her mother."

"As always, her mother has impeccable timing."

"So this is a common occurrence."

"You can say that."

"So it's just me and Serah then?"

"After I brief Rupert, Nigel, and their phantoms, I'll zap back." He paused. "Otherwise, you can always call Kalli." Rafael chuckled. "Then again, she might scare Daniel away."

"Scare him away?"

"Let's just say Kalli looks like she'd fit better in a tattoo shop than a beauty parlor or a black tie, catered event."

"Sounds scary."

"She's anything but. Don't get me wrong, she's pretty, but she'd rather hide behind dreadlocks, tattoos, and leather and lace corsets."

"There's a term for that, right?"

"Some people call it Goth, but she's a bit edgier than that." Rafael snorted. "To be honest, she makes her own style."

"Sounds like an interesting character. Go ahead and let her know to keep alert."

"Trust me, she's good at it." The phone cut out for a second. "Lucy's on the other line. Hold on a second."

"Okay."

"Thanks." With that, the phone clicked, and Matthias was left listening to dead air. He took a seat at the desk and propped his feet up on the corner. He knew he shouldn't, but he was going stir-crazy in this cramped office. Every minute with Serah not in his sight drove him further over the edge. Every minute drove him closer to despising Daniel Blackburn and this stupid television show.

As if in ironic answer to his twisted prayers, the door swung open. Serah, chef's hat askew, strode through the door.

"Dude, I know I told you to make yourself comfortable, but isn't that a little extreme?"

Juggling the phone on his ear, he stifled his grumble. "Sorry. My legs got tired." He took his feet off the desk and swiveled in his chair. "I'm holding for Rafe."

Serah nodded. "Daniel's leaving for a few hours. Hope your phantoms are ready."

"Rafe's on the other line with Lucy."

"I just got done talking to her. She's probably telling him the same thing I just told you."

So he was the last on the chain to get notified? Was this where her priorities lay? "So you felt it necessary to call her first before talking with me?"

"I was on my way to tell you. It's a force of habit to call Lucy first." Shaking her head, she raked her hands through her corkscrew curls. "I seriously didn't think it would be a big deal. Sorry."

She took another deep breath of air. "I thought Rafe was in charge of this operation anyway. Why are you so concerned? I'm still safe."

"Rafe is in charge of the overall mission. My mission is to protect you. Anything that has to do with your protection concerns me." Why was he taking this so personally? Lucy was her best friend. Of course she'd go to her first.

"Noted." The ire in her voice cut into him like his favorite dagger. Damn it. He could never do anything right when she was around. How was he supposed to complete this mission?

"I apologize, Serah. I've not had a mission like this in some time."

"What sort of missions are you used to?"

He wasn't ready for these questions. Not now. Hopefully not ever again, if everything went according to plan. He'd do his part and then take that mission in Siberia if he had to. He needed to get away from her before it was too late.

"Nothing a woman of your caliber should ever have to burden yourself with knowing."

"It can't be that bad."

Oh, but it could. It would destroy any chance of redemption he'd had. If he were Serah, he wouldn't forgive him. "I don't want to talk about it."

Serah nodded. "Believe me, I understand. More than you realize." She exhaled a deep rush of air. "I can tell that you blame yourself for something."

Shit. She was starting to remember. That was why she was taking this angle. She wanted to dig in deeper. He couldn't risk it. "It's a common habit, actually— demons and humans alike. Not much to talk about."

"I see." Serah pushed a curl behind her ear. "Sorry I didn't run the news by you first. I am actually going to prepare dinner and wanted to know if you liked something in particular."

"Anything will be fine. As long as it's not hardtack."

"I learned how to cook at the River City Culinary Institute, not in a Civil War army camp. How does lasagna casserole sound?"

Casserole? Was there any meal that could not be made into a casserole? He might not be up on the whole culinary scene, but he'd heard quite a bit about casseroles over the years. He wrinkled his nose.

"Why does everyone always turn their nose up at the word *casserole*?"

"It's a bunch of leftovers thrown together in a dish."

"Don't let my Nonni hear you say that."

"What's so special about your casserole?"

"Do you like lasagna?"

Matthias nodded. He'd eaten it while on a mission in Italy during World War II, guarding one of the Infernati's most infamous minions. "I haven't had it in a while, but it was tasty. I ate it when... never mind."

Serah blew out a frustrated breath.

Just because he wasn't that forthcoming with his personal stories of woe didn't mean he couldn't do his job. He gritted his teeth.

"It's still lasagna, just made a little differently."

"If you say so."

"I know so." She raised her chin defiantly. Bloody hell, he hated when she did that. It drove him mad.

The phone clicked back over. Bloody hell twice over. Leave it to Rafael to cool his lust. "Still there, Ambrose?"

"One moment." He covered the receiver. "Deleon picked back up."

"I suppose you want some privacy so you can continue your manly talk of battle plans and strategies?"

"Something like that."

"Fine. I'll be in the kitchen." With that she spun around and marched out the door.

Matthias winced. It was for the best. The less she knew about him the better. He took a deep breath and went back to the phone. "Serah just told me Daniel left to run a few errands. Are the phantoms ready?"

"As ready as they can be." Rafael chuckled. "Rupert and Nigel almost turned me down, until I told them who they would be helping."

"Oh?"

"It appears Serah has quite the fan club at the soup kitchen."

Matthias arched an eyebrow. "Umm, should I ask?"

"Apparently no one makes soup quite like her."

Matthias shook his head, a smile curving his lips. That didn't surprise him in the least. If she cooked as good as she looked, he was done for. He'd get the chance to sample her skills in a bit. At least he could taste one thing Serah offered without being strung up by his fingernails. "I wouldn't know. I haven't tried her cooking yet."

"Too bad."

"You don't need nourishment to survive though."

"That doesn't mean I'm going to turn down a home-cooked meal. Especially one cooked by Serah SanGermano."

"Why not eat your fiancée's food."

"I'm not quite certain it is safe for demon consumption."

Matthias cringed. "Lucy lets you talk this way about her domestic skills?"

"She's the one who said it, not me." Rafael cleared

his throat. "But back to business. I'm going to discuss our plans with our two British phantoms. I'll call back in an hour."

"Sounds good. Be safe." With that, he ended the call.

He exhaled long and hard. No. Those two had it all. An open and honest relationship. He'd never have that with Serah. That sort of honesty would only send her further away. Right now, that was the last thing he wanted.

Chapter 27

WHAT WAS THE DEAL WITH THAT MAN? HE HAD TO BE the biggest ass she'd ever dealt with. Well, not far from it. But part of him intrigued her. To the point of distraction. Not a good thing where heat and flame were involved.

She cranked off the water and heaved the stock pot from the sink. Lugging the heavy pan to the stove top, she grumbled beneath her breath.

"Let me help you with that."

And there went her concentration. His spicy, woodsy scent wafted through the air and right up her nose. She inhaled deeply. God, she loved that scent.

Stupid man!

"I've got it," she said. Water sloshed and splashed, hitting her in the face.

He came to stand behind her. "I insist," he said, his breath inches from her ear.

She shivered. Her body melted. Her hands shook. More water sloshed over the side and splashed onto the floor. He needed to stop whatever it was he was doing… before she did something she would regret.

"I don't know what you're doing, Matthias." The pot slipped in her hands.

"Just let me help you," he whispered.

Serah's breath caught. Her pulse raced. Her body, of its own volition, pressed back against him. As her body melded into his, she gasped. He was just as turned-on.

"I... I banned you from the kitchen," she breathed out, her hands trembling. The water continued to slosh over the side.

"Did you?" He snaked his arm around her and pulled her closer, grinding his hardness against her backside. Heat pounded its way through her body, from her head right down to the tips of her toes. Electricity zinged across her skin. What on earth was he trying to do?

"I'm going to drop the pot."

"Are you?" Not a man of many words, was he? And her words were fleeting as well. More energy roared through her body. Her fingers tingled.

This sort of energy wasn't safe. It was volatile. It would burn her to a crisp if it continued. But her body made up its own mind. She leaned her neck back, her head resting on his chest. "What are you doing to me?"

"Nothing," he said with a quick nip to her earlobe. It was a wonder that she still managed to grip the pot handles. "Serah, turn around and give me the pot." He chuckled, the rumble reverberating through her body. "I do know how to at least boil a pot of water. There's no grease involved, right?"

Serah managed a nod. So this is how he pushed his way into her kitchen? Seduction? Sadly, it was working. Reluctantly, she pulled away from him and turned to face him. His onyx gaze burned brightly, despite the darkness. She held out the pot, her hands still shaking like leaves in a windstorm. Matthias reached out, his hands brushing hers. Who knew a simple act of handing someone a pot could evoke the most intense sensations.

"Give me the pot, Serah. It's heavy and you've clearly got other things on your mind."

Yeah, she had other things on her mind, all right. And it was all his fault. She should have known he had ulterior motives. But what exactly were those motives? "Fine, take the pot." She thrust it out toward him.

"Careful!"

But it was too late. The force of her hands sent water flying up out of the pot and down Matthias's new shirt. He jumped backward, water dripping down the black linen onto the checkered floor below. Thank goodness the shirt was black instead of white. That was one view she couldn't handle.

"I told you to be careful."

"Sorry," she mumbled. "You made me uncomfortable."

"I'm trying to be friendly."

Friendly? This was more than friendly. This was positively delicious.

Matthias scooped the now-empty pot from her hands and set it next to the sink. He reached to unbutton his shirt.

Her eyes widened, giving saucers a run for their money. "What the hell are you doing?"

"Taking my shirt off." He plucked open another button.

She rolled her lips over her teeth. "Why?"

"It's wet. It needs to dry." He reached for the other button.

Serah gulped. She stood riveted, watching his fingers work the buttons. Her pulse thumped in her ears. She balled her fists at her sides. "I suppose you didn't bring a change of clothes with you?"

"I'm not psychic. I didn't know you'd douse me with lukewarm water." The shirt spread open, exposing a hair-sprinkled pectoral. She'd already seen it, so why did it keep affecting her this way?

"I said I was sorry." She sucked in a breath and turned away. She had to. If she continued to gape at the work of art that was his body, she'd melt right into the black-and-white ceramic tiles.

"I know." He turned her to face him. "I've tried keeping my distance from you, Serah. I can't do it anymore."

Close your eyes, her practical side warned.

And miss the positively delicious view? Her naughty side thought not. Curiosity always won in the end. Serah opened her eyes. The linen shirt hung off his shoulders. Droplets of water trailed down his chest, and farther down the contours of his abs to pool around his navel. Her fingers yearned to trace the droplet's path.

"You confuse me. One moment you're distant. The next moment, you're kissing me. Then you go back to brooding."

"I've done some bad things, Serah. Unforgivable things." Matthias raked a hand through his sandy brown hair.

"Yet, here you are, protecting me." What would one tiny touch do? He obviously needed some comfort. She took her fingertip and traced the long, jagged scar just above his left pectoral. "How did you get this scar?"

His muscle twitched against her finger and his breath hitched. "It was a long time ago."

"I wish you'd open up. I'd be able to trust you more."

"Trust this."

With that, he crushed her to him. With his thumb and forefinger he raised her chin, angling her gaze to meet his. Those onyx eyes seared into her. His large hands roved down over her bottom and back up to lock in her curls.

Did people really kiss like this? Like that scene from *Gone with the Wind* where Rhett finally gives Scarlett a kiss to remember. But Serah wasn't Scarlett, and she wasn't quite sure she'd be able to pull away from Matthias, let alone slap him.

As if eager to feel those hard lips against hers again, her lips parted. A ragged breath escaped her mouth. Her practical side managed to ball her fists. She should resist him. He had secrets. Dark secrets. She shouldn't trust him. But oddly enough, she did.

She relaxed in his arms and unballed her fists. She wrapped her arms around his neck and ran her fingers through the hair at the nape of his neck. She pulled his mouth to hers.

"Serah. You don't know what you're doing."

"I beg to differ," she breathed against his lips. She punctuated her sentence with a swirl of her tongue against his lower lip. Electricity zipped between them. She grabbed his sodden shirt and flung it from his body. Maybe she could seduce the truth out of him. Then again, who exactly was being seduced? Him and his smooth talking—he was just as guilty as she was.

With more daring than she had possessed in the past ten years, she moved her hands down his pecs and swirled her finger along each contour of his six-pack and brushed her fingertips along the muscles that tapered down to his hidden bounty. His body tensed against her ministrations.

"We can't do this here. We're in your kitchen."

"We're only kissing. No sanitary concerns there."

Matthias nodded. "I don't want to take advantage of you."

"Seriously? You're not taking advantage of me." She swirled a fingertip along his nipple. Hot energy fired inside her. "Why is there so much heat when I touch you?" Serah asked.

"I think you know why, Serah." Matthias yanked her against him again, his grip more fierce and intense. "I'm warning you, Serah. You don't know what I am."

"I know you want to kiss me. What's so wrong with that?"

"You might not like it."

Like hell she wouldn't. So the guy was an ass at times, but he did know how to kiss. And they'd already kissed anyway. "I kissed you already once. I liked it then."

"You did?"

His inquisitiveness caught her off-guard. Yet somehow she found it a turn-on. "A lot."

"You seriously don't know what you do."

"Maybe I don't, but right now I don't care."

Matthias growled deep within his chest, the vibrations reverberating against her body. He hoisted her up against him. She wrapped her legs around his waist, her hands frantically digging into the corded muscles along his shoulders. His heat throbbed and radiated against her, right down to her core. "We can't do this here," he drawled, with a leisurely lick along her earlobe.

"Fine, the first door on the left then," she gasped out. Who knew the room she'd set up as sleeping quarters would get more action than sleep. "Lock this time." Oh God, she couldn't even manage complete sentences anymore. She was doomed.

Matthias's mouth moved to the base of her neck

where her pulse bobbed. His tongue traveled with slow, sensuous strokes against each throbbing beat.

Throwing her head back, Serah moaned. Fingers clawing into his hair, she pulled him closer. "Please?" she gasped out. Not wanting to prolong the wait any longer, she took both hands and craned his head to meet her gaze. She brought his lips to hers.

Allowing her tongue to swirl along his lips, she prodded them open. Hunger and lust combined as she swept into his mouth. Tongue darting and gliding with Matthias's, Serah murmured against his lips. Taking his lower lip into her mouth, she nibbled his tender flesh. She pulled her lips away and gazed up at him. "I'm through asking nicely."

"I can't resist you any longer." He plowed across the kitchen, scattering utensils, pots, and pans in his wake. The clamoring echoed faintly in her ears as other, more passionate, senses took control of her body.

Without missing one step, Matthias kicked open the door, swung around to catch the doorknob behind him and draw it closed. He flipped the light switch and snapped the lock in place.

"A bedroom?"

Serah felt her cheeks flush more. "I've pulled a few all-nighters. Makes it a little easier."

"Very convenient," he murmured, tracing his hands up and down her curves. It amazed her how even through the layers of her dress and jacket, his touch still sent shivers of pleasure spiraling through her.

He laid her gently on the twin bed, fluffing the pillows beneath her head. "The bed's kind of small. I don't want to break it."

"I hardly use it anyway." Serah's hands moved up the expanse of his chest and across his shoulders and down over his biceps. The hard muscle flexed and bunched as he scooted next to her.

He took her hands, held them in place above her head and looked down at her. "Are you sure you want this?"

"It's just sex."

He let out a sharp breath. Surely he wasn't expecting more? They were nothing alike. They were just frustrated and needed some release.

"Yes, just sex."

With that, he lowered his mouth to hers, their lips joining again. He nibbled and suckled her lips, prodding them open with his tongue. It was like their tongues were made for each other. They swirled, laved, and slid along each other in perfect harmony.

God, he was good. Then again, he had centuries of practice. Centuries, her mind screamed. He probably had a lot more experience than she did. She tensed against his body.

"Did I do something? Do you—" He abruptly ended his question.

"How many times have you done this?"

"I'm not inexperienced," he said, his hands moving to unbutton her chef's jacket. "But it's been about four centuries, so I'm a little rusty."

Four centuries? And here she complained to Lucy about her four years of forced celibacy. "I'm rusty too," she said, her hands working the buckle of his belt. Ripping it open, she threw the belt to the floor and eagerly tugged at the button and zipper. She offered a secret prayer that he'd ditched the boxers. The easier the access the better.

Matthias returned the favor, ripping open her jacket and sending buttons flying in every direction. "Too many clothes," he murmured, tracing his tongue along her collarbone. His hands moved into her hair, loosening the ponytail at the nape of her neck. Her curls fell to her shoulders.

"I love your hair," he whispered against her lips. Fingers tangled in her curls, he pulled her head closer.

His hands continued their delicious ministrations, swirling massaging and stroking each curve of her body. Gripping the tie of her dress, he yanked, sending the fabric falling off her body.

"You're so beautiful." He pushed the dress off her shoulders. "No slip? Maybe you're not as pure as I thought." His fingertip traced against the lace of her pink pushup bra.

"Told you," she gasped out.

"Nah," he said with a long lick down her cleavage. "You're still pure."

Oh no. He wasn't stopping now. She might have pure blood, but that didn't mean she had pure mind. She reached for his zipper and yanked it down.

She caught a glimpse of black-and-red polka dots, shielding his manhood from her view. "I was hoping you'd lost those," she said tracing her fingertips across the silky fabric.

Matthias gulped, the pulse bobbing along his neck. She might as well give him a show. With a reluctant breath, she moved back to her own body, tracing her fingers up her sides and over her back.

"What are you doing?"

"This." She unhooked her bra, letting it slip off her shoulders and off her body. She moved her hands back down her body to trace along the hem of her matching panties.

"You are a temptress," he groaned, pushing her down against the pillows.

"No, I'm just demonstrating how you undress."

"Clothing has changed a lot since I last did this." Matthias said, placing kisses along her collar and down her cleavage. "Could you help me?" He blew a long breath over one of her nipples.

Her nipple pebbled instantly as his breath swirled around the sensitive nub. Hot moisture pooled between her thighs. "I can't concentrate," she managed to breathe out.

"I imagine that means I'm doing a good job?" He swirled a tongue across one nipple, his calloused fingers kneading the other. His other hand roamed down her stomach to trace along her navel then lower, to graze the elastic band of her panties. She never knew foreplay could feel so good.

"Please," she gasped, her hips grinding up against his hands.

"Are you sure? I don't want to complicate our arrangement."

"It's just sex." But was it really? She'd had sex enough to know that nothing ever felt this explosive before. Then again, she'd never done it with a demon before. Maybe that's why. But seriously, did it matter? She just wanted to feel his body against hers.

"Yes, just sex," he murmured, his mouth moving lower, between her breasts and further down her stomach. With slow, almost agonizing movements, he slid her panties down her legs and off her feet.

"Much better," he murmured.

"I know what would make it even better." Serah reached out to grab the waistline of his cargo pants. "Getting these pants off you." To finish her sentence, she traced her fingertips across the bulge of silk popping from his pants.

Matthias groaned. "You know not what you do."

"Oh, I know exactly what I'm doing." She laced her fingers into the fabric and yanked both pants and boxers down. She had never thought that particular part of the male anatomy to be attractive. Until now.

It jutted out, the rosy tip beckoning her to reach out and touch it. She'd never seen one so thick. He was definitely more than a handful. It was pure torture keeping her hands to herself.

Nibbling her lip, she fought back the urge to reach out and trace her fingertips against the bulging veins. Would he like it?

"Is something wrong? Are you scared?"

Hell no, she wasn't scared. Not in the least. She finally found her voice. "Can I touch you?" She flashed an attempt at a seductive smile. "There?" Her gaze roved over his hard length.

He reached out and snagged her wrist, wrapping her hand around him. She moved her hand up and down, enjoying the sensation of soft skin, veins, and hardness sliding in her hand. Then it throbbed. Her heart thudded. God, it felt so good.

"Serah," he groaned. "I can't hold back any longer, but I need to know if you're ready."

Ready? She was more than ready. She was ready to burst. "Trust me, I'm ready," she said with a long stroke up and down.

His breath hitched. If she kept moving her hand like that, he wouldn't last much longer. With as much willpower as he could muster, he pulled Serah's hand from his member.

"You are going to be the death of me," he growled, his hands stroking the smooth skin of her thighs. He shouldn't be doing this, but she had him so worked up. So hot. He couldn't resist.

"Please touch me," she said, her tongue darting along her lips. "Like I did you."

How could he refuse such a heartfelt request? He traced his fingertips across her inner thigh. With his other hand, he crept around, stroking and kneading her buttocks.

She inched her legs open, giving him full access to her most sensitive regions. There wasn't a part of her that wasn't beautiful. With slow, sweeping strokes, he traced his fingers through the soft curls crowning her mound. He moved lower, brushing a fingertip across her clit. She gasped, her body quivering against him. He circled again, pressing a little firmer into her mound.

She squeezed her eyes shut, her body thrusting upwards. "Oh God. Please."

"What do you want?" he whispered, tracing his tongue along her earlobe.

"I need you inside me. Now."

And there was no place he'd rather be, either. He nodded. With that, he pulled her legs up around him and pushed forward. Taking her lips with his, he thrust deep.

Serah groaned, latching her legs around him. He

wanted her to savor this. He didn't want it to be just sex. He wanted to make love. He thrust hard but pulled back slow. God, she was so tight. He thrust again, hard and slow. Her body pulsing against him, she moaned.

"Faster," she breathed.

"I won't be able to stop if I go any faster."

"Who said anything about stopping?" She tightened her legs around him and thrust her body upward. "Please?"

With that, he completely lost control. He slammed in and out, faster and harder. Her walls tightened around him with each thrust. He looked into her eyes, astonished to see them open and glowing with lust. Her breath was ragged as she clung to his shoulders, her fingernails digging into his muscles.

Her tongue swirled around her lips. Matthias took her tongue in his mouth, the tempo meeting each thrust of their bodies. Serah clenched even tighter around him, moaning against his mouth. She threw her head back, her body rocking against his.

"Oh God, Matthias!" She shook against him, her body undulating wildly. He groaned, his own release imminent.

"Please," she gasped. "You need this."

Oh God, he did.

"Serah!" he roared through gritted teeth. His cock pulsed. He thrust one final time, to the hilt. And then he felt it, as spasm after spasm rocked through his body. A loud, guttural groan burst from his mouth. With that, he collapsed against her, his tongue still tracing along her lips.

"Wow," she breathed, her fingers laced in his hair. "Four centuries, huh? Could have fooled me."

What the hell had he just done? He pulled away. Curse his overactive libido. It would be the death of him, if it hadn't been already.

"We shouldn't have done that." Matthias grabbed his pants and yanked them up. "I need to be honest with you, Serah."

"Honest? It was just sex, not a marriage proposal." She looked up at him, her gaze pleading. "Don't worry about it."

"There are things I haven't told you. Now I've taken advantage of you."

"I wanted it. I was taking advantage of you."

Matthias shook his head. "You won't want it anymore after I show you exactly what I've done. You'll hate me in the end. But I need to show you. Trust me."

"What the hell is your deal?"

"I didn't want to do this. But it's the only way."

Damn it, the last time he said that she ended up locked in a changing room with only her watch for protection. "Do what?"

Matthias closed his eyes, put both hands on her shoulders and spoke some words in Latin.

The first image came like a lightning bolt. No, her mind screamed. He couldn't be. But the images didn't lie. And the memories came flooding back.

He was the one who had kidnapped her. He was the one who had her thrown in that dungeon. But why was he in the dungeon with her? Shaking her head, she pushed Matthias away from her.

More memories assaulted her. Matthias's arms wrapped around her, comforting her. Kissing her, caressing her. With as much passion as he had shown her earlier. Matthias fighting the Infernati guards. Was he protecting her or not?

Then he did the same thing. Put his hands on her shoulders and spoke Latin. He'd deceived her. Tricked her. She always wondered why she couldn't remember Belial's goon kidnapping her and her first imp. Now she knew why. Matthias Ambrose was that goon. She gave herself to him? Her stomach roiled.

"It was you!"

"Serah, let me explain." Matthias reached for her hand. She snapped it away. "You tricked me."

"I was trying to protect you."

"Is that what delivering me to the leader of the Infernati is? Protection? You almost had me killed."

"That was not what I was trying to do."

"What the hell did you do to me?" She grabbed at her dress, pulling it closed. She scurried off the bed and yanked the ties of her dress closed.

"I removed your memories to ease your suffering."

"Yeah, right." He expected her to believe that crazy line? "You were trying to erase your evidence."

"The moment I saw the mark on your hand, I knew what Belial planned. It started as a kidnapping." He grabbed Serah and swung her to look at him. His onyx gaze blazed. "I swear by all that I have lost that in the end, I tried to rescue you. You are more valuable to the world alive than dead. Even someone like me knows that.

"He never told me you were a Pure-Blood. He said he needed something to bargain with."

She flung out her leg and kicked him in the shin. "Try your pathetic story on someone else, Matthias."

The sudden movement sent Matthias stumbling back. She ripped herself from his arms. She'd had sex with him! A heartless assassin. Someone who sells out to the highest bidder. The bile rose in her throat.

"There are other reasons. Reasons I can't explain. Just know that I am sorry."

"Sorry?" She yanked open the closet door and grabbed a new jacket. She buttoned it up and slipped on her shoes. "If you're asking for forgiveness, you've come to the wrong woman."

"I don't expect forgiveness. I just wanted to come clean." Matthias raked his fingers across the stubble on his chin. "The only way I knew how was to give you your memories back."

"They weren't yours to take." Fumbling with the last two buttons, she sucked in a deep breath. "You seduced me on purpose, didn't you?"

"No. I have feelings for you, Serah."

"Yeah, right. If that was the case, you would've told me sooner." She spun around, and narrowed her gaze. "You make me sick."

"I don't expect you to understand, Serah." Matthias's onyx gaze pleaded. "I wanted to ease your suffering. Sometimes forgetting is the only way."

"You can ease my suffering by getting the hell out of my sight."

She spun around and squeezed her eyes shut, the tears threatening to spill down her cheeks. What the hell? Anger she could understand. Sadness, though? *Screw him*. She balled her fists. Too bad she already had. Things were totally and thoroughly fucked up.

"I never meant—"

Shaking her head, she gave him a dismissive wave. "Just shut up and get out."

He blew out an aggravated breath of air. "As you wish."

The door swung open and without further word, he left.

At the click of the door shutting, Serah buried her head in her hands. If she was going to be sad, she might as well go down with a waterfall.

She crumpled at the foot of the bed and buried her head in the sheets.

Chapter 28

MATTHIAS DIDN'T BLAME HER ONE BIT. IT WAS ALL ON him—his fault. But it was for the best. Serah would be better off without him and his twisted set of morals.

He leaned against the door. It was for the best. They'd never have anything anyway. It was for Serah's own good. No matter how hard he tried to reaffirm his decision, it still cut straight to his heart.

An assassin with a conscience? He snorted. A dangerous mix.

"You must be Matthias."

The haunting voice carried across the kitchen and tickled his ears. Not a human voice. Not Infernati either, since no stench lingered.

Matthias spun around.

She smiled as she lounged against the buffet. A mop of hair of myriad colors fell around her face and down her shoulders. A crimson lace corset left little to the imagination about her womanly assets. There was no mistaking the demon side of her as she stood there clad in a leather skirt and fishnets. Tattoos of ivy and roses vined their way across her chest and down her arms. A leather thong was tied around her neck, and whatever was tied to the end of it nestled snugly in her cleavage. She blew a bubble and smacked her blood-red lips.

She fluttered her heavily mascaraed eyelashes. "Finished gawking already?

"Kalli, I presume?"

"Ding. Ding. Ding. We have a winner." She bent down and picked up his shirt from the floor. "Had a little accident, did we?"

"Serah dropped the pot."

"That's not like Serah, even when she's having an *episode*." She shook out the shirt and tossed it to Matthias. "There, all fixed."

"What are you doing here?" he asked, throwing the now-dry shirt on.

"Lucy told me to stop by and check on you two."

"Serah is in her sleeping quarters."

Kalli arched a brow. "She's not the one for midday naps either. What the hell is going on?"

Kalli yanked at the leather strap, freeing the pendant from its confines. She placed her arms on her waist.

The pendant! Matthias's blood turned cold. He'd never forget it. He'd bought it from a peddler in the village where he lived. He was courting Josephine at the time. She had fallen in love with the pendant instantly. He only had a few coins in his pocket, but the peddler could see how much they fancied each other and gave them a deal.

It was simple, yet elegant. A ring of pewter engraved with ivy vines. He'd recognize it anywhere. And now this woman wore it.

Was she the one who had killed Josephine and their unborn child? He clenched his fists. He never knew which side had done it, but signs always pointed toward the Paladins. They were angry at him for not aligning himself with them—at least that's what Balthazar had said when he first took him under his wing.

"Is something the matter?"

Matthias lunged at Kalli and grabbed the necklace. "Where did you get this?"

"It's just a plain ol' pendant. Hardly worth anything."

It might not be worth much to her, but it meant the world to him and he wanted it back. "If it's not worth anything, why wear it?"

Kalli plucked the pendant from his hands and looked down at the pendant. She traced the carvings with a gentle fingertip. "I like simple things, Ambrose. Is that a crime?"

"Could have fooled me."

"A medieval pendant goes perfectly with my Goth attire."

"Still, I'd like to know where you obtained it."

"If I said Sotheby's, would that help ease your tension?"

This wasn't the time for sarcasm, not when his mission only held on by a single thread. The moment Serah notified Rafael and Lucy of his involvement in her kidnapping, he would certainly be sent back to limbo and lose any chance to redeem himself with the Paladin.

"Someone I knew had a pendant like that."

"And someone I knew gave me this one."

"Who?"

Kalli reached up and traced a fingertip across the ivy designs. Taking a deep breath, she took a seat at the stool next to the buffet. "Well, this wasn't how I expected this to go."

"Expected what to go?" Matthias crossed his arms. "Just tell me you killed her quickly and that she didn't suffer."

Kalli balked, pulling her hand away from the necklace, surprising Matthias. "Seriously, you think I killed her?"

"How else do you explain the necklace? Josephine wouldn't just give her most treasured piece of jewelry away." Matthias's jaw twitched as he fought back the memories. "I saw our home. A Paladin had been there. I sensed it."

Kalli motioned to the other barstool. "You need to sit down to hear this, Matthias."

"I'll stand. Did you end it quick or did you make her suffer?"

"Damn it all, Ambrose." Kalli reached out and grabbed his hand. "It wasn't a Paladin. It was that bitch Salome. She made it look like we killed her."

Salome? The one who had made him this way? "No one is that good. Not even Salome."

"Trust me, she is." Kalli exhaled deeply. "If you don't believe me, why don't you just grab one of my memories? They never lie."

"You know of my skill?"

"I've been tracking you for centuries. Kind of hard not to notice." Kalli chuckled. "None of your victims ever remembered what hit them."

"So tell me about Josephine. What about our child?"

Kalli bit her lip. "It's gruesome. I don't know how to say this."

"You can just show me."

Kalli nodded. "Sounds good to me."

Matthias took hold of Kalli's shoulders and said in Latin, "You will allow me to journey into your oldest memories of the year 1228, to my village near Münster."

The odor of brimstone clung to the air. Kalli Corapolous swiped a piece of auburn hair from her brow and raised her nose for a better scent. The Infernati were nearby. Scanning the horizon, she spotted a plume of smoke looming. *The village*, her mind screamed. It was one she'd passed through numerous times.

God's teeth! Kalli shook her head and winced. It was times like this that she dreaded being a demon.

Even after eighteen hundred years.

The smoke appears fresh. I might still have time.

She raised her hands to the sky and allowed the freezing cold portal winds to pull her toward the village.

She flung ice and snow from her plain, brown kirtle and grabbed the silver dagger hidden in her skirts. The faint sound of a baby's cry set her senses on edge.

"Too late, you Greek bitch."

Kalli spun around. The woman threw her head back as deep rolls of laughter thundered from her mouth. A long swath of raven hair swirled around her. A gown of crimson damask clung to her ample bosom. She'd heard stories of this one.

"Salome, what did this village do to merit such destruction?"

"Nothing. I grew bored."

"You are as cruel now as a demon as you were in your human life."

Salome cackled, a sinister smirk curving her lips. "Some say crueler. Especially when someone crosses me."

Kalli lunged for her, a growl ripping from her lips. She had to stop Salome.

"I *said* you were too late." Salome snapped a finger. Tendrils of black-and-gray smoke swirled around her. When it had cleared, Salome was gone.

"What in the deities?" Kalli had never seen a *Peragrans* like that before. No mists, no snow, no ice or frost. Only that thick, dark smoke. Was it even a *Peragrans* at all?

Kalli searched the village. Thatched huts smoldered everywhere. The people huddled together, soot covering their faces. No one appeared to be injured. Not the Infernati way at all.

"What happened here?" Kalli asked, scanning the crowds.

"She's a witch," mumbled someone from the crowd. "Why else would the demons themselves come to take her away?"

Cursed humans and their backward ways. "Who?"

"Josephine." A girl, no more than twelve, wiped soot from her cheek. She pointed down toward a blazing cottage.

"Aren't you going to do something?"

One of the men shrugged, indifference clouding his face. "A right fitting end for a witch, I say."

The scent of brimstone still lingered. Bloody hell. They'd been enraptured by the Infernati.

"Well, you all might see a witch, but I still see a person who needs help." She grabbed her dagger and kept it poised in front of her.

"You're a witch too! We should've known." The crowd lunged for her. She slashed and stabbed. It was worse than enrapturement. They were *animi mortui*. Dead souls. Human bodies controlled by demons. It was fights like this that caused her to truly despise the Infernati.

Slicing her way through the crowd, she made her way toward the burning straw-and-mud hut. With a final thrust, she pushed her way inside. She threw her hands at the door, charming the house with protection. The remaining dead pounded and shouted as they tried to enter.

Flames licked and flicked her skin. There was only a brief moment of pain until the skin healed itself—a minor inconvenience when saving a human life. The smoke billowed. Coughing and sputtering, she swiped the smoke from her face.

She sucked in a deep breath and exhaled toward the fire. The long blast of air extinguished the fire.

She pushed through the tight quarters, tripping over a broken table. "Is anyone here?"

A gurgling moan came from a pile of rubble in the back of the building. Kalli rushed forward and started digging through the ash and debris.

Then she saw the hand. A very feminine hand with blood trickling down its dainty fingers. Kalli reached out and took it in hers. She felt life, but it was fading fast. "Save yourself," the woman's garbled voice said.

If only she could. "No. I'd rather save you." With a wild frenzy, she threw rocks, wood, and dirt from the pile. Then the woman's face came in sight. A strand of blood-soaked flaxen hair hung across her brow. Her pale blue eyes pleaded.

Kalli's stomach roiled. She might be a demon, but she still had a heart.

"Please," she gasped. "My baby." She coughed, and

blood trickled from her mouth. Kalli flung more debris from the woman's body. What she saw chilled her to the bones.

"Your baby. It's gone."

A loud sob rent from her lips. "No!"

Kalli reached up and stroked the woman's brow. The wounds were too severe. She couldn't heal her. She shuddered. This wasn't an extermination. This was a deliberate act of vengeance. They wanted this woman dead for some reason. "I'm sorry."

"Husband. Please find him." She reached for the blood-soaked necklace around her neck. "Tell him I love him."

Kalli nodded. Reaching around the woman's neck, she untied the leather string. "I will."

The woman coughed as more blood dripped down her lips. She reached and grabbed Kalli's hand. "Please make it stop."

Kalli closed her eyes, fighting the tears that threatened to spill. She took the woman's hand and traced her fingertips along the woman's palm. She might not be able to save her, but she'd not let her suffer. Feeling the numbing energy flowing between them, she scooted next to the woman, still grasping her hand.

The woman breathed a deep sigh. "Thank you," she whispered. With that, she took her last breath.

Chapter 29

SERAH WIPED HER TEARS AND SAT UP ON THE BED. Scrubbing fingers through her tousled curls, she took a deep breath. Matthias was the one who robbed her of her memories. She couldn't change the past. It was what it was.

She looked across at the mirror and cringed. Mascara ran down her cheeks, her eyes red and swollen. She made Snooki's mug shot look like a centerfold. And Daniel would be back anytime. Not that she cared. She wasn't doing the show any more.

She didn't care about the contract. She'd find a way out of it. She only cared about her dignity. And that only held on by a single thread, thanks to Matthias Ambrose.

"Asshole."

Then again, maybe that's what they wanted. For her to give up. Too bad Nonni wasn't here. She always had a way to lift her spirits.

I did not raise you to give up, Nipotina. Serah sighed. No, she only ran away and hid their true nature. If that wasn't giving up, she didn't know what was.

"Why, Nonni?" She swiped her hand across her eyes to wipe away the mascara gone wild. "Why did you hide?"

Her necklace and watch warmed against her skin. She shook her head. Leave it to Nonni to communicate through jewelry. "Why?"

Because you needed to find yourself first. Now go into that kitchen and finish what you started.

With that, the necklace and watch cooled down. Nonni had left the building. Yep, vague as ever. But Nonni did have a point. She needed to step up and kick ass. She'd start with Matthias Ambrose first.

She patted her necklace. *Thanks, Nonni*. With that, she threw open the door and stormed out of the room. She needed to give him a piece of her mind.

She turned the corner to enter the kitchen.

"No!" she heard an anguished shout. The sound chilled her to the bone. She'd never heard a man sound so tormented in her life.

She froze. It was Matthias. He sat with head buried in his hands, his body wracking with sobs. Kalli sat next to him, her arm wrapped tight around his shoulders.

What on earth was going on? Was he that broken up about losing this mission?

He reached out and grabbed Kalli's shoulders. "The babe! What happened to our babe?"

Serah gasped. It wasn't the mission. It was a tragedy from his past. Matthias had been a father. He had a family. He had a wife. She shivered as prickles of guilt washed over her. She should be angry at him, but all she wanted to do was comfort him.

But Kalli was already there, offering him her shoulder. Serah sucked in a breath. What was Kalli doing here anyway?

Serah clenched her fists. What was coming over her? *Jealousy, that's what.*

Why in hell was she jealous? She should hate Matthias. He had kidnapped her, stolen her memories, and kept his dirty little secret. So what if he gave her the memories back. Too little, too late. She should hate him. But all she felt was pity.

"Salome took him. She sent him away. I tried to find him, but I never could. I assumed she killed him. That's her usual *modus operandi*."

"I had a son?" Matthias looked up at Kalli.

She reached for his hand. "Yes. I sensed a boy. Just know that I tried everything to find him."

Matthias nodded. "I know."

Serah had to get out of there. This wasn't her business, and, as secretive as Matthias had been about his past, he wouldn't want her there anyhow.

She turned to leave, bumping one of her hanging pots, the clamor echoing through the room. Great. No way was she getting out of this one.

Kalli looked up and Matthias turned to meet Serah's gaze, his onyx gaze still clouded with sorrow.

Matthias drew his lips straight, his jaw ticking. "Serah."

"I was going to start supper, but I can do it later." She'd never felt so out of place, to say nothing of feeling like an outsider in her own kitchen. Serah inched backward out of the room.

Kalli scratched her forehead, her eyebrows scrunched. "What the hell happened to you? You look like a raccoon."

"Nothing. I fell asleep in the back room and forgot I had makeup on."

Kalli arched an eyebrow. "Since when does sleep make your eyes all puffy like that?"

Kalli was always too smart for her own good. Even though Kalli said she couldn't read her mind, Serah often wondered. "I had that dream again."

"The fire?"

Matthias spun around, his gaze alert. "What fire?"

"It's a dream. I'm with Nonni in a closet. There's a fire and then I wake up."

Kalli let out a sharp breath. "Still, I don't like it." She leaned over to Matthias. "Everything okay here?"

"Yes, but there are complications with my assignment."

Kalli narrowed her gaze. "What sort of complications? I thought we got that issue resolved?"

"Another complication, I'm afraid."

Serah slunk backwards out of the room. Maybe she judged Matthias too soon. Maybe he really was trying to redeem himself.

"I know Serah can be stubborn at times and a bit thickheaded, but she's a good person and is in terrible need of protection."

"I don't deny she needs protection, but there are certain circumstances that prevent me from doing my job."

What was he trying to do? Set himself up for failure? After what she just witnessed, that was the last thing he needed right now. He needed something to keep him occupied. Something to ease his pain. She'd at least give him that.

"What sort of circumstances?" Kalli massaged the back of her neck. "Because the Fore-Demons are not ones who reassign missions that easily. Just ask Rafe."

Serah finally found her voice. "Matthias and I had a little disagreement earlier. It's nothing that a little compromise can't fix."

Kalli waggled her brows. "Oh, really?"

Serah rolled her eyes. "Not that sort of compromise. *Jeez.*"

"Oh, darn. Well, my job here is done. Lucy wanted me to check on you. Despite the mascara, things look fine." She brushed her fingertips over Serah's face. "There, all fixed."

Kalli reached back and loosened the leather thong that hung around her neck. She placed the pewter pendant that dangled from it on the counter and slid it toward Matthias. "Something tells me you need this more than I do."

"Thank you, Kalli."

"You're very welcome. I'm relieved actually. I was afraid I'd given Josephine an empty promise. I don't like breaking promises."

Kalli swiped a red dreadlock from her cheek and stood. She held out her hand. "I'm glad we're on the same side now. I always admired your abilities."

Matthias's lips curved into a wan smile. He took Kalli's hand in his and clasped it in a sturdy grip. He shook his head and stood, crushing Kalli to him in a tight hug. "Thank you. Thank you for easing her pain."

Serah's breath hitched and her heart clenched. Seeing him embrace Kalli sent her skin crawling. She shivered. Matthias was not her ideal man, but something about him called to her. And now he was attracted to Kalli. Then again, Serah had told him he made her sick earlier and that she never wanted to see him again. What did she expect?

Why the hell did she have to like him so much? After all, he was the one who almost had her killed.

Almost. Didn't he try to save you in the end?

Ugh! It was crazy what he did to her—what he still did. She shouldn't like him. He'd been a demon for hire and had obviously done terrible things in his past. Kidnapping her couldn't have been his worst crime. Why the hell did she care so much about him?

Even when he acted like a complete asshat, she cared. Absolutely crazy. She gritted her teeth and clenched her fists. Yep, she was pathetic.

Kalli pulled from the embrace first. She turned to Serah and arched a brow, a knowing smile curving her lips.

Yeah right, she couldn't read my mind. That expression said it all.

"If you scowl any harder, your face will stay like that forever."

"Sorry, I was just thinking really hard."

Kalli shrugged. "If you think any harder, diamonds are going to pop out of your ears." She yanked at her skimpy lace corset and blew a giant pink bubble.

"Are you saying I have a brain full of coal?" Serah crossed her arms. Then again, sometimes she felt like it.

"Good point. Not a very good quip, huh? As much as you try to hide the fact, there is more in your brain than you realize."

Kalli strode toward her and wrapped her arms around Serah, pulling her into a friendly embrace. "It's perfectly all right to be attracted to him," she whispered. "Just so you know, he's attracted to you too." She offered Serah a sly wink.

Yes, Kalli was much too shrewd for her own good.

With that, she pulled from their embrace. "Mind if I use your office? I know how all that poofing affects you."

Serah nodded. Secretly, she wished Kalli would stay.

She didn't want to be alone with him. Part of him scared her. Part of him intrigued her, and, well, the other part of him—she'd seen where that had ended up.

So what if they were attracted to each other? So what if he kissed like a professional? So what if she was more than eager to jump his bones?

He'd been a mercenary. He'd battled for both sides. What's not to say he wouldn't switch sides? Maybe he was playing both sides right now? After all, hadn't Balthazar said as much in the alley? That Matthias had upheld his part of the bargain?

And then there was Daniel with his always smiling disposition. Maybe they were working together?

"Thinking hard again?" Kalli asked, breaking her from her thoughts.

"Yeah, something like that."

"I'll leave you to it then." Kalli threw her hand up in a dismissive wave and strolled off toward the office, the door clicking shut behind her.

"Why did you do that?"

"Do what?"

"Cover for me."

"I wasn't covering for you." She crossed her arms in front of her. "I just didn't think it was the right time to discuss it."

Matthias nodded. "Well, thank you anyway."

"What*ever*," she said, attempting to sound indifferent. "Now, if you'll excuse me, I need to start supper."

Matthias blew out a breath and adjusted his shirt. Serah sighed. The naughty part of her wished it were still on the floor. "I need to talk to you about this, Serah."

It was not the time or the place to have thoughts like

that. And she definitely wasn't ready to discuss his involvement in her kidnapping either.

Serah crossed her arms. "I've got other things to deal with right now. The TV show, remember?"

"As you wish." He reached in his pocket and palmed his phone. "Rafael will be checking in soon anyway." He swiped his finger across the touch screen. "I might just call him myself."

"I'll let you know when supper is ready. Maybe then we can talk." She owed him that.

"Would you like me to get the pot at least?" Matthias offered a friendly smile. "I can't have my shirt drenched again."

"Fine, if you really want to."

"Yes, I want to."

"Knock yourself out." She handed him the pot.

Matthias took the pot beneath his arm and filled it with water. He carried the pot across the kitchen and set it on the stove. "I'll let you take care of the rest. You've seen what I can do to a kitchen."

"Don't remind me." She reached for the knob to light the burner.

Matthias reached for her shoulder. "Serah, are you sure you don't want to talk now?"

She stiffened. Part of her wanted to talk, but part of her still wanted to keep her distance. *For crying out loud, could anything go easy once in a while?*

"I'm not ready yet."

Matthias nodded, turned, and headed toward the office.

She twisted the knob to increase the flame. With a deep sigh, she leaned against the counter and stared into the placid pot of water. If only those molecules knew what was going to happen to them in a matter of minutes. If it was anything like what was going through her heart right now, she really felt bad for that pot, especially when the water started to boil out of control.

It was better this way. It had to be.

Chapter 30

"YE SHOULD GIE HIM SOME HAGGIS," FARQUHAR SAID, his voice meowing in her ear. Serah adjusted the Bluetooth headset to turn down the volume.

"That's just cruel."

"Wha's that sayin'? Don't knock it if ye haven't tried it."

"I have tried it."

"Wha'ever, lass." Farquhar sighed. "Why did ye no invite me tae dinner?"

"I just assumed you and Inanna would be busy elsewhere."

She stirred the sauce in the pan. She took a long breath, savoring the aroma of simmering tomatoes and spices. Her nose twitched. Something was off. She scanned the spices, spinning the rack. She never missed a spice before. Stupid Matthias. Now he was affecting her ability to cook.

She took a spoon and dipped it into the sauce. Maybe tasting it would help narrow the problem down. She brought the spoon to her lips.

Ick! She'd never tasted anything so vile in her life. The tomatoes had been fresh. Not a spot on them. Yet it tasted like rotten goat cheese.

She spit out the sauce. No effing way. She should have known Matthias was up to something. She reached for the knob to turn down the flame. It would not budge.

The flames burst from beneath the pot. A giant bubble

burst, sending the stink up in the air. The rank odor of rancid Limburger cheese set her nostrils burning. The sauce continued to rumble and roil as the bubbles grew bigger. It was solidifying.

"My recipe didn't call for this."

She yanked open a drawer and grabbed the first implement she could. She gripped the shiny meat cleaver, ready to strike.

"Get the hell out of my kitchen," she shouted, waving the cleaver in front of her.

A low, primitive growl was the demon's response. He, she, or whatever it was, kept growing out of the pot, as thick plumes of black smoke swirled around it. The pot was like a magic lamp, but the genie coming out wasn't so nice.

Two arms formed, the thick red sauce dripping onto her floor. Her sauce was indeed ruined.

"I said get the hell out."

"I was invited," the demon gurgled out, its head popping up like a bubble. "I don't have to leave."

And from what she remembered, the Infernati made their own rules anyway. And who exactly invited this freak? Matthias? Daniel? Kalli? Nah, Kalli had better taste than that.

"Wha' is wrang?" Farquie's Sottish burr rang urgency in her ear.

In all her excitement, she forgot the imp was on the phone. "I got a problem with the sauce."

"Wha' kind o' problem?"

"It's attacking me."

"Wha'?"

The demon in the pot spewed hot sauce from its

mouth, spraying her in the face. With a deep sardonic roar of laughter, the demonic marinara man leapt from the pot and lunged for her.

"It's a demon," she breathed.

The demon lashed out its hand, more sauce spraying in every direction.

Serah managed to duck to the ground and roll across the floor. With a quick leap up, she pulled open a drawer and yanked out another tool. Gripping the spatula tight in one hand, the cleaver in the other, she somersaulted across the checkered floor and jumped to her feet.

"Where's yer bodyguard?" Farquhar asked in her ear. Thank goodness she still had reception.

"I kicked him out of the kitchen," she managed in between ragged breaths.

"Inanna an' Ah are on our way."

She wouldn't risk her friends' lives. "No. I have it under control. Stay there."

"Ye sure?"

"Yeah, I'll call you right back." She clicked the end button and stuffed the phone in her pocket.

With fluidity she didn't know she possessed, she snapped back her arm and let the meat cleaver fly. It cut clean through the demon's saucy head, slicing it into two. More sauce spewed across the room.

"Got you now you demonic pile of crap."

The demonic roar of laughter echoed—quite literally—throughout the kitchen. *What the hell?* Serah glanced upwards, her heart plummeting. The sauce separated, and two equally menacing demons formed from the ooze.

Things aren't ever that easy.

"Arrgh!" the twin demons bellowed in unison. Their fangs glinted with menace. Serah had never seen fangs that long and sharp. What kind of demons were these things? Then again, she didn't have time to figure that out. She had to defend herself. Talk about a kitchen nightmare.

"There's more where that came from." Serah launched the silver-plated spatula right between one of demon's glowing red eyes.

It dodged to the right, the spatula barely scraping its ear. Throwing back its head, it let out a deep chortle. The other demon joined in, lunging at her. This was getting worse by the minute. She had to do something.

"You will die!" it growled out. More sauce swirled, its body fully regenerating. It slashed out its hand, snagging her by the ankle. More demonic laughter rang in her ears as it pulled her toward the pot. What was it going to do, boil her to death? The other demon grabbed her other leg, helping its twin drag her across the checkered floor.

Oh, God. She really had to do something now. But how?

She couldn't let this self-replicating demon win. It was bad enough it had already ruined her prize-winning sauce. She gripped the legs of the buffet with all her strength. No way was she giving up that easily.

Then she heard it. The door flew open. A warm gust blew into the room. Had Matthias found a way to break the demon code and enter somewhere he wasn't welcome? She sure hoped he had.

"Let go ov her!" the rich feminine accent sang through the air. *Edie?*

"Edie!" Serah shouted, fear creeping through her veins. "Get out!"

"No! You need help." Her tone remained calm, yet strangely assertive. "Zee demons must be stopped."

"How do you know—"

"Zere iz no time for talk. Use zee necklace."

Serah blinked. *She knew about the necklace? What was she?* She craned her neck for a glance at her sous-chef.

Edie threw her hands in the air, a giant ball forming between her palms. She closed her eyes. Cloaked in a flowing purple toga instead of her usual chef's jacket, she threw her head back. Her red hair swirled around her face. Warmth emanated from her body. She'd felt that warmth once before. When she met Minerva.

Another goddess? No freaking way! Then again, she didn't have time to contemplate it. She needed to vanquish these pesky demons.

"Use it!" Edie implored. "Now!" With that, she threw the giant ball of violet energy at the demon on the right. It howled and screamed, then burst into a million pieces of light and vanishing with a loud burst of air. Edie fell back and crumpled to the ground.

Serah had no choice but comply. She allowed her own warmth to pool around her neck and spread through the rest of her body. She looked down. The diamonds in her necklace sparkled and glowed. What was going on?

The locket continued to radiate, the heat and energy coursing through her entire body. Her head pounded and her toes tingled.

Close your eyes, someone whispered in her head.

Serah wasn't in a position to argue, so she squeezed her eyes shut.

Harness the power. Control it.

How in the hell did she do that? It wasn't like she'd

done yoga or anything to become one with her inner chi. She'd have better luck milking a billy goat.

The answer is in your heart. She didn't have time for this cryptic shit. She needed to kick some Infernati ass. Why did everything have to be so danged confusing?

She kept her eyes closed. In her heart, huh? Fancy that particular organ thumped wildly against her rib cage. She took a deep breath. With that, she concentrated on her heart. She visualized all the warmth of her body surrounding it, pouring energy into it. Confidence pounded its way through her veins. She kicked out her foot, sending the demon reeling back.

The demon grunted and righted itself. Wiping some trickling red sauce from its brow, it hunched low.

"Die, Pure-Blood bitch!"

"Uh, no thank you."

"Arrgh!" It lunged forward again.

Serah dove to the left, slamming against the side of the buffet. Adrenaline pumped through her body, her pain at the back of her thoughts. She didn't need a bodyguard after all. She was doing fine all by herself.

"Ha. Ha. Ha! Got you now." The walking mound of marinara spread his slimy lips into a mocking grin. Slithering along the ground, it reached out and grabbed Serah by her shoulders and turned her to face it.

Heart still pounding and full of energy, Serah stood her ground. Feet firmly planted to the floor, she stood tall.

"Isn't that pot a little small for both of us?"

"Where you're going, size doesn't matter."

She knew what she had to do. It was time to trust her heart. "I'm not going anywhere."

"Oh, yes you are, and I'm going to take you there."

She squared her shoulders. "No, I'm not." With that, she closed her eyes. She sent all her heart-energy shooting through her body, right to where the locket rested on her collar. She threw her head back and let the energy rush through her.

"Aggggh!" the demon gurgled. "What have you done?"

She opened her eyes. The sauce-man flailed its arms as flames lashed out from beneath it. It lunged forward in a last-ditch attempt to take her to hell with it.

Serah spun out of his grasp and snatched another sharp knife from the counter.

"I'm pretty sure I just vanquished your ass. See ya, wouldn't wanna be ya." She sent the knife flying, lodging deep in the demon's chest.

"Bitch," it garbled out. With that, it burst, sending marinara sauce spraying across the kitchen walls.

She slumped against the counter, tightly gripping the edge. *What in the hell had just happened?* She turned toward the counter and rushed toward Edie. Leaning down, she brushed a wisp of hair from her cheek. She hoped she wasn't dead. Then again, if she was a goddess, Edie was probably immortal.

"Are you okay?"

Edie murmured, her eyelids fluttering open. She reached up, and brushed a fingertip across Serah's chin. "*Oui!* Now that you are safe."

"What goddess are you?"

Edie sat up and stretched out her arms. "You should know. I'm a good cook."

"I thought Bacchus was a guy."

Edie rolled her eyes. "He's the god of wine. I am the

goddess of food." She sighed. "Unfortunately, I'm not that well-known." Her sigh turned into a smile. "Not that I shouldn't be. I've helped so many famous chefs achieve their lifelong goals."

"Well?"

"Edesia's my name. Food is my game." She stood up, allowing her garments to billow about her. "I'm not supposed to be here. I just wanted to make sure you remained safe. I owed it to your grandmother—to you!"

Her grandmother was a blessed woman, in more ways than one. "So, you're the goddess of food?"

"*Oui!* I am!" Edie smiled. "But you do not need much help with that."

"Thanks, I think."

"You're welcome."

A loud pounding echoed on the door. Matthias's voice boomed. "Serah! Are you okay? Let me in!"

"I must go. Matthias, he is a good man. He will take care of you." With that, Edie spun around, allowing the warm mists to envelop her. A loud pop echoed in the air and then she was gone.

Serah flew backward from the percussion, only to find herself caught by two very muscular arms. Her head crashed back against more muscles. The familiar scent of ginger and spice wafted to her nose. Matthias. Had he seen Edie?

"Edie," she murmured.

"Edie isn't here." A gentle hand swept a blob of sauce from her cheek. He took her into his arms and cradled her against his chest. Fingers laced into her hair, stroking her neck. Maybe Edie was right.

Letting out a deep sigh, she snuggled up against his hard, muscled chest. "I'm just going to order a pizza instead," she whispered, as the events of the ordeal finally took their toll.

Chapter 31

"WHAT THE HELL?" SERAH MUMBLED, RUBBING HER temples. She groaned as she fought to open her eyes.

"Shh," Matthias whispered, pressing a warm cloth to her forehead. He brushed a strand of hair from her cheek and dabbed away some rancid sauce.

"The demon," she moaned. She attempted to pull herself up. "Edie."

Matthias placed a gentle hand on her shoulder. "Edie isn't here."

"Goddess—Edesia."

"Shh," Matthias murmured. His breath hitched. "Goddess? Another one?"

She forced her eyes open, grabbing Matthias's shoulder. "You did it, didn't you?"

Matthias's gaze narrowed. He stepped away from her. "No. If I wanted to kill you, you'd be dead already." He turned to the window. "And I sure as hell wouldn't have had another demon do the job."

He did have a point. He was a trained mercenary. He knew how to kill. But he had also kidnapped her. What's not to say he wasn't still working for the Infernati?

Then again Edie had said he was a good man. She was a goddess. Weren't goddesses all-knowing? And why did she want it kept a secret? She shook her head. After a year of all this weirdness, she knew better than to question things.

"I need a shower," Serah mumbled, taking a whiff of her sauce-covered chef's jacket. "I smell like I fell in a sewer."

"I called Kalli for cleanup."

"Thank you."

Matthias crossed his arms. "It wasn't me, Serah. I swore to the Fore-Demons and Rafael that I would protect you. I might have done some reprehensible things in my past, but one thing I've never done is broken my word."

"Balthazar doesn't seem to think so."

"I did what was asked. They were the ones who broke the vow."

"I'm still trying to understand why."

Matthias took a deep breath. "It's complicated." He took a seat next to her on the bed. "I don't expect forgiveness. I wouldn't forgive myself either."

"I just want the truth." Serah sat up in the bed. "You owe me that at least."

"If I said you couldn't handle the truth, would you understand?"

"Sorry, that line's already been used." She reached down and slid a finger across a splash of sauce. "If I can handle a demon in a pot, I think I can handle what you're hiding."

Matthias nodded. "I kidnapped you, but not for money. I was already planning on retiring before the Infernati contacted me."

"How noble of you. You did it for free." Serah rolled her eyes. "Not a good way to get on my good side."

"I did not do it for free."

"Then what did you do it for? Notoriety?"

"You said you wanted to know. Let me tell you."

"Fine. What did the Infernati have on you that was so bad you needed to kidnap a Pure-Blood?"

"I didn't know you were a Pure-Blood. I thought you were just the succubus's friend."

"So that makes it okay?"

"No. I am not saying that at all. If I knew their true intentions I would have turned down the mission."

"It still doesn't make it right."

"I know!" He reached out and grabbed her hand. She should have pulled away, but instead she allowed him that one touch. "Let me explain."

"Okay. I won't say another word, unless you ask."

Matthias nodded. "I was married before. I joined Emperor Frederick II in 1228 to go on his crusade."

"The Holy Roman Empire?" She had gone to Catholic school, after all.

Matthias nodded. "I was raised near Münster, in modern-day Germany."

"Like the cheese?"

Matthias scowled. "No, unfortunately not. Let me continue. My wife, she never told me she was with child."

Serah cringed as he told the story. How he'd taken a blade through his chest. How he thought an angel was taking him to the Promised Land. But it wasn't an angel. She was a demon. She'd turned him into a demon for her own pleasure. Serah's stomach roiled.

Salome. She remembered the story from her years at Catholic school. It was only fitting that Salome would choose the Infernati in her demonic afterlife.

"She showed me what the Paladins had done to my village. It had been burnt to the ground. My wife had been torn to pieces, she said. Then she told me about the babe. How she tried to save it."

But she had lied. Kalli had shown him the truth. How the villagers had been manipulated by the Infernati. How they tried to kill her. Kalli had shown him his wife's final moments, how she eased her pain.

But one thing disturbed Serah the most. The baby had been ripped from his mother, quite literally. She clenched her fists. Of all the sick and demented things she'd heard in her life, this had to be the worst.

"I'd always believed the baby had died. I'd been conditioned to believe the Paladins had killed everyone in the village. The truth is, Salome killed Josephine and our child because I chose them instead of her."

"That's disgusting."

"Kalli happened to be in the area and she saw the fire. The villagers attacked her as she rushed to my wife's aid. Unfortunately, she was too late." A tear crested along his eyelid, ready to drop. "Kalli had to burn the village. They'd been changed to *animi mortui*."

"Sorry, my Latin stinks."

"Dead souls—zombies."

Yuck! And here she thought zombies were only a voodoo creation. *Who knew?* "So what does all this have to do with kidnapping me?"

"Salome never killed my son."

"She raised him as her own?"

Matthias shrugged. "I haven't any idea. Kalli said she'd tried tracking him for years, but she never found anything."

"And Kalli's a pretty good tracker, from what I've heard."

"Salome can be pretty sneaky. She's evaded quite a few trackers over the centuries. No one knows quite how she does it."

"Okay, so go on."

"Belial called me in. He knew I was planning on retiring. He told me he had an offer I couldn't refuse."

Offers like that never boded well. "What sort of offer? Your prized horse's head in your bed?"

"I should have known something was amiss with that sort of offer, but I knew one thing. When Belial wants something, he gets it—one way or the other."

"What was the offer?"

"I was to kidnap you or my only remaining descendant would die."

Serah's heart plummeted. Her stomach heaved. She wasn't sure she'd react any differently if she were in his shoes. "Oh."

"He said Salome had hidden the child so the Paladin couldn't find him. I didn't believe him at first. After all, Salome had told me they both had died." Matthias sucked in a ragged breath. "But he had proof. He had the babe's swaddling cloth and a toy Josephine and I had bought shortly after we were wed to prepare for the family we wanted."

"How horrible."

Matthias nodded. "I took the mission, but when I saw the mark on your hand, I knew what they were planning."

She looked down at her hand. She'd never seen the scar until after she and Lucy had opened the chest. It freaked her out. She hated it. "So when you found out I was the world's biggest superhero, you decided to change sides?"

"I was already planning to change sides." Matthias pushed a curl off her brow. "You are more important to the world alive. If you died, the world could have died with you. If I saved you, I would also help save the world."

"Either that, or you've watched one too many episodes of *Heroes*."

"Is there a need to be so flippant?"

"It's just something I do. I think I've been hanging around Lucy too much."

"Lucy can be a tad sarcastic at times, huh?"

Serah nodded. "She sure can. So you did this all to save the world, eh?"

"Yes." He sucked in a deep breath. "But there's a part of me that did it for myself too, Serah."

"What do you mean?"

"There's something about you that draws me to you." Matthias's onyx eyes sparkled. "When I kissed you, I meant it."

Serah's heart thudded. She didn't have the guts to tell him she meant it too, even when he held her captive. Heck, he still held her captive. "I'm glad."

Matthias quirked a brow. "You're glad?"

"Yes," Serah replied with a smile. "I like meaningful kisses." God, she sounded so lame.

"Why do you try to hide from your true nature?"

Serah froze. Now that was a bomb she didn't need him to drop right now. "Huh?"

"I just bared my soul to you. I think it's only fair that you do the same."

She gnawed her lip. Damn him for always making an excellent point. She'd been hiding all her life, it seemed. Nonni always kept her protected. She gulped.

"The dream I mentioned to Kalli?"

Matthias nodded. "I remember."

"It's not a dream."

Matthias nodded. "I imagine it's more of a nightmare. They are easily overcome."

"It's not a nightmare either. It's reality." She took a deep breath. "I was young—just turned four. I don't remember much, but what I do remember has haunted me my entire life."

"What happened?"

"My family was visiting Nonni. We were all playing Candy Land. I had just passed Lord Licorice's Castle." She clasped her hands together and wrung her fingers. "Nonni was just about to draw a card when we heard a loud hiss.

"I was about to ask what it was. Before I could, Nonni jumped up and grabbed me. She rolled into the closet and threw a blanket over us. Just then, the entire house exploded.

"My parents weren't so fortunate. They didn't make it to safety in time. Nonni was my only living relative, so she took me in.

"I remember hearing the fireman say it was a gas leak. Shortly after, Nonni packed up our remaining things, and we moved to Michigan."

"It wasn't a gas leak."

Serah sucked in a ragged breath. "I figured as much. Especially the way Nonni packed up in the middle of the night. Later on, when I got older, I thought maybe she was hiding from the mob." Serah snickered. "We are Italian, after all."

"If only it were the Mafia. Your chances would have been better."

"Thanks for boosting my confidence."

"But you still haven't answered my question. Why do you keep denying your destiny? The world needs you."

"I'm not a hero. I'm not that smart. I do dumb things. I gave my half-demon friend a cursed chest, after all."

"You put it in safe hands, from what I can tell."

"I helped destroy her shop. If it weren't for Kalli, Lucy's shop would still be under water."

"Things happen for a reason. There are no coincidences."

"I killed Nonni."

Matthias blinked. "What do you mean? I was told she died of a stroke. Hardly something that you could have caused."

"It was the day of my birthday. Usually I spent the evening with Nonni, playing cards and watching old movies." She wiped tears from her cheek. "Nonni called and said I didn't have to come if I didn't want to. She knew someone had given me tickets to a concert and she didn't want me to miss my favorite band. I felt guilty the whole time. I didn't enjoy the concert at all."

"What happened?"

"The hospital called me. Nonni had a stroke and was on life support." Serah couldn't stop the tears. They fell from her lids, down her cheeks. She gulped. "I stayed by her bedside. I never gave up hope. But Nonni had always told me she never wanted to live like that. So, when the doctors told me there was nothing more they could do, I had them turn off the machines.

"She said to me once that if she wasn't able to see

me through to my destiny, she'd find a way. I guess this is her way." Serah reached down and ran her fingertips across the locket.

"Your Nonni loved you very much. You're lucky to have had her." Matthias ran his hand across her forehead.

"I can't help but think that there's more." She brushed her fingertip across the locket, one stone jiggling at her touch. "Oh no. A stone's loose."

"Huh?"

"One of the diamonds. It's loose." She wiggled her finger over the stone, just like a kid would wiggle her first loose tooth. The stone popped out. Serah caught the diamond in her hand.

All of a sudden the locket flew open. "What the hell?" God, she was really starting to hate that expression.

"There's something inside," Matthias said, pointing to the now-open locket.

Serah took the locket and turned it over. On one side was a picture of her mother. On the other side, a folded piece of paper. Serah took out the paper. Behind it was a picture of her father. Shaking her head, she brushed her fingertips across their photos—the only reminder she had of them.

Unfolding the paper, she breathed in deeply. She squinted to read the ornate print.

"Damn it, Nonni. You know I can't read Latin."

"Do you need me to translate?"

Serah nodded. She went to hand the letter to Matthias, until she caught a glimpse of some of the words.

"Wait." On second thought, maybe she didn't need a translator after all. Tracing her fingertips across the words, she read. "Actually, I don't!"

The key is in your hand. Stand Watch and Face your fears.

"The key is in my hand?" Serah groaned. "Stand watch and face my fears?" Her Nonni couldn't have been any more cryptic. It was her specialty. Sadly enough, Serah missed it.

"Can I have a look?"

"Have at it." She handed him the scrawled note. "I'm as clueless as I was before the locket opened."

She glanced down at the locket, looking at the tiny hole where the stone once fit. Picking the stone up with her fingertips, she placed it in the empty socket. The locket snapped shut and locked.

"It's the key!"

"What?"

"The stone." She brushed her fingertips across the stone again. It loosened and fell, the locket snapping back open. "See?"

Matthias nodded. He plucked the stone from Serah's hand and looked closer. "There are two tiny prongs at the bottom. Not visible to the *human* eye."

She took the stone back and held it up to the light. Sure enough, two silver prongs jutted from the setting. "But how come I can see them?"

"Let me rephrase: They are not visible to the *normal* human eye."

"Of course," she said with a snort. "But what does 'stand watch and face your fears' mean?" Serah threw up her hands. "I'm stumped."

Matthias reached up and snatched her wrist, his hand encircling her watch. "Your grandmother was clever."

"Huh?"

Matthias pointed at the *W* on the slip of paper. "Look. *Watch* is capitalized." He then moved to the *F*. "And so is *face*, but none of the other words are written that way."

"I hate to blow a hole in your theory, but my grandmother wasn't very good at grammar."

Matthias shook his head. "I think it was deliberate." He examined her watch. "There." He pointed to a spot on the watch. "See the gap there?"

Serah glanced down to where Matthias pointed. A tiny spot, but it was still large enough for the stone to fit. She took the stone and placed it in the gap. It snapped into place.

The watch face creaked open, revealing another compartment. Serah glanced inside. Sure enough, there was another folded piece of paper. She reached in and plucked it out. "Another note, it appears."

She unfolded it and began to read.

> *My Dear Seraphina,*
>
> *Let me start out by saying how incredibly sorry I am that I left you without answers. I thought I was protecting you. My time is drawing near and I don't want to keep you in the dark any longer. I just hope it isn't too late.*
>
> *You have now discovered the key to unlock your destiny. I wish it didn't have to be this way. I wish I had made different choices. After the fire, I decided to run. I thought that keeping you hidden was the only way to protect you. I was wrong.*
>
> *As you have already figured out, you have*

special abilities, as do I, and your great-grandmother before me. It is believed that we have a rather angelic ancestry. Every female born from this line has had these powers. I tried to mask ours and hide in the shadows, but I now see how wrong that was.

I know you enjoy your uncomplicated life. But life needs to be lived to its fullest. And sometimes complications help us grow to become better people.

You are destined for great things. I do not want you to have regrets, as I did. Claim your destiny. Do not cower in fear.

Love,
Nonni

"Wow." She handed Matthias the note. "Apparently an angel is my great-great-great-a couple times over great-grandmother."

Matthias shook his head, a wide smirk curving his lips. "I knew there was a reason Minerva took such an interest in you. Angels are known for their wisdom."

"Looks like you and my grandmother have a lot in common."

"What's that?"

"You both were trying to save your only descendants."

"There's one difference."

"What?"

"She's going to succeed."

Serah's heart clenched. In all the excitement, she'd forgotten that he'd given up his descendant for her. "Oh God, I'm so sorry."

Matthias shook his head, brushing her tears from her cheeks. "Don't be sorry. I made this decision, not you."

"I know, but it still must be hard for you."

"I told Balthazar that I'd risk my remaining blood if it meant saving the world from the Infernati. I still feel that way." He'd sucked in a long breath. "Sure, it hurts that I will see my lineage die, but the world will be a better place."

"There has to be a way to save them."

"That's the problem. I don't even know if this descendant is male or female. And Belial and Balthazar weren't that forthcoming with information. I don't even know if what they told me was true."

She had to do something for him. She felt in her heart that this descendant did exist. He risked his life to protect her. She owed him something. "I know they're out there, Matthias. I can feel it."

"What are you saying?"

"I'm saying that we're going to save the world... your descendant included."

Chapter 32

"I DON'T EVEN KNOW WHERE TO START. THEY COULD be anywhere in the world."

"You have something that belongs to them."

"What?"

"This." She reached out and traced her fingertip across the pendant dangling from Matthias's neck. "It belonged to your wife, so it would belong to your descendants after her death."

"Kalli said she tried tracking the child for several years after the incident."

"Even you said Salome was sneaky, but one thing may have changed. Maybe the descendant is far away from her. Maybe Kalli will have better luck now."

"It is indeed and interesting theory."

"Kalli grows bored at the salon. A mission like this might liven things up for her."

"If she's up for it."

Serah grinned. "This is Kalli. She lives for this sort of adventure."

He admired her willingness to help out, even after she'd discovered his dark secret. But he would not put her friends in danger. The best way to protect Serah was to protect those she cared about as well.

"I'd rather take care of my own family problems." He reached out and took Serah's hand in his. "You should understand that, right?"

Serah nodded. "I do." She reached out and took his hand with her other, softly stroking. The sensation of peace washed over him. God, he loved all the feelings Serah evoked in him.

"But what do we do about Daniel?" Serah asked. "Have you talked to Rafe yet?"

"I talked to him earlier. Lucy and he are on their way. The phantoms haven't seen anything out of the ordinary." Matthias blew out a breath. Something about Daniel didn't add up. He was too perfect. One thing he'd learned over the years—no one was perfect, especially those who seemed too perfect. But the vibe that Matthias got was one from someone who was clean of conscience. He'd never felt a vibe quite like that and still had doubts. "Daniel went back to his hotel. Nowhere else. It looks like he's heading back now."

He decided it was best to let Serah know his thoughts. "I have concerns about Daniel. I've heard about this before. Humans who have been influenced by the Infernati."

"So he's a minion?"

"Worse. Minions know the Infernati to be evil and join anyway. There are others who are led astray by lies and trickery. They've been taught that the Paladins are the problem and the Infernati are the ones doing the world good." He clenched his fists. In a way, he'd been tricked the same way. Unfortunately for Salome, that plan had backfired. He never fully joined their sick and twisted cause.

"They genuinely believe they are doing the right thing." Matthias ground his teeth. He truly hated what the Infernati had done to humans. More than ever. Especially what they were trying to do to Serah. But for some reason, even Daniel's situation frustrated him. And he didn't know why.

Then again, he was a Paladin now. That's why. He was one of the good guys now—of course he'd take things more personally.

"Everything okay?"

Matthias nodded. "Sorry. It's my first mission with the Paladins, so I guess I'm taking it a little personally."

"Makes complete sense, actually." Serah smiled. "I've noticed one thing about working with the Paladins. You all tend to take missions very personally."

What did that mean? Then again, they had sex. You couldn't get any more personal than that. But even Serah had said it was just sex. And he saw how she interacted with Daniel. He wanted her to act that way with him, damn it.

"We are dedicated to our cause. Is that so wrong?"

"Not in the least." A cold blast of air swung the door open. "Looks like Rafe's here."

Matthias nodded. "Why don't you go catch a quick shower and get cleaned up?" He brushed a tomato chunk from her hair. "And I was starting to get excited about that casserole too. Leave it to the Infernati to ruin my supper."

"I'll make it up to you, I promise." With that, Serah pushed open a door in the far corner of the room. If only he could join her and make it up to her.

With a deep sigh of regret, Matthias strode out of the makeshift bedroom. Rafe stood in the kitchen with arms crossed, his glare penetrating. "What the hell happened here?"

"A demon got in, that's what."

Rafe nodded. "Marinara sauce? The Infernati get more creative as the days pass by. Has Kalli been notified?"

"Yes." Matthias snickered. "As have Farquhar and his playmate."

Rafe grabbed Matthias by the collar of his shirt. "How did this happen?"

"It wasn't me."

"Why would I think it was you?"

"I don't know. Maybe the way you are grabbing my shirt and glaring at me?"

"Oh, sorry." Rafe let go of the shirt and straightened the collar. "She's Lucy's friend, and I have yet to trust you completely."

"With reason."

"What's that supposed to mean?"

"I'm surprised that Serah hasn't told Lucy or you yet."

"Told us what?"

Matthias knew he should tell Rafe. Of all the Paladins, he should understand. After all, he'd had his own share of familial issues. "The assassin who kidnapped Serah?"

"You know who it was?"

Matthias nodded. "I do."

"Who?"

"It was me."

"I knew I couldn't trust you." Rafael gritted his teeth and with the swiftness only a demon could possess, he plowed his fist into Matthias's jaw.

Matthias reeled backwards. He would not retaliate. He would not fight back. After all, he deserved the beat-down Rafael was sure to give him.

Rafael swung again, this time catching him in the eye. "Why aren't you fighting back?"

"I deserve it."

Rafael growled and slammed him in the gut. "You better start explaining yourself, or I'll send you back to the Council, one piece at a time."

"I'd like an explanation too."

Lucy stood there, hands on her waist. Her amber eyes flickered. "And why is there spaghetti sauce splattered across the walls? Did Serah lose control of her powers again?" She took a deep whiff of the air in the kitchen. "Never mind an explanation. I need a big explanation."

"Someone invited a demon in." Rafe tossed a sidelong glance toward Matthias.

"Who?"

"Not me," Matthias murmured. "I care for... this mission. For the first time I feel alive. Free."

"Why don't you tell Lucy what else you did? She will find it as interesting as I did."

A deep scowl furrowed Lucy's brow. "What did you do?"

They weren't making this easy for him. Then again, he didn't deserve easy. "I was the one who kidnapped Serah."

"You did what?" Lucy's eyes flamed. "Fucking priceless. The Fore-Demons really messed up this time. Everything they do, they do for a reason? I'd really like to know their reasoning for this."

"I truly do not know," Rafael replied, crashing into one of the barstools. "But I told Matthias he could explain."

"Explain how he kidnapped my best friend and delivered her to one of the high princes of hell?" Lucy snorted. "It better be a damned good one."

He wasn't one to air his dirty laundry, but if it got

them to understand, he'd hang it from the highest pole. "It started the day I was turned demon."

And he told the story again. He'd recite the whole bloody history, as much as he had to, if it would make them understand. He watched both Rafe and Lucy cringe as he related what Kalli had told him. How he'd been led to believe the Paladins had done it. How Salome had tried tricking him. But her plan had backfired. Instead of joining the Infernati, he hadn't chosen a side at all.

Then he talked about Belial. How he blackmailed him into taking the kidnapping assignment. How he used his last descendant as leverage.

"But I swear to you that as soon as I found out what Serah was, I knew what I had to do. I wanted to be a Paladin. And certainly a Paladin would choose to save the world, not just one descendant."

Rafael nodded. "They would. It is a hard decision to let your family go. One I know well."

Lucy flashed a sympathetic smile toward her fiancé and wrapped her arms around him. "I always knew something was up. Serah isn't the type to forget. She remembers the strangest things, like what Fergie wore to the Grammys five years ago. Have you told her?"

Matthias nodded. "I did. I gave her the memories back, but I should have done it sooner. I waited too long."

Rafael's gaze narrowed. "You slept with her, didn't you?"

"Rafe!" Lucy shouted, slapping him on the shoulder. "Jeez!"

Matthias nodded. "I did. We both got caught up in the moment. It was just sex. She has feelings for Daniel."

"Daniel?"

"They had chemistry. I saw it in the way they worked together."

"They were cooking. Serah could have chemistry with a turtle if you hand it a whisk. She isn't the type to just fall in bed on a whim."

Could have fooled me. Then again, he wasn't complaining.

"No. This is different. They have a connection."

Lucy shook her head. "She would have told me if that was the case."

"What did she tell you?" Matthias asked.

"She said he was friendly and nice but when he started asking questions about her life in Chicago, she felt uncomfortable."

"I saw what I saw, but it doesn't matter," he said with a shrug. "I'm only here for her protection. I'll be assigned a new mission when this is done."

Rafael shook his head. "If you say so."

Lucy smirked. "Protecting Serah is a full-time job, my friend. You'll be here a while."

The fresh scent of orchids and spice wafted into the room. *God, she smells good, especially after a shower.* Heat pounded its way into his body, straight to his cock. He bit his tongue. Not now.

"Very funny, Lucy. I'm learning how to protect myself rather well." She ran her fingers through her damp curls. "Did Matty-boy here tell you how Edie and I took down the sauce thing all by ourselves?"

"Edie?" Lucy raised an eyebrow.

"I'll tell you later," Serah said with a nibble of her lip.

Lucy snorted. "Oh brother. Too bad your demonic cleaning skills aren't the greatest." Lucy traced her fingertip through a splash of sauce. She brought it to her nose and winced. "Ick. Poor sauce."

Serah shrugged and ran her fingers across her necklace. A cocky smile spread across her lips. "Whatever."

Matthias cringed. He knew one thing. When people became cocky, they became dangerous. "Serah, don't even think about it."

"Wow, only a day on the job and he already can read her mind." Lucy smirked. "Serah, you've got your hands full with this one."

Serah looked at her friends. Rafael's jaw ticked but Lucy had a lopsided grin. Serah's gaze widened. "You told them? Jeez! Is nothing private here?"

Rafael crunched his fist in his palm. "I am Matthias's handler. He is required to tell me *everything*."

"Well, don't worry. It won't happen again—right, Matthias?"

"Not if I want to stay on Rafael's good side." But he wasn't completely averse to the idea of succumbing to pleasure with her again. Not that he had a chance in hell of it ever happening again. If it kept her safe, he'd do another four centuries of celibacy—if he had to.

"Good answer, Ambrose." Rafael relaxed his stance.

"I know Matthias told me not to even think about it, but as I was showering an idea hit me and I wanted to try it out."

Lucy arched a brow. "Some of the best ideas come while in the shower." She rubbed her chin in thought. "Not sure where I heard that, but it sounded good. So what's your idea?"

"The necklace helped me vanquish the demon, right?"

Matthias nodded. "Yes, it did." He was proud of her,

yet slightly disappointed. Once she learned how to harness all of her powers, she wouldn't need him anymore. He'd have to move on to a new mission. He'd probably never see her again. Then again, after what he had done, she probably wouldn't want to see him anyway.

"Well, I figured I could use the necklace to do other things."

"If you are looking of ways to increase your productivity, I'd look elsewhere, hon," Lucy said with a chuckle. "Our powers are not to be overused." She turned to Rafe. "I assume the same thing goes for Pure-Bloods, right?"

Rafael nodded. "When people misuse their power, bad things happen. I've seen good demons—and humans—go bad."

Matthias couldn't agree more. He'd seen his fair share of power-hunger on both sides, Infernati and Paladin alike.

"How well you people know me. I was just going to try and harness some of that cleaning mojo Kalli likes to sling around."

"Well, that would make Kalli's life a little easier." Lucy smirked. "You know how she hates getting called at all hours of the day and night because some imp invaded your dinner party." She snorted. "Let's not forget that one wedding. That poor cake never stood a chance. I never knew an imp could throw that far."

Serah crossed her arms. "All these demons hate me just for being born. How fun is that?"

"It sucks, I imagine." Lucy certainly didn't sugar coat things, which oddly enough added to her charm.

"Fine, so you'll let me try it out then?"

"Sure, and if it doesn't work, it's nothing that a professional can't handle." Lucy pulled out her cell phone. "I've got Kalli ready on speed-dial."

"Thanks for the vote of confidence," Serah said with a frown.

He hated that frown. It made him shiver. He wished she could never frown again. He reached out and took her hand in his. "I know you don't particularly care for me right now, but I know you can do it."

"Well, at least one person trusts me." She leaned in and whispered, "Thanks." She gave him a quick peck on the cheek. What was that for? His whole body sizzled. Sparks flew through his veins. Bloody hell.

"Here goes nothing." She closed her eyes and stood tall. She threw her hands up in the air, and her head flew back. With that, a large burst of light flew from the necklace, bathing the entire kitchen with warmth. The shimmers of light trickled away to reveal a brilliantly clean kitchen. The counters and floor sparkled. Every utensil and pot gleamed bright. It was so clean that Matthias could eat off the floor if need be. She could definitely give one of the Paladin's best cleaners a run for their money.

"Is it safe to open my eyes now?"

Lucy and Rafael stood there, mouths agape—just as amazed as he was.

"Well?"

Lucy finally found her voice. "It's safe. Really safe."

Serah inched her eyes open. "Wow!" she gasped. "I did that?" She covered her mouth, shock still evident in her gaze.

Matthias nodded. She was indeed special. He would do

everything in his power to keep her safe. He owed it to her. He owed her his life. She helped him in so many ways.

"You are an amazing woman, Serah SanGermano."

"If you think I'm amazing, you should have met my Nonni." She smiled, her hand drifting across the locket again. "She wanted to protect me."

"We all make mistakes, Serah." And he was living proof of that. He'd made the biggest mistake when he accepted that mission. He wished he could take it back—every bit of it. But what was done was done. He'd live with it. Then again, what other choice did he have?

"You did what you thought you had to do to save your family. My Nonni did the same thing."

Matthias nodded. "I wish we could have met under different circumstances, Serah. Believe that."

"I do."

"Good."

Lucy cleared her throat. "We're still here, you know. Should we get back to business?

"A few of the phantoms are hovering around the hotel to check for anyone or anything that seems out of place. So far, nothing. Either this guy's record is extremely clean, or he is working for a demon who is."

"I'm betting on the last one," Matthias added.

Rafael's expression grew pensive. "Oh?"

"He mentioned my name to the person he was talking to on the phone." He hadn't thought much of it at the time, but now that he did, it made perfect sense.

"So it could be a demon who knows you?" Serah asked.

Rafael smirked. "There isn't a demon—Infernati or Paladin—who hasn't heard of Matthias Ambrose. As much as I hate to admit this, you're a legend."

"I wish I had a legend worth talking about. Not one because I fought and killed a lot of demons." Some legend that was.

"I read your record before you were assigned. The Paladins you killed… they straddled the line of right and wrong. They all deserved the fate you dealt them."

"If you say so." Matthias blew out a deep breath of air. Every time he took a mission, he worried that it would take him over the edge. He almost had with Serah. His mind wandered to the sex, her body against his, her fingers digging into his shoulders. Never mind. He already had stepped *way* over the edge.

Lucy took a glass from a cupboard and headed toward the refrigerator. She pulled out a bottle of soda and unscrewed the cap.

"So how are we supposed to proceed with Daniel?" She poured the brown, fizzy cola into the glass and took a sip.

"It's too late to cancel the show."

They all spun around to see Daniel standing there with his arms crossed.

Chapter 33

UH OH. BUSTED! EXACTLY HOW LONG HAD DANIEL been standing there listening?

Lucy gulped down her soda, nearly coughing on the drink.

"Why would we want to cancel the show?" Serah asked in a feeble attempt at nonchalance.

"No need to hide. I heard enough of the conversation."

"And what are your plans for us?" Matthias asked. He moved closer to Serah, wrapping his arm around her. Warmth spread throughout her body. She relaxed against him, as if she were truly protected. Then again, protecting her *was* supposed to be his job.

Daniel blew out a long breath. "Do you want the long version or the *Reader's Digest* condensed version?"

"I don't like anything condensed. Not soup, not orange juice, and especially not reading material."

"I figured as much. Let's see." Daniel paced the floor, scratching his chin. "My early life in Chicago wasn't the greatest. My mother, she was heavy into heroin. There isn't a time I recall when she was ever clean. The state bounced me around from foster home to foster home. Then I turned eighteen and aged out. I did not want the same life my mother had. I was determined to make something of my life." He took another breath. "I was a big-boned person. I worked out and kept myself clean. I took a job as a bouncer at a club downtown."

"I read all this on your online biography," Matthias said, his gaze penetrating.

"You asked for the long version."

Matthias nodded. "Fine, continue."

"Thank you," Daniel replied, leaning against the counter. "While I was working the crowd one night, I met Sally. She said she was a producer, and thought I had the look of a star. It was weird. It was like she knew exactly who I was. Being young and determined, I never questioned it. That's how I ended up on *Princes and Paupers*."

"Great show, by the way." Lucy smiled. "One of the only reality shows I liked. Too bad it lasted only two seasons."

"Sally's choice. She wanted to move to cooking shows instead." Daniel shook his head. "Completely surprised me because I don't think I've seen the woman eat at all while we worked together."

"That's the California mentality," Serah murmured. "Eating is a sin there."

"Perhaps, but even the skinniest supermodel binges every so often." Daniel shrugged. "Anyhow, I did like the show's idea. I'm also someone who enjoys a good meal every so often, so it was a win-win situation. Then your audition tape came through. There was something about you. Sally's interest was intense. More than I had seen with other audition tapes. She made the legal team rig up a contract, which I've never seen before with any of the other guests. I just assumed she really wanted you for the show."

"What can I say—no one can resist my charms."

"Then Sally told me the truth. She said she was a

member of an anti-demon taskforce that was designed to rid the world of evil."

"What did you tell her?"

"I told her she was crazy," Daniel said with a chuckle. "Who wouldn't. Demons? Yeah, right." His gaze grew serious. "Then she showed me videos. Demonic possessions, demon attacks, demon everything. It was very convincing. She said she needed both of us to help win the war."

"Wow." Serah chuckled. "YouTube has some freaky stuff on it, but most of it is totally fake."

"You'd think so, but there was something very real about these videos. It was disturbing."

Matthias turned to Rafael. "Are the Paladins aware of any human militia or organizations determined to wage a war on demons?"

Rafael shrugged. "I'd have to discuss this with the Council. As far as I know, the only humans who can truly fight a demon are the Pure-Bloods. Even priests are inept when it comes to exorcism."

Matthias turned back to Daniel and crossed his arms. "So what is your reason here?"

"Sally wanted me to get Serah to join the cause. The TV show was the excellent backdrop."

"What cause?"

Daniel took a deep ragged sigh. "The Brotherhood of Enlightenment."

Rafael narrowed his gaze. "I've never heard of this organization."

"No one has. We have only fifteen members as far as I know." Daniel drew his lips tight. "But after I reported in to Sally, she told me the mission had changed."

"How did it change?" Serah asked. She dreaded Daniel's answer.

He took Serah's hand in his. "She told me we had to kill you all. She said you all were demons and that you had been tainted by their influence."

"How did she know this?" Matthias asked.

"I gave her your name."

"So it's someone who knows Matthias?" Serah asked. She turned to Matthias. "How many humans know you and your name?"

"The humans who knew my name have since parted this world."

"So Sally was right?" Daniel asked, nervousness lacing his voice. "You all are demons?"

"Uhh…" How the hell were they going to get out of this one? "I'm not a demon."

Matthias leaned in and pushed her hair from her ear. "I'll take care of it." He directed his gaze toward Daniel. "Yes, we are demons."

Daniel reached into his pocket and drew out a switchblade, his eyes wide and alert. "Stay back."

Matthias approached him with slow cautious steps. He held out his hands. "Put your weapon away, Daniel. We aren't going to hurt you. We are here to protect humans."

"Sally told me you would say that." He lashed out the knife at Matthias. "She also said you were deadly and not to be trusted."

Matthias raised his hands above his head. "I'm unarmed. Feel free to search if you don't trust me."

Daniel continued to scowl, but he did shut the knife and shove it back in his pocket. "Fine. Just because Sally told me to not trust you, doesn't mean I don't."

"But you just drew a weapon on us." Serah came to stand next to Matthias.

"I'm confused." Daniel said, his green eyes clouding over. "Sally said all of you were evil, but everything I've seen is just the opposite." He shook his head.

"She said the Paladins were demons and had to be vanquished and that we needed Serah to do it."

"Only the Paladins?"

"Yes, you demons are called Paladins right?"

"What about the Infernati?"

Daniel scrunched his brow. "Infer what?"

"Sally didn't tell you about the Infernati?" Matthias asked, his face stern.

"How about your weapons? Did she tell you that the only blade that can kill a Paladin is one that has been forged in the fires of hell? That the Paladins actually have the blessings of angels? Did that slip her mind?"

Daniel balled his fists. "No!"

"The Infernati are the real enemies, Mr. Blackburn. Not the Paladins. We are your friends."

"So do you believe us or not?" Lucy asked, her voice calm and collected.

Serah had to do something. "Daniel, you trust me, don't you? I don't just let anyone make tiramisu with me, you know. Not even my best friend."

"That's because you won't let me use rum like any other respectable cook." Lucy snorted. "Then again, I'm not known for my culinary expertise, either."

"Captain Morgan and coffee don't mix. Trust me."

"You never know until you try it." Lucy said, a small grin curving her lips.

"Let's not and say we did." Serah wasn't in the mood to talk about Captain Morgan and its many medicinal qualities. "You know I'm more of a wine girl, anyway."

"Alcohol snob."

"See, Daniel? I trusted you enough to invite you and your crew in. I can see you're a good person too. I sense it. You don't really want us to die."

"You're right. I don't." Daniel sighed. "But why would Sally target the Paladins and not the real evil-doers. That makes no sense."

"Sally Lohman right?" She ran the name through her mind. "Do you have a picture of her so we can see if anyone recognizes her?"

Daniel shook his head. "No. She's very private. I knew something big was up when she decided to be a part of the show. I told her I wasn't going to kill anyone. It wasn't in my contract."

"A contract. How appropriate." Serah rolled her eyes. "Does this woman get her jollies from keeping her people slaves to contracts?"

"Slaves." Matthias gritted his teeth. His face hardened. "She's a demon."

"A lot of people use contracts to keep things under lock and key. Prenup anyone?" Serah smirked. "Don't get married without one."

"Demons like contracts too." Matthias said in a muffled tone, his gaze moving to the floor. "Especially one demon."

"Who?"

"Salome."

Chapter 34

HE SHOULD HAVE KNOWN IT WAS HER FROM THE get-go, but he let himself get distracted. And, as Daniel proceeded with his story, it made perfect sense.

She was building herself an army. She'd been building one when she first turned him to the demon side. Now, with one of the seats of hell open for the taking, she'd need an army even more.

And she was not one who was above using humans to get what she wanted. Kalli had shown him that.

"She hasn't been spotted on earth in almost thirty years." Rafael said. "She was always one who liked her presence to be known."

"Have you ever fought her?" Lucy asked, gazing up at Rafael.

"Once. Remember the incident I told you about? The thing in the early eighties?"

Lucy's eyes widened, giving a slow nod. "The antique Model T?"

"That would be the one." Rafael shook his head. "She has the strangest *Peragrans* I've ever seen. Smoke instead of frost. It's weird."

"It's not a *Peragrans*." Kalli strode in from the office, the frost following her. "I've only fought her twice. The one time—" She flashed Matthias an apologetic glance. She turned back to Rafael "And with you in the eighties."

"She has a strange ability to transport herself without using the portals of hell. We're still trying to analyze it."

"Do you honestly believe Sally Lohman could be Salome?" Serah asked, her brow furrowed in concentration.

"They aren't very creative when it comes to fake names, if that's the case." Lucy said.

"And she changed her plans when Daniel gave her my name."

Daniel nodded. He shook his head and sucked in a ragged breath. "She told me they were protecting the world and doing good. Killing innocent people isn't good."

"How do we know that we can trust you?" Matthias asked. He was working for the enemy. He didn't want to take any chances.

Kalli nodded. "I can't read your mind either. So whoever you're working for is powerful."

Daniel sighed. "I'm confused and frustrated." He took a seat at the dining table and put his head in his hands. "I wouldn't expect you to trust me. But trust this. Tomorrow, when we film the show, her people will be there. They are going to ambush you. Even with my help, you all are doomed."

"Comforting thought," Serah murmured.

"After you feed them the tiramisu, and the credits have run, her people are going to kill you."

"Wow. So she plans on airing the show, even when I'm dead? How heartless. There's got to be something we can do." Her sapphire eyes pleaded with him.

He wouldn't let them near her. He'd take a blade if he had to. He was training to become a Paladin. The worst he would get would be a few years in limbo to recover. It was worth it. "I won't let them take you."

He hoped it was enough to ease her fears.

"If Sally is truly a demon, then the people working with her are demons too." Daniel shook his head. "They'll be mixed in with regular people. Can you tell the difference between a human or demon?"

"The Infernati have distinct odors," Rafael said. "But when mixed in a crowd of humans, it is hard to differentiate between the two. I really don't want to kill innocent people if I don't have to."

"What do these odors smell like?"

"Rotten eggs, Limburger cheese, moldy goat cheese, boiled cabbage." Serah wrinkled her nose. "And that's only the less-powerful demons."

"Don't forget the county landfill and the River City sewer system." Lucy added for good measure.

"So basically, like shit." Daniel scrunched his face. "Thank goodness I can't smell it."

"Sad thing is, those dumb Infernati don't know how rancid they smell either."

"Is there anything that can kill these demons?" Daniel asked.

"Silver blessed by an angel is the only way."

"Maybe I could just finish Sally off when I go back to the hotel room."

"Too obvious," Matthias said. He wouldn't let murder stay on anyone's conscience, especially someone Serah had feelings for. He didn't care what Lucy and Rafael said. He saw the way Serah comforted him. He had seen the kiss earlier too. It was sweet and tender, the way two people in love should kiss. Not hot and explosive like the ones they shared.

Truth be told, Matthias actually liked Daniel—despite

the fact that he was working for Salome. He could see that he was a man who worked to get where he was. Even when Salome handed him a career on a silver platter— maybe not the best analogy—Daniel still worked hard. Daniel would have done well on his own. And that only made him angrier.

Besides, he was a demon. Daniel was human. It was a better, safer combination. A demon and a Pure-Blood together? Not likely in this century or the next.

Besides, he should be the one to kill Salome. She had taken away everything he held dear. He'd not let her take another. He had to protect Serah.

Rafael nodded. "Matthias is right. Not to mention it would be a suicide mission. Every one of Salome's demon servants would be after you. It's better to act as if nothing has changed."

Daniel's eyes flashed with worry. "I don't know if I can do that."

Matthias grabbed his shoulders, his gaze narrowed and intense. "You have to. You're an actor aren't you?"

"Reality star and actor aren't always synonymous," Daniel mumbled.

"You have to try, Daniel. You want to help save this town, right?" Matthias pulled him closer, baring his teeth. "You want to save Serah, don't you?"

Daniel nodded. "I like Connolly Park." He gulped. "And Serah."

"Good. So you will try?"

Daniel nodded. "I will."

He loosened his grip and stepped back. "Is there anything about Sally that we can use against her?"

Daniel shook his head. He held onto the counter and groaned. "How could I be so stupid?"

"You aren't stupid, Daniel," Serah said, wrapping her arms around him. She patted his shoulder and stroked her fingers through his shiny blond hair. Matthias yanked his eyes away.

"I am too. I let myself fall for Salome, or Sally, whatever-her-name-is's story. She played me like a fucking fool."

Matthias had to say something. "You're not the only one, Daniel. She did the same thing to me. She's a cold, calculating bitch. It wasn't your fault at all." He hoped it would help ease his distress.

Serah looked up, her sapphire eyes warm. She gave him a wide smile. *Thanks* she mouthed.

Nodding, he turned his gaze toward the window above the sink.

"I just wished there were some way to separate the demons from the humans," Serah said, pulling away from Daniel. "If only I could just shove silver down everyone's throats."

"Very funny."

"I have an idea."

Everyone turned back to Daniel. His lips curved into a wry smile. "What would happen if a demon ate silver?"

Kalli shrugged. "They would die, more than likely, but I think they'd avoid anything with silver nuggets in it."

"I saw a news report once about a guy who used to eat silver, because he thought it would cure his diabetes," Serah said. "His whole body turned blue. It was so weird. Would the same thing happen to demons if they ate it?"

"Who in his right mind eats silver?" Matthias asked. Then again, humans did the strangest things to keep themselves healthy.

Lucy shrugged. "Silver does have some medicinal benefits, but I bet the guy was using colloidal silver." Was she a hairstylist or a doctor? She seemed to know a hell of a lot about these things.

"Colloidal silver?" Rafael winced. "Sounds disgusting."

"It's silver particles suspended in a liquid. Some idiots claim it cures everything. I'm not one to diss alternatives in medicine, but it's a little crazy." She snorted. "And they will keep trying to sell this *amazing* cure until they are blue in the face—literally."

"How in the world does an ordinary hairstylist know all this?" Matthias whispered to Serah.

Serah snickered. "You forget she took two years of med school."

"Seriously? Hairstyling instead of becoming a surgeon? Who is crazy enough to do that?"

"Lucy. And she's not crazy. It was the best decision she's ever made."

Great. He'd just insulted Serah's best friend. This wasn't going well at all. "Sorry, I didn't mean to—"

Serah smiled. "No worries. Everyone thinks the same thing when they hear the story. But you just have to know Lucy, then you'll know why." She laid a reassuring hand on his chest. The zings tingled and chased through his body. She leaned in, her breath inches from his ear. "Oh, she's afraid of blood too."

"Afraid of blood?" Then again, the Sexubi weren't the bravest where blood was concerned. This was going to be a gruesome battle. Would she be able to fight?

"Don't worry. Infernati blood doesn't scare her."

"So would liquid silver work on demons?"

Rafael nodded. "The effects of silver are magnified where demons are concerned. The problem would be getting an angel's blessing on such an unusual weapon."

"How long does it take?" Matthias asked. "Didn't you recently visit with an archangel?"

Rafael nodded. "The weapon had already been prepared and blessed. I just needed to claim it."

"They got my katana to me rather quickly," Lucy said.

"You are royalty, that's why. That and having a bunch of loosed demons ready to take over the world helped a little."

"Stop rubbing it in, Rafe." Lucy gave him a playful punch to his shoulder. "But isn't this just as dire?"

"Even if the last Pure-Blood is killed, it will not affect the Paladin or Council's actions. They will still exist and function as before." Rafael sucked in a ragged breath. "Not that I agree with that standpoint, of course. I think the world needs Pure-Bloods—more of them actually." He angled a sidelong glance at Serah. What in the hell was he suggesting?

Of course, she'd need to breed more Pure-Blood women, thought Matthias. Which is why he could never be with Serah. They wouldn't be able to have children. Then again, Lucy was living proof that a demon and human could mate. However, if they could have children, the demon bloodline would taint the Pure-Blood lineage.

"Right now, I don't see that happening, Rafe." Serah slunk away from him and toward the wall. She tugged at her chef's coat. "I don't see myself anywhere near a steady relationship to raise a family. That, and I don't think I'm good mom material."

"You'd be a great mom, Serah." Daniel sidled up next to her. "You're a good cook, you're generous, and from what I've seen, you're always ready to help someone out." He took her hand in his.

Matthias's jaw twitched and he balled his fists. Why did seeing Daniel comforting her hurt so much? He was the better person for her, regardless of how he'd been conned by Salome. He managed to control the growl ready to rumble in his throat.

Daniel continued to stroke her shoulders. "I would have done anything to have a mother like you."

What kind of pickup line was that? Not a good one if he was trying to woo Serah.

Serah smiled. "I'm a little young to be your mother, but thanks for the compliment."

"A lot young, actually. I'm older than you."

"Not by much."

"True, but you'd still make a good mother. Trust me, I know."

Interesting attempt at seduction. Not at all how he would have done it. But who knew what Daniel's plans were? So he gave them info about the Infernati's attack. Big deal. Demons could be double agents as well. But if they wanted this plan to work, that's what Daniel would have to be.

"When is Salome expecting you back?" Matthias asked, breaking up the talk about motherly love.

"Around ten or so. I figured we had a couple pans of tiramisu to make."

Matthias turned to Lucy. "Where can we find this

silver substance? I'd like to try some before we go with the plan."

"That homeopathic store in Green's Corner probably sells it. I'm in the Rotary Club with the owner. He might work me up a deal." Lucy grabbed her cell phone. "Believe it or not, some alternative medicine does work." She pushed a button and headed toward the office.

"I can transport there in a matter of minutes," Rafe added. He followed Lucy to the office. "I'll do it in private. I know how Serah hates it. Daniel probably won't like it much either."

With that, he shut the door behind them.

"We could use the silver instead of the alcohol. I bet it would pack a better punch." Daniel smirked.

"We don't want it to be too obvious. I suggest mixing it in with the alcohol, so it blends in together," Serah suggested. "Like the afterburn from a really spicy chili."

"The kind that sneaks up on you. Yeah," Daniel said with a nod.

"If you need someone to try the silver, I'll do it." Kalli twirled her tongue around the loop piercing her lip. "So what if my face turns blue—I'll just shave my head and try out as an extra for the Blue Man Group."

"But you're a woman," Matthias said.

"It's the twenty-first century, jackass," Kalli said with a roll of her eyes.

"I know that, but why call it Blue Man Group, then? I thought the idea was to make names and titles more—as humans say—politically correct."

"Because," Serah said with a wide grin. "The Blue Man or Woman Group doesn't have as nice a ring to it."

Women! So sarcastic. Like a breath of fresh air, nothing like the women he first knew. But he couldn't imagine Serah any other way. And, frankly, he didn't want to.

"Ahh, I guess that's makes perfect sense."

"Seriously, though." Kalli lounged against the counter, examining one of her black-lacquered fingernails. "Let me try the silver before it's blessed. We need to make sure it works."

"Don't you want to fight?" Serah asked Kalli. "I saw how well you kicked Larissa's ass."

Kalli grinned. "I'll stick out like a sore thumb in that crowd. I'd be better off in the background."

She meant to put herself in danger to protect her friends? Serah was lucky to have friends like that. In a way Matthias was jealous. As a demon, he'd never had any close friends, save for Balthazar, and he'd seen where that had ended up. But relief always overpowered the jealousy. These people were here protecting Serah— keeping her safe. He'd be forever grateful.

"Can't you change your appearance?" Matthias asked. She was one of the oldest and most powerful demons. Surely she had enough power to change?

Kalli twirled a dreadlock around her finger. "My kind can only change their appearance every five years. I have about six more months left," she said with a smirk. "Besides, I happen to like this look."

Matthias knew there would be no chance of getting Kalli to change her mind. "I just worry that you might injure yourself. Then what good would you be to the Paladins?"

Kalli leaned in, hands on her hips. "I know what I'm

doing. I've done it before." She patted him on the shoulder. "But thanks for the concern. I'm oddly touched."

"Protecting Serah means protecting her friends as well." Matthias crossed his arms. "But if you want to be the guinea pig, there isn't anyone stopping you."

"Perfect! I'll go in and make the arrangements with Lucy." With that, she spun around and strode toward the office and shut the door with a quick snap.

"Interesting," Daniel said, scratching his chin. "At first sight, I thought she'd be someone you wouldn't want to meet in a dark alley. However, there's this vibe about her that left me calm and relaxed."

"Don't judge a book by its cover." Serah winked at Daniel. "That will only get you in trouble."

"Something I am learning quite well today," Daniel said with a sigh. "How could I be so stupid?"

Matthias's heart clenched. He really felt for Daniel. They had a huge thing in common. They both had been duped by Salome. Matthias had had centuries to realize her treachery. Daniel, on the other hand was a human, with not nearly so much time on his hands. He hated Salome now more than ever. But he also needed to let Daniel know he wasn't alone.

"Don't beat yourself up, Daniel." He took a deep breath. "Salome is known for her skills as a temptress. Even when she was human, she had those skills."

Serah arched a brow. He loved that expression. "I thought she lived during biblical times?"

"Biblical being the operative word."

"No way!" Daniel shook his head. "She's *that* Salome? What in the hell have I gotten myself into?"

Matthias took Daniel's hand in his, his gaze stern yet

gentle. He couldn't have him losing control. Not now—
not with Salome and her minions so close. "Nothing we
can't get you out of. All we need is your trust."

Daniel nodded, placing his other hand on top of
Matthias's—an action that filled him with joy. Odd, yet
extremely comforting. "I trust you."

"Good." He withdrew his hand from Daniel's. It
was time to get down to the problem at hand. He
needed as much information as he could get. "Does
she have anyone else that she works with. Pictures?
Names? Anything?"

"She mentioned meeting with an old friend after the
Paladins had been exterminated."

"Any names?"

"Sally isn't one to give out names." Daniel pounded
his fist onto the counter. "She was so damn secretive. I
should have known."

"She can be very persuasive. Many have fallen for
her ploys."

"I've dealt with shifty and shady people all my life.
I have no excuse."

Was there any getting through to him? Humans could
be so stubborn at times. He thrust his face inches from
Daniel's, his eyes hard. "That's the difference. She's a
demon, not human. She has powers."

Daniel nodded and took a big gulp. "Okay. I understand."

Did he really? Regardless, he would soon enough.
Matthias pulled away and scraped his fingers through
his hair. "I felt the same way when I learned she'd
deceived me."

"How long ago was that?"

"Nearly eight centuries ago."

"Dear God, you're old!" Daniel covered his mouth. "Oops. I'm so sorry. I didn't mean to be so blunt."

"No need to apologize. I am indeed a rather weathered individual." He proceeded with more questioning. "So there's no one else except Sally's old friend?" He wondered if Balthazar was her old friend. He and the sauce demon were the only two Infernati he had come across recently. Then again, there was the demon that had come pretty damn close to getting Serah in an accident.

Then there was Balthazar to consider. What part did his old mentor play in this fiasco? It was no coincidence that both Salome and he showed up in Connolly Park right around the same time. The two had worked together before. That, and the fact that his descendant was of interest to them all. Salome was the demon who had stolen his son and altered his family line, after all.

He wanted to spit. He clenched his fists. Heck, he wanted to kill the bitch. But that itself was too humane a punishment for the hell she'd put Daniel through. For the hell she planned to put Serah through.

There was no mistaking the obvious. He loved Serah. He'd always loved her. But she deserved someone more human. He was a soulless abomination, not worthy of her. And for that, he'd protect Daniel too. He had a soul Matthias could only dream of possessing.

Why did this have to hurt so much?

Because love isn't all roses. He glanced up at Daniel and Serah. They made a perfect couple. He would not stand in the way of their happiness.

Serah arched a brow, her lips drawn. "Everything okay over there?"

"Yes," Matthias said with a nod. "I was just running ideas through my head."

"Care to share?" Daniel asked.

Not really. "I am just hoping these effects take place immediately. Like Rafael, I don't want to risk innocent lives."

Time was of the essence. They needed to act fast.

Kalli strolled back into the kitchen, smiling wide. "Rafe will be back soon. After I take a swig, we'll have our answer."

"Are you absolutely sure you want to do this, Kalli? It could kill your human body."

"Nothing I haven't gone through before."

"You are brave."

"Anything for the cause."

Daniel smiled. "It is good to see such dedicated people. Sally would delegate such things to one of the lesser people in the group."

"And you seriously didn't get the Jim Jones vibe from her at all?" Serah asked with a soft chuckle. "Tell me you didn't drink the Kool-Aid."

"Flavor-Aid, actually. Those poor people at Kool-Aid always get blamed. It was all caused by demons, you know." Kalli shook her head. "What a terrible mess. Thank God I didn't have to clean that one up."

Matthias nodded. He'd heard about that incident. After that, he vowed never to take a mission that would harm another innocent life. Then Belial had blackmailed him. He wasn't one to break a vow. He fought as hard as he could in Belial's dungeon to get Serah out of there. He thanked God and all the angels that Belial hadn't had the forethought to kill Serah first. And thank goodness for Lucy and Rafe. They had defeated Belial and sent all those demons packing.

With a giant whoosh, the office door swung open. "We got it!" Lucy pumped two small bottles above her head triumphantly.

"Is that going to be enough?" Serah asked, her brow tense with worry. "Those bottles look kind of small."

Rafe strode out of the office, cardboard box beneath his arm. "Don't worry. I stocked up."

"I volunteered to try it out before you take it to get blessed." Kalli grinned. Looking as happy as a lab rat that had no idea what it was getting into, she jumped up and down with eager anticipation. Then again, she'd lived for over two thousand years. She was far from stupid.

Matthias wasn't going to let up. "Are you sure? I'm the one who's protecting your asses."

"My ass? Do I really look like I need protection?" She flew up in the air and flipped backward. She sprang up again and cartwheeled across the floor. The sound of silver scraping against a scabbard echoed throughout the kitchen, and Matthias found a fine saber pressed dangerously close to his heart.

"Point taken," he said. With calculated slowness, he pushed the blade away.

"I hope so, or I'll make another point." She gave the saber a quick flourish and sheathed the blade. "I'm testing the drink. No one will change my mind. Or I'll find a way to change it for them."

With a sly smile, she patted the scabbard. "Works every time." She plucked a bottle from Lucy's hand. "Let's get this show on the road."

Chapter 35

WAS SHE BEING SUICIDAL OR JUST PLAIN INSANE? SHE slit the security seal with her fingernail and untwisted the cap. Bringing her nose to the bottle, she shrugged. "No scent."

Serah reached out and snagged the liquid from Kalli. She wasn't going to let one of her friends go down to protect her. "That saber doesn't scare me. Are you sure?"

"For the five-billionth time, *yes!*" Kalli bellowed, her hand still gripping the hilt. "I've lived over two thousand years, Serah. A nice long sabbatical in limbo could be what the doctor ordered."

She was willing to let this thing kill her? Something wasn't right here. What the hell was going on with her? But Serah knew one thing. When Kalli made up her mind, there was no changing it.

"Okay, if you say so." Serah handed the bottle back to Kalli.

With a sly grin, Kalli raised the jar high. "Bottoms up." She pulled out the medicine dropper and dripped a little of the clear liquid on her tongue. "It doesn't have a taste. Bonus!"

"That's a relief." It was the last thing Serah wanted, a secret weapon that was too obvious.

"Anything yet?" Daniel asked.

Kalli looked down at her cream-colored hands and

frowned. "Not yet." With a swirl of her tongue, she traced the tip of her labret piercing.

"Uhh..." Serah said, pointing her finger. Right above Kalli's tongue piercing, where she had dropped the silver, a blue dot had formed. It expanded, growing larger by the second and coating half her tongue. "I think it worked."

"Really?" Kalli stuck out her tongue and looked down at it. "Hell, yeah, it did." She pulled out a pocket mirror and flipped it open. Sticking her tongue out further, she shook her colorful dreadlocks around her head. "I kind of look like a Chow Chow that got in a paintball fight."

"We'll have to use more," Lucy said, examining the other bottle. "We need more than their tongues to turn blue." She snorted out a chuckle. "Don't even go there, Serah."

"Me? You're the one who was about to. Your head is always in the gutter."

"We can put it in their water and wine, right?"

"Great idea. I think I can get away with putting some in the mascarpone filling too."

Daniel cleared his throat. "We're supposed to prepare it on the show."

"Yeah, but it takes six hours to firm up." Serah grinned. "The one I make on the show will be made correctly. The ones we actually serve will be poisoned."

"Sweet. Sally wants me to inspect all the ingredients beforehand." He looked around the kitchen. "Inspected."

Serah giggled. "I think that's the shortest inspection I've ever seen."

"What can I say? I'm thorough."

Matthias turned to drill Daniel with a piercing glare. "You need to act as if everything is normal. Can you do it?"

What's with his sudden attention to Daniel? It's as if his mission was to protect Daniel instead. Strange.

Daniel gulped, and his eyes widened like a kid about to get reamed by his dad. "I will do whatever it takes."

"Good." Matthias smiled, his gaze softening.

"Anything else we need to worry about before Matthias and I head to limbo to get this silver blessed?" Rafael asked.

Matthias drew his lips tight. "I can't leave Serah unattended."

"It isn't safe to travel the portals alone," Rafe stated. "With such important cargo."

"What about Kalli?" Serah blurted. Anything to keep him close. Yep, she had it bad.

"As much as it pains me to say this," Kalli said with a smile. "Matthias is a stronger fighter." She turned to Matthias. "You'll only be gone for an hour or two at the most. Lucy and I can protect Serah."

Matthias offered a reluctant nod. "I understand."

Maybe they could eliminate the middleman all together. "Gerardo's an angel. Can't he just bless them?"

"Guardian angels are earthbound angels, so no." Leave it to Matthias to rain on their parade.

Daniel shrugged. "You know, earlier I felt like I was being followed. The presence didn't seem demonic though." He chuckled. "I'm probably just being paranoid."

"No, you're not." Rafe reached into the box and set several more bottles of colloidal silver on the table. "You were being ghosted."

"Ghosted?"

"I had a couple phantoms keep tabs on you." Rafe shrugged. "We couldn't be too cautious."

"Sally never said anything about ghosts or phantoms either. This is getting even wackier." Daniel rubbed his fingertips together. "Then again, she left out a lot more serious things." He shook his head, no hiding his disgust with himself there.

Poor guy, thought Serah. Something told her he'd get over it and move on with his life. She'd help him in any way she could. She owed it to him.

"Phantoms and demons don't usually revolve in the same circles." Rafe smirked. "But I helped Nigel and Rupert out of a jam, and they were repaying me the favor."

"Oh. Wow."

"I can have them stand down, if you like."

Daniel shook his head. "No, just make sure they keep their distance. If I could sense them, and if Salome is as powerful as you all say, then she may sense them too."

"Will do." Rafe nudged Matthias. "We need to see the Council now. The sooner we get these bottles blessed, the sooner Serah can get the tiramisu made."

Matthias nodded. His gaze caught hers. "Will everything be okay for about an hour?"

An hour? It takes that long to get a couple bottles of silver blessed? What can we do in the meantime. Swap cookie recipes? "It'll have to be. Kalli's here to take over your bodyguard duties."

Kalli squared her shoulders and raised her chin. "I've done my fair share of guarding every so often. I once guarded an Egyptian queen."

"Cleopatra?"

Kalli snorted. "Heck no. Much too proud for my tastes."

"Oh so you had nothing to do with the asp?"

Kalli nodded. "She was a proud woman. She would rather die than be humiliated by the Romans."

"So it wasn't about love?"

Kalli leaned in. "It hardly ever is."

Matthias slanted his eyes at Kalli, his jaw taut. "Enough."

"Love shouldn't be tragic," Kalli added, ignoring Matthias.

"But it is." Matthias stiffened and turned to Rafe. "We've wasted enough time. Let's get going."

Serah wished she knew how to help him. He needed more than a quick romp like they'd had earlier. He needed someone to console him. Hug him. Show him love still existed. Because Rafe's and Lucy's PDA obviously wasn't enough.

Speaking of Rafe and Lucy, they gave each other a quick kiss and Lucy straightened his leather jacket. "Think of me as that cold portal sucks you in."

"I always do. It's what keeps me warm."

Serah pretended to gag, coughing and sputtering. "Spare us the display already."

"You'll know what it's like soon enough," Lucy said with a friendly swat to her arm.

Not if she continued down this dark path of obsession—obsession for Matthias. She wanted to be the one to hold him, the one who he confided in. The one she wanted to confide in.

They had a lot more in common than she thought. They had both lost their families. They both felt guilty about it. She couldn't ignore that they had some kind of connection. Not that it was a healthy one, but it was still there.

"I think I'm fine right where I am." But was she? She'd have to be for now.

"Okay," Lucy said with a frown. "But you should be happy too."

"I am happy. See?" Serah gave her best attempt at a toothy grin. "But we need to concentrate on other things now."

Matthias nodded. "Serah's right. We need to go—*now*."

"Yes," Rafe said, giving Lucy another quick peck on her cheek. "We can continue this later."

Lucy smiled. "Okay, babe."

Matthias took her hand in his, tingles zinging from just that touch. His dark gaze burned her, in a totally good way. "I'll be back soon, Serah. I promise."

"Okay." She withdrew her hand from his, electricity zipping across their skin. What was it about his touch?

You like it, dumbass.

Without further words, he turned around and strode to the office. Rafe followed right on his heels. The door blew shut behind them.

Yes. She did like it. Way too much. Who was she kidding. She loved it. She loved his hands when they stroked and roamed all over her body. She loved his lips against hers. She loved all the naughty things they had done in bed. Yep, she was really fooling herself. She loved him.

Well, that made things complicated, didn't it?

"Shit. I'm getting tired," Serah said, with a yawn. She rubbed her eyes. She'd had a long day and just wanted to curl up and go to bed. Perhaps she could battle the brisk early-winter air by snuggling in some cozy fleece blankets in front of her warm fireplace. That would keep her toasty. Alas, they still needed to make their poison tiramisu.

"What you need is some extra strong coffee to jolt your senses." Lucy smiled. "I can at least brew a strong pot. I'm not completely helpless."

"Be my guest." Serah extended her arm to the coffee pot in the far corner. "As long as it's a machine doing things for you, it's all good."

Lucy shrugged, grabbed the carafe from the machine, and filled it up with water. "What kind of beans do you have?"

"Costa Rican Dark Roast."

"I've never had that blend before."

"It's delicious. It has a faint hint of dark chocolate and figs."

"Sounds like a fancy chocolate bar, not a coffee, but I'll give it a try." She pulled out the grinder and canister and scooped out way too many beans.

"Are you trying to kill me?"

"The stronger, the better. Trust me." Lucy covered the grinder and pushed a button, and the grinder roared to life. She poured the grounds into the top of the machine and turned it on.

The woodsy aroma of coffee filled the air, wafting to her nose. Yep, Lucy could at least brew a good pot of coffee.

"Smells good," Daniel said.

"I'm good for one thing in the kitchen, huh?"

Serah nodded. "Indeed."

Lucy opened a cupboard and pulled out Serah's

second-favorite cup, a tall mug that said "This cup's for you." Her favorite one had been melted, thanks to Matthias. She pulled the half-filled carafe out and poured some coffee into the cup. "I don't do cream or sugar. You're on your own there."

She replaced the carafe and the machine resumed its brewing. Gotta love automatic drip.

"Probably a good idea," Serah said with a chuckle. She ripped open a pack of I Can't Believe it's Not Sugar and sprinkled it into her cup. Coffee wasn't something that she spent hours on, so she relied on the delicious mixes that Café Du Jour provided her. Sure it wasn't real, but it tasted damn good. She pulled out the bottle of white chocolate caramel creamer and cracked open the lid and poured some into her coffee.

Without any warning, Lucy's phone went off. The *smooth* crooning of Justin Bieber filled the room. Lucy blushed as she flipped open the phone. "Hello."

Daniel grinned. "Nothing to be embarrassed about. I've met Justin before. A wonderful kid."

Lucy smiled and nodded, followed by widening eyes. "What?" she asked, her voice booming with surprise. "Really? That's amazing."

Despite the surprise, she didn't seem overly worried, which only piqued Serah's interest more.

"What's going on?"

Lucy pulled the phone from her ear and covered the receiver. "Hold on," she whispered. She went back to her conversation. "So they came and took him, just like that?"

Took who? What was going on? Now Serah was starting to worry.

"Frankie, calm down. I know you wanted to give him a party." Lucy shook her head. "He knew they were coming and he didn't tell us?" There was a brief pause as Frankie said more. "I'm sure he just didn't want us to make a big to-do about it. I'm sure he'll be fine." Lucy blew out a deep breath. "Rafe and the other Paladin who is guarding Serah have gone to limbo. I'll ask if they can find anything out when they get back. We're trying to make poison tiramisu and are waiting for the main ingredient." She paused again. "Okay, I'll tell her. Bye, hon." She hit the button to end the call.

"Oh, brother," Lucy breathed. "Something weird just happened at the shop."

"What?"

"A group of angels came and took Gerardo away."

"Wasn't he going to be reassigned to a human child?" Serah asked.

"It wasn't earthbound angels that took him. It was heavenly hosts, I guess. I hope he's okay."

"Me too. We'll have to have Matthias and Rafe investigate when they get back." If anyone could get answers it was those two. They could either charm with their looks or threaten with their muscles. She prayed it was the former. She never cared much for violence.

"Angels too?" Daniel threw back his head and chuckled. "It just got weirder again."

"Yep. After a while, it will all seem normal, though."

"I hope." Daniel shivered. "And to think I was freaked out when I auditioned for *Supernatural*."

Supernatural? He was cute, but she didn't really see him as a Dean or Sam Winchester. "Sorry that didn't work out for you."

"Sally wasn't too thrilled about the idea anyway." Daniel shrugged. "She said it would be a conflict of interest with our work with the Brotherhood."

"More like some of the episodes would make you suspicious of their organization. I mean they made angels villains. Who does that?"

"Hollywood." Kalli said, pouring herself a cup of coffee. "Artistic license, you know. By the way, not all angels have angelic intentions. Matthias can tell you all about that."

Serah nodded. He had mentioned it briefly when he related his story to her. But it really shouldn't have surprised her. If demons could be good, what's to say an angel couldn't be bad?

Speaking of Matthias, where were they? It had been over an hour already. Then again, she was not known for her patience. "How much longer? I'm worried about Gerardo."

"Frankie said Gerardo was happy to see these angels and willingly went with them." Lucy took a sip of her coffee. "Ahh, just the way I like it."

"So you think he's okay?"

Lucy chuckled. "Even if he were in trouble, he can hold his own."

No lie there. She'd seen the way he fought. Still, she worried. There was nothing they could do now. She'd have to wait for Matthias and Rafe.

God, she hated waiting.

Chapter 36

IT WAS BRUTAL, BUT AT LEAST IT WAS SHORT-LIVED. Matthias brushed the frost and ice from his head and shoulders. He scanned the room they'd ended up in. A red jacquard divan sat in the far corner, with two matching pillows bedecked with gold tassels guarding each corner. Candles lined the alabaster walls, their flickering shadows dancing across the walls. The polished, black marble floor shined bright.

The High Council chamber. Where many demons had waited to speak to the oldest and powerful of the Paladins. Where he had waited, a mere five days earlier, to get his first mission.

Rafael took a deep breath. "I remember the last time I waited here."

"When."

"Right before I went to Earth and met Lucy. Amazing how views can change, based on our attitudes. It was dark and foreboding then. Now it's light and peaceful."

"It seems confining to me."

"Nerves do that to people."

"So how does this work?"

"Well, I've never actually witnessed a blessing. I'm not the best person to ask."

"Thank you for trusting me, Rafael."

"Rafe. All my friends call me Rafe. Despite our initial differences, I know you're a good man, Matthias."

"Matt." He allowed Rafe his arm. With a smile, Rafe grasped his elbow. Matthias returned the favor. It was nice to finally belong, to have someone call him a friend and mean it.

Two giant, gilt doors swung open. Astra strode into the room, flicking her black, barbed wings. "The Council will see you now." She spun on her heels and flapped her wings. Could she fly or was it all for show?

"I can fly. I just choose not to." She flashed a wry smile. "Everyone asks me the same question. I was just saving time."

Rafe leaned toward him. "I take it she didn't greet you your last visit?"

Matthias shook his head. "Leonidas did."

Imagine that, one of the bravest warriors of ancient times, a Fore-Demon. Even for a demon it was still surreal.

"Did he regale you with all his war stories?" Rafe took a right turn down the candlelit corridor.

Astra grinned. "They are fascinating stories, though."

Indeed, they were.

Astra stopped in front of double, silver doors. Ornate carvings bedecked the surface, and angel wings framed each side. He hadn't paid much attention before. Being summoned by the all-knowing and all-powerful Fore-Demon Council had a tendency to do that. He was as nervous as hell the first time he met them. He reached out and ran a finger across a delicately carved vine of ivy. It was beautiful.

"The silver is blessed. It's the most effective way to keep the Infernati from attacking the council." Astra snapped a finger and the doors swung open.

He took cautious steps inside, Rafe and Astra following behind him. Astra flicked her wings and took flight, zipping to the empty seat on the dais.

Leonidas sat next to her. Gerard Butler he wasn't. He'd been near sixty years old when he fought his last battle. His hair and beard had long since grayed. He pulled at the garment swimming around him, as if he longed to wear something else. Still a fighter, even after almost twenty-five hundred years.

"Welcome back, Deleon and Ambrose. I hear you have an interesting request."

Matthias bowed. "We need to have some silver blessed."

"Don't you have weapons there already?"

Matthias nodded. "Yes, we do, but there will be humans where we expect to meet the Infernati. We need a way to separate the innocents from the demons." He reached down into the box at Rafe's and his feet and pulled out a bottle. "These bottles have liquid with silver particles in them. We plan to serve food infused with it tomorrow."

"Interesting," Astra said, flicking her dark hair from her shoulder. "Isn't that a remedy humans take on earth? How is this going to work?"

"If too much is taken, human skin can turn blue or gray over time. When a demon ingests it, the results are a little more immediate."

"And you've tested it?"

"Kalli did, my lord." Rafe said. "Her tongue turned blue."

"We expect the results on Infernati to be much more severe, after it has been blessed."

"I have to admit, this is probably the most interesting

request we've had in a while. I assume you need this right away?"

Both Matthias and Rafe nodded.

"I will send a request to have an angel join us post-haste." Leonidas closed his eyes and threw his arms up in the air. He slowly opened his eyes again. "Hopefully the angel on call isn't inept. Things can get pretty messy when done in haste."

Astra harrumphed. "Tell me about it. Thank goodness we got that situation under control."

A soft mist formed, swirling and spiraling around them. The mist solidified into a giant, glowing ball, which shattered. Sparkles of light burst into a million brilliant pieces.

"Did someone order an angel?" He scanned the room, flicking the bright white plumage behind him. He continued to scan the room, then locked gazes with Rafe.

"¡*Dios Mio*, Rafe! What are you doing here?"

Rafe's mouth gaped open. "I could ask you the same."

"You two know each other?" Matthias whispered.

"Gerardo."

"Lucy's guardian angel? I thought earthbound angels couldn't do blessings."

"They promoted me."

"This quickly? Weren't you at Lucy's shop earlier?" Rafe asked.

"Guess so. And a good thing too. My first blessing is something for Serah?" He jumped up and down with giddy delight. "¡*Muy bueno!*" He glanced at the bottle in Matthias's hand. "Is that holy water? Isn't that already blessed?"

"Colloidal silver, actually."

"Are you going to try to poison demons? You aren't supposed to use the weapons in cold blood, you know."

Of course they knew that. But Rafe gave kudos to Gerardo for keeping their best interests in mind. "No, we aren't going to vanquish them with it."

"What will it do?" the Latino angel asked.

"It will turn them blue when they ingest it. We plan on putting some in the tiramisu that Serah will serve to the guests on the show."

"Wow! What a great idea. Serah always thinks on her toes."

"Daniel's."

"The guy working for Salome?"

"Daniel's had a change of heart. He's helping us."

Gerardo pursed his lips. "I'll bless these, but they won't work if the person using them doesn't believe in the Paladins."

"I understand. We haven't any other options. Please help us?" Matthias asked.

Gerardo smiled, and the bright blue feathers on the shoulders of his shirt fluttered as he sashayed up to them. "You don't know me, so I'll let it slide this time. You never have to ask me for help. I'm always willing to help my friends."

Matthias nodded. "I've heard good things about you."

"Serah's a sweetheart. She deserves to be happy." Gerardo's brown eyes sparkled mysteriously. "I can see it in your eyes, Matthias. You'd do anything to make that happen, right?"

With a soft gulp, Matthias nodded. "I would."

"Good. Now stand back. I need some space to work my mojo."

Matthias and Rafe stepped back. Gerardo knelt before the box of bottles and scratched the dark goatee grazing his chin. "*¡Dios!* What was that word?"

Matthias cringed. Gerardo was likable, but he was new. Would the angel get the words right? He couldn't afford for the blessing not to take.

"Is everything okay, Gerardo?" Astra asked, her voice laced with worry. Her barbed wings flicked up and down.

"I'm fine." Gerardo reached into the pocket of his aquamarine, pleather skinny jeans and pulled out a brown, leather-bound book. "When in doubt, read it out."

He thumbed through a few pages and tapped his finger. "Ah, here we are."

Wings spread wide, Gerardo cleared his throat. "By the power of all that his holy, I Gerardo, of the fifth order of Cherubs do humbly ask for your blessing on these weapons..." He counted the bottles. "Twelve bottles of colloidal silver for the Paladins Rafael Deleon and Matthias Ambrose." With that, he drew his hand across the box. "This I ask."

A warm breeze swept through the room, circling them. Just as quickly as it came, it evaporated. Was that all there was? He'd expected more—holy water, incense, and burning palms.

Fifth Order of Cherubs? He'd been promoted that quickly? Most angels that he knew of started out lower, around the twelfth order or so. To be promoted that much in a matter of a day meant he was one powerful angel. He had to admit, he didn't look anything like what he imagined a cherub would look like.

"All blessed!" Gerardo said with a grin.

"That's it?" Matthias asked, wonderment evident in his tone.

Gerardo nodded. "Beginner's luck, I guess."

"Don't let Gerardo fool you. He's an excellent angel. His disguise as a human fooled three Paladins."

"Impressive."

Gerardo's cheeks reddened. Must be the cherub in him. "Rafe, you flatter me. And here I thought you didn't like me when we first met."

"Water under the bridge, friend." Rafe reached down and grabbed the box. "We need to head back. Don't be a stranger. You know how much Lucy cares about you."

"¡Si! I will never abandon our friendship. Lucy will understand. She's good like that. Frankie I worry about. He won't have anyone to argue with." Gerardo shook his head. "I'm sure Kalli can fill in."

"She's doing a smashing job so far." Rafe smiled. "She's got some great ideas to help Lucy with the shop too."

"¡Bueno! I knew she would." Gerardo waved his hand and wing. "But don't let me keep you. You have some mean and nasty Infernati to take care of." He turned to Matthias. "Serah is lucky to have such a dedicated Paladin watching over her. Keep her happy. A pleasure to meet you, Matthias." With that, Gerardo whipped his wings around his body and vanished into the mists.

Keep her happy? What did the effeminate angel mean by that? He didn't think he'd ever get used to all this cryptic stuff. But that didn't mean he wasn't going to try.

"Let's head back. Serah has some kick-ass tiramisu to make—and hopefully it will help us kick some Infernati ass as well."

~~~

"I'm getting nervous." Serah gnawed on a fingertip as she swished the remaining coffee in her mug. "It's been way longer than an hour now."

"Maybe they stopped for a beer afterward," Kalli said over her second cup of coffee.

"Not now, Kalli."

"Just trying to lighten your mood. Sorry." She set her mug on the counter. "I'm sure everything's fine."

The door to the office flew open, the gust rattling the pots and pans.

Kalli grinned. "See?"

Matthias and Rafe stepped back into the kitchen. Swiping snow and ice from his shoulders, Matthias allowed a wide grin to spread across his face. It was amazing. He was amazing.

"The silver is blessed," he said, his voice as smooth as butter. Serah didn't need this now, when they needed to concentrate on Gerardo and the tiramisu.

"Something happened to Gerardo," Lucy said, rushing to Rafe. "Frankie called me. Some angels came and took him with them."

Rafe nodded. "I know."

"What happened?" Serah asked. "We're worried about him."

"He was promoted. He's no longer earthbound."

"What does that mean?"

"He's a cherub now," Matthias said, setting the box on the counter.

Serah scrunched her brows. "Aren't they pudgy little babies?"

"Stupid human painters," Matthias mumbled. "They always misrepresent what they do not know."

Kalli snickered. "My fault. I was a muse for a while. It was better to keep our secrets by misleading the artists."

"A cherub? Really?" Bemusement flooded Lucy's face.

Rafe nodded. "In the fifth order too, which means he's strong."

"I always knew he had it in him." There was no mistaking the pride in Lucy's voice. "Was he the one who blessed the silver?"

Matthias nodded. "He was."

"Good. That means we're well protected." Serah grabbed one of the bottles. "Looks like we've got some tiramisu to make."

"Let's get crackin'," Kalli said, popping open the egg carton.

"I never pegged you for the domestic type," Serah said. "But nothing surprises me anymore."

"Don't let the lace and fishnets fool you. I've done my fair share of baking and cooking, enough to last a millennium or two." Her ruby-red lips spread into a wide smile. "Besides, we're cooking up trouble for the Infernati. That's an opportunity I can't afford to miss."

"I'm so lucky to have friends like you." Serah grabbed Lucy and Kalli in her arms and hugged them both.

"How many bottles do you think we need?" Matthias asked.

Serah pulled out of the friendly group hug and shrugged. She turned to Daniel. "How many people are going to be there?"

Matthias let out a sharp breath. He clenched his fists.

Did he still not trust Daniel? After all the information he gave him?

"Is something the matter?"

Matthias gave a slight shrug. "No."

"Whatever."

Lucy wrapped her arms around Serah's shoulders. "Can you put aside the animosity for now?"

"Fine." She angled a glance back to Daniel. "How many?"

"Fifty people."

Serah did the math. "Let's make three, nine-by-thirteen pans." She shook her head. "No. Four. We need to show the final product for the show. Let's do half Kahlúa and the other half silver. If we quadruple, we'd need exactly a cup of Kahlúa. So one half cup each." She pulled open a drawer, pulled out two half-cup measures, and set them on the counter.

"Sounds good," Daniel said.

"Let's get busy," Kalli said, throwing the cupboard door open. She pulled out a bowl and spun it around on the counter, where it glistened as light reflected off it. "Silver mixing bowl? Can you actually cook with it too?"

Serah nodded. "I guess once something's blessed by an angel, it becomes usable in all applications."

"Bonus. A weapon of mass destruction and a utensil of mass enjoyment in one." She gave the bowl one final spin.

Rafe turned to Lucy and zipped up his leather jacket. "It looks like everything here is fine for now. Let's head home."

"No poofing tonight?"

Rafe smiled and shook his head. "No, I want to spend time with you. If I have to do it in your cramped sardine can of a car, so be it."

Lucy smiled and wrapped her arms around Rafe. She looked up at him and kissed his lips. "And here people always told me that demons were bad."

"Nope, just the Infernati giving you all a bad name." Serah's lips curved into a wide smile. Those two were perfect for each other. She wished she could have a man as strong, gentle, and sweet.

"So, you okay if we leave?" Lucy asked.

Serah nodded. "We have it under control." She turned to glance at the bottles sitting on the counter. "How much do I owe—"

"Call it an early birthday gift."

"My birthday was over three months ago."

"Okay, a really early birthday gift, then."

"Fine, whatever."

Lucy strolled over and gathered Serah in her arms. "Rafe took care of it," she whispered. "He used his Paladin Express card. He never leaves limbo without it."

She couldn't tell if Lucy was joking or not. The Paladins and Fore-Demons were a strange bunch. "Umm... okay."

"So it's been taken care of by the Fore-Demon Council. No IOU needed." Lucy gave Serah a quick hug. "See you tomorrow, girl."

She turned to Matthias, giving him a knowing gaze. "It's a pleasure working with you, Matthias." She held out her hand.

"Matt," he replied. "The pleasure is mine."

Matt? What the hell? He was on a nickname basis

with them now? What was she? Boiled cabbage? No,
she was worse than that. She was a brussels sprout.

Lucy smiled. "Take care, see you tomorrow, *Matt.*"
She turned and winked at Serah, like he would give her
the same pleasure.

After the earlier sex, his actions pretty much said
it all. He wanted to keep his distance. And probably
a good thing. Bad things happened when you mixed
business and pleasure. Take a look at *Bodyguard*. The
moment Kevin and Whitney got together, their whole
world blew apart.

Lucy looped her arm through Rafe's. "Cramped sardine can, here we come." With that, she let Rafe lead
her out.

"Can I measure?" Kalli asked eagerly. It was weird.
She'd never seen Kalli so ready to ax the demons.

"Are you okay?"

"I'm fine. I can't help much tomorrow, so I wanted
to make it up to you. I figured helping prepare the food
would be as good a way as any."

Serah smiled. "Ahh, okay. You are more than welcome to help." She handed Kalli the Kahlúa. "Have at
it, hon."

"Yay!" She unscrewed the cap and poured the dark
liquid into the measuring cup. Pushing the bottle to the
side, she reached for the silver. Cracking open the lid,
she poured the clear liquid in with the liqueur. Swishing
the cup, she mixed the liquids.

So far so good.

She glanced over at Matthias. He stood in the shadows, his facade unrevealing. Arms crossed, he glanced
up. Sorrow flashed in his eyes.

"Did you want to help?"

"I don't want to burn down another kitchen."

"There's no oven involved."

She wished she knew what was going on with him. He was passionate enough. She'd seen that earlier, but now he was distant, aloof. She didn't like it. *Bodyguard* be damned. She couldn't stand Kevin Costner and Whitney Houston anyway.

"I insist you help." She handed him a bag of ladyfingers. Soaking them in alcohol and silver was simple enough. Something so easy even Lucy could do it. "All you need to do is roll them in the alcohol and silver."

A tiny smile curved his lips. "I can handle that, I think." He leaned in, his breath inches from her ear. "Thank you, Serah."

"You're welcome, Matthias."

He didn't correct her. That answered her question.

Chapter 37

IT WAS TORTURE BEING SO CLOSE TO HER AND NOT reaching out to stroke those luxurious curls. He had to refrain, however. He didn't want things to be any more complicated than they already were.

Serah covered the last pan of tiramisu with foil and put it in the fridge. She took out the pan she had made earlier with Daniel and unrolled the foil.

"Anyone want a slice?"

"Me!" Daniel said.

"Me too." Kalli licked her lips. "If it's as good as that filling we just made, I'll be in heaven."

"You ate some of the silver-tainted filling?" Daniel asked, concern etched across his face.

"Blessed silver doesn't hurt the Paladins," Kalli said, giving the spatula a lick.

Daniel nodded. "Makes sense."

Matthias supposed he should have some too. That way he could have a little piece of Serah. "I'd like some."

"All righty then." She grabbed a knife and cut four slices of tiramisu. With a warm smile, she handed him a plate. It looked delicious. Layer after layer of ladyfingers lay nestled in a bed of fluffy filling. A sprinkle of cocoa dusted the top. A chocolate-covered coffee bean sat on top, giving the cake a simple elegance. He scooped up some with his fork and took a bite.

The mixture of coffee, cream, and mascarpone exploded along his tongue. He'd had tiramisu before, but not quite like this. Delicious was an understatement. More like divine.

He angled a covert glance at Serah, who handed a plate to Daniel. She patted his shoulder and giggled cheerily.

Divine, indeed. Just like the woman who'd made it. He gritted his teeth and fought back the emotions that brewed. It was better this way.

"Can I bring a piece to Sally? That way she isn't suspicious," asked Daniel.

"Great idea," Kalli said, grabbing the knife. She slid the knife through the tiramisu. "Any to-go boxes?"

Serah nodded and opened a cupboard. She pulled out a small, foam container and handed it to Kalli. "Here."

"Not much of an environmentalist, are you?"

Serah smirked. "Spare me the lecture. They're recyclable."

"Okay." With that, she lifted the cake server and plopped the tiramisu into the container. She closed the lid and handed it to Daniel. "There you go."

Daniel smiled. "Thanks."

The sound of wind chimes echoed through the kitchen. Daniel sighed. "It's probably Sally."

He set the foam container down and reached into his back pocket. With a nod, he tapped on his screen. "Hello?" He blew out a frustrated breath. "We had to make an extra pan. We forgot about the display." There was a pause. "We're just finishing up. I'm bringing you a piece so you can try it."

So far so good. The guy was a natural. He would have eventually made it on his own, even without

Sally's—Salome's—help. Too bad he'd gotten wrapped up in the wrong crowd.

"I'm leaving now, Sally… All right… See you soon. Bye." With that, he mashed his finger on the screen and ended the call. Matthias decided right then and there that he'd help Daniel straighten out his life. After all, if he could do it, Daniel could too.

"So?"

"She doesn't seem suspicious." Daniel shook his head. "Doesn't mean she's not. But she's not pleased that I'm late."

Typical Salome. Controlling and callous. If he could march right into that hotel and give her a piece of his mind, he would. He would not let her corrupt another human—or demon for that matter.

"You'd better get going," was all he said. He bit his tongue.

Serah nodded in agreement. "The last thing we want is her angry right now."

Daniel nodded. "She wants me back here at nine. The taping starts at eleven o'clock. Is that okay?"

A sly smile curved Serah's lips. "It will have to be. If you try to defy Sally—Salome—whatever—she may become suspicious."

"Okay!" He wrapped his arms around Serah and pulled her into a tight embrace. Serah returned the hug, her arms wrapping just as tightly around him.

Matthias stifled the growl. Why in the hell did he have to be so jealous? Serah needed someone like Daniel, someone with a clean conscience. Someone who hadn't lived almost a millennium.

Daniel fit the bill perfectly.

Daniel withdrew from the hug and gave Kalli an equally warm hug. Daniel then turned to him. "Thank you for allowing me to help, Matthias." He held out his hand.

"Call me Matt." He took Daniel's hand in his and gave him a hearty shake. He glanced over toward Serah, her face in a tight scowl. *What now?*

He gave Daniel a pat on the back. "Be careful, friend."

Daniel smiled. "I will." With that, he gave a quick wave and made his way toward the front door.

Matthias blew out a breath. Maybe some of this jealousy would abate with Daniel gone. He could only hope so.

"I'm heading off too." Serah said, grabbing her keys from the wall.

"Not without me, you're not."

"Not this again."

"I don't want a repeat of this morning. You are too important to—the world. I can't lose you."

Kalli arched a brow. "I think I'm going to go poof. I have a feeling you two need some alone time."

"No!"

"Sorry, but I think it's best for both of you." Kalli gave them no chance to answer. "Don't worry, I'll use the office." She spun toward the office and strode off.

"You've been acting weird all night, Matthias. What is the deal? Daniel is harmless. I saw the way you looked when he hugged me."

"It's complicated."

"Yeah, sure." She spun away from him.

He reached out and grabbed her elbow, bringing her to face him. He took her chin and angled her face to meet his gaze. "I worry about you, is that so wrong?"

"No," she breathed out.

He allowed his arms to reach around her neck and wind his fingers in her curls. He knew he should resist, but the damage had already been done. He lowered his lips to hers. With slow tentative sweeps, he pressed into her mouth, his tongue sweeping against hers. A soft moan escaped her lips as her teeth grazed against his tongue. It was too much. His member pulsed and throbbed.

He couldn't do this to her. Not now. It was the excitement from the impending battle that affected him. He'd seen it in battle before. But not like this. Not so tender or caring. Bloody hell. He was in love, that's why.

He withdrew from the kiss. "Sorry. I didn't mean to take advantage of you. We can't do that again."

Her lips trembled and her sapphire eyes clouded. "You're right. We can't."

Those words cut him to the core.

———

They rode home in silence. Serah turned the corner and pulled into the driveway. She just wanted to go to bed and make the night go by faster.

It was a hard task with Matthias so close. She glanced down at her phone. How did she miss all these calls? A number she didn't recognize. She pushed the button on the machine to get her messages.

"Farquie, where are you baby? The human went out on a date. I'm all alone."

Serah shivered. She really didn't want to know.

"It's me again, my little pussycat. You're not answering your cell either."

A cell phone? Where the hell was he hiding that?

Now she was worried. It wasn't like Farquhar to miss Inanna's *calls*. She dialed the number that appeared on the caller ID.

"Farquie?"

In all her excitement over the show, she'd completely forgotten her sidekick. What kind of human was she?

"No, it's Serah. Farquhar isn't here."

Inanna gasped. "Oh shit. Farquie's going to be pissed."

"I already know you can talk and that you're imps, Inanna."

"Oh. Whew," Inanna murmured.

"I talked to him earlier when I was fighting a demon. I told him to stay home. He obviously didn't listen to me."

Serah sighed. How could she have done this? "He spends all his time with you, so I assumed you two were together."

"He cares for your safety," Inanna purred. "You stay home. I will go out and look for him."

"Is it safe?"

Inanna laughed. "No one will suspect me. I'm just a stray Persian, far from my home."

"If you say so."

"I'll call you back when I learn more. I have a good sense of smell, you know. Who needs a bloodhound?"

"Okay," she said, a huge lump in her throat. "Inanna?"

"Yes?"

"Be careful."

"Always."

With that the call ended. Serah slumped to the floor.

Matthias appeared in the doorway, concern flashing in his dark eyes. "What's wrong?"

"We totally forgot Farquhar. Now he's gone."

"What do you mean gone?" Matthias leaned down and pulled her up into his arms. She rested her head on his chest, her tears trailing down.

"Inanna said she's been calling him all day and he never answered or called back. It's not like him. I was so engrossed in our plans, I let one of my friends down."

"Did you not tell him to stay put?"

Serah nodded.

"Did he listen to you?"

She shook her head, a sob bursting from her mouth.

"I know you aren't going to like what I'm about to say, but I'm going to say it anyway." He cradled her head to him, his hand softly stroking her hair. "He made his own decision. Whatever happened to him isn't your fault."

He raised her chin so that their eyes met. "I've also tussled with the imp. He knows how to hold his own."

Matthias was right. Despite his size, Farquhar could indeed fight with the best of them. "I know, but I still worry. What if it was Salome? What if she's the one who got him."

"Salome isn't one to just kill a captive. She likes to make spectacle of things. All Infernati do."

"I hate them. They need to die." She clenched her fists. She had to end them. Now.

Matthias shook his head, his voice soothing. "No. That's what they want. You can't give in to the anger. If you do, you will lose. You could die. I will not let that happen. I—the world needs you too much. I need you too much."

"You need me?" Serah glanced up. His onyx eyes burned. *What did he mean by that?*

"I just feel I have a purpose when I'm with you. I feel like I belong. I feel good."

She nodded. "You need me to live so your mission is a success. I understand."

"It's more than that. I like you."

Like me? He wouldn't even let her call him by his new nickname. He may have been trying to keep his distance because of the mission, but he sure had a strange way of showing it.

"Could have fooled me."

"What's that supposed to mean?"

"'Call me Matt?'" she ground out, pulling from his embrace. "Does that ring any bells?"

"You don't like me making nice with your friends?"

Serah growled, louder than she had ever growled before. "I don't mind that. But you could extend the same courtesy to me if you *like me* as much as you claim to."

"I didn't think you cared for me."

Serah pounded her fists into his chest. "*Are you for fucking real?* I don't just fall into bed with men I don't like or hardly know." She shoved him away. "I feel connected to you." She sighed. "And not just because of our past, either."

"I know, I feel it too. But you deserve better. I saw the way you and Daniel worked together. You need something like that in your life. Not a hardened assassin without a soul."

"I doubt that."

"Doubt what?"

"I doubt you don't have a soul. You've shown it plenty of times." She shrugged. He was probably right. He apparently thought he was too broken to be fixed. But with a little glue, a statue could always be put back together.

"We're a lot alike, you and I."

Bemusement flooded his face. "How so?"

"We blame ourselves for our pasts. Well, I've got a news flash—it's the past. I've forgiven myself. Heck, I've even forgiven you."

"You have?"

Serah nodded. "But you're right, we should keep our distance." Her face fell into a frown. "You need to learn how to forgive yourself."

"My ignorance got my wife killed and my baby stolen."

"No. Your love gave them hope. Salome is responsible. Not you!"

Maybe now he'd get those pieces glued back together. If not, it had been worth the try.

"Good night," she said, storming off to the bedroom and slamming the door behind her. She twisted the lock. Right now, all she wanted was to be alone.

Chapter 38

REALITY CAME BARRELING AT HIM.

He'd tried to keep distant, and that had only made things worse.

Despite the anger and frustration lacing her words, they hit him right in the gut.

He'd been too busy blaming himself he hadn't even bothered to see the truth. He was Salome's pawn in her sick, twisted game of world domination. And he'd fallen for it hook, line, and sinker. What's worse, he'd—no, Serah was right. It wasn't his fault. Salome had taken the only thing he'd ever cared for in this world—until now. He'd be damned if he let her do it again.

"Thank you, Serah. For everything." He owed her his life.

There came a faint scratching at the front door. It could be Farquhar or his Persian goddess coming with news. He prayed it was good news.

He peeked through the peephole. No one was there. The scratching grew louder, more urgent. Obviously *something* was there.

"Who's there?"

"It's Inanna. I found Farquie." Her voice raised a few octaves. "He's hurt."

"Let me get Serah." He whipped down the hall and pounded on the door. "Inanna's here. She has Farquhar. Get out here."

The door flew open. Serah pulled her robe tight and rushed to the front hall.

Inanna stood there, Farquhar's limp, blood-soaked body draped over her back. Her eyes wide and alert, she burst into the room. "There's a note tied around his neck."

Matthias's blood turned cold. Quite a feat for someone who'd already been dead. He clenched his fists. Farquhar coughed and sputtered, blood dripping from his heart-shaped nose.

Serah ripped the letter from Farquhar's neck. "Call Kalli. She can help." She glanced down at one of Farquhar's shattered legs and gasped. "I hope we're not too late."

He yanked the phone from his back pocket. "Call Kalli."

"Calling Kalli," the phone replied. The phone rang three times. Finally, after the fourth ring, Kalli picked up.

"Hello, Kalli's Cleaning Company, how can I be of service?"

Was there ever a time this woman didn't joke? "Farquhar's been attacked. We need you here now."

"On my way." With that, the call dropped.

Despite the fact that Farquhar was really an imp, the scene was still gruesome, reminiscent of that sad commercial he glanced at before turning in for the night. They made even the strongest of demons teary-eyed. Salome had to be stopped.

"It was Salome. I know."

Serah gripped the letter tight, tears streaming down her cheeks. She shook her head. "It wasn't."

She handed him the bloodstained paper. He recognized the handwriting right away. His skin crawled.

My Dear Friend:

If you do not uphold your end of our bargain, this will be the same fate in store for your descendant. He won't be nearly as resilient. I know where he lives and will be more than happy to oblige. Salome is the least of your worries.

Yours,
Balthazar

This time, it was indeed his fault. He should have finished him when he had the chance.

There was a knock on the door. Serah looked through the peephole and opened. Kalli strode in, flinging ice and snow from the mass of hair on her head.

"Where is he?"

Serah led Kalli to Farquhar's bloody and broken body.

"Dear God, they skinned him alive. Bastards." Kalli bared her teeth. "Just because he's an imp doesn't make it any better."

She knelt down, placing both hands on Farquhar's body. She closed her eyes and ran her hands up and down his mangled body. Skin started to heal. Blood faded. His broken tail unbent on its own. A soft mewling moan broke from his lips. He shook out his once-broken leg. Swatting his paw, he bounded up on all fours. "Hi-Yah! There's more where that came frae."

Farquhar's eyes widened. He looked around the room and glanced down to see the blood-soaked floor beneath him. "Mebbe there isnae more where that came frae."

"What happened?" Serah asked, gathering the impcat in her arms. She stroked behind his ears and rubbed the top of his head.

"Ah was jumped by Balthazar th' magnificent—not." He narrowed his eyes at Matthias. "Seriously, ye need tae pick better friends."

"That is not the same person I was friends with."

Farquhar nodded. "He said Ah was gawn tae be an example. Wha'ever that means." He puffed up his fur. "That infernal dobber picked a war wi' the wrong Scot, that's fer sure."

"Honey, let the big people handle it. I like you better like this, and not chopped into little pieces," Inanna said, concern purring from her lips.

"Inanna makes a good point," Matthias said, reaching down to stroke the top of her head.

"Get yer paws off mah lass."

Matthias took his hand away from Inanna's ears. "You're one lucky SOB, Farquhar."

"Why's that?"

"You've got a woman who cares about you."

Serah stiffened, then set Farquhar next to his lady friend. Inanna and Farquhar slunk toward the cat bed and snuggled with each other, wide grins from whisker to whisker spread across their feline faces. Cats can't smile? Yeah, right.

He sidled a glance at Serah. "Lucky indeed," she mumbled. With that, she headed back toward her bedroom.

He sprinted down the hall to join her. "Serah, wait. Let's talk."

She spun around, her sapphire gaze sparking. "You want to talk? Fine, let's talk." She threw open the guest bedroom door. "Privately."

He followed her into the room and shut the door behind them. "I've never been in this sort of situation."

She arched a brow. "How is this any different than any other mission of protection?" She stood there, wearing those cute little shorts and T-shirt, her hands defiantly on her hips.

She expected him to answer when she looked so delectable? He swallowed the lump in his throat. "It's complicated."

"I've got news, buddy. Life is complicated." She reached out and grabbed his hand. "Things would be so much better if you just open up."

Her touch electrified him to the core. He'd already opened up, more than ever. What more did she want? Her fingertips moved in circles around his palm. Even the most innocent of touches sent him over the edge.

"How's this for opening up." He reached out and pulled her to him, his mouth crashing down into hers. She moaned against his lips, her body melting into him. God she felt so good. He let his hands rove and explore as her own hands roamed over his shoulders and down his arms.

All thoughts of talking vanished and more delicious thoughts, of the carnal variety, took over.

Chapter 39

MATTHIAS TRACED A FINGER DOWN SERAH'S SPINE, reveling in the softness of her skin. She blew out a breath and pressed her body closer to his. The heat radiated between them. It scared him at first, but now he welcomed it. He wished it could last forever.

Alas, it couldn't. They were going to go into battle. He leaned over and pushed some curls away from her neck. He nibbled and licked and traced his tongue down over her pulse.

She stirred against him, a deep sigh of contentment on her lips. She stiffened.

"Oh God. Not again."

"Does my touch offend you that much?" he asked, placing a kiss upon her shoulder.

"No, but…"

"What's wrong with two people with similar interests succumbing to pleasure?"

"It's not safe."

"You're safer here with me next to you, trust that."

Serah pulled herself away from him, taking the sheets with her. "There are other things that can harm us, besides the Infernati." She twisted the satin sheet around her, shielding her curves from his view.

"I haven't been that truthful with you."

"Tell me something new."

"Just hear me out. Back in the dungeon, I didn't just try to save you because you were Pure-Blood."

She shrugged. "Let me guess. You saved me because you wanted to jump my bones?"

"I admit, the thought did cross my mind from time to time."

She rolled her eyes. He hated it when she was annoyed. "So why else did you do it?"

He reached out for her hand, flashing her a pleading gaze. *Please take it.* He needed her to understand.

With a reluctant sigh, she allowed him her hand. She took seat on the bed, the sheets billowing around her. "So spill it."

"I…" Why in the hell were these words so hard to say? Those greeting cards made these things seem so damned easy. He wasn't Shakespeare. He couldn't pen her a sonnet. He couldn't even say three measly words. He was pathetic.

"You what?"

"Oh, never mind."

"Fine, whatever." She jerked her hand away and grabbed the sheets. With an exasperated sigh, she headed toward the door. "We have to get ready for the *show*. We've wasted enough time." With that, the door slammed shut behind her.

Yes, she is better off with someone else. Someone with less baggage.

With a frustrated breath, he rose from the bed. He pulled out a gray T-shirt and wrenched it over his head. Rummaging through the other piles of clothes, he grabbed a black pair of cargoes and slid them up his legs. Tightening his belt, he strapped the dagger to his side. He grabbed a few other weapons—a Glock with modified bullets and a couple of silver-infused grenades. Shoving the gun into the holster, he looked in the mirror.

Grabbing his final weapon, a long broadsword, he slid it into the scabbard at his back. He was ready—ready to defend Serah, whether she liked it or not.

———∿∿∿———

Demon men were more complicated that human men. She sure as hell wasn't going to live her life like a *Charmed* episode gone bad. Then again, life with Matthias couldn't possibly be that bad.

"Too bad their Balthazar wasn't nearly as bad as ours—but not by much."

She decided she'd wear something a little less fancy. Ripping the closet door open, she grabbed the first thing she could find. A blue, cowl-necked, cashmere sweater. The material was thin, not too heavy. She should be fine under the hot stage lights.

Why did she have to fall in love with him? She could tell he cared about her too, in his weird, demonic sort of way. She pulled the sweater over her head and yanked it down. She grabbed a nice pair of dressy blue jeans and quickly put them on. Taking a look at the full-length mirror that dangled from the half-repaired door, she shrugged.

Not bad at all.

She quickly headed into the adjoining bathroom and sprayed some detangler on her dampened roots, running a comb through her crazy curls. With a final draw of the comb, she sighed.

"I'd wait until you get there to put your makeup

on." Kalli stepped into the bathroom. She twirled one of Serah's curls around her finger. "Did I ever tell you how awesome your hair is?"

Serah shook her head. "Thanks. When did you get back here?"

"Five minutes ago. I wanted to make sure Farquhar was okay." Her eyes flashed with concern. "Why are you moping around? We're about to kick some big, bad Infernati ass."

"Nothing."

"Want me to do your makeup for you? You'll need more than you're used to."

"Thanks Kalli. I'd like that a lot."

"By the way, he loves you."

Serah blinked. What was she talking about? "Who? Daniel?"

"No, you dumbass. Matthias," Kalli said with an irritated huff.

"What a funny way of showing it."

"He's afraid. Look at what happened to his wife. He doesn't want Salome to do the same to you."

"Seriously?"

Kalli nodded. "I can't read his mind, but when he thinks no one is looking, it's plain as day on his face."

"Then why does he push me away?"

"I suspect that Salome and Balthazar have something to do with it. Even more so after what Balthazar did to Farquhar."

"But he's acted uptight from the get-go."

Kalli exhaled. "Are you daft or just unobservant? He was afraid to tell you the truth about what he did. Then his old mentor and Salome showed up." Kalli took a deep breath. "The less anyone, especially Salome, suspects anything, the less of a threat you are to them." Kalli sighed. "You're already a threat as it is. Imagine if Salome knew that Matthias cared for you?"

Serah nodded. She understood—too well.

"Salome never forgets a thing, especially when someone she turned into a demon defies her. She'll do anything to see him suffer. And if it means, killing you, she won't even bat an eyelash. But that's not the bad thing."

"What?"

"She already plans on killing you. She'll make it even slower and more painful if she knows the truth." Kalli gritted her teeth. "Matthias is dedicated. He'll die himself before that happens."

Well, then. That changed things—a lot. She wasn't just going to draw her out of the crowd. She was going to a hell of a lot more. She couldn't let Matthias risk his life for her.

"Not if I have anything to say about it."

Kalli smiled. "So you see my point?"

"I do."

"Good."

Serah smiled. "So... Do I get more weapons other than the poisoned tiramisu?" She would not sit idly. She would bring these bitches down—one way or the other.

"Huh?"

"You know—daggers or silver bullets or anything?" Then again, her necklace worked pretty damn well the last time. "I... ahh... just want to be safe."

"I'm not stupid. I've seen that look before."

"Really? When?"

"When Lucy fought Belial." Kalli shook her head. "You two are too determined for your own good."

"And that's a bad thing?"

Kalli shrugged. "Not always, I guess."

"So can you hook a girl up or what?"

"Sure, I guess."

"Kalli, you rock."

Kalli grinned. "You said that already." She pulled a silver-inlaid dagger and sheath from her boot and handed it to Serah.

Serah pulled the dagger from its sheath. It was a simple blade—no fancy etchings or jewels. Then again, all you needed was silver. It all sliced the same.

"For your *protection* only. Never anger. Remember that."

Serah nodded and sheathed the weapon. She remembered full well. She'd seen where anger had gotten a few of the Paladins—an extended stint on the Paladins' injured reserve list. Then again, she wasn't demon and she wasn't a Paladin. "Do those same rules apply to Pure-Bloods."

"Frankly, I wouldn't take any chances."

Good advice, actually. Anger never got anyone anywhere, in real life and fiction alike.

"After all the crap we've been through, I don't think I should either."

"Glad we agree on one thing, at least."

Serah wrapped her arms around Kalli and drew her into a hug. "I really appreciate you helping Farquhar. I don't know what I would have done if he had been vanquished."

"No problem. That's what friends are for." She

straightened the collar of Serah's sweater. "I think you're ready to go."

"You planning on riding over with us?"

"Only if we can come tae." Farquhar said, sitting in the hall with a cigar poking out of his mouth.

Already back to cigars. He was indeed on the road to recovery. Serah scowled. "Farquhar!"

"It isnae lit. Jeez."

"Fine," she said, her hands on her hips. "And my answer is no."

"Ye'r nae fun." Farquhar whipped his tail back and forth. "Kalli has given me a clean bill o' health. Right, Kalli?"

"Yeah, he's fine."

"Do you forget? You're a cat." Serah reached down and scrubbed behind his ear. "Having a cat running around a professional kitchen isn't going to go over well."

"Ah can sneak in later on. Ah ken how tae fight." He jumped up in the air and flipped backward. He ended with a quick kick and a punch. "See?"

"Kalli, what do you think?"

"Seriously, I think you're going to need all the help you can get."

"Great! Ah'll go an' git Inanna." He swiveled around and sauntered down the hall, tail swishing in victory.

"Thanks a lot, Kalli."

"It was nothing." With a sly grin, she winked. "I'll go see if Matthias is ready to go."

Serah took a deep breath. It was almost time. If there was one thing to be thankful for it was her nerves. Luckily she could pawn it off on the cameras.

"Okay. I'm ready," she replied, her breath hitching. She flipped the switch on the bathroom lights and closed the door behind her. There was no turning back now.

Chapter 40

THE DRIVE WAS SLOW AND TEDIOUS. MATTHIAS wanted to have some alone time with Serah. He wanted to speak his mind. But then Kalli, Farquhar, and Inanna had decided to come along for the ride.

"I didn't feel that a *Peragrans* would be in good form, especially with humans nearby."

Matthias nodded. She had a point. They needed to exercise caution. They couldn't afford any mishaps so close to the show.

But the cats? Why? They wanted to remain discreet. Having two extremely intelligent felines around would certainly bring up suspicions.

"Ye need tae relax, Matt," Farquhar meowed out. "Inanna an' Ah will be safe."

Serah sucked in a deep breath. There was no mistaking the nervousness. She turned into the parking lot and pulled into an empty parking space. Putting the SUV into park, she clenched the steering wheel tight.

"What's wrong?"

"I'm scared." She turned to Matthias, her bright sapphire eyes swimming. "What if it doesn't work? What if they don't eat it?"

Matthias shook his head, brushing a hand over her shoulder. He didn't care if Kalli was in the car with them or not. He leaned in close. "Shhh. Don't worry. You'll do fine."

"How do you know?"

Matthias allowed his lips to curve into a reassuring smile. "You stood up to me—and lived."

"You're so full of yourself," she said with a chuckle.

"There, I got a laugh out of you."

"So you did." She glanced up at him, her gaze warm. "I'm glad you came to protect me. I don't think anyone else could have survived."

She wrapped her arms around him and brushed her lips across his cheek. How in the hell could he let her go when his mission was done? He loved her. Maybe he could make it work.

"What was that for?" he asked.

"It was a thank-you kiss."

"Yeah right," Farquhar mumbled from the backseat. "Get over yerselves."

Inanna swatted him with her tail. "Now now, baby."

Both Serah and Matthias whipped their heads around. Serah narrowed her gaze. "Seriously. Can't I thank my bodyguard for doing an awesome job of protecting me?"

Kalli blew out an annoyed huff. "He did more than protect you, and you both know it."

"He's not interested in me."

"She's not interested in me."

The words came out in unison. He shook his head. He needed this mission done ASAP. Serah was completely wrong. He was more than interested in her.

"Ye two are actin' like eejits." Farquhar sighed. "Let's go."

Kalli nodded. "I was just about to say the same thing." She yanked open the back door and stomped off toward the building.

Farquhar and Inanna followed, their tails swishing behind them. "Bluidy hell. Stupid arses," he heard muttered in the distance.

"Has she always been a matchmaker?"

"Well, she did try to get Frankie and Gerardo together once."

"What happened?"

"World War Three almost happened."

Matthias nodded. "I see." He swung the door open and hopped out. He'd do anything to ease her worry. "Well, we'd better get going. You have nothing to be afraid of."

He jogged around and opened the driver side door. "You have me to protect you."

"I want more than your protection, Matthias."

His jaw ticked. "What more do you want from me?"

"I want your love, damn it."

You have it, Serah. You just can't know it. "That can't happen," he said instead.

The words tore him up inside.

———※———

"I know you have feelings for me. Why can't you admit it?"

Kalli had said he was protecting her. But was he protecting her from Salome or protecting her from himself?

"Now is not the time."

"It's never the time." Serah clenched her fists. She needed to speak her mind, before it was too late. "I'm not weak, you know. I can protect myself. You're overreacting about this."

"I can't stand the thought of losing you."

"You're not going to lose me. We're going to beat Salome."

"Maybe not today, but some day." Matthias shrugged. "You're better off with someone like Daniel."

"Daniel?"

"You two seemed so comfortable together."

"In a totally platonic way." She rolled her eyes. "I accidentally kissed him and it was weird. Not at all like our kisses."

"Huh?"

"It felt like I was kissing my brother, not a lover." And that was the truth. "That sort of thing doesn't get my rocks off, if you know what I mean."

He raked a hand through his hair, pacing back and forth. "You don't know what you're saying. It's the excitement of the impending battle."

"Fine, then I'm going to ask you just one favor."

Matthias nodded. "I can respect that. What's your request?"

"Let's discuss this afterwards."

"So be it." Matthias's face became more sullen. "After the battle and we've had time to relax. Let's see if you still feel the same."

Oh, she had no doubts at all. Her feelings wouldn't change. She'd never been so sure of anything ever in her entire life.

"That's all I'm asking," she said, a sly grin curving her lips. With that, she stomped past Matthias and headed up the path to the front entrance.

She threw open the door and promptly wished she could close it. She'd never seen her kitchen so busy. There were people everywhere. Cameramen bustled around, testing their cameras. The director adjusted his headset, and began barking out orders. Other people bustled about. Was this a major motion picture or a TV show? What had she gotten herself into?

Then again, she wasn't a coward. She took a deep breath. *You can do it!*

Oh, brother. There she went, channeling her inner Rob Schneider. But any little bit helped.

You know what? I can do it. She had to. Connolly Park depended on her. Heck, the world depended on her. And even Matthias depended on her, even if he was too stubborn to admit it.

"Serah!"

She turned and spotted Daniel over in the corner discussing something with a woman. She took a huge gulp. A beautiful woman. She wore a bright fuchsia sweater that accentuated her more-than-ample bosom, and completed the ensemble with a tight, leather pencil skirt and stiletto ankle boots. The woman snapped her head up to lock gazes with Serah. Her turquoise gaze narrowed. She would've thought a color like that would be dazzling but, on this woman, there wasn't anything brilliant about it. Absolutely soulless. Salome.

She couldn't blow her cover. She had to remain cool. Quite a feat recalling the stories she'd heard about this bitch. She took calm, confident steps toward Daniel and the mystery woman. "You take your production seriously, don't you?"

Daniel grinned. He did not miss a beat. He definitely had Academy Award potential. "Serah, may I introduce the producer, Sally Lohman."

Sally extended her hand, with an unconvincing smile. Men had fallen for her charms? All Serah felt was the desire to yak up her caramel macchiato. Then again, the scent of curdled milk and roses didn't help matters much either.

She took Sally's hand, shivers of revulsion coursing through her. She gave it a quick shake and just as hastily pulled it away.

"I didn't realize so much went into producing a TV show," Serah said in an attempt to make nice with this walking cup of sour milk. "I hope I can make it through the entire taping."

Sally grinned. "I hope so too."

Yeah, I bet.

"Should I show you to the banquet area?" It wasn't much of a banquet room, but it was large enough to serve fifty. Perfect for Salome's little production.

"Certainly."

"I had some of my hired help come in early and set it up."

Hired help. More like hired hand. The magical hand of Kalli.

Serah inserted a key into the lock and twisted. She pushed open the door. "Daniel said we'd have about fifty, so I decided ten tables should be plenty. And there's room for the camera crew." She pointed to the parquet dance floor. "Just be careful. It's new flooring."

Salome nodded. "Indeed, I will." She wove her way between the tables, drawing her fingers across the backs of the chairs.

"Perfect," she murmured. She flipped up the white table cloth and rubbed it between her fingers. "Damask—nice."

Her fingers traveled to the vase of roses in the middle of the table. She traced the tip over a thorn. "Great touch."

"Do you approve?"

Salome shrugged. "It'll do."

Bitch! She'd paid a lot for those tablecloths. She wanted to take that silver and plunge it into her heart right then and there. It would make things easier wouldn't it? *Yeah, right, she probably had a second in command.*

"You're doing great," Daniel said, coming to stand behind her. "That's the best reaction she's ever had to the table arrangements in the history of this show."

"Wow. Charming lady."

"She's tamer than usual." Daniel shrugged then whispered, "I've never seen her like this before. I hope she doesn't suspect anything."

"Let's worry about that later."

Salome came back from her inspection. She put a hand on her hip. "Daniel informs me that you've got a bodyguard. I hope he can make himself scarce during the production. We have a large crew, including our own protection. You will be fine."

"Thank you, I appreciate that. He's in the office, monitoring from there."

"I suppose that will do."

Damn right, it would. "But Lucy stays. We're besties and we do everything together."

"How sweet." She snorted. "What about your sous-chef?"

"She's off-site today, catering a business luncheon." Probably one for Jupiter or Neptune, she supposed.

"Very well. Business must go on, I suppose," Salome said with a shrug. "Be ready. The taping starts in a half an hour." With that, she turned and dismissed them with a rude wave of her hand.

"Yikes! I'd never make it in showbiz."

Daniel sighed. "Yeah, I know. I should have known better, right?"

"Actually that's exactly how I expected a stuck-up Hollywood producer to act."

"Have you met the director yet? He's pretty cool."

"Is he a demon?"

"I hope not. He's always been nice to all of our guests, including Diner Diva."

Then again, it would take a saint to be nice to that lady. Of course, the lady had been so annoying that she got her own spin-off show. Go figure. Serah wasn't taking any chances though, not with so many rotten stenches lingering around.

The odors barraged her senses. Her kitchen had never smelled so rank, never, not even when she cooked Nonni's favorite cabbage soup recipe. It was like she was climbing through a giant landfill with the reek surrounding her. She stifled the urge to gag. What she really needed, right now, was a super-powered gas mask. Like she could be that fortunate. She'd just channel the time she went to visit an old school friend's farm for a week. Who knew pigs could be so malodorous?

"You need to get your makeup on. God, I hate this stuff," Daniel said, wiping some foundation from his sweaty brow. "Adam Lambert I am not."

"Well, I'm not Lady Gaga, for that matter."

Daniel smirked. "Your friend could easily make you look like that."

She didn't doubt that one bit. "Kalli knows not to overdo it with me. She's done my makeup plenty of times at the salon."

"You should be in good hands then," he said. He grabbed her elbow and led her back to the kitchen. "Let's go meet Barry."

"Barry who?"

"Barry Holland."

"I've never heard of him."

"It's reality TV, not a big production." Daniel led her over to a short, pudgy man, who was flipping through a sheaf of pages.

"We're only doing tiramisu? Why doesn't anyone tell me these things?" He huffed. "We'll have to make it work."

Daniel nudged his way in. "I've got a pre-recorded piece on the history of tiramisu ready to roll with it."

Barry spun toward Daniel. "Oh? Whereabouts?"

Daniel bent over and grabbed the pages. He pointed to the middle of one of the pages. "Right here, where it says 'Fade to recorded footage.'"

Barry scratched his head. "Oh, I must have missed that." He glanced over to Serah, scanning her from head to toe and back up again, like she was a calf going to slaughter. His gaze met hers. "Is this Miss SanGermano?"

Serah nodded and extended her hand. He took it. Cold and clammy. Mother of God. He *was* a demon.

"I am."

"A pleasure to meet you, Miss SanGermano. Daniel has told me all about you. And that tiramisu? It's divine."

Surprising he'd know anything being divine. "Daniel's told me a little about you as well."

"All good, I hope."

Serah controlled the urge to smirk. *As much as he knows.* "Yes, it certainly was."

"Good. Let's get you to makeup." He wrapped his cold arms around her hip and led her to an area they'd set up.

"I have my own makeup artist and hairstylist actually. Is that okay?"

"I suppose so," Barry said. "Less work for our people, I guess."

"Cool." With that, she pulled herself from his clingy embrace and called Daniel over.

"What is it?"

"Sorry, to break this to ya, but Barry's not as nice underneath his disguise."

Daniel exhaled sharply. "Aww, man."

And now she really dreaded the situation more than she had before.

Chapter 41

MATTHIAS USED *PERAGRANS* TO ENTER THE OFFICE without notice. Daniel had surprised him. There, he found a laptop set up for him, with a direct feed into both the kitchen and the banquet room. He'd seen Serah's introduction to Salome. She'd always been so vain. She'd kept the same appearance since he'd last seen her.

The only thing that had changed was her fashion.

He clicked over to camera number two. He wasn't quite sure about the director from the start. He'd seen Serah's reaction. He was a demon. Two demons down, fifty more to go.

She headed toward her bedroom-away-from-home and shut the door behind her. Unfortunately, there was no camera there to continue the surveillance.

The door swung open. He looked up. Lucy and Rafe stepped into the room.

"Kalli's doing Serah's makeup." Lucy pushed the door shut. "It stinks out there," she added as she plopped into the love seat and propped her knees up.

"Waterloo was worse," Rafe said without remorse.

Matthias nodded in agreement. He'd hired himself out to humans for that battle. Luckily they had been English humans. It was a bloody battle. Both sides had lost many lives. He'd seen what had happened to the emperor he had once guarded. He didn't like it one bit.

"You were at Waterloo too?" Lucy asked with wonder. "Probably the other side, right?"

Matthias shook his head. "I fought for the English as a hired mercenary."

"Really?"

"In times of war, I've assisted many humans in their battles. The American Civil War and the Napoleonic Wars were two of the bloodier ones." Matthias sighed. "My last war was the Great War."

"World War I? What about World War II?"

"I detest modern warfare. I was a bodyguard during that time. These newer tactics aren't the way I was taught."

Lucy's eyes flashed knowingly. "I understand." He didn't doubt that one bit.

"Who did you guard?"

Earlier, he would've told someone to mind their own business in a not so friendly way, but now he had no qualms sharing. "Benito Mussolini."

Lucy's expression pinched. "Didn't he die by firing squad?"

Matthias nodded. "That was afterwards. I'd already moved to a different mission." He shrugged. "I didn't like where things were going in my life and I vowed to change. People like Mussolini did not fit with those changes."

"We will make sure Balthazar doesn't get your descendant. I promise."

"Thanks. I appreciate that." He really did. It was nice to belong, even if only for a few days.

The singer previously identified as Justin Bieber announced a call. With a small grin, she grabbed her phone and flipped it open. "Hey Kalli. What's up?"

She nodded. "Okay, be right there." With that, she

closed the phone. "Serah's ready for me to do her hair." She leaned across the love seat and gave Rafe a quick kiss on the lips. "I'll see you in the banquet room after they eat their treats."

With that, she popped up from the couch and shimmied to the door. "Bye." She snuck out and quickly shut the door as she left.

"You're a lucky man, Rafe." Matthias clicked the mouse and watched Lucy enter the room.

"I know." Rafe rose from the love seat and came to face him, his silver gaze stern and stony serious. "You could be lucky too, you know."

"Huh?"

"Stop being so stubborn." Rafe threw back his head and chuckled heartily. "Never thought I'd ever say those words to anyone."

"I'm not being stubborn. I'm being practical."

Rafe shook his head, his expression pinched. "If I were practical, I'd be wasting away in limbo, moping for an eternity."

"The Fore-Demons wouldn't allow it."

"In the words of Lucia Gregory, 'Fuck the Fore-Demons. Do what makes you—and Serah—happy.'" He grinned. "I'm completely paraphrasing there."

He'd heard Lucy talk before. Not much paraphrasing at all. "It's complicated."

"Serah loves you. If you do this, you'll end up hurting her more. How about those complications?"

"Daniel is a better mate for her."

Rafe slammed his fist into his palm. "Don't make me beat the sense into you. Have you really looked at how they interact?"

"They get on quite well."

"Yeah, because they're friends, you dolt."

"How can you be so sure?"

"Other than the fact that Lucy told me where Serah slept last night?" He leaned in, his face stony. "The Serah we know doesn't do that with just anyone."

Matthias took a deep breath. Rafe had a point. He'd been so focused on protecting her that he failed to see the bigger picture. He knew she cared for him. And he obviously loved her.

"Just watch the bloody show and you'll see."

Matthias nodded. He wouldn't miss the show. And after they defeated Salome and her minions, he'd make it up to her—any way possible. He'd find a way to make everything work. He'd been ignorant for too damn long. He just hoped he wasn't too late.

—◆◆◆—

"Seriously, I love your hair the way it is." Lucy said, twirling a strand of Serah's hair around her finger. "So bouncy and full of life."

Kalli lounged on the twin bed. "I have to agree with Lucy here. We both have experience in the hair-care field." She smirked. "Can't tell it from this head of hair, huh?"

"I love your hair, Kalli. It's a statement of individuality." Serah smiled. "Not many women can pull off the dreadlock look, except for maybe you and Crystal Bowersox."

"Don't forget Whoopi." Lucy scrunched Serah's hair with her fingers.

"Whoopi too," Serah added.

Lucy blew out a breath. "If I do anything else with your hair you'll look like you just stepped out of a bad eighties hair-band video."

"Fine. I trust you guys."

"Good, because we're right." Kalli handed Serah a tube of lipstick. "Here. The pièce de résistance."

"It's not black, is it?" Serah asked with a quick giggle. It was so amazing how these two women could calm her nerves so well.

"It's rosy pink."

"Darn. I really wanted to shock them."

"They'll get a shock soon enough," Lucy whispered. "By the way, Daniel hooked Matthias up with some hidden cameras. He's got a view of both the kitchen and the banquet hall."

"That's good. I know how he hates being in the dark where my safety is concerned."

"So what's the deal with you two besides the you-know-what?"

Not now. He made it clear he was leaving after this mission. She didn't want her feelings and emotions to complicate things further.

"He's not that into me."

"Bullshit," Kalli said through a muffled cough.

"What she said." Lucy took Serah by the shoulders. "He's crazy about you. Why not just tell him how you feel and see what happens."

Kalli crossed her arms. "He says he cares about you. I bet it's more. Men have a difficult time admitting their feelings."

"He says he has too much baggage."

"Tell him you'll be his bellhop. I see the way you

look at each other." Lucy winked. "I'm a sex-demon so I'm pretty knowledgeable with this stuff. Those gazes aren't just lust."

"Yeah, I love him."

Lucy shook her shoulders. "Then tell him."

"Fine."

"Good."

Her phone rang. "It's Daniel," she said as she answered it. "Hello?"

"We've got about ten more minutes until Showtime at the Apocalypse. Are you ready?"

"Yeah, Lucy and I will be right out."

"Okay, see you soon. Bye."

"All righty," Serah said, shoving the phone into her purse. "It's now or never." She reached over and gave Kalli a hug. "You know when to make your entrance, right?"

"Of course! I've been waiting almost eight hundred years to take down Salome. I can't wait."

She'd have to fight Matthias for that honor. "Don't be surprised if Matthias beats you to the punch."

"I know better than to step in his way." Kalli grinned. "I'm sure I can find a way to keep myself occupied." She cracked her knuckles.

"Okay." With that, Serah opened the door and stepped out.

"Ready?" Daniel said as he loped toward them.

Ready as I can ever be, she supposed. "Yeah."

"I've made things easy for us. There's a teleprompter that will deliver our lines."

"Wow, just like a news anchor. I really feel special." Nothing she could do would calm the nerves building in her. Her pulse raced. Sweat dampened her brow.

Thankfully, the thick coat of foundation Kalli used was waterproof. She couldn't wait to wash that junk off.

"So how do you feel?"

"Like a frickin' clown." She rubbed at some of the foundation.

"Yeah, it's a little itchy at first. After a while you get used to it."

"Sorry. This is the last time for me." She saw where the temptation of fame had gotten her. Almost ready to get annihilated by a legion of angry demons.

"You know," Daniel said, leaning in close. "I really feel you. I'm thinking of cashing in my chips after this."

"But you're so good at it."

"It's time to move onto bigger and better things. Heck, if Snooki can write a book, then so can I."

"What would you write?"

"Fiction, because this stuff is too weird to be considered true."

Serah couldn't disagree there. "You could do a whole Blair Witch sort of deal, how the demons took over the show?" Then again, there are a few weirdos out there who thought that shit was true. Then again, maybe it was.

She dreaded what would happen later. Daniel wouldn't remember anything. Matthias would more than likely wipe his memory—for that exact reason. She didn't have the heart to tell him.

"Wow. That's an awesome idea."

"Places, everyone!" Barry, the demon director, shouted. Her stomach roiled. Her pulse spiked. She couldn't turn back now. The world needed her.

—⁓—

Holy cow! She couldn't believe she had done it. She survived the taping of a cooking show. Even if they had ulterior motives, it was still an accomplishment.

Lucy rushed up and gave her a huge hug. "I can't believe how well you did. I would have lost it completely."

Serah almost had... right in the bowl of mascarpone.

"We're not out of the woods yet," Daniel whispered. "Salome prides herself on the taste test scene."

"Well, let's give her something to choke on," Serah said with a smirk.

"I love that attitude." Lucy grinned. "You got it from me."

"No. I got it from my Nonni. You got it from me."

"Perhaps."

Serah reached in her pocket and grabbed her phone to call Matthias. She needed to hear his voice at least once before she headed into ground zero. She pressed the send button.

"Hello?" his sexy, rich accent hummed in her ear.

Barry snatched her phone and hung it up. That asshole. She was giving him an extra dose of silver when she met up with him.

"We need to film the final scene. Now," Barry said, an evil gleam in his eye. He shoved the phone back into her hand.

At least she got to hear one word before Barry ripped her phone way.

"Barry, what's going on, bro?" Daniel asked as they entered the banquet hall. "You're not yourself today."

"It's my last show."

Serah stifled the smirk that threatened to burst on her

lips. How true it was. It would be his last show—ever. "Moving on to bigger and better things?"

"Yes. I'm about to hit the big time. This has to be the best show ever."

"So far so good, huh," Serah said, taking a seat at one of the tables. "I hope this show helps you explode on the scene." *Literally*.

"Thank you, Miss SanGermano." He turned to the crew. "Places!"

Daniel took the seat next to her.

"Action!"

Daniel smiled. "Welcome back, everyone. We're now going to put Serah SanGermano's tiramisu to the test." He flashed Serah a smile. "Here's how it works. We've got a crowd of hungry food critics waiting in the wings. They will taste your dessert and give you either a pass or a fail." Daniel faced the camera, his gaze serious. "Think it's easy? Well you haven't met these people." He turned back to Serah. "Are you ready?"

Those words held more meaning than these demons knew. "As ready as I'll ever be."

Daniel nodded. "Bring them in, Barry."

Chapter 42

MATTHIAS'S AND KALLI'S EYES REMAINED GLUED TO the computer screen. "Are you all ready?" He asked into his headset—an important staple of a mercenary's gear.

"Yes, ready," Rafe said in a hushed tone.

"Ready," Lucy echoed.

"Good." Matthias scanned the room. Daniel and Serah stood in front of the tables. "Farquhar and Inanna are waiting behind the Dumpsters if we need them."

"Sounds good. Let's rock and roll," Lucy whispered into the headset.

"Bring them in, Barry," Daniel shouted, then led Serah to the front of the room.

Barry pulled a cord and a curtain dropped. The people, all with eager delight spread wide on their faces, found their way to their seats.

"Is everyone ready to try some tiramisu?" Daniel asked, playing into the crowd's excitement.

"Yes!" the crowd shouted.

"Send in the tiramisu!"

He held his breath. Rafe and Lucy wheeled in a cart, the neatly cut pieces of cake wiggling as the wheels jostled. He couldn't believe he was so nervous about someone serving food as he was now.

"Oh wow, Serah. It looks heavenly."

Matthias's breath caught. Would she keep a straight face? He sent out a prayer hoping she did.

"I hope they think so," she said, her smile radiant.

Matthias breathed a sigh of relief. She was doing well. He caught a glimpse at the necklace around her neck. Then again, she did have her grandmother's spirit.

Rafe and Lucy bustled around the tables, delivering the cake and filling glasses with the tainted water. Lucy reached over a table to hand someone a glass, bumping another glass with her elbow.

Matthias gritted his teeth. His fists clenched. Their plans would backfire. "Bloody hell," he growled. He bounded to his feet, ready to burst down the doors of the banquet room. If that water fell on one of the demons, their cover would be blown.

Both Serah and Daniel cringed. She raked her fingers through her hair and gnawed her lip. Matthias scanned the crowd. No one appeared to notice their expressions.

Lucy reached out with her free hand and grabbed the glass. With an embarrassed smile, she righted it, only losing a few drops. She moved on to the next table and finished serving the plates.

Matthias blew out a long breath of relief.

"Thank the Almighty for Lucy's quick reflexes."

"You're welcome," Lucy whispered as she headed away from the table.

Matthias relaxed back in his chair, as Lucy and Rafe carted the remaining cake away.

"Remember to feed the crew."

With a quick nod, Rafe pushed the cart and proceeded to hand out the extra cake.

Where in the hell was Salome? Wasn't this her production? Or was she planning on making a grand entrance. Knowing, her past, it wouldn't surprise him one bit.

He gritted his teeth. "Salome's not there."

"Do you want us to abort?" Lucy asked.

Hell no. Serah was in danger. They couldn't pull out now. "The mission is still on. Salome will show up."

Lucy headed to the corner of the room. "Okay. All the cake is passed out."

"Good."

"And as Marie Antoinette so famously said, 'Let them eat cake!'"

"Oh, brother," Lucy mumbled.

Kalli sneered. "Dumbass. She never actually said that."

Matthias shrugged. "Apparently Daniel is a master of irony."

"Whatever," Kalli said. She watched the first person take a bite of cake. Nothing happened "Human."

Then all hell broke loose. People coughed and sputtered. They reached for water. Spitting out the tainted liquid, the demons burst from their seats, flailing their bluish tinted arms in the air.

It was time to crash this demonic party. "Ready to kick some ass?"

"Always," Kalli said, bursting out the door. Matthias followed, quick on her heels. The sooner they got in, the better.

Kalli reached for the door. "Bloody hell! It's warded."

He grabbed the handle and twisted, the pain burning into his skin. He had to get in there. Serah needed him.

"Open the doors," Matthias roared. The sounds of shrieks and metal clashing ripped in his ear.

"Fuck!" Lucy shouted. "Those bastards have us locked in."

He heard metal clanging against metal. Screams,

demon and human alike, rent the air. His heart pounded.
This was Salome's plan after all.

"See if Daniel can open it."

"He can't!" Rafe shouted amidst the melee.

Matthias's heart clenched. He pounded on the door,
anguished sobs ripping from his mouth. He'd only wept
once before. When he found his wife and child gone.

He wouldn't be stopped. He had to get in there. He
had to tell Serah he loved her. He kicked the door, not
caring if he broke his foot or not. The pain would only
last a second. The pain of losing Serah, though, he knew
he would never be able to bear it.

"Serah, I love you!" he shouted through the door,
hoping by some small miracle that she could hear him.
"I can't lose you!"

"Wow, did I hear what I think I heard," Lucy asked.
There was a whoosh. "Shit!" A loud crash echoed in
his ear.

"Enjoy the cake, bitch."

"Balthazar is here too," Rafe said. "I thought for sure
he'd want you in here."

"He's afraid of me. Afraid of what I've become.
Right now, I've become a man who won't lose the
woman I love.

Kalli sucked in a breath. "I can summon Gerardo."

"It'll take too long."

Kalli blew out an aggravated breath. "Damn Infernati!"

"They'll get what's coming to them." Matthias knelt
at the door, his head in his hands. What could he do? He
was running out of time. He fumbled with his cargoes,
his hand brushing against the grenades he had packed.

"I have an idea." He gripped the grenade tight in

his hand. "Get back, Kalli," he ground out. With that, he pulled the pin, backed up, and tossed it at the door. Hunkering down, he covered his ears and waited for the blast.

"I guess my dessert failed the taste test," Serah said. "Are you armed?"

Daniel nodded. "Rafe slipped me a knife as he passed by."

The demons lunged in the air, grabbing their throats. They spit out the cake.

Daniel's eyes widened, his hand gripping his blade tight. A bulbous, hairy demon dove for him. He jumped back, slicing into its hair.

"Arrrgh!" it shouted, jumping for him again. Daniel crouched and ducked. He spun around and slammed the blade into its chest. It screamed, loud and guttural, blasting into a ball of flames.

Daniel dropped the knife and stepped backward, mortification filling his face. "Holy shit!"

He couldn't flake out now. Not when they needed all the help they could get. "Daniel, grab the knife. You need to protect yourself. Please? We need to save this town before Salome takes over."

Daniel blinked. He reached down and gripped the knife tight, swinging and slashing his way through a crowd of demons. "I am so getting a new job after this."

She didn't blame him one bit.

"Bitch!" one hissed, baring blue teeth. It lunged at her. She stepped to the right, pulling out the dagger Kalli gave her earlier. With a quick slash, she sliced its blue arm off. She thrust it into its chest. It shrieked, erupting into a mound of blue ash.

She caught a glance at her friend. Lucy jumped in the air and kicked one of the demons in the head. She threw a silver star, the blade lodging in its neck. She grabbed the demon by the neck and slammed its head into a pan of tiramisu. She reached under the cart and pulled out her katana. She sliced clean through the demon's neck. His head burst, fire and sparks shooting from its torso.

She glanced across the room. The humans just sat there, not moving, as if they were catatonic, oblivious to what was going on around them.

"Why aren't any of the real people moving?" Serah grabbed an elderly lady's hand and let go. It fell to her side.

"Rafe and I put a spell on the water. Any humans who drink it are entranced."

"Cool." Serah dodged a demoness, her blue fangs bared and ready to bite. Screaming, she flung a battle-ax right at Serah's head. Serah ducked in time, grabbing the demoness's feet and hauling her to the ground.

The ax connected with the mirror on the far wall, sending shards flying. "That's seven years bad luck, you dumbass demon." She slammed the knife into the demon's sternum, the crack echoing in her ears.

Standing, she wiped the dark demon blood from her face. She wished Matthias were there, standing next to her like Rafe had been there for Lucy. But that damn bitch Salome was too smart. She wouldn't give up. She'd find a way, even if she had to blast through that door herself.

"Serah, I love you!" She turned toward the bolted door. Had she heard him? Her heart soared.

She had an idea. She closed her eyes and concentrated on channeling her energy. The warmth filled her body. She pulled the energy into the locket.

She had to break through. She needed him there. She loved him too. She kept her eyes closed and visualized the door bursting open and him rushing to her side.

A loud explosion shook the room. She flew backward, landing against a table. She grabbed ahold of a man's leg. The entranced man just sat there, unknowing, while hell erupted around him.

"Serah!"

She'd recognize his voice anywhere. She spun around. Matthias burst into the room through the hole she'd just made with her necklace. Kalli followed, an AK-47 on her shoulder.

"Matthias!" She wanted to run to him and let him know she didn't care about baggage. She wanted the entire package, baggage included.

All of a sudden, Barry Holland appeared right behind him, an evil gleam in his translucent eyes. Without warning, he grew taller, his fangs gleaming. Talons extended, he swung out his arm, ready to slice. *Balthazar!* Her stomach wrenched. This would kill Matthias inside.

"Watch out! Balthazar!"

Matthias dodged to the left and swung around, pulling out his handgun, aiming it at his old mentor. Balthazar threw his head back, crazed laughter bursting from his mouth. "You picked the wrong time to play hero, Matthias."

"It's never too late." He stood in front of Serah, his

sword drawn, protecting her. Lucy and Rafe joined Matthias, their weapons glistening. Kalli trained her machine gun on Balthazar's head.

"I beg to differ." The saccharin sweet voice did nothing but rankle her nerves. "How dare you turn my minion against me."

Salome stood there, her soulless, turquoise gaze penetrating. She vanished in a cloud of smoke and rematerialized right behind Daniel.

"Daniel," Serah shouted. "Behind you."

But she was too late. Salome vanished in another swirl of smoke and appeared where she had previously stood.

"A pity now that he needs to die."

Balthazar came to stand next to Salome, his fanged grin sardonic. "As does your descendant."

"Show me this descendant." Matthias said through gritted teeth. "I still don't believe you."

"They're in this room," Balthazar challenged. "But who?" Balthazar shrugged, examining one of his talons. "Is it her?" He asked, tracing a finger along a young twenty-something woman's auburn hair. "Or maybe him?" Bal traced another talon down a middle-aged man's cheek. "Or maybe, just maybe, it's her." He laughed loudly as he sliced the cheek of a young blonde.

Matthias shrugged. "Maybe it's none of them."

"Do you dare challenge me? I taught you everything you know."

"Enough theatrics, Bal." Salome swung out her hand, sending Balthazar crashing into the wall.

"Here's your last remaining descendant," Salome said, thrusting Daniel out at them, then flinging him in the air and back in her clutches.

Salome scratched her chin. "I forgot one teeny-weeny detail. He's not your descendant."

"Then what is he?" Matthias gritted out.

"He's your son."

Son? How? The world spun. His heart clenched. He'd seen Daniel's eyes before. His wife's eyes, blue as a placid lake. Daniel had her hair too, the color of wheat. He clenched his fists.

"I'm his son?" Daniel asked, bewilderment flashing in his eyes. "Wouldn't that make him like two when I was born?"

"Silence, you ignorant fool," She yanked him against her, her gaze maniacal.

"How?"

"I've discovered I have a truly fortuitous talent. Who needs *Peragrans* when you can travel through time."

"Time travel?" Serah murmured. "Oh God, even I am baffled."

"I was going to raise your son as my own." She turned to Kalli and sneered. "But Kalli showed up and ruined my plans. I transported myself to the first place I could. I tried to bring your son back in time but I'm only allowed to move a person once. I left him with one of my minions. I knew I'd meet up with you one day. Now we can raise our son together."

"He's a grown man. Wouldn't that be weird? He's already been raised." Serah rolled her eyes.

"I would take Matthias back in time with me to the day Daniel was born."

"To 1228?"

Salome nodded. "You could have your life back."

His life back? He'd never get his life back. He'd

never see Serah again. He'd never be able to protect her—love her like she deserved.

"That's the past. You might give me my old life back, but it will never be the same. I wouldn't have the woman I love."

He angled a sidelong glance at Serah. Her breath caught and her lips twitched. God, he wanted to wrap his arms around her and calm her fears.

"Even when I hold you by the proverbial balls, you defy me?" Her turquoise eyes glinted.

"I'll always defy you, you evil bitch."

Matthias gritted his teeth. He had to act. He had to save his son. He unsheathed his sword and lunged for Salome. "I won't let you take either of them."

He swept the blade up, slicing through Salome's shirt. She threw Daniel down and lunged to the right.

Balthazar growled. "I thought we were going to kill Daniel."

"Belial wanted to kill him. My intentions are different."

Matthias clenched the hilt of his sword. He had to put an end to this. He'd rather languish in limbo than give up Serah for Salome.

"You duped me!" Balthazar howled, lunging for Salome.

She dodged to the right and kicked Balthazar in the head. Ripping a large machete from its scabbard, she swung the blade.

Balthazar gasped, his head rolling from his body, flames bursting from his neck. He fell back into a pile of blue ash and blew away with the breeze.

"You're right, I did." With that, she wiped the blood from her blade with one of Serah's elegant tablecloths and sheathed the blade.

"That tablecloth was expensive, *Salami*," Serah ground out, a hint of defiance flashing in her eyes.

Salome's gaze narrowed. She let out a primal roar through gritted teeth. "You have no respect for your elders. You will pay."

Matthias reached out and grabbed her arm. "Serah, no. Not like this."

"I won't have her torture the man I love."

His heart soared at those words. He would end this— now. "Don't worry, my love. I know what I have to do."

"You sure?"

Matthias nodded.

"Okay."

With that, he sprung in the air and lunged for Salome. He unsheathed his sword and angled the blade, slamming it into Salome's gut. She pushed Daniel to the side and swung, slicing into Matthias's chest.

"Always so brave," she said, pulling Matthias's blade from her stomach and dropping it to her side. Her laughter came with deep roars of thunder. "Look where that got you." She held her machete high, ready to deal the final blow.

So be it. At least he had protected Serah to the best of his abilities. He closed his eyes, ready for whatever death she gave him.

Instead, she stumbled forward, her gasp echoing through the hall. Matthias opened his eyes. Salome slumped to the ground, thick dark blood pooling from her mouth. Standing above her was Daniel, his face sullen, gripping Matthias's blade tight.

With that, Salome's body burst into flames and an eerie pop sent her exploding into a million fiery pieces.

"Matthias!" Serah rushed to his side, and knelt down by him. Peeling his shirt back, shuddered. Blood poured from his chest and down his stomach. She had to do something.

"Kalli!" she shouted. "Do something!"

Kalli came to stand next to her and peered down, taking in a sharp breath. She drew her hands across his wound and shook her head. "There's too much damage."

Matthias gasped, reaching out to grab Serah's hand. She took it, her grip gentle, caressing.

"I… I…" He winced, blood trickling from his mouth.

"Shh," she whispered in his ear. "I know." She knew, she really did. She didn't need to hear him say it. She'd seen how he'd defended her. She loved him too, and that's all that mattered.

And she could save him. She had to. Closing her eyes, she placed her hands on his wound. She pooled all her energy into her hands.

"Holy shit, you scar is glowing," Daniel mumbled.

"Wow," Kalli said under her breath.

Did she dare look? And risk Matthias's life? *Hell no*.

Paying no heed to the conversation behind her, she continued to concentrate. "Heal, damn it! I won't lose the man I love."

Heat shot from her fingertips and she flung her head back. She had to save him. She wouldn't survive if he didn't. Matthias moaned, stirring beneath her.

"This doesn't feel like limbo," she heard him say.

Her eyes flung open. She glanced down at Matthias. The wound left by Salome was just a red, faded line. She wiped a hand gently across his brow and gathered him in her arms.

"No, sorry to upset you, but this is in fact not limbo."

"Good. I don't know what I would do without you." Matthias reached up and brushed a stray curl from her forehead. He sat up and gave a low grunt.

"You need to rest."

"The pain is gone." Matthias reached out and grabbed her hand. "I'm not a man of many words, so I'll keep this simple. I love you." He gathered her close in his arms. "I always have, since I first laid eyes on you." He grunted again as he adjusted her in his lap. "I'm sorry I couldn't find the words sooner. And now I've lost you."

"I wasn't very forthcoming either, you know." She placed a gentle kiss on his nose, down to his chin and back up to his lips. "As for losing me? Not in this lifetime. I love you too."

She couldn't resist any longer. She brushed her lips across his. His arms reached out and crushed her to him, the kiss becoming more demanding.

"Awkward." Daniel stepped back and tried to shuffle away.

"Yeah, I can understand that," Kalli said. "Why don't we let these lovebirds alone for a few."

"A few? They'll need more than a few," Lucy said with a snort.

Serah shook her head. She'd give Lucy that one— for now. She was too occupied elsewhere to care. She wrapped her arms around Matthias's neck and snuggled in his warmth.

Then again, Lucy was right. She definitely needed more than a few. She needed forever, and thanks to Matthias, she had finally found it.

Read on for an excerpt from Book 1
in the Demons Unleashed series by Sidney Ayers

DEMONS
Prefer Blondes

Available now from Sourcebooks Casablanca

Prologue

"WHAT DO YOU MEAN THE CHEST IS MISSING?" RAFAEL Deleon managed through gritted teeth.

Even though the clacking of boots on the polished black marble grated his nerves, he continued to pace the expansive room. Candlelight flickered and flitted, sending silhouettes darting against the ivory walls.

What about his sister? Jacoba had all but begged to join the guard, even though he'd pleaded with her not to. Unfortunately, Jacoba didn't need his approval. She won the Fore-Demon Council over, instead.

Dominic Duvane, shrouded in darkness, stood solitary in the corner of the High Council chamber. A forlorn expression was etched across his face, adding to the already foreboding mood. The news was worse than Rafael had imagined. *Utterly horrible.*

Dominic drew in a ragged gulp of air. "The guards were ambushed."

"Who?" He shook his head. He didn't even need to ask the question. Belial, the bastard prince of northern regions of Hell.

Blasted Fore-Demons!

"Belial's Infernati warriors. Have a seat, my friend." Dominic motioned to the burgundy jacquard and gilt divan in the far recess of the room.

Rafael's heart sank. Dominic meant to talk to him as a comrade and not a colleague. This didn't bode well. He clenched his fists. He couldn't panic. To do so would show weakness. He needed to be strong—or at least appear so.

"What… happened?"

"The Infernati swooped in and torched the encampment." His friend's gaze grew somber. "I suggest sitting, Rafe."

Rafael folded his arms and raised his chin. "I'll stand." He'd receive the news like a man, not a coward. "Say whatever you need to say, my liege."

Dominic growled. "I might outrank you, but I'll be damned if I let you call me *my liege*."

Rafael shrugged. "Too bad we're already damned, Nic."

"The chest was to be our salvation." Dominic blew out an exasperated breath. "Bloody hell, Rafe. Why must you be so stubborn?"

"It runs in the family."

Dominic grabbed him by the arms, his eyes blazing. "Your sister was captured."

"She isn't dead. Our connection isn't severed."

Dominic nodded. "Yes, but who knows what tortures Belial has bestowed upon her." His gaze hardened and he clenched his fists. Jaw ticking, he paced. "I begged her not to join. I stood by you."

Rafael shook his head. "Coby wouldn't take no for an answer. Even if the council forbade her, she would've found a way."

Fighting the thought of his beautiful sister, with her magnificent flowing silver hair and enchanting silver eyes at Belial's mercy, Rafael crossed his arms in front of his chest. "What happened to her?"

"Coby's a hero." Dominic's jaw twitched, the demon blood tears rimming his eyes. "She managed to send the chest away before the guards could take it."

A soft smile curved his lips. Leave it to Coby to save the chest instead of saving herself. Despite his despair, he was still proud of his twin sister. However, he wasn't in the mood for Dominic to divert his questions. His gaze grew stern. "Where is she?"

"I guess I shouldn't hide the truth…"

Rafael arched a brow and leaned against the wall. "Well?"

Dominic sucked in a ragged breath, sending candles flickering. "This hurts me as much as you, you know."

"I do."

His friend nodded. "My sources report she's in Belial's dungeon."

Rafael clenched his fists as he held his anguish inside. Grinding his teeth, he paced. Bloody hell. Only a few of the strongest Paladin warriors had escaped that hellhole, but they were never quite the same after.

"Where did she send the chest?" he managed.

"Earth." Dominic flashed a halfhearted smile, his eyes wide and alert. "Your favorite place."

He didn't even want to think about the chest being opened on Earth. Belial already controlled half the underworld—what would happen if he took over Earth too? But Rafael had to save Coby first. The Paladin needed her. She'd been the one the Fore-Demons had prophesied.

"Too bad I'll be busy vanquishing Belial's buffoons." Rafael stood firm, holding his chin proud. "My sister needs me."

Dominic shook his head. "No, I'm afraid not. You've been ordered to retrieve the chest." His black eyes grew stony serious. "I'll save Coby."

"Ridiculous!" Rafael stormed. He gritted his teeth and clenched his fists. "She's my sister. I need to rescue her. Why should you go?"

Dominic drew his lips into a straight line, his nostrils flaring. "Because I..." He wrenched himself around. "I ordered her to attend to the chest, so the Fore-Demons assigned me to her rescue. It's *my* duty."

"She's my blood. That should trump duty." Rafael steepled his fingers. Why must the Fore-Demons do this? They knew how much he cared for his twin.

"They make their decisions for a reason, Rafe." Dominic turned to face him, blood tears threatening to spill. "In the end, everything will fall into place. I'll see to it."

"Where on Earth is the chest?"

Rafael grimaced. He remembered the last time he'd traveled to Earth for such a large mission. He'd been sent to quell an outbreak of Infernati possessions during the early eighteen hundreds. And those clergymen thought they'd done all the work. Earth wasn't all bad, if you could ignore the mortals and their easily tempted ways.

Not that temptation didn't serve a purpose. As a Paladin Demon, he was taught only to tempt when times were dire. The Infernati, however, chose to be a bit more overzealous with the skill. Money, sex, drugs, and alcohol, to name a few. He'd learned his lesson with temptation—a skill he wanted to live without.

"You know what happened the last time I was sent to Earth for such a large mission."

Dominic shrugged. "I'm sure you'll remind me. You always do."

"Miss Amanda Newell."

The other demon rolled his eyes. "So you slept with a human. Demons do that all the time."

No matter how hard he tried to forget the past, it always came back to haunt him. The time he used temptation for his own good. "She died because I tempted her. I killed her."

"That was two hundred years ago. Times have changed on Earth. Why, they even have horseless carriages now."

Rafael rolled his eyes this time. "I know what the world is like. I haven't completely closed myself off. Even with all their technology and fancy cars and airplanes, one thing remains the same."

"Which is?"

"Humans are still human."

Chapter 1

WHEN LUCIA GREGORY BECAME A COSMETOLOGIST, she never expected this. Here she was, sitting over a bubbling footbath, scraping the calluses off Mrs. Gunderson's bunion-ridden feet and sandblasting her thick, yellow toenails.

Got Lamisil?

Thank goodness for the soothing scent of lavender foot scrub and the protection of latex gloves. This wasn't what she had in mind, at all. But when your nail tech calls in sick again, what can you do? Grin and bear it. Bearing it was easy. The grinning part she still needed to work on.

"There you go, Mrs. Gunderson," she said, a wide smile pasted on her face. "You're all set." With a quick pat of the towel, Lucia—Lucy to her friends—dried the woman's feet. Feet that shouldn't be seen in public.

"Oh dear, you've got it all wrong." Her voice, high and whiny, would make fingernails on a chalkboard sound like a symphony.

"Standard pedicure, Mrs. G." Lucy ripped off the rubber gloves, powder flying, and threw them into the wastebasket.

Mrs. Gunderson huffed and crossed her arms. "Suzie always gives me a paraffin bath."

"That's a deluxe pedicure," she replied, pointing up to the pricing chart that hung on the wall.

"Suzie ain't ever charged me extra."

Suzie ain't here, damn it!

"Okay, Mrs. G."

The door jingled open. Lucy turned her head. In sauntered her 1:30 customer. Then again, was she really even a customer? In some circles, she'd be called a best friend.

"Hey Lucy, I'm home!" Serah said in her worst Ricky Ricardo accent.

Lucy stifled the urge to roll her eyes. Yeah, Serah's jokes were lame, but she still loved her. "What up, Serah Bear?"

"I need a wax." She paused. "Oh, I also came across the coolest chest at the antique store."

Mrs. Gunderson shook her foot and huffed. "Where's my paraffin?"

She wasn't ready to have a full-blown argument with a woman who could use her feet as weapons of mass destruction, so Lucy called over to her second-in-command, who lounged in a dryer seat reading the latest in celebrity dirt. "Frankie, hook Mrs. Gunderson up with a paraffin bath, please. My appointment just came in."

Tossing his magazine, Frankie huffed. "Appointment, my flaming ass. She visits us more than a government official visits a high-priced harlot." The mixture of effeminacy and southern flair rolled from his mouth like honey.

With a dramatic flip of her brunette curls, Serah put her hands on her hips and whipped off her Dolce frames, her sapphire eyes sparkling. "Do not!"

Frankie mimicked Serah and sashayed back and forth. "Do too, hon."

"Yeah, whatever, Frank." Serah gave Frankie an

over-dramatic glare. "You know you want me. When you gonna get back in the closet, big boy?"

"The apocalypse could come, and I'd still wave my rainbow flag. Sorry, toots," Frankie smirked.

Mrs. Gunderson shook her edema-swollen cankle in front of Lucy's face. "Can someone just dip my feet, please?"

Frankie sighed. "Right away, Mrs. Gunderson." Glaring, he swiveled to face Lucy. With a point of his always manicured finger, he mouthed, "You owe me—big time."

He assisted Mrs. Gunderson from the foot spa and led her to the private room where the paraffin bath was located. Poor Frankie. She did owe him. He could have tomorrow off. That always worked.

Serah shook her head. "Why are all the cool ones either gay or already married?"

"Because that's life, *toots*." Lucy ambled toward the shampoo bowls and reached up to the shelf where they kept the wax. "So do you want me to tame those wild bushes or what?"

Serah ran her fingers against her eyebrows. "Are they that bad?"

"Whoever said the Amazon was the biggest rainforest in the world hasn't had the opportunity to explore the wild recesses of your brows."

"Whatever!" With a roll of her eyes, Serah whacked Lucy's arm. She plopped into the chair and leaned back. "Work your magic, girl."

"Sit back," Lucy said as she swirled the wooden spatula in the gooey mass of wax.

Taking the spatula, she spread a layer of wax in

between Serah's eyes. Those eyes always made her jealous, all sapphire and sparkling. Lucy's hazels did nothing special at all. Smacking the wax strip down, Lucy smirked. With a firm grip, she ripped the strip off.

"Ouch!"

"Sorry." Gazing down at the strip, she inspected her handiwork. Success!

Serah chuckled. "No, you're not."

"Got me there." Lucy lined her brow with another thin layer of wax. "So you got another dusty old antique for your collection, eh?" With the same gusto as before, she yanked the strip off.

Lucy's friend yelped. "I should've had Frankie wax me."

"Too bad he's already got his hands dipped in wax elsewhere."

Serah drew in a deep breath. "I swear you enjoy torturing him." She leaned back more as Lucy prepared to deforest the other eyebrow. "As for the chest, it has an inscription carved in old Latin."

Latin—Lucy's least favorite subject in high school. Not because she failed, but because she was able to pronounce and read the language better than any of the nuns in Catholic school. And she wasn't afraid to correct them either. *Talk about getting your habit caught in a knot.*

"So you want me to read it?"

"Yeah, remember how bad I was at Latin?"

How could she forget? Imagine that, someone of Italian descent who wasn't able to decipher a lick of Latin. Lucy pulled off the strip, a little gentler this time. "It probably says, 'When in Rome, get the hell out.'"

"Ha-ha! Funny." Serah's gaze searched hers. "Something about that chest draws me to it." She heaved a sigh. "If only I could open it. It's locked."

Grabbing a pair of tweezers from the shelf, Lucy shook her head. "You got ripped off. A locked box with no key?"

"I bought it as a conversation piece, but when I got home I just had to look inside." Serah winced as Lucy plucked the remaining hairs. "Are you almost done?"

"Yeah." Lucy shoved a mirror at her. "How's that?"

"Perfect. So you'll look at it?"

Lucy arched a brow. Serah's odd interest in this chest piqued hers. "Umm... if it's locked, how will we open it?"

"I meant the inscription, you dork." Serah thrust the mirror at her and bounced from the chair. "I think it will tell us how to open the chest."

Taking a deep breath, Lucy nodded. "Yeah, okay. Meet me here at nine."

"Thanks girl. I owe you one."

"Yeah, sure." She'd just add another item to the long list of things Serah still owed her for.

After two hours of sweeping the floors and cleaning the stations, Lucy flopped down into the dryer seat. Taking a swig of warm Coke, she grimaced. Where was the Captain Morgan when she really needed it? She picked up the tabloid Frankie had been reading earlier and thumbed through the pages. So-and-so's hidden baby bump, someone caught at the beach with someone else, the drunken socialite who went commando and bared all to the paparazzi, the professional bowler who had fifteen mistresses. Each week, everything was the same. Only the names had changed.

The soft rap on the back door broke Lucy's thoughts. Glancing at the clock, she sighed. Punctual as always. Serah was never late. Throwing the tabloid trash on the stand next to the dryer, Lucy bounded from the seat and walked toward the door.

There stood Serah, her arms wrapped around a huge chest. It had to be at least three feet wide and just as tall. How she managed to lug the thing would remain a mystery to Lucy. She looked like she would tip over at any minute. She unlocked the door and let her friend in.

"Whoa! You carried that all the way from your car?"

Nodding, Serah toddled into the shop. "The chest isn't as heavy as it seems. I think it's empty. Where can I put it?"

"I suppose here," Lucy said, pointing to the reception desk. "Let me clear it off." She picked up the display of hair products and set everything on the floor next to the desk.

Serah took in a deep breath and grunted as she tried to set the old chest on the desk.

Lucy rushed over and grabbed the other end.

"Let me help." Tingles of electricity traveled from her fingers through her arms and chest down to her legs and feet. Her toes twitched. Her hand fell away, and the chest landed on the desk with a deafening thud.

Serah's mouth fell open. "Hey, that cost me a lot of money!"

"Your box just electrocuted me!" Lucy retorted, her fingers still tingling.

"It did not." Serah crossed her arms in front of her.

She gazed down at her fingers and gasped. *What the freaking hell?*

"I see, so I am supposed to be gentle with your box, while it's allowed to send jolts of electricity through my body. Look!" Lucy thrust her hands toward her, showing Serah her singed fingertips. "Well?"

"Maybe it's hair dye from earlier." Serah threw her head back in laughter. "And stop calling it *my box*. It weirds me out."

"Whatever. Let me see this *chest* so I can set sail with Captain Morgan. It's been a long day."

Serah shrugged. "Fine by me, if I can stow away."

"The captain says, 'Aye aye. The more the merrier.'" Lucy hunched over the chest and rubbed her fingers across the lid. Tingly, but not as tingly as before. Wiping two hundred years of dirt and dust from the chest, she had her first look. Along with the fading inscription, weird symbols dotted the lid. Then she discovered a title etched deep into the sturdy oaken chest. A box with a title? Strange, indeed. Almost as strange as the hieroglyphics decorated all over the lid.

"*Arca Inferorum*." Lucy said. Now if that wasn't a title to try and scare someone away, she didn't know what was.

"Arca what?" Serah's blank expression filled her face. "What's that mean?"

"It means Chest of the..." Lucy thought long and hard about the last word, and then Dante's *Inferno* came blazing back at her. "Damned."

"Damned?"

Lucy nodded. "Yes, damned. It was probably designed

by some over-devout monk wanting to scare mankind into repenting for their sins. I wouldn't be surprised if there's a 'Made in Rome' stamp on the bottom."

Serah wasn't amused. "Whatever. Just read the inscription."

Lucy wiped away more grime and traced her fingertip over the words. Stronger tingles zipped through her body. "It must be equipped with a security system. Every time I touch it, I get zapped."

"Doesn't happen to me," Serah replied nonchalantly.

"Guess it's my electric personality." She leaned over the chest and began translating the inscription.

"At the beginning of the total eclipse of the winter moon, shall this chest be opened only by one of demon blood. They shall call forth the legions of the underworld. By the power of this one demon will Earth be theirs."

Lucy shook her head. "Yep, it's a hoax. I hope you get your money back."

"Oh my God!" Serah exclaimed, oblivious to Lucy's words.

Bemusement filled Lucy. Her gaze narrowed. "Oh my God, what?"

"There's supposed to be a total lunar eclipse tomorrow night!" Giddy laughter burst from her lips. "This will be so cool!"

It was as if they were kids again and this was their first sleepover. Only they weren't kids. Lucy was pushing thirty and Serah wasn't far behind.

Rolling her eyes, Lucy shook her head. *Here comes another one of Serah's harebrained ideas.*

"Even if what the inscription says is real, what part of 'Only by one of demon blood' do you not understand?"

"There's a demon inside me," Serah replied.

Oh brother, Serah and her demons. "But you usually shut the bitch up with chocolate."

"Even so, wouldn't it be fun to at least try and open it?"

"Whatever," Lucy replied with a shrug. "If you want to wait until tomorrow for me to translate the inscription better, that's fine."

"Demons in a box, how cool."

"Yeah, cool. Too bad demons don't exist."

Acknowledgments

I wouldn't have been able to complete this book if it weren't for several special people. So thanks to the lovely ladies in the In Motion group—Carly, Sharon, Susan, Riley, and Delilah. Your encouragement kept me going when I thought I'd have a meltdown. Special thanks to my mom and my sister Brenda, who helped read and proofread my craptastic first draft. I owe you both—BIG TIME!

Another special thanks goes out to some other special people, including Sharron, Derek, Jody, and Sandra for reading through and helping me tone down Farquhar's thick Scottish dialect. You guys rock!

About the Author

Sidney Ayers loves infusing her stories with humor. What would the world be without a little bit of laughter? She writes in a wide variety of genres, ranging from historical to paranormal to contemporary. A native of Michigan, Sidney still lives in the same town she grew up in. No matter how hard she tries, she just can't seem to get away. Michigan is in her blood.

Strange Neighbors

BY ASHLYN CHASE

HE'S LOOKING FOR PEACE, QUIET, AND A MAYBE LITTLE ROMANCE...

Hunky all-star pitcher and shapeshifter Jason Falco invests in an old Boston brownstone apartment building full of supernatural creatures, and there's never a dull moment. But when Merry McKenzie moves into the ground floor apartment, the playboy pitcher decides he might just be done playing the field...

What readers say about Ashlyn Chase

"Entertaining and humorous—a winner!"

"The humor and romance kept me entertained—a definite page turner!"

"Sexy, funny stories!"

978-1-4022-3661-7 • $6.99 U.S. / £3.99 UK

The Werewolf Upstairs

BY ASHLYN CHASE

SHE SHOULD KNOW BETTER...

Attorney Roz Wells is bored. She used to have such a knack for attracting the weird and unexpected, but ever since she took a job as a Boston Public defender the quirky quotient in her life has taken a serious hit. Until her sexy werewolf neighbor starts coming around...

Roz knows she should stay away from this sexy bad boy, but she can't help it that she's putty in his hands...

What readers say about Ashlyn Chase

"Entertaining and humorous—a winner!"

*"The humor and romance kept me entertained—
a definite page turner!"*

"Sexy, funny stories!"

978-1-4022-3662-4 • $6.99 U.S. / £4.99 UK

DEMONS
ARE A
GIRL'S BEST FRIEND

BY LINDA WISDOM

A BEWITCHING WOMAN ON A MISSION...

Feisty witch Maggie enjoys her work as a paranormal law enforcement officer—that is, until she's assigned to protect a teenager with major attitude and plenty of Mayan enemies. Maggie's never going to survive this assignment without the help of a half-fire demon who makes her smolder...

Praise for Linda Wisdom

"Hot talent Wisdom does a truly wonderful job mixing passion, danger, and outrageous antics into a tasty blend that's sure to satisfy."
—RT Book Reviews

"Entertaining and sexy... Ms. Wisdom's stories have something for everyone." —Night Owl Romance

"Wickedly captivating... wildly entertaining... full of magical zest and unrivaled witty prose."
—Suite 101

978-1-4022-5439-0 • $7.99 U.S./£4.99 UK

Hex Appeal

BY LINDA WISDOM

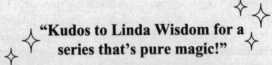

> **"Kudos to Linda Wisdom for a series that's pure magic!"**
>
> —Vicki Lewis Thompson,
> *New York Times* bestselling author of *Wild & Hexy*

JAZZ AND NICK'S DREAM ROMANCE HAS TURNED INTO A NIGHTMARE...

FEISTY WITCH JASMINE TREMAINE AND DROP-DEAD GORGEOUS vampire cop Nikolai Gregorivich have a hot thing going, but it's tough to keep it together when nightmare visions turn their passion into bickering.

With a little help from their friends, Nick and Jazz are in a race against time to uncover whoever it is that's poisoning their dreams, and their relationship...

978-1-4022-1400-4 • $6.99 U.S. / £3.99 UK

Wicked by Any Other Name

by Linda Wisdom

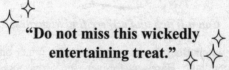

"Do not miss this wickedly entertaining treat."

—Annette Blair,
Sex and the Psychic Witch

STASI ROMANOV USES A LITTLE WITCH MAGIC IN HER LINGERIE shop, running a brisk side business in love charms. A disgruntled customer threatening to sue over a failed spell brings wizard attorney Trevor Barnes to town—and witches and wizards make a volatile combination. The sparks fly, almost everyone's getting singed, and the whole town seems on the verge of a witch hunt.

Can the feisty witch and the gorgeous wizard overcome their objections and settle out of court—and in the bedroom?

978-1-4022-1773-9 • $6.99 U.S. / £3.99 UK

Hex in High Heels

BY LINDA WISDOM

Can a Witch and a Were find happiness?

Feisty witch Blair Fitzpatrick has had a crush on hunky carpenter Jake Harrison forever—he's one hot shapeshifter. But Jake's nasty mother and brother are after him to return to his pack, and Blair is trying hard not to unleash the ultimate revenge spell. When Jake's enemies try to force him away from her, Blair is pushed over the edge. No one messes with her boyfriend-to-be, even if he does shed on the furniture!

Praise for Linda Wisdom's Hex series:

"Fan-fave Wisdom… continues to delight."
—*Romantic Times*

"Highly entertaining, sexy, and imaginative."
—*Star Crossed Romance*

"It's a five star, feel-good ride!" —*Crave More Romance*

"Something fresh and new."
—*Paranormal Romance Review*

978-1-4022-1819-4 • $6.99 U.S. / £3.99 UK